SPELL BOUND

RU EMERSON

ACE BOOKS, NEW YORK

This book is an Ace original edition,
and has never been previously published.

SPELL BOUND

An Ace Book / published by arrangement with
the author

PRINTING HISTORY
Ace edition / May 1990

ISBN: 0-441-77792-9

Ace Books are published by The Berkley Publishing Group,
200 Madison Avenue, New York, New York 10016.
The name "ACE" and the "A" logo
are trademarks belonging to Charter Communications, Inc.

PRINTED IN THE UNITED STATES OF AMERICA

10 9 8 7 6 5 4 3 2 1

SPELL BOUND

Now, magyk is divided into many kinds, the most prevalent of which are two: Green, and Gold. Of Green Magyk, its practitioner is the village witch—woman, man, or most rarely a child. Rarely, for the practice of Green Magyk calls for the utmost intimate knowledge of plants, herbs, barks, flowers, so that a witch might cure ill, prevent plague from striking the village, ensure the harvest or the hunt, smooth the path of true love by means of the proper charm or spell. While they are often held to be evil of intent, it is seldom that this is so, and among our folk, it is most rare that a witch will do harm.

The Gold Magyk includeth all of the alchemyk sciences, and while a sorcerer often seeks the same ends as a Green Witch, the means are different: potions are made using metals and queer distillations, rather than the offerings of wood and meadow, strength of will is of much greater import. There are words and incantations of great length and complexity. Astrologers are also practitioners of Gold Magyk, and all such sorcerers serve nobility and royalty—who else could afford them?

There is one thing these two branches of magyk have in common, sorrowfully, and that is the hatred and fear with which each views the other, and with which the patrons of each view the practitioners belonging to the other.

Green and Gold Magyk, Being a Compendium of the Means, Methods and Differences of Herbal and Alchemykal Magyk Practiced in the Lands of Greater Germany Today, which Includeth Matters from the Sorcerer's Key of Solomon and from the Green Witch's Oral Grammarie. Franz Augustus von Hebbner, Nuremberg, 1595.

Prologue

The air in the small cabin was thickly, richly and variously scented: sweet hedge rose vying with sage and basil, a pungent eye-watering steam coming from a small kettle on the hearth that was mostly pennyroyal and something nasty underlying it. The two windows—glassed, both, sign of prosperity—and the open door let in considerable light, though they let out little of the smell.

Neither of the women inside noticed the odor: One had lived with it all her sixty and more years, the other for nearly thirty. Old Gerthe created her tincture for winter damp and deep cough every year, about this time. The rest of the village stayed clear of the cabin when she did. Her daughter Ilse was as inured as she to the smell. Besides, *she* knew a trick or two to keep the steam from touching *her* nose; wizard's trick, Gerthe would call it. No Green Witch should care about such a smell, or use such tricks. Gerthe disapproved; but then, Ilse thought sourly, the old woman had been disapproving of her, loudly, for years.

Ilse watched the old woman covertly, from under thick blonde lashes that matched her heavy plait. There never had been such a close adherent to the Green Way as Gerthe; nothing save growing things permitted for spells, no encroachment on the sorceries the alchemists called their own. However accessible—and useful—those spells might be, particularly to a woman who had no intention of growing prematurely old, gray and wrinkled as her mother had, nursing village brats and supplying love potions to scrawny, half-witted village lads and pimply lasses. Only daughterly devotion leavened generously with guilt kept her coming to visit every week or so, and brought her to Tannen for four days at a time during spring and fall preparation. Even daughterly devotion, lately, was hardly enough to keep her tongue behind her teeth when Gerthe lashed out at her for some new transgression.

Gerthe claimed not to feel her age, but she could no longer keep up with the demand on her stores. Tannen had grown too much, there were too many accidents of late, too much illness. *Her own fault,* Ilse thought furiously. Aunt Hel—Gerthe's sister—had two apprentices; Gerthe alienated people. Ilse visited Aunt Hel for pleasure, Gerthe because she must.

She checked the tincture, tested the meat Gerthe was drying for her own table, selected two hanging packets from the upside-down forest among the low rafters and settled back to the table with a bundle of dried mint, another of dried lettuce. She was busily powdering them with her fingers when Gerthe came back from checking the fire under her yard kettle. She flew across the small room and agitatedly snapped her fingers under Ilse's nose.

"Not like that, you'll destroy the potency!" she snapped. Ilse dropped mint to the table and folded her hands at its edge. "Pestle and bowl, girl, you mustn't touch it, where are your brains today?"

You swore you wouldn't argue with her, Ilse reminded herself. She got up without speaking—she didn't trust her voice—went over to the shelves and brought back the long troughlike bowl, the flat scoop, and the long wooden pestle. It was a bothersome job, getting flaking bits of lettuce and mint into the bowl using only the scoop, but Gerthe was watching her with those gimlet, narrowed eyes, making certain she didn't use her fingers.

"It's too bad," Gerthe said finally. She settled into the room's other chair, across the table, and went back to braiding straw, crooning the words into it as she worked, embedding thirty bits of different grasses, rose seeds and other oddments into it, making a protective charm for the headman's door. "All I taught you: when to gather, what and how; the words to say and when to say them. You learned quickly and well, best of any apprentice I ever saw. I wish I'd never taught you anything."

"Mother—" Ilse bit her tongue. Let Gerthe spew her woes and be done.

"There are reasons for everything we do. Why can you not accept the limitations and the reasons, do what you are fitted to do and let the rest go? I need you. Tannen will need you when I die.''

Ilse stood so quickly she overset the mortar, scattering mint-scented powder across the table. ''You promised Aunt Hel you would not bring that up if I came to help you.''

Gerthe sat quite still, hands neatly closed over the door charm, eyes wide and cold. ''Did I? Hel never said that; I wouldn't have promised, either.'' She shifted, set the charm aside and stood. ''Tannen does need you. The village is on the main western road, near Neustadt, near three noble hunting preserves. The Green Witch needs to walk a narrow and careful path, to keep the village whole and keep the nobility happy—to keep the King and his chief sorcerer away.''

''Then find a successor, Mother,'' Ilse said icily. ''Get yourself an apprentice who will toady to the titled and happily waste away in this grubby village!''

''Is that what you think I've done?''

Ilse drew a steadying breath. Gerthe waited as though she really wanted to know. ''Mother—I don't know. I *don't*! If this was what you wanted, all you ever wanted, then—you know, I don't. It's your life. But I want—''

''Aye, you want,'' Gerthe said quietly, and her eyes softened for a moment. ''You always did want, only child of mine. It's been your problem, or your fate. Put it from you, child, you're too old for such foolishness.''

''It's not—''

''It is,'' Gerthe hissed. ''Foolish, to think a Green Witch can take what she chooses of the gold magic and come away untainted; more foolish to think the King's sorcerers—here or anywhere—will let you pass unharmed, when they learn what you do!''

''They will not learn,'' Ilse said flatly. Gerthe dropped back into her chair and her brow was furrowed with worry; she chewed at her lower lip. Ilse's anger faded; it wasn't her mother's fault they could not agree. She should not have come. ''Mother, let's not quarrel, please,'' she said finally.

''We won't, there isn't time for it today. Finish that soporific so you can box it up for me.'' Ilse nodded, and went back to grinding mint and lettuce leaves to powder. Gerthe watched her a moment, then picked up her door charm again. ''I only beg, daughter, that if you don't change your ways, you'll use caution and the mind God gave you. Please.''

Please. So unlike her mother that Ilse raised her head and stared. Was that a tear on the old woman's cheek or merely a trick of her own eyes? Unable to speak, she nodded. And Gerthe, with a faint sigh, bent back over her work.

Far down the road, a line of armsmen marched from the western border toward the King's city, with the King at its head. Ladislaus, the King's Armsmaster, estimated they would reach Tannen about mid-afternoon; there was a decent well there, and it would make an excellent long stop.

The road that ran east and west was narrow and dry, thick with reddish dust that carpeted the narrow verge of grass and weeds separating it from the dark, still forest to either side. In another month, the fall rains would begin and dust would be thick mud, the grasses flattened in a ruddy mire. Just now, it was still, the hour of a late August afternoon when golden light touches everything and leaves it looking new, or reformed, or touched with magic or the Philosopher's Stone.

The road ran nearly straight from the border to Neustadt. Within a league of the King's capital, it was a broadly paved avenue, lined with elaborately pruned trees in the formal mode— the influence of King Leopold's French Queen. For four furlongs beyond the avenues, in any direction, the roads were still wide, bordered with tall, thin poplar. Past that, however, roads were narrow, rough affairs. It saved the King considerable expense, and there was after all little wheeled traffic save farm carts and a rare carriage.

At Tannen the road was so narrow that the Armsmaster had to break the ranks down, making them into a slow, weary and overheated snake three times its proper length.

Tired, hot and dusty horses led the procession, bearing tired, hot men who had long since shed cuirasses and plumed mouron helmets to ride in their lightly padded undergarb. Behind them came rank after rank of footmen, choking on the dust the horses made, dragging the butts of their pikes. A distance behind the pikemen were three wagons—bearing supplies, powder for the guns and ordnance and the four exhausted Ordnance Sorcerers who had worked the cannon against Lower Hesse two days and a night running. These added to the plumes of dust, nearly hiding the cannon towed behind the wagons.

At the very head of the horse, under his red and gold banner, rode Leopold I, King of Saxe-Baden and—however temporarily—now also Lower Hesse. He was a tall, powerfully built man, long-legged, broad of shoulder; his hands were long-fingered, square and immensely strong. His pale hair was more than half gray and cut severely short to fit comfortably under the intricately incised and double-pointed mouron. His tanned, seamed face was long and lean, clean-shaven; his nose was too slender for the rest of his face. His lips were full and ruddy, and usually turned up in a broad smile that showed teeth amazingly even and white for a man of his years.

He was not smiling now, and had not done so for most of the day. It had been a long and hard fight against Lower Hesse, a long and hard ride out, the return this dusty, slow walk. He was tired and hot, and at the moment felt every one of his fifty years. There would be celebration when they reached Neustadt. He'd have to muster enthusiasm for that, when all he wanted was cold ale, a cool bath, and a long sleep. He was irritated at thought of the welcome, the celebration, even more irritated with his chief sorcerer, who'd taken his own personal guard and special coach and traveled through the night. He'd have been home hours since, he'd be bathed, rested . . . *Louse,* Leopold thought sourly. If he had not been so tired himself, he'd have been able to defeat Gustave's arguments and made him stay with the caravan.

Ladislaus von Mencken, King's Armsmaster, was at least as tired and as irritated as the King. They'd ridden in silence for most of the day; the Armsmaster had a temper and so did the King; they both knew when to leave well enough alone.

Like Leopold, Ladislaus was graying, though his hair had been black; he wore it close-cropped, his face shaven. He was short, squarely built like his face. Common sense would have dictated he take his personal guard and ride ahead, but Leopold was having none of that, particularly after Gustave left them. *Selfish pig,* Ladislaus thought; he might have meant either man, or both.

Leopold was blissfully unaware of his old friend's thoughts, but he never worried about what other men thought, even friends. Even Ladislaus. Ladislaus had grown up with him, had studied in Paris with him and been at his side through the grand tour of Italy, Greece and Spain thereafter—Ladislaus had married his lovely Spanish wife not long after Leopold wed his

French duchess. He had always been one of the King's most loyal supporters.

Ladislaus shifted uncomfortably as the horses started down a steep incline and came into Tannen. He could almost hear the relief down the lines as he signaled for a halt and the banner bearer repeated it. But as they neared the well, he signaled for an immediate, complete stop. Something was wrong; something afoot.

Tannen was prosperous for a village, but it was still only an ugly straggle of huts fading back into forest, a place where peasants supported themselves by selling wood, scrawny kitchen gardens raised on poor dirt and not enough sun, scrawnier pigs and goats. Ordinarily, whether one stopped or rode past, one saw none of the folk: Peasants avoided their betters whenever possible. Now there was a crowd of them in the grubby, dirt square. Beyond them, a maze of color: a banner, bright capes flaring in an all too brief afternoon breeze, brilliantly plumed hats. The sun touched a drawn sword and cast shimmering light over silent, upturned faces.

Those were Count von Elbe's colors, in the hands of his youngest son. But it was not a day for a hunt. The King rode up beside his Armsmaster. "What chances here?" he demanded. The words trailed off as smoke billowed up in a thick gray cloud, followed by a sheet of flame: A straw roof was ablaze. The common folk drew back as one; the mounted nobles cheered loudly. The Armsmaster's mouth set in a thin line: They were hunting, after all. Hunting a witch.

"Witch," Leopold hissed, and his face went purple with hatred and fury. He turned to the banner bearer. "Tell the men to wait here, find shade. Ladis, pick four men, come with me." And before anyone could protest, the King turned his horse toward the flaming cottage.

Twenty thatched huts, surrounded by pole and twig fences to contain chickens, geese or pigs, lined the road. A cart stood near the well, blocking passage; the aged, thin horse at the traces. With an oath, Leopold edged past it.

Fire shot for the cloudless sky as Ladislaus and his four men pressed past the King. Peasants backed hurriedly away, clearing a path. The leader of the noble party, a young man with a face made ugly by smallpox scars and half hidden under heavy beard, leaped from his horse and removed his broad-brimmed hat. "Milord—your Majesty," he added in surprise, and bowed low. "Your Majesty comes at an excellent time. There have been rumors of late, among the servants in my father's house, of a witch daring to press beyond the herb-lore tolerated in such folk. Knowing your Majesty's feelings on the subject—" The peasants stirred unhappily, subsided into still, watchful silence again as Ladislaus dismounted. "We rode to check upon the rumors, and lo! We found the witch."

"And you execute her without trial, young von Elbe?" Leopold demanded sternly.

"My Liege, no. We cornered her at the well not an hour ago and sought to prove her by means of the Green Mark. She made some sort of light spell to dazzle our eyes, and escaped us. But it is after all daylight, and so she did not escape far. She went there, to her own cottage, and she herself has set it alight from within, no doubt fearing the tests she would surely fail."

Ladislaus peered, nodded. "There's no mark of fire from without, my King." He shrugged. He cared little for magic so long as it left him alone, and he was tired. "She has chosen her way; let her burn." He spoke without much conviction, and his eyes slid sideways to watch Leopold: The King was becoming fanatic about witches in his old age.

Leopold urged his horse forward and turned to face the crowd. "No witch may choose her own death! And this of sorcery is purest treason! Douse that fire and bring her forth!" There was a shifting among the villagers; even thick-sensed and tired as he was, Leopold felt their resentment. "Do as I say, or this entire village will be proven with her, as having harbored a witch and a traitor!"

A child broke into a high, terrified wail. It was the only sound. Men and women formed a silent line and passed buckets from the well; Jacob von Elbe and his friends urged them to the task. Leopold pulled his horse back into the shade and gestured his Armsmaster to his side. Ladislaus slipped one leg free and draped it across the saddlebow.

Something was wrong; it worried him. To convince the King, though: "Leo, my friend, it is late." Leopold waved a dismissive hand.

"Bother the hour, Ladis. I dare not let this pass; look at these people! Let a witch learn sorcery? Would they revolt, could they then use guns against us should a witch learn control of ordnance? I will not have it!" He glared at his Armsmaster.

"I told you before; these witches get above themselves. We should stamp them out, all of them—this is what happens when we do not!" He brought his temper under control with visible effort. "We finish this one here and now. Remind me to devise a minor reward for the von Elbe lad, and also to fix a fine against him—he would have let her suicide. And a fine against Tannen."

The Armsmaster nodded, but inwardly he was seething. It reeked of Gustave. Leopold of all men, parroting his sorcerer as though simpleminded. And he must be simpleminded; anyone could see this active persecution would make trouble—not only unhappy commons but young von Elbe and his like getting above themselves.

Ladislaus turned to watch the smoldering hut. It worried him; this sudden unpleasant business so near the end of the road. As though someone had overlooked them. Evil—he shook the mood with difficulty as a weeping old woman was dragged from the smoke-filled hut.

She went white and silent when von Elbe clapped iron rings and chains about her throat and wrists. *Iron to still a witch and break her power; fire to kill her.* Leopold smiled with cold satisfaction. Her reaction to iron was enough to name her witch, of course. Not enough under the present laws to more than question her. The King was thorough in his questioning: He put the entire list to her. There was no answer. One of von Elbe's friends noted her lack of response in a small book. The Green Sign was found on her shoulder; another mark just below it was found—faint, perhaps a bruise or an old scar. To men searching for the Cold Mark, it was damning. Von Elbe touched her face with his iron blade and she shrieked in agony. A blistered burn came up along her cheek where the knife had touched. One of the village women moaned and covered her face with her hands.

Leopold gazed down at the witch. "Confess and abjure, woman; I'll permit them to strangle you before you are burned."

"I am not—" The words were dry as the road behind them. She coughed. "I am a Green Witch, nothing more. I swear it by God himself."

"No!" von Elbe shouted.

"Silence!" Leopold thundered. "She is an admitted witch, and we have sufficient proof in the two marks. I have no more time, and no need for further proofs. She is set in her way, stubborn and intransigent. Burn her alive.'' The witch's cry was topped by a raucous cheer from the hunters.

Von Elbe ordered two of the village men to bury the end of the iron stake they had brought; others piled brush and wood around it. Jacob von Elbe himself shackled the old woman in place. One of his friends pulled a bundle of still smoldering straw from the roof, blew on it until it flamed, and handed it to him. He smirked, thrust it into the brush; flame roared up. The witch screamed once, horribly. There was no sound then but the roar and crackle of fire.

Leopold turned to face the villagers. ''Reflect, Tannen, on your good fortune that I do not hold you accountable for this woman.'' He turned to ride away; something brilliant and green whirled into being just before him. The horse plunged aside, came back under control as the King exerted an iron hand on the reins. Villagers melted into the shadows.

A horrid laugh tore the King's eyes from the whirling light; there was a woman on the roof of the half-burned cottage—a young woman, tall and wild-looking. Blonde hair hung wet down her back, a long green shift clung to damp skin. ''Murderers and fools!'' she shrieked. The words echoed, bounced from hut to hut and were swallowed by the thick forest.

Ladislaus forced his horse between the King and this new threat. Out of the corner of his eye, he could see the King's personal guard trying to decide whether they dared break the King's command and come to his rescue. Those men who did start forward stopped just beyond the well as though they'd struck a wall. *Oh, God, circling spell,* he thought in horror. *And we six in it!* ''This is Leopold I, your Liege Lord!'' he bellowed. The rest of his words were drowned in a hellish laugh; two armsmen were thrown by their terrified mounts; a third crouched low in his saddle and wept.

''And that woman was my mother!''

''Ah, sweet Jesu,'' Ladislaus whispered. The King had burned a witch, but not the right one.

If Leopold was frightened, it didn't show. ''Mother or no, she was a witch and a traitor, to practice sorcery! I but obey the law in burning a traitor!''

''Law! You set the law! Do not *dare* excuse yourself so!''

''I need not excuse myself—''

''Silence!'' the witch roared. Leopold sat his horse, stunned, with his jaw hanging; no one had ever spoken to him in such a manner. "She was not the one this poxy young rake sought—I was. I, Ilse! And I do not fear any of you. Why should I? I wield both Green and Gold Magic, and where one cannot serve the other does!" She dug bare toes into the straw thatching; this King and his men must not see her tremble in her grief—they would think it fear. She must not weep! She had only gone to wash the reek of pennyroyal from her hair, Gerthe had been no proof against their iron and fire, Gerthe had done nothing to deserve them. *My fault, my fault, ah, Mother, no!* But as she glared down at the stunned, pasty noble faces, she felt a surge of pleasure. They were afraid of her; look at the young hunters easing away from her, just as those filthy peasants had!

They will have cause to fear me. Mother's bones will have company! Ilse drew a deep breath and began the spell, the first forbidden spell she had learned. And she vanished.

Her voice echoed in the still, dusty streets and seemed to come from all around them. "For the death of my mother, you shall pay, all of you! Jacob von Elbe, your father will bury you before the snows come and none of those who ride with you shall live to father sons! Armsmaster Ladislaus, you will die before Midwinter, and you, King Leopold, had best call home your son and give your crown into his hands, for you will follow your friend within days." A terrible silence followed her last words, broken by a roar like cannon: The witch's hut went up in a ball of bright green flame. Another engulfed the stake and its hideous, blackened burden.

The shadows were long when the King again took his place at the head of his army. A cloud of dust hung over them, marking their progress toward Neustadt. A white and shaken Jacob von Elbe rode away with his subdued friends. The villagers of Tannen gathered near the well and gazed in fear at the rubble that had been a cottage and the puddle of iron that had been a witch stake. There was no body, no sign of Ilse. None of them expected her to return; many prayed she would not.

Jacob von Elbe no longer rode hunting after that—for boar or for witches. But it did him no good; a month later, he was riding back from the City during a heavy rain. A falling oak flattened him face first in the mud and drowned him.

Ladislaus took to his bed with a severe chill not long after the first snows. The King sent physicians and the sorcerer Gustave sent his best apprentice. The Armsmaster's daughter Sofia came from the Queen's side to nurse him herself, but he died the day before Christmas. Two mornings later, the curtains were drawn back from the King's bed to reveal Leopold, eyes open and staring in terror at the red silk canopy; though his sorcerers had surrounded the castle and the bed with charms, though one of them had slept the whole night in a chair nearby, he was quite dead when they found him. The covers and hangings of his great bed were singed as if by fire.

18th May, 1637, Neustadt
Henriette, Queen Regent of Saxe-Baden,
to her Cousin, the Duchess Marie Helene,
Greetings:

I thank you, cousin, for your most welcome letters and messages. I hope you are quite well, and that your comfortable niche in hotel society as a patron of the literary arts continues. I see that I must one day visit Paris to observe first-hand the changes since I left.

I am indeed grateful that you keep me up to date on my son's activities. I am glad to hear he is sensible at cards and dice and does not drink to excess or brawl—though of course I did not fear he would. Does he still maintain his flirtation with the Valois girl? And you did not say this time of the gossip attaching him to her mother, with little Marie as facade? Marguerite de Valois is a widow, there would be no scandal; she is my age, but that can only be good experience for a green boy.

But it is of no consequence as he comes home before month's end. Though I would approve a Valois marriage—Marie is of good lineage—this Will of Leo's prohibits. Consider, Marie Helene! Conrad must wed a girl of Saxe-Baden. There is logic in that, I suppose: With so many Germanic kingdoms, so many factions and all aggressive, Leo wished to strengthen national feeling. And so it might. But I must give a homecoming ball at once; Leo thought his son would choose a woman more readily so, and he must wed before year's end! It is not *pratique*, that. But then, alas, poor Leo was not *pratique* in such matters. I only hope my son has become sensible where he was sensitive; the boy who went to France would die of shame at the very thought of the whole business. I have argued with the Regency Council until my poor head aches, and nothing changes; Leo decreed it, the ball stands.

I have my own hopes, however. Do you remember Magdalena von Mencken—that lovely Spanish woman you met when you visited me so long ago? You said then how odd a couple they were, she and my husband's red-faced Armsmaster, how adorable the daughter. Well, poor Magdalena is eight years dead, and Ladislaus remarried—a disastrous affair, truly, a woman of mean station who resembles a horse and brought two dreadful nearly grown daughters with her. Poor little Sofia has been a rose smothered by cabbages in that household—she looks much like Magdalena, but is even smaller and daintier. I brought her to court as one of my young ladies two years ago, in hopes of countering her truly horrid home life—the stepmother was working her like a drudge!

I flatter myself I had made a certain progress when old Ladislaus died, and Beatrix insisted her stepdaughter return home for mourning. Well! Deep mourning is three months over, and Sofia still walled up with those ghastly women. Beatrix sends me excuses, but they are very poor ones—mourning, mostly—since she then offers her daughters instead. Do they not also mourn?

And such daughters! My dear cousin, do you remember the second son of that Polish Count, the one who wore gowns and wigs and ladies' makeup? With that nasty little beard? Then you have Isabelle and Johanna, save that lad was more graceful and refined!

It is a touchy matter: I do not wish to stir up bad feeling with the girl still under Beatrix' hand, and I can hardly make a command of it when it is merely a matter of my ladies. But you know I get my way. I shall have Sofia back at my side eventually. And of course, attendance at the ball will be by command of the Regent's Council: she must come to that, stepmother or no. It is my intention that Sofia von Mencken will wed my son.

Do write again soon and give me all the gossip. I hear your sister has named her most recent daughter for me. I suppose I must send a decent gift, though I fear knowing Anna-Lise, that is the only reason she had the child christened,

Henriette.

1.

There. Sofia dumped the gray rag back in the bucket of soapy water and stood, slowly. Hours on her knees on cold stone left her feeling old, and the first moments on her feet, her eyes swam. She eyed the flags and sighed. Clean for the moment. Johanna's dogs would be at the door momentarily, and they always found plenty of mud to walk through before they came begging to be let in. *Nasty, yappy little things.* At lease *she* didn't have to bathe the dogs; Johanna had announced loudly that she didn't trust "Schmutzie Sofie" to get them clean. For once Sofia had let both nickname and implied insult pass; so long as those dogs were not added to her burden of chores.

But how could she help being dirty, *schmutzig*, when her load of those chores was so much greater than that of her two stepsisters? Beatrix liked to pretend her two daughters were being groomed as perfect housekeepers. In practice, of course, the few tasks assigned either Isabelle or Johanna were done by poor ancient Otto or Drusilla, his wife—or by Sofia.

Sofia sighed, took the bucket to the back door to empty, and carefully did not look at her hands as she rinsed and dried them. She could have wept at the sight of those little hands. Her nails were short and ragged like a boy's, her palms callused, the skin across her knuckles red and chapped.

But she could do nothing about them, nothing about anything save keep her misery behind an impassive face and wait. Show nothing; give those three women no certainty of how unhappy they made her. Pray the Queen would win the battle of wits she presently politely fought with Beatrix.

First sun came through the open shutters and shone red in a puddle halfway between the fireplace and the door to the sitting room. She had a little time for herself at this hour, before Beatrix and her two precious daughters would waken. Sofia had never appreciated early mornings until she realized they were the only hours she could have uninterrupted. The rest of the day she would spend waiting on Beatrix, cleaning up after Johanna and Isabelle, or doing heavy chores like scrubbing the kitchen floor, chores suited to servants rather than the eldest daughter of a Count, one who was—had been—Queen's Lady.

Ah, Father, you great fool, if you have known would you have done it differently? She doubted it. He had remarried indecently soon after Sofia's Spanish mother died, claiming his girl needed a mother. He could never have loved Beatrix; after the first year he seldom even spoke to her. Sofia had openly loathed her from the first, and Beatrix never bothered to hide her own hatred of her stepdaughter. But Ladislaus was too inflexible and stubborn to ever admit he'd made a mistake.

Poor stupid man. He'd had Beatrix to wife for nearly seven years and had seen nothing: Sofia's deep grief, her shock and indignation at her father's haste to remarry, the way the three had treated her.

She'd complained to him once only, when Beatrix took her rooms for Johanna and put Sofia's few remaining belongings in the bare little room that had been his grandfather's vault. Ladislaus called her spoiled and ungrateful and had slapped her. She'd never complained to him again.

"It's not fair," she whispered. Nothing was. Her dresses were plain and dark, ill-fitting and years out of fashion. Beatrix had sent her pretty gowns back to the palace, claiming they were unsuitable for a girl mourning her father's death, but Isabelle and Johanna had worn ordinary bright-colored gowns for months. Her hair had lost its curl from living in a hard knot at the back of her neck, or under a scarf; her eyes were tired, her narrow face that owed much to Magdalena's Spanish blood was drawn, sallow and pinched. Even old Drusilla did not look so worn.

The two years as Queen's Lady seemed distant these days; more distant than her years with her mother. She had nothing to show for them. Beatrix had taken the things she had brought home; Isabelle wore the silver and pearl bracelet, Johanna the gold locket. Neither girl could fit her gowns, her shoes or gloves, but Beatrix sent most back and kept the rest in a chest in her rooms.

She had nothing of her mother's save two gowns—years out of fashion, and so not worth stealing or ruining. And a dowry of two thousand marks, but she could not touch that without marrying. Ladislaus had of course been too concerned with Saxe-Baden and his King to worry about a husband for his daughter; Beatrix had done nothing to urge him to the point. *I do not understand her,* Sofia thought. *She cannot touch the money Mother left. Why not marry me away or send me back to the Queen? She must know Queen Henriette would never take Isabelle in my place! She ought to be glad to be shut of me.*

But Beatrix was an extraordinarily jealous and narrow woman: She thought of nothing save social standing, the advancement of her own daughters, money and fashion. Sofia infuriated her: That the Queen dared prefer that dark-skinned, ill-tempered little creature! She should permit as many girls as possible to have the honor of serving her; who was she to reject two such fine maidens as Isabelle and Johanna? And then for Beatrix to discover after the man was dead that Ladislaus had left his daughter the income from his country estate for a dower! Who would want her? If any did, the Queen's patronage would guarantee her a husband, that money should have come to Beatrix! But it would revert to *her* should Sofia not marry by the time she was twenty-three.

Beatrix was a plain woman: dark, large-boned and strong-featured: Both daughters were much like her. Isabelle was pale and chinless like her father, her light eyes slightly protuberant, eyebrows and lashes nearly white. Her hair was a muddy gold, too thin and lank for fashion. She wore ill-matched artificial side curls that never stayed where they were pinned. Her nose was long and pointed; she breathed—noisily—through her mouth.

Johanna's hair was a dull brown that frizzed in damp weather. Her mouth was too wide, usually set in a dissatisfied line that matched her mood. When she was crossed or irritated, she found ways to play dirty tricks on her stepsister or her own sister—or she kicked her dogs or tormented them. Her teeth were large, and the front ones stuck out.

Sofia, with her black hair, wide and slightly slanted black eyes, tiny hands and feet, made all three women look even larger and more awkward than they were. Her mouth was small and sweet when she smiled—seldom any more. But her chin and her temper both owed to Ladislaus: Where her mother had been sweet and forgiving, Sofia was stubborn, strong-minded, a fighter.

Beatrix knew her stepdaughter's strength; she'd had enough examples of it over the years. Deep down, she might have realized the girl was much prettier than her own daughters, though she would never have admitted it even to herself. And so it gave her deep satisfaction to watch Magdalena's daughter scrubbing floors and the front steps. Her shoes were heavy and ill-fitted, her plain skirts kirtled over an unfashionable quilted muslin petticoat never very clean, her hands as red and chapped as any kitchen servant's. Once she'd waited upon the Queen, once Count Walther Grossland had tried to pay his address to her. Now she scrubbed floors, and Count Walther had recently sent his man to make discreet inquiries about Isabelle's dowry.

The Queen was a difficulty; Beatrix worried about that now and again. But Henriette was a soft woman; she, Beatrix, would win this battle of wits.

Sofia put her bucket in the far corner and left the kitchen before old Drusilla came in to ready breakfast. She liked the old cook, but Drusilla fussed over her and still acted as though Sofia were in mourning. Sofia could scarcely explain to anyone how little she and Ladislaus had cared for each other. For Ladis, there had been only his King, his duties. Sofia remembered his open affection for her mother, but like most men he had wanted a son. He ignored his daughter unless she angered him.

Sofia remembered being frightened of his temper and his bellowing rages when she was small. She'd gone from fear to contempt to a mild dislike when he was about, no conscious thought of him when he was not. But she would never, ever forgive him for Beatrix. *May he rot in hell with that old witch he and the King burned,* she thought viciously as she started for the stairs. That made her feel guilty and unhappy. Poor old woman, it hadn't been her fault—not if Court rumor had been true. She had not sought power beyond her own at all. She had cared for the hurt, for ill children, or blessed the huntsman's arrows. A true Green Witch nurtured, she didn't destroy; Magdalena herself had consulted a nearby Green Witch now and again, for advice on herbs and her beloved roses—

A knock on the great outer door stopped her, and she waited

in the large, cold hallway as Otto went to open it. *Who would call at such an hour?* Those few friends Beatrix and her daughters had left knew not to call before midday. Tradesmen used the kitchen gate and the back door.

Otto came back with two rolled sheets of pale blue paper tied with darker ribbon. As he handed them over, a delicious fragrance of roses enveloped her.

"A messenger, in the Queen's livery, Lady Sofia," Otto said. Beatrix could not dissuade him from addressing her so, though she certainly had tried. "He said one was for all the household, the other for you personally." Sofia stared at the scented paper, gazed up at the old servant, wide-eyed.

"What do you suppose—?" She inhaled another breath of red-rose and turned it over, rather uncertainly. With a sudden, decisive movement, she took the one marked with her name and slid the ribbon down. It was not waxed into place, nor was the other: Simple enough, then, to satisfy her curiosity as to the other message and yet have it taken, apparently unopened, to her stepmother. And after all, *she* was household!

The paper was gilt-edged, the ink a darker blue, the familiar writing a beautifully flowing script that was all swirls and sworls and flourishes. It had been too long since she'd read the Queen's hand, and at first she could make nothing of it. Then: "To the Lady Sofia Magdalena von Mencken, greetings; by command of Her Royal Majesty's Grace Henriette Marie Eleanor Marguerite de Bohun: Know that three days hence the City of Neustadt will hold celebration to greet Crown Prince Conrad, who returns from Paris to take up his duties. As only child of Ladislaus von Mencken, the Lady Sofia is given heir-right for this time to the seat in the Pavilion of Nobles reserved to the King's Armsmaster, and commanded to attend the welcome ceremonies." It was signed with a great swirl of letters, of which only the "H" was legible, and sealed with the Queen's seal. Sofia swallowed disappointment—she hadn't *really* believed this would be an order to return to the palace. Of course she hadn't. . . .

"The Queen commands my presence in Father's seat, out in the parade square. The Prince is coming home."

"Time enough," Otto said tartly. Sofia smiled faintly and shook her head.

"He would have come at once when the King died; the Queen told me so. But the roads were impassable, and the King had insisted the Prince finish his studies no matter what."

"Aye. Well." Otto pulled a long face. "Who knows what the old King really intended? They say old Leopold's Will specified odd things. I hear he didn't trust his sorcerer to leave the lad alone. Or that he didn't trust the Queen—"

"That's not so; *I* know." Otto accepted that readily; Sofia had been at Court, the Queen's confidante. "Besides, she is Regent, he must have trusted her a little." Sofia slipped the ribbon down the second roll of paper, hesitated before unfurling it. "It is curious to make him wait until he is twenty-five. A man's grown at twenty-two, I would say."

"Perhaps the King knew a thing or two of his son, that he didn't trust *him*."

Sofia laughed. "What a thing to say! Leopold scarcely *saw* Prince Conrad from his fourteenth birthday; he's been away for most of the past eight years. I daresay he'll find it odd and a little dull, coming here after France." She stared at the paper in her hand. "Otto, just look!" The old servant came to stare over her shoulder, and his lips moved, slowly; Sofia impatiently read the message aloud for him: "By order of Henriette, Queen of Saxe-Baden and Regent to his Royal Highness, Leopold Gerhard Karl Conrad, Crown Prince of Saxe-Baden and Lower Hesse, to the nobility of Neustadt and Saxe-Baden, and their unwed daughters: Know that our beloved Son shall return home within the week, to take up his duties as Heir to our late, beloved Consort Leopold I.

"By the terms of the King's Will, the Prince will wed a maiden of Saxe-Baden. To aid the Prince in his choice, and to carry out the terms set by our beloved Consort, we have ordered a ball in four days' time. Invitation is made hereby to the noble households of all degree to come and celebrate the return of your Prince."

Sofia blinked as she rerolled the invitation and deftly slid the ribbon back into place. "A ball. How wonderful!"

Otto shook his head as he took the invitation from her fingers. "Poor young Prince. I wonder how he'll fancy being on display like the prize in a horse race!"

"What of the noble women of Saxe-Baden?" Sofia retorted. "Being sent for like so many rolls of colored silk for the Crown Prince to pick through! Or rolls of homespun, he's been so long in Paris."

"Remember when you were a small lass and your lady mother took you to a party for the Prince, Lady Sofia? I remember; you said he was spoiled and snobbish, but your mother reproved you and said he was only shy.''

Sofia smiled and touched his hand. "Think of your remembering such a thing; I'd forgotten it. He hardly spoke to anyone. I thought him insufferable." She sighed. "Think what so many years in Paris will have done for him; he'll consider us very dull. And years out of fashion.''

"Perhaps not. Perhaps he's old enough and wise enough to know better what things matter.'' Otto cast a practiced eye at the beam of sun crossing the hall. "It's not long before my wife takes the trays up; I'll give her this to carry. *She* ought to know you've seen this.''

"Beatrix? She can't hide it from me, Otto. There is no way to keep a ball a secret! Besides, the Queen will surely—'' She forced herself to stop, shamed at her outburst. *Will surely what, Sofia? Send her household guard to steal you away from Beatrix, since all polite requests have failed?* She felt smothered, all at once. Was there no escape for her?

Otto went down the narrow passage to the kitchen; Sofia turned the roll of scented paper over in her hands. It was not so bad as that; Beatrix was nearly out of excuses. She would have no valid excuse against the welcoming or the ball. There was always a way; she must not let herself panic so.

Poor Otto. He moved so slowly, looked so awful of a morning. He was too old for the tasks he had to manage. Beatrix kept him because of Drusilla's cooking and because it was cheaper than hiring a trained lad. Her innate snobbery would not let her do without a skilled man to answer the door—a younger lad with more strength might not be as cowed by her, or come as cheaply; a green lad would be absolutely unacceptable. "If I had the running of the house,'' she said to herself, "I would pension him, he and Drusilla both, to the old cottage below the garden, or to the country estate. If I had—'' She thought that too often, for too many things.

She tucked the message in her sash and walked across the sunlit hall. Prince Conrad had been a pretty lad, all golden hair and golden skin, blue eyes that might have warmed if he'd ever smiled. A strong chin and good hands. No doubt he'd grown into a proper fairy-tale Prince. The new Paris fashions would not look foolish on him as they did on the garish La Modes, or on the older men who tried to copy them. He would know all the dances; perhaps he would dance with her, perhaps they would find things in common, perhaps—

No, she told herself firmly. She knew better than to daydream such things. "Look at yourself," she whispered. "You, with your odd dark skin and black eyes, those dreadful hands and that dull hair. He will never look at you; if he does, he'll only laugh."

Beatrix would gown her daughters to draw all eyes—*away from their ugly faces, I hope,* Sofia thought sourly. And Beatrix was only one mother of many who would read that invitation. A Prince as the prize! She laughed. "There will be panic among the silk merchants and the cobblers."

A dark little creature in an old yellow gown would never stand a chance of catching the Prince's eye.

But—everyone would be there, by command. Somehow, she would elude Beatrix and catch the Queen's eye. If she could not—she must provide for that, not make herself a false hope— if the Queen could not help her, or would not, then there was another way. A presentable young woman, one who was neat, daughter of a Count and two years Queen's Lady—one with a dowry of two thousand Marks—that would not attract a Prince, but there was only one Prince. There were many border Counts, many younger sons of such Counts. It wasn't the thing she wanted. But if she couldn't return to Court, she would take what she could.

She opened the front door to check the walkway and the steps. Both were still clean. Beatrix became furious if the two stone steps weren't spotless, if the hall itself did not look as though no one lived in the house.

So she had perhaps an hour to herself; enough time to look at that yellow silk. The fabric itself was hopeless: brocaded when now the fashion was heavier stuff, taffeta, draped and bunched and folded. But she could perhaps find a collar for it, or enough lace in one of those dreadful old stiff ruffs once the starch was soaked from it.

But in her room, she sat on the narrow bed and stared at the small window with its pane of oft-mended glass. She could see the Queen's banners and the official palace mourning banner through that window. So near, so completely out of reach. Ah, God, why even bother?

"Why," Sofie demanded of the wall, "can I not be like Mother? What is wrong with me? Mother would have found a way around Beatrix, long since." She laughed; it was a tiny sound, almost a sob. She let her head fall into her hands and swallowed. ''Ah, Mother, I hate that you left me.''

There was no answer, of course. After a moment, she sat up again, sniffed and blotted her eyes with her sleeve. The yellow gown was near the bottom of her clothing chest, wrapped in its soft wool shawl. It was in worse shape than she'd remembered: It was wrinkled, the bodice stained with a dark juice—Johanna had jogged her elbow and the mark had never come out. The hems were torn in the back. Rolled up inside a sleeve was the stuff that went with it: ribbon, lace—it needed washing—underskirts. She spread it out and stood for some time looking down at it. She finally shook her head. It was hopeless.

But under the yellow were the two gowns she'd saved to remember Magdalena by: a deep rose velvet and a white day dress with a wide skirt embroidered in soft pink. There were no spots on Magdalena's things; no rips in them. Sofia bundled the yellow away and laid the white over the rose. "It might work. If I put the two together—I might manage it. But I'd better find a place for them in the back of my press, and only work on them mornings, so *they* don't catch me at it." Even more wonderful, pinned in a small muslin bag, nearly invisible against the underskirts of the velvet, Magdalena's favorite ear drops—small silver rosebuds, now sadly tarnished. She fastened them to the inside throat of her bodice for safekeeping.

Her stepsisters had ruined fabric before, had stolen things. Though not recently. Not since Sofia had caught Isabelle in her room with one of the Queen's gift gowns and its beaded velvet shawl in her hands. Isabelle's eyes had been a magnificent yellow and purple for a full week; it had been worth every minute of Beatrix's punishment.

Her fingers snagged in the skirt as she turned the hem, and she winced, scowled and glared at them. They were dreadful. She needed narcissus root, comfrey, lady's mantle for them: The kitchen garden had comfrey, but the other two—she'd need to get Drusilla to dip her a measure from the stuff Beatrix used, or she'd have to find her way to the apothecary's. A proper lotion might make the difference; her hands were beyond mere soaking in oat water. Practicalities occupied her; she brought out scissors and a needle and set to work.

Ilse stood very still in the small shed near the kitchen, where the garden tools were stored. Above her head were the bundles of her s and dry flowers Sofia had hung—she was the only one to tend the vegetables, the small rockery with its herbs, the warm wall with the French and Spanish roses that had been Magdalena's bridal present to the house. The witch gently detached her thought from the third-floor bedroom that had been a vault, let the soft red apple fall. The situation was not what she'd have chosen, but she could use it. And those earrings—how odd. She remembered them, remembered the dark-eyed and gracious Spanish lady who had come several times to talk to her mother. Spanish witchery, her mother had called those silver earrings. They'd once been true rose petals. Not genuine Green Magic, something entirely foreign, a potential danger to the wearer. Magdalena had been unaware of that, and Ilse's mother had overlaid them with a spell of her own, to take away the unpleasant residue of left-over power. Whatever they had been, they were Green Magic now—they were also Gerthe's by her own interference, and so something Ilse could use.

Her face bore new lines, her eyes were haggard. There was an edge to her look, something that might have been madness save her magic was strong, her spells precisely worked. *Three deaths; why do I not feel release yet?* She reached overhead, unerringly selected a brittle piece of rosemary and held it to her nose. *Remember.* Ah, she would indeed remember.

"To keep the mind firm of purpose, an infusion of fennel, or a sprig thereof worn in the hair . . ."

An Oral Grammarie, Being the Means
Whereby the Green Way Is Taught

2.

Beatrix took the news of Sofia's invitations without remark, on first hearing of them. But then, Beatrix had never made open objection to the Queen's requests for Sofia's return to the palace, either—that was not her way. And so Sofia was hardly surprised when Beatrix waited until a scant hour before she was due at her father's seat to summon her to the mistress sitting room. It was nearly midday, but the older woman was still eating breakfast: tea and cold toast. Drusilla had put back the shutters, a thing Beatrix seldom did so soon after wakening, but the reason for that became immediately clear.

As Sofia came into the room, her stepmother's eyes widened and she set her teacup down with a clatter. "Before God and all the saints, look at you! Is that what you mean to wear this afternoon?"

Sofia bit back a caustic retort, and somehow wept black fury from her eyes. "It is the best thing I have, Madam. It is clean and properly mended."

"It's disgusting!" Beatrix snapped. "I had no idea you intended to shame us in such a way! Before God, I think you do it deliberately! You will *not* leave this house!" Her voice made the glass cover in her bedside lamp ring. "Go to the kitchen; there is work, and that rag is fit for nothing else!"

Sofia's eyes narrowed and her hands tightened into hard little fists under the cover of her skirts. But years of experience told:

She kept her voice low enough that her stepsisters, hovering in the hall, barely heard her reply. "By your leave, Madam, you know the state of my wardrobe. The small dress allowance set aside for me by my father has not come to me these past six years. You returned such gowns as the Queen gave me this past year, and you have refused those she has sent to me since."

"Silence, Miss!"

"So please you, I shall *not* be silent." Sofia overrode her firmly. Beatrix stared at her in surprise. The girl never spoke back; this was not a good sign. Not with the ball approaching, not with the Queen raising a fuss once again, and so many household problems that began and ended with money. "The Queen commands me to occupy Father's seat. I could wish I went better gowned, but that is of little import against a direct royal command." *Something even you dare not ignore, Lady Beatrix.* She did not say that, but it hung unpleasantly between them.

Beatrix sat up straighter, her pale eyes glittering; the milk jug overturned in her saucer and the whole breakfast tray wobbled alarmingly. "I will *not* have you disporting yourself unattended amid noblemen!"

"I do not disport, Madam," Sofia said quietly. Her stepmother's eyes narrowed even more. She particularly distrusted the girl when she made such an outward show of politeness. "But in this, Madam, neither of us has a say. It is an order. Queen's order."

"I shall not have it," Beatrix said flatly. "You will not go; I shall send word you were taken ill."

Sofia laughed. "Send word that I am ill, and the old King's physicians will be on the doorstep within the hour. Have you forgotten?" The look on the older woman's face was grim; she remembered. A reception five years before, when the Queen chose new maidens. Beatrix held Sofia back by a plea of illness and sent Isabelle instead, but the Queen had returned the girl with bare thanks—and sent two physicians, a young sorcerer and an apothecary, for Sofia.

"A maid alone—" Beatrix began, one last attempt to work matters her own way.

"If I take Drusilla as chaperone, she will needs must stand in the hot sun for hours; she is old and would take ill. I daresay the household would prefer its dinner tonight. No man will annoy the Armsmaster's daughter. But I would never disgrace Father. His seat is flanked by Herr Braulen of the Furrier's Guild and Count Ernst Gustav von Elbe, elderly men of good repute both. I could not be in better company." She drew a deep breath. Beatrix glared at her, but she was momentarily defeated and they both knew it. "There is no excuse to hold me back." Sofia kept her face straight but her eyes were wicked; it was foolish—even dangerous—but she couldn't resist one parting remark, knowing Isabelle and Johanna were pressed to the door, listening. "Do you fear the Prince will spy me in Father's chair and spirit me away on the spot?"

"Out. Out!" Beatrix screamed. The breakfast tray hit the floor with a crash as she began fighting her way from under the comforter; Sofia turned and fled.

"Unfortunate she has such a carrying voice," she murmured as she hurried down the stairs. It would have been amusing to open that door and see her stepsisters fall in. "And what would Madam have made of that?"

Not much, most likely. Beatrix would accept any excuse her girls gave her and let them go. She seldom punished them. Neither Isabelle nor Johanna had manners, or social grace: Isabelle's shrill giggle cut through conversation; that dreadful laugh must have dissuaded suitors. And Johanna's manners at table were atrocious; she did not own two unstained bodices. Or sleeves: Beatrix would be well advised to do as army captains had begun to do, and put buttons along her sleeves to keep her from wiping her nose on them.

Well—she would not think of them for a few hours; this afternoon was hers. She drew her mother's brave red shawl across her shoulders and stepped into the street.

The city was festive, and there was color everywhere: flowers at windows, on doorsteps, in the hands of burghers and in the hair of their wives and daughters. Banners in Prince Conrad's colors—red, orange and black—had been hung from balconies. Folk stood in the squares several deep, hung from windows, gathered in doorways in such tight clumps it seemed impossible anyone could breathe.

Sofia looked up to see Drusilla setting out two enormous bouquets of red roses on Beatrix's balcony. Johanna was hanging over the edge of hers, pointing out people to someone behind her and screaming at her dogs. Despite so much noise down in the streets, Sofia could hear yapping and a pained yelp from one of the dogs as Johanna kicked it; over that, Isabelle's cutting voice and that awful laugh. She hurried on down the street.

There might have been a way around that order but Beatrix had not found it. Then, Beatrix knew little about Court. She knew fashion, the names of the most recent colors and where to put face patches, the forms of address. She knew all there was to know about every unwed noble in Saxe-Baden.

If only that order had been for her return to the palace! Well, she must make the best of this she could: Accept the honor with grace, talk with sweet old Count Ernst—it had been too long since she'd seen him. And—well, it was exciting, all this; and she would be able to see more of Prince Conrad than the top of his head. She'd never come close to him at the ball; sensibly, she would pull her old, reworked skirts close and slip into the crowd unnoted.

The ball—she remembered her dream of the night before, and she blushed. Every thought she'd denied herself down in the hall when the invitation came—herself as the beauty of the ball, all in gold and white, pearls and filigree on her brow, her hands dainty and white, and the Prince holding one of them as though it were a rare rosebud, gazing at her with wide, awed and adoring eyes, while her stepmother and stepsisters stood against the wall gnashing their teeth. There was more; she didn't dare remember it just now. *How silly dreams are! He'll never even see me!* But she found herself humming a merry little dance tune as she slid through the crowd and made her way toward the City gates.

There were four ranks of chairs under a splendid canvas awning in the old King's colors, with cushioned seats for those granted the right to sit there. The Armsmaster's place was in the front row, near the flags and just behind the King's separately covered dais. The pavilion was finely crafted, the chairs covered in red velvet. Gold leaf touched the patterning of the carved arms. She felt shabbier than ever.

She'd forgotten how nice Count Ernst Gustav could be; how insufferable the furrier. Herr Braulen cast a disapproving glance at her, spared another for her gown, shuddered visibly and turned away from her to watch the road. The Count leaned close and whispered against her ear, "One can tell when they've only just risen from the mud and begin to see themselves as somebody, can't one?" His voice came up to normal volume. "How are you, lass? You are missed at Court. I was sorry about your

father, I never had a chance to tell you.'' She swallowed hard—
it had been so long since anyone spoke kindly to her, she could
have wept. She managed a smile instead.

''I'm well, Sir. The Queen was kind enough to give me Father's seat—for the day, you understand—and so here I am.''
She was uncertain quite what to say about Jacob, if anything.
Word had it his middle sons were still grief-ridden over their
youngest brother. The Count saved her the worry.

''Well, then, you could hardly hold it longer, could you?
'Less the Prince wishes a fairer Armsmaster than his father
had!'' He laughed, and Sofia laughed with him. ''No, I knew you
weren't back with the Queen, and when my lady met Lady Beatrix last week, she heard you were unwell. Would have thought
you were abed and wasting away, for all my Ursula told me, and
I'm glad to see it's not so.''

''I'm fine. Honestly, Sir.'' The Count patted her hand and
turned away to speak to his son Gerhard. Sofia leaned from
under the canvas awning to try to see past the furrier. It was hot
in the sun, unpleasantly so, and the dust was thick already. The
furrier cast her a chill glance and she smiled at him mock-
sweetly—the warm turn of her lips ill-matched by cold, dark
eyes. He blinked and blushed like a boy, and left her alone after
that.

Sofia's smile slipped as she sat back, and her hands clenched.
Unwell! What was Beatrix planning? She could just hear the
woman! But—why would she? *Perhaps she thinks to slip hen-
bane in my evening tea, and so covers herself beforehand,* Sofia
thought dryly, and that restored her humor, but the Count's words
sat in her stomach like undigestible bread. Why would Beatrix
spread such an untruth? For gain? To prevent her stepdaughter
from the Prince's ball? The lie preceded the invitations by several days, though; and Beatrix knew from experience illness
would not serve. To see Isabelle or Johanna—or both—in the
Queen's service? Surely she could not believe either girl had a
chance, with or without Sofia at the palace! *Whatever she thinks
to do, she'll be sorry she thought of it!*

But it was too hot for anger to hold, and there was too much
to look at—and the rising volume of conversation from the commons jammed six-deep near the gates told her the Prince was
near. There had been excitement in the air before; now it rose
to a fever, until it seemed the very air would crackle with it.
The air *was* crackling on the battlements of the old town, where

cannon had been placed to either side of the gate: two cannon to each side, four Ordnance Sorcerers to work the powder spells. The air up there sparkled and briefly coalesced; children screamed in terror or delight, women covered their ears or hid against their husbands' doublets. Flame and a bellowing roar burst from the thick pipes.

Sofia reveled in the echoing blasts and let it all carry her along. She leaned forward, fingers plaited together in her lap under a fold of skirt, scarcely breathing, as the first horseman came into sight.

They must have stopped short of the City to refresh and to wash themselves and their horses, for there was no sign of the dirt and wear of travel anywhere. The lad leading the procession carried the pike with the Prince's banners and colors. His jacket was unwrinkled; his dapple gray and his saddle shone. His broad-brimmed hat bore three plumes: red, orange and black.

Behind him came four young men in the uniform of the Saxe-Baden cavalry, and behind them twelve pikemen—even their boots bore no sign of dust. There was a space, a drummer, a longer space, two cavalry officers and a small company of picked horsemen. Behind them, a man so splendidly dressed, for a moment she thought this must be the Prince himself, but his skin was olive, his hair dark. *He looks like a Prince, and surely he's French!* But one horselength behind the Frenchman, there unmistakably came Crown Prince Conrad.

Sofia realized that she was holding her breath and expelled it in a rush. Her cheeks tingled and burned, her chest hurt, and she felt extremely annoyed with herself, embarrassed by such a foolish reaction. But Prince Conrad was a glorious sight. He was much taller than she remembered, of course: taller than the old King. His hair was pale gold, as was the narrow moustache, the touch of beard between a firm chin and a rather finely shaped—if at the moment tightly set—mouth. His eyes were shaded by his hat, but might have been a deep blue or hazel. Capable, long-fingered hands lay across the reins, ready to direct his gray if necessary. His legs were well muscled under the smooth-fitting red breeches, and he sat his horse with an erect grace.

But even if he had been plain of face and common, his garb would have caught the eye and held it: He wore lace at his throat, cuffs and boot-tops. A perfect riot of feathers tumbled from the gold lace band of his hat, mingling with pale gold hair, elaborately curled. A gold lace band ran from his right shoulder to his left hip, holding the red velvet and gold and gem-crusted scabbard which in turn bore his thin-bladed rapier. All she could see of *that* was the hilt: a swirl of basketry to protect the back of the hand, but the end of the pommel was encrusted with tiny pearls and brilliants. His gloves matched his hat to perfection; the breeches of a deeper red were wound about at the knee with an even deeper red and tucked into boots of supple leather, wide-topped and slouched. His spurs were gold, elaborately chased; rubies winked from the hinges and the center of the rowel.

He inclined his head in the direction of the pavilion and smiled as he waved, then turned away to wave at the crowd near the gate. The people there cheered. Sofia closed her eyes and fought an overwhelming disappointment. *You knew he would never see you, for all your clever remarks to Beatrix.* His eyes had gone right over, or through her. He'd looked over, or through, everyone on the stand. Prince Conrad's smile was a wide flash of fine, even teeth that went no higher than his upper lip.

Snob. After seeing him, she'd found herself hoping for better, and hating him because she hadn't been able to find it. He hadn't changed; people never did. He might be a grown man, he might use that sword with skill, might rule Saxe-Baden three years hence, but he was still the snotty little boy she remembered. *That will teach you to remember dreams,* she told herself sourly.

"Eh?" Count Ernst Gustav turned and she blushed; she'd spoken aloud and not realized it.

"Nothing, Sir. Just—thinking."

"Ah. And small wonder, young Sofia. He's a fair pretty lad, isn't he? I hope he's got compassion and brains under that fluffy hat, since he takes his father's crown three years from now." He laughed and nudged her slyly. "And what a pleasure for you lasses tomorrow night, eh?"

"Well—I hope so, of course." Maybe she *was* overly sensitive; the Count apparently hadn't noticed those coldly distant eyes. Perhaps he'd been too dazzled by the overall appearance of the Prince and his escort.

It didn't matter. She mustn't let him matter; she would not let foolish dreams lift her spirits again.

But Prince Conrad's ball—there would be kind men there, men such as Count Ernst Gustav. He would dance with his old friend's daughter. Others would. Or if Beatrix sought to keep her from dancing, she could speak with them.

She *would* somehow speak with the Queen. That above all; truly, nothing mattered so much as that.

Beatrix would keep her busy very late tonight to "make up" for the past hour. Well, she would manage somehow. In the meantime—she settled back in the chair that had been her father's. So many people out there, and even most of the women were taller than she. She hated being trapped like a child among so many folk, where she could see nothing but bodies. Beatrix would put her hard to work as soon as she returned; she might as well spend another hour at leisure before she went home.

"The paths of the stars control a man's destiny. But he must have proper interpretation of that destiny, and so a skilled astrologer is much sought after."

Green & Gold Magyk

3.

The cheers were still echoing in the streets outside when Conrad came through the great carved double doors, passed down the white and gold tiled hall and into his mother's small study. Henriette had watched his arrival from her long balcony, but she was still a young woman and still light on her feet; by the time he'd peeled off his gloves and sent his escort to the stables and then on to the barracks, left his personal entourage and his best friend Dominic in the hands of his father's First Steward, she was seated on her favorite blue and gold sofa, waiting for him.

Conrad's whole face lit up as he came to her side and knelt to kiss her hands. "Ah, Mother! It's been too long, but you're as fair as ever."

"He's not only learned how to dress himself in Paris, he's learned flattery," Henriette said in her soft, light voice. She still had the least of accents. Conrad had forgotten her habit of addressing him in that manner; it still charmed him and warmed his heart. She caught his face between her hands—long-fingered and deft, like his—and kissed his forehead. "But you must be tired. Perhaps you'd prefer to rest now, and talk later?"

"After eight years, Mother, bar the odd short visit, I absolutely refuse to kiss you and leave you! Besides, I am not really tired. We took the journey in easy stages. I wish—" He paused to search for words, took the seat next to her when she patted the cushions. "I wish the greeting had been—frankly, I know they wanted it, but I wish they had not.'' He spread his hands helplessly.

"And he has not lost his shyness,'' Henriette broke in with a warm, understanding smile. Conrad cast his eyes up, but smiled ruefully back at her, and for one moment the resemblance between Leopold's French Queen and his heir was quite striking. "I thought the University, the French Court and the Hotels would cure you of that, my dear son. I cannot think how you came by it, either—your father certainly was never shy a day in his life.''

"And you were so full of charm there was no room left for such foolishness,'' Conrad smiled. Henriette laughed. "I—it's not so bad, these days, honestly. But—all those people, Mother, just to see me! I think I learned much in Paris, but not to be the center of so much attention.''

"Of course not. One grows used to it in time. And for now, at least, it is behind you. Take some wine, it's a Florentine I had brought in last year. Rather nice. And a cake. Or, are you hungry? I can have meat and bread and soup brought.'' Conrad shook his head. "Your time is already taken up, the next days, I fear; you will have little to yourself after this.''

"I don't care, it's why I came home. Father kept me idle too long, Mother. I'll sleep this afternoon, then begin what needs doing. Though I am not certain I know anything useful. I can speak English, Court and Southern French—that last thanks to my good friend Dom, whom you will love. Or I hope you will; he's exiled for an entire year and he came with me at my wish, since he dueled on my behalf—''

"Dueled?'' Henriette inserted into this rather headlong flow.

"Over his sister—an insult. Dueling's illegal, of course.''

"It was when I still lived in France. But only a year for that—? Oh. I remember, you spoke of him in your letters. He is a Valois.''

"Cousin of some sort to the old regime. No threat to the throne, of course, but the Bourbons find them useful, and although Dom is a second son, his brother the Duc dotes on him and the Duc holds vast and influential sections of Avignon. I was saying? Ah—French, Italian, a little—and of course Spanish, but Portuguese has been beyond my skill. I have studied fencing, the English guns, which need no sorcery—strategy and tactics, ah, and of course, music and dance. I learned mathematics from a Moor exiled from the Spanish Court and romantic poetry from a Countess; I read all the classics not absolutely forbidden—and, one or two of those forbidden,'' he added with a candid grin, ''when we could find them.''

''In short, you went through the course your father planned for you, and learned those things I hoped you would when I insisted Leo send you to Paris instead of dull Nuremberg. Good. Leo's advisors want to talk to you about the terms of Leo's Will. Are you up to discussing it with me now? I prefer you not meet his men cold.''

''I thought it was all settled.'' Conrad put his wine aside barely tasted. ''Father's Will was very specific.''

''The Will holds without challenge.'' Henriette drew a deep breath and squared her shoulders. ''I will not apologize for Leo's Will. He did not consult me, as you must know by its contents. I was only surprised to find he trusted my acumen and diplomatic abilities and named me Regent. I do not understand this age he chose for you, and I am truly sorry about the marriage provision. An alliance with France or Spain would serve the country quite well and I know you had hopes of the little Valois—this is your friend's sister, is it not?''

Marie de Valois, Conrad reminded himself firmly. *Marie, not Marguerite.* It seemed months, not days, since he'd attended Marguerite's last reception—some new opera, two impoverished poets; the reception had been dull, Marguerite adorable. *Would it shock Mother?* Would she understand her son's obsession with a woman her own age? He certainly had no intention of ever telling her about Marguerite. It didn't matter anyway; he might have persuaded his father to accept Marie, but Marguerite would have been the scandal of the Continent. ''I knew I would have no voice in the matter, so did Marie,'' Conrad said finally. Henriette touched his arm.

''But you hoped Leo would consider the worthier aspects of such a match. Had he lived, perhaps he would, though your father considered me a singularity, rather than representative of French noblewomen. He *was* insular, you know.''

''I know.'' Of all men, he should.

''The worst of it—I think—was brought about by this curse; he made the Will after, only days before he died.''

It still made little sense. ''Poor Father! He must have been wild when Ladislaus took sick!''

''I have never seen Leo so,'' Henriette said simply. ''He was terrified, I think, but he would never confide such a thing in me.''

Conrad shook his head. "At least one good thing has come of all this. I shall not have to put up with old Ladislaus scowling at me across the conference table!" Henriette made a distressed little noise, and her son laughed humorlessly. "Yes, I know, Mother, and I'm sorry to offend you. But the old man was impossible unless one was Father. That does remind me," he added as he stood and stretched. "Where on my list of advisors to see is Father's pet sorcerer, Gustave?"

Henriette's distress visibly deepened. She watched Conrad anxiously as he began to prowl the small chamber, examining ornaments and paintings with a critical eye; she was not fooled, he was nervous and doing that to avoid having to look at her. He had always done that when he was being stubborn. "Conrad, listen to me. You mustn't offend Gustave."

"Why?" Conrad held a tiny glass bell by its rose-shaped handle. It chimed when he moved it. "Will he turn me into a boar, or a demon? Or feed me to his pet Kobold?"

"Conrad, please! He was third sorcerer under your grandfather. He's been a sorcerer so many years, he knows so much— You and he don't like each other, I know. But I implore you to remember that you must coexist for three years at the very least."

"I admit it, most unhappily. But I warn you, I will obtain my own man the moment I am allowed to. I met a man in Paris not long before I left; Pietro, a Spaniard. He and I got on well; he and his two apprentices would come at any time, if I asked it. I despise Gustave; he despises me; how can he possibly work to my benefit if he feels that way?"

"Conrad—!"

"If he is so very powerful, why did Father die?" He turned and came back to her side, took her hands and kissed them in turn. "I'm sorry, Mother, I did not mean to distress you. But I will keep Gustave no longer than I must. And listen. I have an astrologer, my own man. He's coming by carriage; he had to, since he's quite old. You'll like him; he's French, and quite talented. His name is Nicholas de la Mare."

"Nicholas?" Henriette gazed at him in astonishment. "But I know him! He was at Louis' Court. He is one of the finest astrologers in all France! He studied under a man who studied under Nostradamus himself! Conrad, how did you ever persuade him to come here?"

"If you heard Nicholas speak on the subject of Court life as it has become, you wouldn't ask," he replied with a grin. "In fact, if you're wise, you won't ask; Nicholas will tell you, in fine detail. He can be garrulous, when he's not at his business. But I know he is good, and he likes me—he says he does. It's odd, though: He cast my horoscope twice recently, and none of it seems right.''

"Oh?''

"Well—not to my eyes. He said I must be patient; you know I'm not that. Now, Mother, this ball.''

Henriette sighed. "The ball, tomorrow night. The Council insisted, and if you knew how difficult they have been you would not wonder why I was not able to gain you more time, at least to rest from your journey. There will be a dinner, formal but small. The Regent's Council will be formally presented, along with the Ducal Council Leo established. He said it gave the nobles a place to shout at each other and disagree with Leo's policies, but keeps them from whispering the same things in secret, or across the border.''

"Border problems?'' Conrad asked sharply. Early in Leopold's reign two Rhinish Counts had gone across river to make a pact with King Erhardt of Saaren. Leopold had dinned the need to watch for such treason into his son's head at an early age, and Conrad had a strong dread of it.

"No. Rumors a year or so ago, no action and no rumor since.'' Henriette consulted a list on the small table at her elbow. "After the dinner, your time is unstructured, but of course you'll need most of it to ready for the ball.''

"Of course.'' His face and voice were both blandly expressionless, but his mother still knew him.

"My son—!'' Henriette spread her arms wide in a very French shrug. "Do you think I like it, that your father did this?''

Conrad shook his head. "I know better. But you know that scarcely helps: I feel like the prize in one of old Louis' gambling dens. I—imagine, Mother, what it was like riding through the streets, with every girl of fifteen or more looking at me as though I were a trout she was about to bring in.'' Henriette gazed at him with widening eyes and burst into laughter. Conrad scowled, but his mother's laugh was as infectious as it had ever been, and he found himself joining her. "Now, Mother, please! I wasn't amused in the least at the time!''

"Poor boy. And so you smiled that stiff smile and gritted your teeth. Well, but this is not quite the same.''

"It is worse. There will be no horse between me and those women."

Henriette laughed again and shook her head. "Most of them will be much too abashed to approach you without invitation. Besides, all you need do is find a girl of acceptable parentage and wed her."

"All!" Conrad mumbled darkly.

"All," Henriette agreed calmly. "Preferably an attractive girl; people like their Queens pretty, and you yourself must look at her for many years to come—and get children on her. You will want one with social graces. Don't look so, that is very important. Imagine year after year wed to a woman who drinks soup with an ear-breaking slurp."

Conrad let his head fall back and he laughed loudly. "Mother, you're terrible!"

Henriette shook a finger at him. "Listen to me! You cannot divorce like the fat English king did; your people will never stand for it. And you've a long life ahead of you. Once the ball begins and you stand in the midst of Saxe-Baden's finest maidens will not be the time for common sense; I know. So decide between now and then what you can bear to live with. Choose the best of them—and if you are reticent, you can always have a mistress or two." She fixed him with a hard look. "Mind, now! I doubt your father did so, because one woman was nearly more than *he* wanted! But—"

"No." Conrad shook his head. "I can't—I don't think I can."

"It *is* your choice, son." Henriette considered this, smiled faintly. "That much of it, at least."

Conrad looked at her, down at his hands. "If you'd seen the French King, bundling his mistress and his wife together in one household—I just—I don't think I could." He considered a moment, sighed. "I hadn't meant to tell you; you'll laugh. But Nicholas cast my horoscope not long before I left Paris. There was a girl, he said I would marry her. But—not just because of Father's Will, because I wanted to. He said something—the Queen, the ball, another, three women, all bringing together as one. It didn't make any sense, and he wouldn't explain any more than that. But—" The muscles at the corners of his mouth bunched; his eyes were unfocused and distant.

"I dreamed about her—that night, and one night on the road, coming here."

"What did she look like?" Henriette asked softly.

"Odd—I don't remember. Beautiful, of course." He laughed quietly. "Silly, believing in dreams." He held the rose-handled bell to his ear and swung it gently. "I don't, of course. This was like—oh, a song, a tale. Perhaps I had too many of those before I left Paris, they're all the rage just now."

"I know." *I must meet this Nicholas; I must learn more of these dreams.*

And she must do something about poor little Sofia. That dreadful Beatrix had so far proved her match. But the girl must attend the ball, and Henriette would find a way to spirit her away from her *soi-disant* family long enough to talk to her.

One of her stewards had seen the girl in the Armsmaster's seat, and Henriette could have wept at his description: that harsh, mistrustful look about her eyes and mouth. *I worked so hard to soften that sweet child, and Beatrix has undone it all in so short a time.* Worse, the look of her: her hair unattractively bundled back in a hard knot, her hands chapped from hard work, grayed and ragged skirts. Surely they could not have been as horrid as Bernhard said!

She would keep the girl's name from her lips just now, though. If Conrad knew his mother intended deliberate matchmaking, he'd turn stubborn; he'd never even look at her. But the same could be said for Sofia. Proud, stubborn children, both of them.

Conrad stifled a yawn, caught his mother's eye and laughed tiredly. "Sorry, Mother. One more of those cakes of yours, a little wine to keep it company, and I'll go sleep. Dom is probably already asleep; he's not much of a horseman. Are the apartments next to mine still unused? I'd like him close."

"Yes to all of that." Henriette filled his cup. "Your mouth is sagging, you need rest. Gustave sent word; he hopes you will see him when you're free."

Conrad broke the crisp little cake in two and stuffed half in his cheek. "Let me see if I can still translate. Gustave wants me to rush to his chamber at once." His eyes narrowed as he chewed and washed the cake down with wine. "Well, I have no intention of doing that. That much ends here and now. Don't look at me like that, Mother; I know all about the next three years. But I will not crawl, I will not let him order me around like a child or a servant. There are plenty like him in Paris; they press constantly for advantage, and any petty advantage edges them a little higher. Gustave comes to *me* from now on, when I say."

"I don't think that is a very good idea."

"Perhaps not. Running at his every little command is a worse one. Don't worry, I will make clear to him it is my choice, I will not involve you. Deal with him yourself as you choose. And I will leave him be until I've slept." Conrad stood, patted his mother's shoulder. Henriette looked up at him, her mouth pursed and her brow knitted. "He's not so powerful as he thinks, Mother; honestly. You know he's not; he's old and entrenched, and he knows enough tricks to bolster whatever true sorcery he *can* wield. If we give him a free hand, God knows what he'll be like in three years." Henriette nodded finally, tilted her face so he could kiss her cheek, and watched him leave.

He was so very handsome—he took after her family for features, fortunately, not poor, plain Leo's. And there was heart and charm under that shy armor of his. He and Sofia—she was more certain of it than ever. They were so very alike, once one got past the prickles. And so—how to go about it?

"Patience is all things: there is always one right moment to begin a spell."

An Oral Grammarie

4.

The night sky was cloudless and a full moon eclipsed all but the brightest stars. The hour was midnight and in the Old City portion of Neustadt only the watchman was abroad. In a few houses, lights still shone: women putting the final touches on gowns for the Prince's ball the next evening. The von Mencken house was dark, however, and had been since the watchman's second round. In her small room, Sofia heard his boots shuffling across the cobblestoned street, heard the creak of his lantern. As he moved away, the crickets and pondfrogs began to serenade once more. Had she opened her eyes, she'd have seen the long slender, black shapes crawl across her ceiling, shadows of the wrought balcony.

She kept her eyes closed, her body relaxed, her breathing even and quiet. Isabelle and Johanna were up to something. The entire afternoon and evening, while she'd sewed and mended and attached beads and feathers to bodices, the sisters had eyed her sidelong, whispering and giggling. They were so transparent! Poor fools, they never learned—fortunately for Sofia. The afternoon before they'd been acting much the same, and Sofia had walked on eggs until she found the cause: Isabelle had wound string at a hand's height above the floor, just at the head of the main stairs. Just like her: Anyone might have sprung that trap, including Beatrix or old Drusilla, who most likely would have broken her neck.

Well, it was partly her fault; try as she might, Sofia had not been able to hide her pleasure and excitement at the prospect of the ball. *She* was no competition, of course—each thought the other to be that—but anything Sofia wanted so much, she must not have. A broken leg would excuse her absence; even the old King's sorcerers and physicians would be unable to mend that in time. And it would keep her from the Queen's retinue as well. She didn't doubt they had reasoned that; it was their sort of cunning. The very thought had made her ill.

We shall see, Sofia thought grimly as she wound up the string and stowed it in her pocket. But retaliation was dangerous, the ball was too near, Beatrix eager for any excuse to keep her from it. Unfortunately, ignoring the girls was no answer: They simply increased the unpleasantness of their pranks.

And oh, to give them a taste of their own: She'd salt Isabelle's sheets and watch her break out in a glorious rash. Last time Isabelle had not left her bed for nearly a week. Or an emetic herb for Johanna's cocoa—but she couldn't. *Am I afraid of Beatrix?* No, she was sensible; it took sense and intelligence to know an opportunity and not waste it. Better to let vengeance slide and attend the ball; she'd have last laugh on them all when the Queen took her back at Court.

Besides, she would enjoy watching her stepsisters bedizened within an inch of their lives, simpering and giggling at the Prince. *They* would never see the humor of it, Beatrix certainly never would. Others would. And Sofia intended to be there to share in the joke.

But that string trap of Isabelle's—Isabelle had watched Sofia wad up the string, and she had smirked defiantly. *Oh, I would put a little sand in the toes of her shoes, where she'd never notice it until she came out in blisters,* Sofia thought furiously. But Isabelle could barely walk in French shoes, she could not walk barefoot with any grace. To watch her dance—!

And if she were Isabelle—Did the girl realize how unattractive she was, plain-faced, oversized and awkward, loud and graceless? Was she aware how often young men put on a polite face and made a quick escape? Johanna must know, after that disastrous picnic with little Heinrich, a fourth Duke's son, not wealthy but pleasant-looking. Outspoken, however: Johanna had come home weeping because he had been appalled by her inability to eat neatly and he'd told her so. No one would ever love her, she had wailed.

Not all suitors cared whether a potential wife was fair as

Queen Henriette; many did not even care if she was well-behaved, modest, able to run the household—so long as her dowry was a proper one. Young women like Johanna and Isabelle needed more dowry than either had to attract a husband. Even the men who looked beneath an uncomely exterior found the interior even less fair.

Well. It was too bad, but none of her fault; Beatrix encouraged them, they encouraged each other. And she could conjure up no pity for either of them just now, not when she was still awake at midnight waiting for the next hideous prank. What would this one be? There was a shuffling noise on the bare boards of the hallway; a board not far from her door creaked. She was about to find out.

A smothered giggle, a hissed, impatient warning: Two white-clad figures stole into the room. One halted just inside the door, shielding a light, while the other crept toward the bed. Sofia lay still, waited until she could feel breath against her forehead, and lunged.

Johanna squawked as her would-be victim's hand clamped around her wrist. A pair of long scissors clattered to the floor. Johanna twisted wildly and grabbed for them. Isabelle flew into the room, but Sofia was already sitting up, Johanna in one hand and the scissors in the other. Isabelle stopped as the points came up; Sofie's eyes glittered in the candlelight.

"How kind of you, *sisters*. Did you intend to trim my hair tonight? Shorter than Father's was, or merely in such a manner so that I'd not want to show my face at the ball? Or did you have another use for those scissors?"

"Don't you dare call me sister!" Johanna retorted sharply, and with her usual grasp for the important part of a conversation. Isabelle hissed "Shut up!" against her ear.

"Yes," Sofia agreed evenly. "Shut up, Johanna, unless you have something to say about these scissors, and the hand you had wrapped around my hair when I caught you."

"Prove we intended anything," Isabelle said sweetly. "Mother won't believe *you*."

"Why should I care? I know; that is enough for me. You'd like to run away, wouldn't you, Johanna?" The girl glared at her sullenly. "But you must get away first, and I am stronger than you are." Isabelle took a step back and glanced toward the door, and Sofia snapped, "And you! You'd leave her here and run screaming for Mother, wouldn't you? I wouldn't, Isabelle.

One more step and something very unpleasant will happen.'' Johanna shrank away from her as far as she could; Isabelle set her lips in a thin line over her protruding teeth and edged forward. "I wouldn't try to take them back, either. The points are quite sharp, *sister*; you might hurt yourself. Your mother would not like it if you bled all over your new nightdress.''

"You wouldn't dare—!''

"Oh? Wouldn't I? Why don't you stop these stupid tricks? You don't do them well, neither of you has the brains. Isabelle, it might have been Beatrix who caught your string and fell, did you think of that?''

"I'd have warned *her*," Isabelle said flatly.

"Ah. And blamed the setting of it on me; how dreadfully clever of you. Did a street boy teach you that one, or did you make it up on your own?'' Isabelle glared at her icily. Sofia glared right back, and Isabelle's eyes shifted to a spot just above her head. "Why don't you simply leave me alone, and I'll do the same for you?''

"Why should we?'' Johanna demanded. She yanked her arm free and scuttled away. "You're an insult to us, Schmutzie Sofie.''

"That's nice, Johanna, coming from you,'' Sofia said. "Father's marriage gave your mother rights, it didn't take mine away. I am a Count's daughter and a Queen's Lady; you two are daughters of a widowed gentlewoman, nothing more. You should at best be treated as my younger sisters, accountable to me.'' Isabelle snorted rudely. "I do not care about that if I ever did. I would rather leave this house and never see either of you again. I am sworn to serve the Queen two more years; I should wed.''

"Who'd have you?'' Isabelle demanded scornfully, almost covering Johanna's blurted, "You can't! The money, the money your father set aside for—'' She squawked as Isabelle trod savagely on her foot. Sofia laughed triumphantly and clapped her hands together.

"I wondered. Thank you, *sister*, for the information! So Father left me a dowry and, let me guess, like Mother's fund, Beatrix has no access to it. Oh, that must infuriate her! She is so fond of money, and so profligate with it. What—does she think I will sign it over, if you three make my life miserable enough? Or is there some limit upon it? If I remain unwed, perhaps?'' Silence. Both girls looked at each other, then at their feet. "You don't lack for nerve, do you? Beatrix has Father's money, his income from the crown, this house, the country estate. Or has she spent that?''

"That's not your business—"

"It *is*. I don't really care, though. But my dowry, any money my parents left me, you will never see," Sofia said grimly. "I swear that." Silence again. "We never liked each other, Isabelle. We never will. Let me be, I'll leave you alone."

"Why should we?" Isabelle demanded. "Johanna was right, you are an insult to us, you're grubby and ill-tempered—how the Queen puts up with you, I cannot imagine." She smirked. "But perhaps she no longer does; she hasn't sent for you, has she? And all Neustadt knows how you look, how you scrub floors and weed the cabbages. She hasn't come to free you from your rightful place after all, has she?"

Isabelle had that one gift: She knew what would hurt most. Sofia stood so suddenly that both sisters started back from her nervously. "Get out of here, both of you! If you try anything else to keep me from the Prince's ball, I swear you'll never leave your apartments without a mask the rest of your lives!"

"You'd never dare!" Isabelle said, but she didn't look very certain.

"Don't trust your luck, Isabelle. And don't push me. I'm Ladislaus's daughter. Remember what Father was *really* like, instead of all that sentimental drivel you tell your friends. Father never forgot a wrong, he never gave over a grudge—and he knew how to make the best of his revenge. Now get out of my room!"

Isabelle opened her mouth, shut it again without saying anything, and left, dragging Johanna with her. Sofia closed her eyes briefly, let out a held breath, and went to shove her clothes chest across the door.

"Is she ashamed of me?" Sofia whispered as she tossed the scissors behind her bed. "Am I so awful as that, that even the Queen rejects me and won't tell me?" It couldn't be; the Queen had borne a loss of her own, she had so little time—but she could have said, she could have done something! She could— Sofia sniffed. "Perhaps it's as well; if she saw me like this! Or if Mother did. I never thought—I'd be—glad Mother was dead, and—and couldn't see . . .'' She swallowed tears and dragged a hand across her eyes. The skin was rough and a nail snagged in her hair. She sniffed again, gave it up and rolled into her comforter, burying her face in the feather pillow so no one would hear her cry.

· · ·

The lower halls were hers for only a short while the next morning. That was just as well, considering how she felt: short of sleep, low-spirited. A steady stream of folk came to the doors: visitors for Beatrix to the double front doors, the furrier's assistant to the rear with two small muffs—ridiculous frippery, Sofia thought, considering the season and the heat. He was followed in short order by the cobbler's lad with shoes—one pair yellow, the other blue with white flowers. They were enormous and awkward-looking; the platform connecting heel to toe was edged in gold. *As if they weren't tall enough.* Sofia laughed shakily at the thought of Isabelle stumbling about the polished ballroom floor in those yellow shoes, one predatory hand clutching the Prince's shoulder while she simpered and cackled that dreadful giggle in his face.

Her dress was done: The plain rose-colored gown was now an overdress with underskirts of the white and burgundy day gown. By careful scrimping, she had managed a white collar and sleeve lace. Her plain dark slippers would have to do, but she had left the skirts long to cover them. Her hair—there would be no time to curl it, even if it would take curl. But a wide band of velvet and roses would hold it back; it would at least wave from the plait. The silver ear drops shone dully.

Beatrix had still said nothing, but she was so busy turning her two sparrows into finches, maybe she'd forgotten her stepdaughter.

There'd been a package the day before, from the palace. Beatrix had intercepted it, made scandalized noises over the really quite modest neckline of the French-cut pale blue taffeta. She had not returned it, though, perhaps fearing a confrontation with the Queen; it had vanished into her rooms, the note the Queen sent had gone into the fire. At least the Queen did think of her; things were not as bad as Isabelle had said, as Sofia had convinced herself in the low hour of the night.

She made more trips to the kitchen doors: one for a hideously large shawl brooch in silver and enameled red Beatrix had ordered for herself, again for hats: lofty, silly affairs, like the shoes, all feathers and silk roses. Then again, the hats might hide portions of their faces, which could only be a good thing. . . . Sofia grinned maliciously as she gathered up the bits of fur, the shoes and the hats and started up the stairs.

A towering shriek echoed down the hall and stopped her in

her tracks. Isabelle, hair flying loose, feet and legs bare, corsets all unlaced, hared down the hallway. "Mother! *Mother!*" Sofia watched Isabelle dart into her mother's apartments. Whatever that was about, she had better stay away from it. She tiptoed up the rest of the stairs to the landing, set her bundle on the trestle there, moved silently down the hall to the narrow flight to the next floor and her own room.

"Sofia!"

Her heart sank as she turned. Beatrix, her morning gown hanging half unfastened, her hair flattened from the linen cap she slept in, her color dangerously high, stood in the doorway and beckoned imperiously. Sofia squared her shoulders, and went. "Yes?"

Beatrix glared at her. "Don't be pert! 'Yes, Madam' from you! What have you done to Isabelle?"

"I—Madam? I've done nothing!" Beatrix flushed, but another wail from Isabelle drew her attention, and Sofia looked at her miserable stepsister. Isabelle was blotchily red on her arms, her face, the leg she was furiously scratching. But Beatrix was watching Sofia, eyes narrowed and suspicious. "She's got a rash."

"Of course I've got a rash, you stupid, worthless girl! *You* did it!" Isabelle wailed.

Sofia shook her head. "I didn't!" Even to her, the denial sounded forced, her voice high and nervous. "If it's only a rash, her sleeves will cover it tonight—"

"How dare you say that, when you did it to keep me from going to the ball!" Isabelle screamed. She threw herself across the room. Sofia backed away as Isabelle snatched at her sleeve and then her hair. "Mother! Remember the salt in my bed four years ago, and the nettles before that?"

Beatrix yanked Sofia off her feet by her plait and pushed her into the wall with one large hand. "Did you salt Isabelle's bedding?" Sofia shook her head. "Or nettle it? Answer me, you sullen thing, did you do anything to cause that?"

"I didn't, I swear—!" Beatrix slapped her, rocking her head back into the wall. "What should I say? You don't believe me anyway!" Beatrix slapped her backhand, snapping her head the other way. "Madam," she added bitterly. Beatrix's hand left her ear ringing and a taste of blood inside her cheek.

"Daughter, go to Drusilla, have her prepare a cool bath. There is oil of witch hazel in the pantry, put that in. Tell her to go to the apothecary for you. I'll come shortly.''

''Yes, Mother.'' Isabelle cast her stepsister a triumphant smile and sped away. Beatrix turned back to Sofia.

''I do not know what to do with you. Your father commended you to my care—do not interrupt me, you wretched girl!'' She brought her hand up purposefully and Sofia shut her mouth. ''Your father married me so you would have a proper mother; he was not fitted to raise a girl of fourteen and he knew it. I tried to turn you from a wild thing into a proper maiden, but look at you!'' Her eyes crinkled; a corner of her mouth came up in the chill expression she fancied a smile. ''Dirty, foul-mouthed, ill-behaved little thing that you are, do you really think the Queen wants you at Court? And what man would have you? Do you think your mother's money would compensate a Duke's son for such a face and a temper such as yours? You're fortunate I keep you here; a husband would have beaten you into a shivering, cringing wretch by now, or killed you in sheer irritation at your nasty ways.'' Sofia shifted under Beatrix's arm; Beatrix slapped her once more. ''Have you not had enough? Answer me!''

Sofia's ears rang and her cheeks throbbed, and she was trembling so with fury she could not keep it from her voice. The ''Yes, Madam,'' she finally managed satisfied Beatrix, though. The woman must have taken the tremor for fear.

''Good. You and I will go upstairs now, and I will lock you in your room for the day. Perhaps lack of a meal or two will tame you.''

''The Queen's command, the ball—!'' The words tumbled out before she could stop them. She bit her lip; winced as her teeth touched swollen skin and she tasted blood. Beatrix shoved her toward the door.

''Be silent! I did not give you leave to speak! You upset my darling Isabelle. I will not have my daughters upset today of all days. But I will not stop you attending the ball, since you are fool enough to foist your filthy little self upon it. I will unlock your door just before we leave. But I warn you, if you come in that shameful rag you wore to the welcoming, or if I hear of misbehavior on your part, you'll pay for it dearly.''

Beatrix propelled her out of the sitting room and up the stairs. ''I have indulged you these past months; considering your father's death and all the ugly gossip about witches and cursings, it seemed only proper. But you always did give yourself airs, and two years of living above your station made it easy for you to forget your true place in the world. So you've taken advantage of my kindnesses, haven't you, Sofia? Spend your time in this room constructively; think on your sins. Consider how much trouble you've caused, absenting yourself today, when there is so much to do. Think in shame of Isabelle.'' She added irritatedly as the door closed: ''Wash your face, you stupid girl, there's blood on your lip!''

The latch clicked down and the heavy key turned ponderously. Sofia nursed her hot, aching face and listened to her stepmother's retreating footsteps, to the mumble of voices below: Johanna's eager, malicious question; Beatrix's sharp reply. Then silence.

She knew there was blood on her lip: It was swelling where her teeth had cut. And it hurt; Beatrix had meant to bruise. Sofia brushed hot, furious tears away and poured water into the cracked washing bowl; her hands were shaking. The cold cloth helped a little. She sat on the hard stool near the room's only window and stared at blue sky, a few small clouds.

It was a shame Isabelle hadn't thought to dose Johanna's sheets herself—that rash was Johanna's work, beyond any doubt. Johanna hadn't wanted Isabelle's competition, she'd hated Sofia for catching her the night before. She'd taken both of them in one trap.

That didn't matter, not just now. Beatrix couldn't *believe* all she'd said! No one could possibly be such a hypocrite! Or a liar—

Panic set her heart to thudding. Surely Beatrix *would* unlock the door when the time came? What if she did not? What if she chose instead to keep Sofie prisoner in this out-of-the-way room—what could Sofie do about it? All very well to say, ''Queen's command,'' but what—actually—would Queen Henriette do to Beatrix? She had done exactly nothing so far; had Beatrix thought of that?

''You will not remain locked in, however Beatrix plans.'' Someone had whispered against her ear. Sofia clapped a hand over her mouth and cried out at the pain of that touch. No one was there, no one! ''Do not fear, there is nothing to fear. Trust in what I say; and I say that Sofia von Mencken will attend the Prince's ball this night. There is a destiny for you to fulfill, and a place in certain horoscopes. Trust, and wait. . . .'' The whisper had been fading; on that last word, it was gone. Sofie drew her breath in on a faint sob and clung to the rough stone wall for support. She would have fallen without it. A ghost? Her mother's shade? Magic?

A trick, it must be a trick! But who would bother? Isabelle or Johanna would simply come upstairs to harass her through the locked door. She stared: On her small table was a nosegay—it had not been there a moment before.

Her heart beat wildly, and she was afraid to touch the flowers. This *was* magic; invisible speakers, things which appeared from nowhere—and magic was not safe. It changed people, people died from dabbling in it. But in confronting magic, they said, one must be brave, or at least not show fear. Her mother had never feared Green Magic. Sofia took a steadying breath and laid two fingers on the tiny bundle of flowers, then picked it up. They were so fresh there was dew on the roses. What did it mean? Every plant meant something. She and Henriette's other ladies had deciphered bouquets often—it was a harmless pastime, a means of sending messages when one could not talk. Those were only messages, of course: Only a Green Witch could actually work the magic represented by a bouquet. She laid a finger on one of the earrings she had pinned inside her bodice and felt easier.

There were two red rosebuds, surrounded by white petunias and a single tiny fern. The cord holding it together was woven of clover and tied in a bow. "Do not despair; all your dreams and ambitions fulfilled; love." She gazed at the little nosegay in rising astonishment. It gave her hope beyond the mere message in it: The giver had kept the message simple, so she would know it. And if it was literally meant—that meant magic, Green Magic. She feared sorcery. *But God protect me, I shall not fear Green Magic if it somehow serves me.*

She set the flowers aside. With this unexpected time, she could hem her gown properly and stitch her few seed pearls about the throat. It was hard to thread the long, thin needles with single strands of silk and to funnel the slender pearls onto the needle. Her hands still shook, her nails snagged the fabric.

The morning was gone before she finished. She shook out the dress, laid it across the bed and stepped back to eye it critically. A ribbon would be nice: a wide, burgundy ribbon a little darker than the overdress, to sash the bodice. Well, she didn't have one.

"I don't care," she whispered flatly—and not very truthfully. "Simply to be there will do. Though," she added wistfully as she hung the dress and underskirts on pegs and fluffed out the skirts, "it would have been nice to have that lovely blue taffeta. And—if someone did notice me—" The Queen would; she could be certain of that, since Beatrix would not be at her elbow to stop her. The woman had not thought of that, had she?

She thought about that and smiled. Perhaps it would sort itself right after all. She stretched luxuriously, kicked her feet free of the heavy old shoes and lay back on her bed. Why, just to lie down and nap in the middle of the day, what bliss!

In a small room down the hall, the last occupiable level of a turret that was slowly decaying, Ilse leaned back and smiled. "I knew I could manage it. The child is young and pliable. Already she sees only what I choose, not the long blade of grass woven among the clover that means lies. Poor simple child! And when the door is left to *me* to unlock, the girl will weep with gratitude; she will be mine. And through her, when she does my bidding, two houses will be obliterated at a single stroke." She was laughing and crying all at once. "Ah, Mother, after tonight you *shall* rest!"

"Arrogance leadeth a man from learning and from his search for the greatest touchstone of them all; and yet as a man's knowledge grows so often does his arrogance."

Notes to the Key of Solomon: Green & Gold Magyk

5.

Conrad stood in the exact center of a carpet bearing the family crest, and let himself be dressed for the ball. He was the only still human in a blur of activity. Twenty men moved around him, helping, waiting their turn—or, having performed, paced anxiously around him, watching as the final product was prepared. The first Master of the Bath had tested the water in the golden tub that had been Leopold's, a second added rose-scented salts, a third stood ready to wash the Prince's back, a fourth with scented towels, warm from the fire. An apprentice sorcerer stood with them: He was responsible for keeping the bath water hot no matter how long the Prince chose to soak.

Now clean and dry, Conrad moved an arm, a leg, his head as directed by those given the honor of dressing various bits of him, and gazed at a portrait of his father without actually seeing it. So many dressers! He felt rather silly, in truth, and more than a little shy. Fortunately, he was not expected to talk to his dressers. And he had to admit, a man needed a horde of dressers for a night like this. His clothing was far from ordinary everyday garb, and he needed the time to think.

Dom had sent two of his own men in to assist. Conrad had felt particularly foolish at first adding men to the crowd already in his rooms; then he worried his own dressers might be offended—one never knew what might offend a status and position-conscious noble, after all. But the two were quiet, deferential, and they knew how to wrap the new boot hose, how to attach falling lace. Both items were of sufficiently new mode as to require Parisians, the only men who knew how to deal with them.

This is what I must learn to live with, he realized; it was another of those little things that brought him up short, things he'd never thought of before at home, seldom in Paris. But then, a Prince in Paris was only another foreign Prince attending the University; nothing remarkable. He had made do with two men, now and again borrowing the special skills of his friend Dominic's dressers. As King, he would choose his dressers for political reasons. The men in his chamber now were his Father's dressers, noblemen Leo had wanted to honor, or those he could ill afford to alienate.

Well, he felt self-conscious still, but it was not unpleasant.

So much had happened in two days—that ride through the City streets, his first moments with his mother. How fortunate he was, having a mother with her fabled beauty still intact *and* a shrewd brain! Henriette was worth several marks on his side of the paper. He could only hope she was not balanced—or over-balanced—by Gustave.

Gustave. God, what had he done, forcing a confrontation with his father's chief sorcerer so soon after his arrival? "Lower your head just a moment, your Highness." He inclined his head, felt lace soft against his cheek, vaguely heard his man's, "Merci," and murmured a response.

He had known his first meeting with the man would be extremely tricky and unpleasant; he had wanted it over; he'd wanted to assert himself, to let the old man know from the first he was no longer an easily awed child—if he had ever been such a child. Had he underestimated Gustave, done it wrong? A night's sleep, a day of speaking to his father's men, worrying the thing with Dom between such meetings—he still didn't know. And it worried him. Gustave was the sort who got even when he felt he'd been slighted.

And Conrad had slighted him from the very first: He'd turned down Gustave's suggestion for a cozy reunion in Gustave's apartments or an alternative cozy meeting in Conrad's apartments, and had sent back a formal command, seals and all, that stated Crown Prince Conrad would be in Leopold's throne room at fourth hour. There was no mistaking the tone it set; and the meeting was on bad footing from the first.

But if I'd gone to his rooms like a truant boy or an erring apprentice, or let him come to mine, he'd have won right then, Conrad reminded himself. *And I would have been so angry with myself I would have poured that anger on him at once. I kept my temper for a while. And maybe because of that I learned something—if I can sort it out of the dross.*

Gustave—he hated the man: his looks, his voice, everything about him. He was at least seventy, practically tottering, unclean and wrinkled, set in his ways, and Conrad doubted he had ever been better than mediocre. He was unimaginative, and if he had made progress in his alchemic studies over the past forty years, no one knew it, including the Queen. Most of his spells were worked by his chief apprentice these days, a young, solemn Italian named Augustine.

Gustave had been precisely on time—lateness was not one of his faults, but that was because of his pride in the enormous watch a patron in Nuremberg had given him years before. He had wheezed his way toward the dais where Conrad stood, stopped short of it and inclined his head—a gesture as between near equals. "Prince Conrad, it is so good to have you with us again. I trust Paris was not too—mmmm—unpleasant, they say the people are quite mad, and—mmm—the streets foul-smelling."

Conrad had been appalled by the man—his air of casual possessiveness, the eyes bright with malicious secrets, Gustave's irritating habit of pausing and humming tunelessly while he sought the word he wanted; forgotten, too, the ancient, greasy ruff the man wore with his gray everyday robes. But most of all—*How could I have forgotten his hair?* he wondered as his collar man rearranged his lace. *That horrid, repellent wig!* Gustave was dark and short, dark-eyed, his face seamed. He looked, Conrad thought, more like a farmer than an alchemist save for the marks of colored chemicals on his fingers and robes, and that he had all his teeth, sure sign of sorcerous intervention at his age.

He had been bald as long as Conrad could remember, and since he was both cheeseparing and forgetful of his appearance, his wig was badly made, ancient and ill-fitted. The color had once been a dreadful purply red, but that had faded over the years; now it was an indeterminately dusty color owing to neither purple nor red, and hair had dried and fallen out in great patches. He had a habit of running his fingers through it, so

often the whole thing hung grotesquely off the back of his head
or over one ear. It reeked of rancid oils and overlaid scent, just
as the rest of the man did. Conrad had been reminded of his
formal presentation at the French Court. Midwinter, it had been,
and he was certain no one had bathed since All Saint's Day,
including the King, his Queen, and his mistress.

"Your left foot, your Highness." Conrad came back to the
present enough to steady himself on the man's back and let him
slide the soft white glove leather boot into place. "And now, the
right." The second boot went on. New, but he'd never have
known it; they fit like velvet stockings.

Gustave had continued speaking, but Conrad had heard little
at first: Renewing this detested acquaintance and finding it worse
than he'd remembered had shocked him. It was just as well;
from the few words he caught, Gustave had been at his unctuous
best, oiling out a welcome composed of spurious happy memories of a baby Conrad, of the child Conrad who had adored
"old Gustl." Conrad had to hold up a hand to silence him;
possibly he would have continued in that vein all afternoon otherwise. "That is enough, thank you. I consider myself wel-
comed. And you may as well know at once, I brought home my
own astrologer. Nicholas de la Mare should arrive this afternoon. You will of course give him every courtesy." He had rehearsed that speech, and it sounded good when he finally used it.

Gustave had smiled broadly, revealing his even, white teeth,
but his eyes narrowed. Suspicious. Not unexpected. "Call me
Gustl, dear Prince, as you used to. But I am hurt; why a French
stargazer? It is a waste of time and money, one man who only
makes horoscopes. Send him back, Prince; you do not need
him."

The old man never gave up; he had judged wrong, though,
thinking to win a grown Prince by babying him. *Unless he was
trying to goad me.* "I never *did* call you Gustl," Conrad had
said evenly; the sorcerer's smile had vanished. "As for my astrologer—I prefer my own man."

Conrad blinked, and his room momentarily swam into focus.
They were adjusting his white silk jacket while one of Dom's
French dressers let the collar fall properly.

*Gustave wasn't pleased, but he didn't make me lose my tem-
per, either. One to each of us? No. I should have waited.*

Because Gustave's expression had roused him to full fury, it
reminded him of too many unpleasantries, too many attempts

on the old sorcerer's part to manipulate him. And that expression of heartbreak over a wayward young Prince was not very convincing: Gustave's eyes had narrowed to mere slits and his face was nearly purple.

"You cannot bring your own men here! You are three years from King, and *I* am in charge of Gold Magic here!"

Conrad's fists had clenched; ah, to strike that suffused face! "I am Prince, nonetheless, *sorcerer*. Watch how you address me! Nothing in Father's Will denies my right to my own men; I only may not supplant any of the council." *Yet*. He hadn't said that. He hadn't had to; Gustave knew he thought it.

"You will not supplant *me*, young Prince." Complacency edged the sorcerer's words. "You would be unwise to think it."

And that, Conrad thought ruefully, as a chair was brought so he could sit and his Master of the Hair could work, *was the worst thing he could have said.* "How dare you threaten me! Whatever rights Father gave you, he *sired* me, Gustave."

"I was Leo's trusted man and his father's, you upstart bratling!" Gustave had shouted so loudly the guard in the hall came running.

Conrad had barely resisted slapping him. "I am heir to Father's throne, and in three years I will rule Saxe-Baden. Let us be candid with each other. We never liked each other, you and I. You are a poor sorcerer, or lazy, I am uncertain which." He wondered that he sounded so very in control of himself when he was shaking in his boots. "Why is it, Gustave, that a mere Green Witch killed three noblemen—and you did nothing to stop her?" Gustave had been white to the lips and for once he had nothing to say. "Go now, sorcerer." He wondered then if he had pushed too hard. But Gustave had merely bowed and walked from the throne room. Conrad had watched him go. The man worried him—Gustave had paused just outside the doors, and Conrad would have sworn he was smiling. As though he had somehow just gained what he wanted; as though the matter had been played the way he'd planned.

Conrad blinked himself back to the present moment once more. His dressers had finished; someone came forward to hold a mirror.

I look too young was his first thought. The white jacket with its gold buttons, the white lace collar—quite plain, compared to those currently worn in Paris—the trousers with their discreet gold striping along the complex slashings, the smooth-fitting knee boots. Lace fell from his cuffs over the backs of his hands, covering the dueling scars that crossed the left. His hair had been simply curled and fell across his shoulders; the broad-brimmed hat was white, with a single red plume jutting rakishly from the band just above his left eyebrow. He wore a gold lace sword belt, no sword.

They'd left his face alone; Conrad had insisted upon that, and he thought his dressers were pleased. He wouldn't miss the new Parisian fashion of face-painting; he'd given the small velvet and pearl box of beauty patches back to the lady who'd made him the present originally. Even Dominic, very much of Parisian society, thought the preoccupation with face patches to be an inordinately silly waste of time.

"Your Highness looks dashing," one of Leopold's men ventured finally. Conrad smiled.

"Thanks to all of you, everything is where it belongs. The ladies will no doubt be dazzled." They laughed dutiful appreciation of the rather wry joke. Conrad gave himself one more look, then turned away. He looked younger, yes: something else—vulnerable? What a dreadful thought! It was a ball, an opportunity to meet his subjects, to dance with noblewomen of his own land—that was how he would view it. And so why did he feel like someone in a tale or a play, the young hero who goes out into the world with a smile, who finds love and tragedy all at once? He laughed. *I am no tragic Prince, no love-struck hero!* All the same—"Pray it go well tonight," he whispered, so softly no one heard. He was nervous, suddenly. On such a night as this, anything could happen. Anything wonderful . . .

"Now, of all green things most complex is the rose: for there are colors, and shades within colors, and scents. Each means a different thing, as does a rose in bud or full bloom, or full-blown. Only those wielders of Green Magyk most skilled, most powerful, most secure in their knowledge, will incorporate roses into a spell."

An Oral Grammarie, Green & Gold Magyk

6.

Sofia paced the narrow space between her cot and the wall with its still locked door. She finally made herself return to the bed and sat on its edge. There was nothing left for her to do: Gown, slippers, hair and skin were as fine as she could make them. She'd slept for two hours by the bell in the town clock, but the good that had done was eroding rapidly under a growing attack of nerves. Beatrix wouldn't come. No, she *would* come, but she'd open the door only to smirk in Sofia's face and lock her in once again. No, she'd come but not even undo the door, she'd come only to wish her errant stepchild a pleasant evening and remind her again to think on her sins. . . . *She dares not.* She'd whispered that to herself so often these past hours, the words no longer meant anything.

The nosegay lay on her wobbly bedside table. The petunias were fading, the clover still oddly fresh, considering how warm it had been all afternoon. The roses were beginning to open. She held them to her nose. The heady fragrances soothed her frayed nerves—but only for a moment. For down in the street she heard the clatter of hard wheels on hard stone, the slam of the front door and women's voices. Above all, Isabelle's grating laugh.

She rushed to the window and stared down. There was a carriage and there, just being handed in, was Beatrix, unmistakable in her deep violet silk cloak. Trailing behind her, shoving at one another for pride of place, were Isabelle in palest pink and Johanna in lavender.

Sofia stared in stunned silence as the carriage edged into the heavy flow of horse, foot and wheeled traffic all heading up the hill to the palace. "No! Please, no, don't leave me!" Her voice wouldn't go above a whisper, but Beatrix wouldn't have heard a shout. She was gone, the heavy door locked. Sofia burst into tears.

She could not stop weeping; when she finally did, her head ached dreadfully, she knew her eyes were swollen and red. It didn't matter; the sun was nearly down, Beatrix had not come; Drusilla had a key to this room but she had not come either. She might not even know Sofia was still here. *Try the door. Break it!* Fool's hope; it was thick, the lock strong. No use. She turned away from the window.

Her heart lurched once, painfully. There had been no sound of lock or hinge, no footstep, but the door was wide and a woman there, a long taper in one hand, an unlit silver lantern in the other. Tall, slender, richly gowned, coifed and scented. Sofia steadied herself. This was no time to fear. She caught up the nosegay and held it out. "Is it yours?"

"Mine? Of course it is mine."

Sofia shook her head. "Why? Who are you? And how is my door open now, when Beatrix left it locked?"

The woman laughed, a nice, sweet laugh so like Magdalena's, Sofia found herself vaguely comforted. "Now, which of these things shall I answer first? I am Ilse, and a friend—of yours. Someone who has kept an eye on you for a goodly time, though this is the first opportunity I have had to counter anything the Lady Beatrix has done. As for your door, why, locks are nothing, if your reason for wanting a door to open is sufficiently pure. Mine is, for I am here to see you attend the Prince's Ball. You have a destiny to fulfill, child, one you cannot fulfill if you sit in this chamber and weep the night away."

"Destiny," Sofie echoed. "I did hear you. Earlier. But, then—whose horoscope?"

"Why—Prince Conrad's, of course," Ilse replied with another gentle laugh. "What other matters tonight?" Ilse set her candle on thin air and left it at shoulder height. Sofia stared at it, then turned her astonished gaze on the woman who'd borne it.

She could see her clearly now: Ilse was tall and golden, her hair dressed in ringlets and rosebuds, a straight fringe covering her forehead nearly to her brows. Her gown was a blue so dark as to be nearly black; the full sleeves were slashed to reveal a pale blue and gold lining that also showed under the swagged skirts. She looked and smelled noble, rich, delicious—totally out of place in this miserable little room. Sofia made her a small curtsey. "Then, I thank you for freeing me, Lady, and I shall be on my way at once."

Ilse barred her way. "Wait. I offer more than an unlocked door, if you will take it." Sofia waited. "Much more. The Prince, for instance."

"The Prince?"

"The Prince. Do you not want him? Every noble maiden in Saxe-Baden wants him, why should you not have him?"

Sofia leaned against the wall and folded her arms. "And who are you, to offer me that?" Ilse smiled. "That was a stupid question, wasn't it? You are a witch. Any Court Lady or noblewoman could make that nosegay, but only a witch could speak to me from afar as you did." Silence. "Am I wrong?"

"You are not wrong."

"Then—did the Queen send you?" But that must be wrong; royalty and Green Magic? Henriette could have made such a nosegay, but she would have sent a sorcerer.

Ilse shook her head. "I came of my own accord. You need aid—mine, since no one else has given it to you. Do their reasons matter?"

"No. Nor do yours. Perhaps I had better go as I am, with thanks for your aid against that door. I do best, it seems, if I depend on no one and nothing but myself."

"Do you? How well have you done so far, prickly little one? Are you always so untrusting of folk? Never mind; listen instead. One moment, what have you to lose? You can walk to the palace in that gown, follow your plan of 'if' and 'perhaps,' and maybe the Queen will take you, and maybe you must return to Beatrix's slaps and petty angers—or starve in the streets or the woods. I can offer better—fair garb, and a Prince." Silence.

"Why, then, what sensible maiden would deny you? But you have not said what it will cost me."

"You *are* untrusting, poor creature. Do you think I want your firstborn or some other such rubbish? Did you not listen? I am a friend to you. Say I owed your mother a favor, and this is by way of repayment. It is little enough I would do.''

''Opening my door *was* enough; dress me in magic and I am a dead woman if the old King's sorcerer finds out. We both are, if I utilize Green Magic in the palace, or if you do and I am with you. How can you suggest such a thing, with Gustave still in command of the magic up there?''

''But who will catch me?'' Ilse demanded lightly. ''Old Gustave despises all Green Magic, I know that; but I know Gustave also. And you have lived at the palace, young Sofia; who there is better at sorcery than Gustl? But he is old and not much good. I have myself been to the palace five times this past year, and once spoken with him. He did not even know me then for what I am.''

Sofia ran her hands through her hair. ''Don't—I cannot do this, it's not safe.'' Ilse applauded silently.

''Of course it is not—not entirely. Nothing is in this world. But you will be safe, I swear it by your mother's memory, so long as you do exactly as I tell you.''

Sofia's gaze went distant and vague for some moments. ''Barring harm to the Queen—no, it must depend upon what you tell me. But what you say is true: Nothing is safe, and I can do what I must. But I still do not understand why you come to me.''

Ilse spoke slowly, choosing her words with care. ''Because I myself cast horoscopes for the Prince, and for this night. Because you are the child of Magdalena von Mencken. Because you yourself are who you are, and were born when you were. By all of that, you shall go to the ball, and to the Prince—and win not just his attention or his troth, but his love.''

''Love,'' Sofia said, and her mouth twisted. ''You have seen me; have you seen him? I doubt either of us is capable of love. Does love matter?''

''So bitter so young,'' Ilse mocked, and Sofia's cheeks burned. ''But we are wasting time; the ball begins soon and there is much to do. Stand still.''

She lit a slender branch at her candle and from that lit the silver lantern. Lavender-scented and colored smoke curled around them; a curious pale light, like early morning sun on a winter's day, filled the room. Ilse looked at the girl critically, walked all around her twice, silently. When she stopped, there was a white rose in her hands: a damask edged in yellow.

''White, for purity of course,'' Ilse said with the least turn to the corner of her mouth. "And gold, to draw the eye. Look at the rose, child, and repeat my words. White for purity, gold to draw the eye."

"White for purity, gold to draw the eye," Sofia said obediently. Her mouth had gone dry; she was suddenly afraid of what she had done. The room swam, a faint music and the scent of spring's first roses touched her nostrils. The witch vanished behind swirling gold and white; the white damask rose seemed to hang before her eyes. There were currents behind it, like a river, surrounding her, enclosing her, enfolding and touching her, clothing her. . . .

"Look," Ilse commanded. She stood behind the girl and a little to one side, and between Sofia and the suspended candle there was now a glass. Sofia laid her fingers against her lips to stop a startled cry. *Who is that, all in gold and white?* Her hair fell in shoulder-length curls, crossed her forehead in a dark fringe. Tiny, pale silk flowers were scattered like stars across the dark of her hair, silver combs held the thick length above her nape. A delicate necklace of gold-edged pearls and opals circled her throat, sheer lawn and deep French lace lay across her shoulders. Her overskirts were white taffeta edged in gold thread, the underskirts white figured with white and gold rosebuds. She could feel stockings—finer than any she'd ever owned—caught up in wide silk garters.

She gazed at her hand then, everything else momentarily forgotten: It was her capable little hand, but her skin was soft, the nails clean and uniform, buffed to a soft shine. "Ohhhh." It came out on a long sigh. "Thank you—"

"Do not thank me yet, child. Wait until evening's end, to make certain it all happens as you wish it. But the beauty is yours, I merely clothed it."

There was an odd undercurrent to the witch's words—satisfaction and malice, neatly mixed. Sofia scarcely heard it; she had put aside wariness with fear, and now the heady rush of excitement buried the last of her worry. She would draw every eye, her stepmother would be wild with fury! And as for Isabelle and Johanna—! "But I haven't shoes—!" She lifted the skirts with all her old Court grace: stockinged, tiny feet there, but her old slippers were gone. Ilse laughed.

"Shoes take another spell, Sofia. And an important one. You've had no dancemaster these past months, and the Prince has brought new dances from Paris. Others will stumble through them awkwardly, but you will not, for the proper shoes can guide you. Hush now.'' Sofia turned back to the glass. *Never* had there been such a gown! She smoothed the skirts with hands that gloriously, wonderfully, did not snag the fine material. And then Ilse stood beside her, now holding two creamy lavender roses, tightly budded. *Musk rose, the Queen's Silver Mother brought from France.* The perfume was unmistakably fruity, and Sofia was suddenly keenly aware she'd eaten nothing since early morning. Ilse pressed the buds into her hands and folded her fingers around them.

The fragrance grew and this time the music was unmistakable; a solemn court piece, but bubbling over, under and around it was a dance that made her feet tingle. Her toes felt compressed, enclosed, but gently: as though the shoes themselves were aware she had worn old and outsized ones for so many months, that she had had no fine shoes and had not danced since her father's death. Sofia lifted the hems of her skirt to find a velvety slipper of a creamy lavender, its heels worked in deeper violet and gold, a tiny gold fringe at the toe of each.

''Rose petal slippers,'' Ilse whispered. ''Not one woman in three hundred could have created them. They live only so long as your foot is in them, mind that! Do not take them off this night.''

''I won't.''

''You look pale. Have you eaten?'' Sofia shook her head. ''We cannot have you fainting at Prince Conrad's feet, that is *not* in my horoscope, and would ruin everything.'' In spite of herself, Sofia grinned at that, as Ilse had no doubt intended. Ilse delved into a deep pocket on the inside of her cloak and brought out a packet containing seed rolls and an apple which she cut into wedges. ''Eat quickly, we haven't much time.''

Somehow Sofia got one roll and half the apple down—she couldn't taste them at all—rinsed her apple-sticky fingers in her basin and dried them on her pillow. ''I am ready.'' *So calm you sound, Sofia Magdalena von Mencken!* Ilse caught up a cloak of gold figured in white, set it across her shoulders, and stepped back to study the effect.

''You'll more than do. Here, one last thing. Take up the nosegay; set it against the throat of your cloak.'' It warmed briefly under her fingers and became a brooch, a flat gold rose surrounded by buds, and she could feel the least weight at her earlobes: Questing fingers removed one of her mother's silver rose earrings. They shone as if they'd been burnished, and her skin tingled at the contact. Ilse took the wire from her fingers and placed it back in her ear.

Ilse doused the lantern by pointing at it, took up the candle and pressed it, still burning, between her palms until it dwindled to finger size and vanished with a faint pop. She hurried Sofia out of the small room. That had been the only weak moment in all her spells. Even a young woman untrained in magic might understand what remained, but she had not seen. Ilse smiled contentedly as she closed the door on the two blood-red rose petals that lay on the floor, between bed and door. *Red rose petals, child, that's for death. Yours and his.*

Otto was in the lower hall, lighting candles for the sconces flanking the entrance. He turned and stared in astonishment; his mouth worked, and tears ran down his face. Sofie caught his hands between hers. A scent of roses—spicy, musky, sweet— washed over him. Had he been more alert, he might have caught the faint reek of witch, for Ilse made no effort to hide it and Otto was ordinarily quite sensitive to the odor of witch.

"Ach, little one, you're more fair than your Lady Mother," he whispered finally. Sofia smiled and flushed with pleasure, but shook her head. "It's so," Otto insisted. He turned his head to call Drusilla, and only as he turned back saw Sofia's companion. Where had she come from? So many women had come to the house this afternoon, but he had never seen this one before. Ilse touched his arm; his eyes glazed, his hands went limp in Sofia's, and she let them drop as though they'd burned her. She spun around to set herself between Ilse and the old man.

"What have you done? He is old and his heart is not strong!"

"I will not hurt him," Ilse snapped. "You cannot walk to the palace like that. Such fine garments call for a fine coach, a driver and a footman." Sofia shook her head stubbornly. Before she could speak, Drusilla came into the hall. Ilse's spell brought her up short. Sofia put her fingers in her mouth and bit them to keep from crying out.

"Cook, do you hear me?" Ilse spoke so softly, her words scarcely carried across the room. Drusilla nodded. "Good. And you, old man?" Otto nodded in turn. "Go then, old man, into the garden and fetch me large green cabbages, four of them. Bring me also the branch of an apple tree, and two leaves from the horseradish that grows against the wall. And you, woman: I want the largest, the ripest, the fairest white rose in the garden: one that has yet lost no petals. Cut the stem short, and bring it at once to the kitchen door. You, Sofia,'' she added as she went after them, ''will wait here.''

''No!'' But to her horror, she could not move. Ilse's golden hair caught light from the kitchen as she followed the servants. Sofia closed her eyes and shuddered. The Prince. Was being wife to the old King's heir worth so much? *It must be, now I have begun this.*

Ilse returned finally and gave her a deep curtsey. ''Your coach waits at the front door, Lady,'' she said. ''And I will tell you now, the coach driver and the footman are your servants. I have changed them. Not as much as I changed the rose, which is now your coach; the horseradish, now two horses; the cabbages which are wheels; the apple branch which is a whip. The man and his wife will return to their forms without harm or memory of this.

''But I have used magic, and so you must listen carefully to me. Your life and mine depend upon it, and so do your servants.'' Ilse laid a gloved finger lightly across Sofia's lips. ''Hear first, then swear. Do not remove the slippers. Give no one your true name.''

''But—but the Queen will know me, others will!''

''Will they? Perhaps so. That is not what I said, though. You must not *give* your name should anyone ask it. Do you not know that names can be used in magic? I used yours tonight, to control so much magic. If you tell your name, the spells will dissolve on the instant. Do you understand?''

She did, and the threat was terrifying. Herself changing in the midst of the ballroom, the servants changing in the courtyard and the certainty of Green Magic about them all . . . But she was committed now. She would not think of the magic, there was no use to that. *Accept what comes, take what is, as you see it.*

''You remain so calm, that is excellent.'' Ilse must not be able to read her thoughts, or hear her thudding heart. ''Guard the earrings well, they are your mother's protection and they seal the spell as your name began it. And you *must* leave the ballroom by the last stroke of midnight. I am sorry for that, I know the ball will go until first light, but I cannot hold so much magic longer than that. As it is, I can only do so by remaining close to you and so I, also, go to the Prince's ball.''

"You will fit in wonderfully," Sofia said. Ilse shook her head. "No one will see me once we are there."

"Why?"

"Because it takes too much power to work magic for you and conceal what I am at the same time. Far simpler and safer for us both, if I conceal myself instead."

"That is none of my worrying, then. I will not look for you once there, even though I know you are about. I will keep the slippers on my feet, Mother's roses in my ears. I will not speak my name, whoever asks it. And I shall remember to leave by midnight."

Ilse set a light kiss on her brow, and held the door so Sofia could precede her into the street. She stopped short on the bottom step and clapped her hands together in delight: The coach was all white and gold; its tall wheels reached nearly as high as the door handles. Two matched white horses with gold harness pulled it; a coachman in black and gold sat on the high seat with a long silver-handled whip in his hand, and the footman in matching livery stood at Sofia's elbow, ready to hand her in. The door shut behind them, the footman climbed onto the seat beside the driver, and the coach eased out into the road.

There was little traffic now; they passed a few women and their escorts afoot; four young men on dark horses clattered up the cobbled way. The journey to the palace was a short one, over almost before Sofia could enjoy it—she had only ridden in a true coach twice and never in such splendor.

The high, crumbling stone wall of the old outer ramparts loomed up before them. Lanterns hung from bars inserted between the stones to light the road. Beyond heavy wrought gates, the grounds were broad and smooth, expanses of lawn edged with poplar and hedges. There were lights everywhere, small rectangular ponds shining golden and reflecting shimmering light against flowering shrubs and carved wooden benches. And then the palace itself: ablaze with lights from turrets to gates, banners fluttering in the least of evening breezes, the enormous silk flag hung above the great double doors. Waiting to receive all guests were three of the old King's senior staff, resplendent in brilliant red and white. *Red for true love, white for purity,* Sofia thought rather wildly. Her ear caught stately music as the carriage came to a halt.

She heard Ilse speak to the footman, who at once climbed back onto the seat. The carriage rolled back toward the main gates. *Not leaving them here in danger,* Sofia thought. She felt pleased at that, and thought better of the witch. Ilse hissed a reminder against her ear: "You are alone now; the guard and the guests cannot see me, remember that." Sofia gathered her skirts and moved lightly up the stairs.

The double doors opened before her; two smiling servants bowed as she passed. Sofia swallowed. *Too late to change your mind, even if you were fool enough to do it.* She did not hear the startled hiss from one of the two men when Ilse passed him unseen—but not unsensed. *Witch.* Ilse heard, and a satisfied smile turned her lips.

Sofia walked the carpeted hall in silence, scarcely seeing the servants, the high-ceilinged beauty of the passageway, scarcely aware of anything but the tightness in stomach and throat. *I should not have come,* she thought in panic. *I'll do the wrong thing and ruin the spell! They'll know, someone will know I've used witchcraft, or consented to it. I could burn for what I do!* She mastered an urge to turn and flee.

She heard music again: a sprightly dance, laughter and a babble of voices. She passed men in the King's red and white livery who smiled, the warmth in their eyes a reflection of her beauty. Now and again, recognition. Uneasiness touched certain of them as Ilse came unseen behind her. *Witch.*

Sofia stopped at the entrance to the ballroom and gazed out across the room. She'd learned dancing in this room. It was beautifully conceived, from its painted and gilt ceilings and magnificent chandeliers to the great expanses of window and marble floors. But she had never seen it filled before. There were folk everywhere, talking, eating and drinking, watching the formal pattern of twenty brilliantly clad couples dancing. Sofia brought her chin up, and waited. And Ilse waited with her.

"Sorcery doth not concern itself with spells of love; that is a mundane matter such as Green Witches use. The Gold Way is above such mundanities."

Green & Gold Magyk

7.

Prince Conrad was bored and trying not to let it show. For two hours, he had stood in a reception line composed of himself, his mother, two distant royal cousins and the Senior Steward. He had smiled, bowed, planted kisses on innumerable hands—or in the air just above them—and had heard so many different names, he'd lost track after the first four Annas. He had had girls and their mothers flutter eyelashes at him, giggle when he smiled; one poor thing had stumbled and torn her skirts free of her bodice. At least no one had fainted—yet. The royal cousins had made their escape when the first dance began; the Senior Steward had escorted the Queen to her throne. Conrad stood alone, seeking some specific goal, trying not to see the coy looks cast his direction from all over the ballroom.

He moved through the crowd, smiling at everyone, somehow managed to not quite hear invitations for the next dance, whispered remarks. He felt as much a fool as he had feared he would: on display, for sale to the highest ante, stakes in a game that he wanted no part of. Compared to his Marguerite, even to young Marie, these were raw children, these girls! How could he choose among such babes?

Or worse than babes: There once more was that dreadful girl in pale pink, another in light lavender with the lowest throat of any present—*Indecent with such a bony chest!* he thought indignantly—and the grim-faced harridan in deep violet behind them.

All three staring at him hungrily. Every time he'd looked across the ballroom the past hour, they had been nearby, ready to catch his eye, watching. Stalking him. . . . He shook himself, brought up yet another forced smile for them and moved on. Behind him, one of them squealed, "He smiled at me; he did, Mother, didn't he?" and the other laughed—his ears rang with that laugh, and it silenced conversation all around them.

He silently, imaginatively cursed his father once again, and fetched up at his mother's side. Henriette touched his hand and smiled as he looked at her. He smiled back but shook his head faintly. None he'd seen in the reception line that met his standards—the standards he would doubtless have to lower considerably before year's end, if not before the end of the night. "The pink and purple she-wolves, Mother; who are they?"

"You were introduced, my son." Henriette smiled and Conrad laughed bitterly.

"Hours since; they were among the first, weren't they? I remember the one in violet; she practically thrust her bosom into my face, and her nose needed tending. I do not remember the name." Henriette leaned forward a little, gazed around the room and sat back again.

"I might have guessed. That is Beatrix, second wife of Leo's Armsmaster, and her daughters."

Conrad stared at her. "Oh, no! How did she change so much? She was the fairest lady, and she spoke with the loveliest accent—"

"That was Magdalena, his first Lady. I liked Magdalena. No, this is the second wife; the daughters are hers from a first marriage and none of Ladislaus's." Henriette laughed mirthlessly. "The Lady hopes I shall have them at Court."

"Ah, God," Conrad moaned, and her laugh was lighter this time.

"She *hopes*; I cannot say I am distressed to disappoint her."

Conrad shifted, looked at Isabelle from under his lashes. "But Ladislaus had a daughter, don't I remember—?"

"She should be here. Beatrix said something in passing that she was not yet ready when they came, and sent them on ahead. Odd, where is she?" Henriette scanned the ballroom rather anxiously. "I shall be very cross with that woman if she delayed the child."

"Oh." Conrad dismissed that with a shrug. He wasn't certain he remembered any daughter. Or maybe he did, a skinny little thing with black hair that would not stay where it belonged and a biting tongue. Yes, at a party in his honor; she had been rude and Magdalena had made her apologize. "I dare not remain here with you, Mother; I feel safe here, and I'll never find the nerve to move again if I don't now." Henriette laughed, but her eyes were sympathetic. Conrad gazed out across the dancers, the musicians, the milling nobles and noblewomen. A definite direction to go would be nice, just now; a goal to reach.

A few faces stood out now: Gustave in the middle of the shallow stairs, watching the dancing with an insufferably superior smile. The sorcerer's assistants and younger associates were dancing, eating, enjoying themselves.

Dominic, brilliant in shades of blue and a mound of dazzling lace, surrounded by a sea of color—Neustadt's La Modes had discovered him. Conrad grinned, wondering how Dom was managing to behave himself; Dom had burst into gales of laughter on the ride through town at sight of that garishly clad, madly overdressed crowd on their balconies. Poor creatures, so certain they were up to the latest fashion.

Conrad wouldn't go there; young Count Ederrin and his fellow La Modes irritated him, and he really should find a partner for the next dance; people were beginning to get restless, waiting for him. The steps leading down into the ballroom—he could see from up there. Gustave was there, but Gustave would scarcely bother him, not after the debacle in the throne room.

The sorcerer was smiling gently, and that made Conrad suddenly wary. Why did Gustave look so pleased with himself? He was up to something! He wouldn't dare cause mischief here—or would he? The Prince walked back across the ballroom, smiling until his teeth ached. He stopped at the base of the shallow steps as though he'd hit a wall, and stared. Something truly was wrong. Gustave no longer seemed so smug; the smile looked as if it had been pasted in place and was at wide variance with the startled eyes.

A tingle ran along Conrad's senses, and he forgot Gustave entirely; *Something is about to happen. Something is afoot.* The scent of roses surrounded him as he turned; he gazed across the wide stairs and up. Everything slowed, until it seemed he stood forever, not even breathing, gazing at the dark-haired beauty in white and gold to match his own.

• • •

At first he saw nothing but glorious black eyes in a small, pale face. He blinked, took a step back, blinked again, and saw her properly. She was beautiful in a foreign manner, small, dainty, clad in white and gold as fine as his own. Her hair swung just free of slender shoulders as she turned her head to gaze out across the room. One fine-boned hand held the train of her skirts, the other lay gracefully against her throat, and he thought she hesitated; thought for one dreadful moment she might turn and flee.

She must have felt his gaze, for she turned almost at once to look at him. Conrad smiled; Sofia descended a step as he went up one. The scent of roses enveloped him, but it did not quite mask another scent—something his father's servants had felt. Something he knew, not from experience or anything innate, but because he was meant to notice it: Witch. *God, ah God, where? Not this lady!* But it was near her, too near. And yet no one stood within five paces; the nearest person was Gustave. Gustave—he stood like a marble statue, eyes wide with fear. *Witch!*

Not a witch, not here, not tonight! Not amid all Saxe-Baden's nobility! They'd—they would kill him, for letting a witch in, kill this lady, burn the palace—

He saw her, suddenly: The witch stood just behind the girl. Golden hair, midnight blue gown—the scent of witchcraft was overwhelming. Her eyes met Conrad's; she smiled and laid a possessive hand on the girl's shoulder. He could have wept; she was all his heart's desire and a witch's toy, both at once.

"No," he whispered. "No, please." He must get help—but who, and how? The witch was within reach, the nearest armsman well down the hall or out in the garden and unready for violence on this of all nights. *Stop her yourself, if Gustave cannot or will not.* The sorcerer had not moved a finger's worth; the witch glanced at him and the satisfaction in her face told him Gustave was under *her* control. Marigold in the Queen's garden, ash bows in the barracks—all he had here was his sprig of purple prunella, dried and fitted into the tiny amethyst bottle hanging from his neck, under his shirt. Prunella was a safety against possession, they said; the liquid in the bottle was a sorcerer's distillation and proven. He reached for the string, fingered the throat of his shirt frantically. It was gone. The witch held it against the white skin of her throat, and suddenly he could not only see her very well, he could hear her, though she was not speaking aloud. *Did you want this, Prince? It's a pretty little French thing, but no protection against such as I.* She let it fall.

Sofia's mouth was dry and her heart was beating too fast. Ilse just behind her, the Prince before her, but after that one brief smile, he had gone white and still; she might not have been there for all of him. *I knew it would not work! He has seen her; I am lost!* With Ilse at her back, Conrad where he stood, Gustave cutting off retreat to her left, there was nowhere for her to go. She clasped her hands together to stop them shaking; the movement drew Conrad's attention. *What will they do to me?* she wondered miserably, and in that moment, she looked so woe-begone Conrad's heart went out to her. He took her hand, brought it to his lips and held it there. Ilse's spell caught him, wrapped around them both, and was complete.

His voice didn't want to work; it barely reached Sofia's ears. "Sweet Lady, will you dance with me?"

She made him a curtsey that was grace itself; the smile came back to her face and lit her near-black eyes. Why had she doubted? It *would* work, of course it would. She would see it did. "My Prince, I will." His eyes were a deep blue; they warmed when she answered him, and her heart turned over.

Conrad kept her fingers in his as he turned to lead her through the watching people, past his smiling and astonished mother. Henriette had no nose for witchery, but it was unlikely she would have noticed anything amiss. She *had* come after all! Had she planned it, arriving late to draw his eye the way she had? Conrad was practically glowing, and as for Sofia—Where, she wondered, had Sofia garnered such a gown? Who had managed such wonderful things with her hair? Henriette watched them contentedly; she had needed to do nothing after all, only look at them! They might have been created for each other.

All the same—she gestured, and her steward leaned down. "Find Nicholas de la Mare for me."

Ilse stood beside Gustave and whispered against his ear. "Look at them, sorcerer. Are they not a pretty pair?" Gustave's pale eyes showed white all the way around, and sweat trickled down past his ear. "But look at Prince Conrad's people. Why, one would think they scented—magic? Sorcery? *Witchcraft*, perhaps? Not yet, perhaps—but they will. Shall we stand here like dear friends, my Gustave, and watch the word spread?"

Silence as the music ended. Ilse laughed and Gustave would have shuddered if he had been able. "Should we wager, you and I, what they will do? Once enough of them realize their Prince is bewitched, that he is under a common Green love spell? Poor Gustave," she cooed. "You thought yourself so clever! When did you first sense me tonight? When I came through the palace gates—or have you developed a better ability to scry than you once had? And can you remove a love charm, Gustave, or is that still beneath your dignity?

"I know what you intended, Gustl: You thought you would overwhelm me as I came down the stairs and denounce me as witch—not any witch, but the one who cursed a King and saw him die just as she said he would. Do you really think that would have made Conrad like you, or trust you? You would not have controlled him; but I do. Don't I?" Ilse laughed nastily. "What a pity it did not work. But you aren't good enough at what you do, are you, Gustave? It doesn't matter—you will not need to fret how to remove a love spell, Gustave.

"Because your Prince will die tonight at the hands of a noble mob, and so will the Armsmaster's daughter. And you—you should be grateful to me, considering the alternative—that Conrad would discover you *knew* I would come, that I would bring that child in response to the horoscope cast by his Frenchman. Their ashes to keep company with my mother's ashes, Gustave." Silence again. "Perhaps I will let you live, Gustave. Would you like that?" She looked at his face and laughed. "His lips cannot move, but his eyes say, 'Please, Ilse!' Yes, perhaps I shall see to it that you live, Gustave. Prince Conrad would not, would he? If he knew. And if he were alive tomorrow to see you dead."

She cannot be real. Conrad was dizzy with happiness, astonished every time he took her hand in his and felt warm fingers. There were roses, tiny silk rosebuds twined in the curls over her ears, silver roses in her ears; the heady scent of white damask roses surrounded her. The music ended and his hands tightened on hers. "I dance with no other lady, save you—this night or any other."

She averted her face and blinked aside tears; her eyes were brilliant as she looked up at him. "Then I shall dance with no one save you, Prince Conrad, ever again." She bent her head and Conrad's lips brushed her hair.

What have I done? She was not thinking clearly; she had not thought clearly in a long time—had the witch's spell touched her, or was it spilling over from the Prince? Love, the witch had said. She had not considered the consequences of the Prince's love; it wanted to soften her. *The Queen*—She could leave him now, go to the Queen, tell her—she would not; she knew she would not even as she thought it. She was afraid, yes. More than that, though: Conrad would never understand, and she would lose him. Him and all that went with him. She must not weaken; her future and her very life were at stake.

The Queen was watching the dancing when Nicholas de la Mare came up beside her, but now there was a faint line between her brows. "Look at them, good sir," she said in a low voice and in French. She glanced up.

The old astrologer looked at her thoughtfully, then out across the ballroom before replying in that same language and in a voice which would not carry beyond the two of them. "Madame, I do. Who is she?"

"She is Sofia von Mencken—the lady we spoke of this morning."

"Ahhhh." The astrologer contemplated her for some time, then turned back to the Queen. "So this is the child. You have an excellent eye, Madame. She is lovely."

"And so she is. But—something is not quite right out there; something does not feel right to me."

De la Mare nodded. "I felt it as soon as I entered this room, Madame, and I tell you frankly I do not like it. I cast the Prince's horoscope four times, and each said that noble maidens would come to this ball tonight but only one would command his attention. And she was born under the Archer—as you tell me this girl was. But there was more: magic, Madame. Sorcery, I thought; now I am not certain."

Henriette's gaze followed Conrad across the dance floor. "Magic. Riddle me this, if you can: How did Sofia come by that gown, when her stepmother treats her like the lowest of servants? And—and why has she come alone, and late, and not with her family?"

The astrologer looked where the Queen's glance went. "Dieu, what a creature is this? Madame, to your last question the answer is simple: Look, please, upon that sweet maiden and then upon the daughters of the monstrosity in purple! But for the rest—"

He sighed vexedly, then fished in the pocket of his plain black doublet for his clarifying amulet. By chance, his gaze lit on Gustave as his fingers curled around it. The breath hissed through his teeth and Henriette looked up at him in sudden alarm. "It explains itself, Madame. There is witchery here! And a witch to work it."

"Magic—?" Henriette glanced around the ballroom; she still *saw* nothing.

"Magic." He drew the amulet from his pocket and held it out. "Here, I beg, set your fingers upon this trifle and look at your husband's chief sorcerer."

"That woman—she was not there before! Who is she?"

"Ask rather," the astrologer said grimly, "what she is, and how she came. And I ask myself, why does the maiden who dances with your son—a child whose every move bespeaks her purity of body and soul—why does she come to this ball with a witch who reeks of ill purpose and vengeance?"

"My good friend, no! The woman who stands with Gustave? She—she is a lady, look at her!"

"She is a witch, and she holds Gustave prisoner. She is waiting for something, and I wager it is no pleasant thing. Madame, there is danger here."

"No." But Henriette felt a sharpened awareness and the first pricklings of fear as she looked for Conrad and Sofia. They stood near open doors into the rose garden, totally absorbed in each other. That alone must create keen disappointment among the hopeful young women and their parents, but there was more tension in the air than simple jealousy could account for.

Tension, anger—her eye touched on old Count Hensil as he turned away and nearly spat; she saw the word "witch" on his lips, on those of his Lady, and both were pale with fury. A few paces away, Lady Beatrix in that dreadful purple was violently shushing Isabelle, who sulked and nursed the arm she had used to point before her mother slapped it down. "Nicholas, did you see that?"

"The stepsister has only just realized who is dancing with the Prince, and her mother fears they could be burned with the same torch, if the child is named witch."

"It is not possible. I know Sofia. She would never willingly league herself with a witch!"

''Madame, please, let your steward take you away, let those such as myself who are protected in some way deal with this.''

''I cannot, Nicholas.''

''Your people—''

''They will do nothing, I know they will not. Especially if I am here.''

The astrologer sighed. ''You know them, Madame, and I do not. But the witch makes no move save to watch and speak to Gustave now and again; nothing will happen right away. I will get young de Valois to help me; perhaps he can persuade the Prince away from his lady and from the ballroom. Send for Augustine in the meantime, please—though what he can do, I do not know.'' He shook his head. ''I thought the Prince wore a specific talisman against bespelling!''

He was gone, working his way through the crowded nobles to find Dominic. The Queen watched him go, and her eye caught another man, standing where old Hensil had been, watching the dancers. She went cold with foreboding, for there was the final ingredient to this disaster. Gerhard von Elbe, elder brother of dead Jacob—half-mad Gerhard, who had sworn death to all witches. He was standing stiffly, white-faced, watching her son, watching Sofia, and she needed no sorcery to know what filled his thought.

Old Count von Elbe had brought his wife, two daughters and three sons. His daughters had come simply for the pleasure of a royal ball and new gowns; they were both too country and down-to-earth to be a Prince's choice, practical and sensible enough to accept that. They at least were finding the festivities to their liking; their brothers—particularly the youngest—were not.

The Count had voiced hopes that Gerhard might remember he was a free man and take note of eligible maidens himself, but he had not made any efforts to do so. It had been eight months since Jacob's death, but he still wore the look of a man in deep mourning and he glared at dancers, scowled blackly when women laughed.

He had cared greatly for his brother, had ridden with him when he found the old witch in Tannen, cheered when Jacob put the torch to her. He'd nearly gone mad when Jacob was found face down in the mud, like a common peasant! And the witch who had cursed him was still alive, somewhere. But no one sought her.

When the change came, well into the ball, it was subtle. But Gerhard knew as soon as he laid eyes on the Crown Prince and his Lady. "She's witched him," he whispered. Arno Hessen, a cousin of his who had been keeping an eye on him most of the evening, turned and looked at Gerhard.

"Gerhard, no," Arno whispered against his ear. "He's simply in love with her. Who would not be?"

"No! She's witched him. Look at his *eyes*!"

Arno's breath went in on a little hiss. The Crown Prince's eyes were unfocused, open too wide, his gaze glassily fixed. "Witch." The word slid out almost without sound, and he found with the utterance he believed it implicitly. Witch in the very palace!

Gerhard shook his head and touched his cousin's arm. "She is not the witch, but there is one, I sense her. I can feel her."

"Succubus?" Arno asked; his wary gaze darted from Sofia to his cousin, back again. How could one tell? Gerhard grabbed his arm, turned him toward the double doors and the three shallow stairs. "There!"

"There's nothing—"

"There is! Near the sorcerer, see him?"

"Of course, but—" Arno's voice trailed off. Perhaps it was Gerhard's insistence; but there was someone—someone hidden. And his nostrils tickled with the scent of witch. "Why does the King's sorcerer not act if there is a witch?"

"I do not know or care," von Elbe whispered. "Spread the word, quickly, Arno, and I will. This is—This cannot be." He slid back through the crowd.

"Look at them, Gustave. Do you see the word on the lips of the men nearest your Prince? 'Witch,' they whisper. Do you wonder what they will do, Gustave? Do you wonder what they will do once they see *me*, Gustave?" Silence. "You hate me, don't you, Gustave? For seeing your weaknesses and exploiting them. I shall give you a little longer to hate me, Gustave; are you not grateful? And I cannot yet decide whether to see you burn with the Prince." Sweat shone on the old sorcerer's face and darkened his robe.

Ilse gazed out across the ballroom thoughtfully. Conrad and Sofia, oblivious to the mutterings and chill looks around them, were seated near an open window, talking. "Perhaps I shall let you *all* live; it seems to me suddenly too easy, too painless. Like—letting an old woman die of smoke in her own hut, rather than binding her with iron and burning her alive. A new plan— not impossible, no." She considered this for some time, then slowly smiled. It was not a nice smile. Gustave paled and made another effort to free himself, but Ilse merely laughed and shook her head. Gustave's shoulders slumped; he remained firmly in her control.

They had conversed, speaking so easily they might have been friends for years; the silence between them was not uncomfortable. Conrad smiled happily. "Why is it we never met before?"

She seemed to come back from a long distance. "Perhaps we have."

Riddles; she used them now and again. "No. I would remember you. But, please—tell me more of yourself. Do you ride?"

"I did, until they sold my father's horses. I always rode, but I do not care to hunt."

The Prince laughed with delight. "Then that is another thing we share, besides chess, and music, and a fondness for Spanish roses! I have already turned down three boar hunts since I came home, and I cannot tell you how many people in Paris thought me a fool because I would not hunt the King's tame deer. Now, I do enjoy the company of a good peregrine. Do you like birds?"

. She shrugged, smiled. "I have never had one. But I like the look of a falcon. Those wonderful eyes! Is it a pleasure, loosing a bird and knowing it will return when you call it?"

"Pleasure mostly; a little guilt to take a free creature and bend it to your will." He grinned ruefully. "I seldom tell that to anyone; even my friend Dom thinks me strange on the subject."

A small pang; his words touched her and opened something that had been closed for hours. *Where have I been? I have lost myself in this man!* That had not been her intention; she had set her purpose and meant to stick by it, but he was not what she had thought. He loved her because of witchery, but he liked her of his own, and for herself.

She must be careful; her judgment was clouded, and she feared the spell on Conrad was spilling onto her.

• • •

Augustine and Nicholas de la Mare stood beside the Queen, watching as Conrad led Sofia back to the dance, oblivious of the growing number of hostile nobles. "Something must be done," the apprentice said anxiously. "I examined the Prince's safeguards myself; he was proof to witchery! And Gustave—"

"Let Gustave care for himself; the Prince is your first concern. Have you another talisman or must we find the one he lost?"

"We could set upon both women," Augustine said through clenched teeth. "I could manage the girl easily."

"No," Henriette whispered. "Please, let us make no fuss if it can be helped. Her reputation—"

"Her reputation is already in danger, Madame," Nicholas said vigorously. "But whatever her part, she has Prince Conrad's fingers in hers. I fear to simply separate them. Go, my young friend, find that charm and if you do, put it upon the Prince's person. Go, man, hurry!"

Conrad finished the complex steps of the galliard with no conscious memory of it, and came across to take his partner's fingers in his. She smelled deliciously of roses: musky red, fruity pink—that rich lavender that had been Marguerite's favorite. He had not thought of Marguerite in hours; he would never again associate the Queen's Silver rose with anyone but this lady.

With—"What is your name?" Why could he not remember it?

"My name?" She gazed blankly across the ballroom; a small frown crossed her face. "I—I cannot tell you. I'm sorry, I can't."

He frowned now. "I don't understand. Why?"

Color darkened her cheekbones, faded, and she shook her head. "I—I can't. Please, please don't ask."

"I've distressed you. Forgive me. Tell me when you can, swear you will."

A very odd expression in her eyes, gone before he could begin to try and identify it. "I will, I swear."

"Seven minutes, Gustave," Ilse whispered. She giggled. "Seven minutes until midnight."

Gustave let his eyes sag shut. He was ill with her spell, exhausted from his attempts to break it. *She is mad, truly mad,* he thought; the thought gave him no comfort. Seven minutes. Would she kill him then, kill all of them? She had changed her mind so often this past hour, had spoken in such fragmented bits he had no idea what she might do when midnight came. He was too worn to care at the moment. And the mere thought of arguing his case before the Regent's Council—trying to save himself from Prince Conrad's fury, if they both lived—he was not certain he could bear it. He had served two Kings faithfully, had pursued his craft thoroughly if not brilliantly—and because of this woman, they'd count that for nothing.

He felt her stiffen in anticipation. Two minutes before the hour! He'd lost five of what might be his last minutes worrying. *Fool! You might have used them to seek out the means of her death!*

But what was wrong with the woman? She was glaring across the ballroom and for one moment, he thought she might throw herself into the crowd—she was visibly exerting self-control. He tried to see what had upset her so: Prince Conrad and little Sofia von Mencken—surely not. They were still wrapped in their own little romantic fog, so much so that neither noticed they alone danced, while ominously silent men—there were no women anywhere near the dance area—surrounded them.

But then Gustave saw, too: That dandy of a Frenchman slipped easily through the crowd, easing his way through close-packed men and onto the dance floor. And dangling from his fingers, a small amethyst bottle. Talisman. Ilse hissed in fury.

"Conrad!" Dominic caught his shoulder.

The Prince looked at him impatiently; the music faltered, died. "Dom? Can't it wait?"

"No." Dominic stepped forward, detached Conrad's right hand from Sofia's left, pushed the little bottle into his friend's palm and closed the fingers over it. "You must have dropped this; I thought you might like it back."

"Dropped—" Conrad swayed as the talisman and Ilse's spell met. It hurt. He let go Sofia's other hand, wrapped both tightly around the bottle. Sofia cried out in surprise as the clock bell tolled the first chime of twelve. She must go, she must! But Conrad—She hesitated, torn; a suddenly visible Ilse came across the ballroom, scattering men and women, and grabbed her shoulders. Sofia twisted in her grip, subsided with a little cry of pain.

Panic. Men backed away from the dance floor and the undoubted witch. Others fought their way forward, to reach her and take her captive. "Kill the witches!" someone near the windows bellowed; the cry was taken up, drowning out the final chimes of midnight.

Dominic still had his friend's arm; otherwise Conrad would have fallen. Ilse's spell was gone, the talisman cool against his hand. *Witch.* He barely saw *her*, save as a backdrop for the girl. Sofia would not look at him. "Why?" he demanded harshly.

Her eyes filled with tears. "I—I didn't mean—" She got no further. Across the ballroom, long brocade drapes went up in flames and someone was shouting, "Kill them both, kill the witches!"

"You stupid girl, I'll murder you for this!" Conrad lunged for Sofia's throat but Dominic grabbed his shoulders and grimly hung on. Ilse's laugh echoed across the high ceilings, topping the screams of frightened women, men's shouts, the crackle and roar of fire. She backed toward the door, taking the girl with her, smirked as men backed away from her, fighting the pressure of other men behind them, fighting to avoid the touch of witch's skirts. Without warning, they vanished.

"Mother! Where is she?" Conrad was having difficulty breathing. Thick smoke from burning curtains was blowing into the room.

"She's safe. Your stargazer got her out! Your own safety, my friend, think to it!"

"No, I can't—!"

Dominic clapped a hand across his mouth, not gently. "What will you do here, eh? Your nobles have gone mad. If this were a time to fight, I would fight, but it is not. Come out of here!" Conrad ground his teeth, slammed a fist savagely into the wall. "And hurry—that little bottle will not protect you from fire!"

There were hysterical men and women everywhere, the French doors clogged with people. Conrad let Dom lead him out through a window. By the time they broke free and reached the relative safety of the lawns, nothing could be seen but smoke and fire; flame had found a way through the roof.

Guards came from inside the palace, from the barracks, from down in the city. Fire lines were quickly and efficiently organized, but the damage was done: The ballroom was gutted, the roof fell in, and only determined effort grimly assisted by the Prince himself prevented its spread. Most of the men who had attended the ball were long since gone, and only a few, including von Elbe and two of his sons, remained.

The rest had gone to find the witches—or any who were foolhardy enough to shelter them. Their cries could be heard echoing through the city streets.

"To cure infestation by a witch, or witches, when it is very great . . . fire will burn not only the creature but the dwelling in which such an abomination is found."

Mallius Heber, *Destruction of the Green Way and its Adherents*

8.

Conrad's throat hurt from the smoke, but the fire was under control, finally. The oily smell of burned wood, the odor of burnt flesh threatened to make him ill. He would not be ill; he would show nothing. Men watched him—openly curious or covertly; he would not satisfy their curiosity. *How does it feel to be under a witch's spell? Learn that for yourselves, and leave me alone!*

His mother had come; he'd persuaded her back to her room and somehow managed to avoid her questions—managed to keep her from asking most of them. Dominic—thank God for Dom, who had worked as hard as any man to save the rest of the palace and who would keep his wonderings to himself. Dom's hand was tied in blue cloth that had been one of his boot wrappings—he'd somehow cut it rather badly.

Conrad turned away as men came from the blackened shell of building with yet another horrid, blanket-wrapped bundle. Four men dead! Gerhard von Elbe, his cousin—two others now, neither recognizable.

Gustave—he would have left Gustave to burn, but Augustine had got him out, robes and shoes smoldering.

Well; he had names for both women, thanks to his mother: Ilse. Sofia. There was nothing more he could do here; perhaps it was time to go join the hunt for witches.

Dominic came after him. "Where are you going?"

"Where do you think? Don't try to stop me, Dom."

The Frenchman shook his head. "You go, I go with you. The stable is that way—"

"There isn't time."

"Why run through this entire city afoot? The mob—pardon, your young nobles—have a considerable start. Get Parsifal. You can stay on him bareback."

He could; but he had forgotten how much work it was, and he had his hands full for several minutes. "I shall break my neck," he mumbled. Parsifal's sensitive ears twitched; one rear hoof slipped on damp cobbles. Just behind him, Dominic swore loudly.

The streets were ominously silent. But there were men—small clutches of them who ran when the horsemen came into sight, single men who vanished over fences and into doorways; frightened faces at windows that pulled back into darkened rooms. They entered a small square just as the roof of a thatched storage building fell in a cloud of sparks. Men stood, grimly silent, before it; defiant faces, hard eyes. Conrad looked down at them and prayed his face was as unreadable—inwardly he was terrified. *They tried once to burn me, these men.* How could he possibly deal with them? *What would Father have done?* But he was not Leo.

"What is this?" Silence. Dom stirred behind him, readying his English pistols; the click of the hammer was unmistakable. "Why do you burn a poor man's storage?"

"Witch—" one of the men said flatly.

"There was a witch," another began, but less certainly. To Dominic's audible dismay, Conrad slid down to stand before the men. One of them was a border noble; he recognized the man's colors. "We thought—"

"You thought, my Lord?" Conrad prompted as he hesitated again.

Use of the title brought about a subtle shift: Men who had been a unit of destruction moved a little apart. They were men addressed as "my Lord," but this man—

The borderer inclined his head. "Your Highness, we thought we saw a witch go there."

"And so you burned it." Conrad's voice had taken on strength. "But there was no witch, was there?" The man shook his head. His eyes were now fixed on a spot just in front of his feet. "Before God, man, anyone might have been there! A beggar, a servant girl gone to fetch her master ale from his private store! To whom does this hut belong? Does anyone here know?''

"It's Johann the baker's storehouse," someone called out. A crowd of city people had gathered, unnoticed, in the past moments. "He kept his sacks of wheat and rye flour here."

"Then I suggest that Johann the baker be found," Conrad said, his voice pitched to fill the square. "And let him set an honest price on the loss here, so that those who did inadvertent damage might recompense him for it." By some quirk of mind, Conrad remembered the name that went with the colors. "You will see to it, will you not, Count Grunnen? For this—accident?"

He thought the Count might argue, and so did the Count. But the heat and excitement of the hunt had left them. "Your Highness, of course we shall. For the accident."

"Good." He turned, took hold of Parsifal's mane, pulled himself onto the gray's back and rode off. Dominic looked them over carefully; men backed away nervously as he eyed them in turn.

"You terrified me, my friend," he said as he caught up to Conrad.

"It wasn't such a terrible chance; they're trained to obey royalty. I merely reminded them."

"They did not remember that earlier, Conrad. Remember, please, that I have two bullets, one in each gun, and even I cannot dispatch eight men with blades—two hands, two rapiers.''

"Two hands, two rapiers." Conrad laughed lightheadedly. He'd been terrified, facing those men, but he'd done the thing right. It was a dangerous, heady feeling, cowing an unruly mob. "You'll remember those faces for me?"

"Of course; I always remember things, don't I?"

Conrad laughed again. "Why do you think I never play cards with you?"

His amusement faded as they rode into the next street. Men and torches everywhere; men looking for two witches. If anyone else found them first . . . Someone was shouting not far ahead. Conrad dug his heels into Parsifal's ribs; the horse leaped forward and Dom cursed again as his Gabriel followed at a bone-jarring pace.

Another fire, this one a pile of brush in the midst of the street; Conrad found it easier this time to exert his will and make the men put it out. A number of angry burghers were easier to deal with; they backed away from the two noblemen—boys, really—who'd tried to drag their women into the street.

It was late, getting cold and damp. Conrad scarcely felt the chill and the hours swam one into the other. He had never spoken so much, so quickly, in his life—but he was getting better at it, developing confidence by the moment.

The house guard found him well up near the north wall of the old city. He took the messages they brought from the Queen, promised to return to the palace at once. But as soon as he and Dominic were out of sight, he turned aside once again.

"Conrad, you promised—"

"Go back if you want, Dom. I can't." Dominic grumbled, but he stayed.

They were back on the main street once again, not far from the palace. Conrad pulled Parsifal to a halt and stared. Two days ago, it had been cheerful, sunlit, brilliant with late spring flowers and brightly clad maidens; tonight, it might have been a preview of Hell. Men with torches fled down the cobbles before him, other men came uphill; horses and men ran from side alleys and gates or vanished through them. Women's voices and sleepy men's voices came from windows and doorways. "Before God, Dom, where did they all come from?"

Almost under the horse's feet, women's voices—he recognized them, suddenly: the woman in purple, her daughters. "Silence, both of you! We are nearly home, you will forget all this, trust what I say. Johanna, stop whimpering, and Isabelle, I cannot walk so fast, my shoes are tight and so are my stays."

"Mother, I'm afraid—" The whispers echoed through the narrow streets; they were near, not as near as he had thought. He saw shadows now: red-edged shadows of three women, cast by torches high on the street above them.

"Don't be, Isabelle, it's all right. You looked lovely tonight, both of you, I was so very proud. Shhh, Johanna, don't talk, wait until we're safe indoors."

"But, Mother—" The contrast to frightened whispers was shocking; Conrad's whole body jerked.

"Shh, no, Johanna—"

Johanna's heel drummed on the paving stones. "I'm trying to

tell you, why won't you listen? That girl with the Prince tonight, that was our Sofie!'' Her voice echoed between tall buildings.

Isabelle's rose shrieking to top it. ''You fool, shut up!''

''Run!'' Beatrix shouted. Three women came flying out of the shadows, running madly toward an open garden gate. The cry of ''Witch!'' was all around them and men came howling from all directions. A torch flew end over end to fall onto a long balcony; another followed. A third. Fire shot up the curtains of an open window.

Dominic set Gabriel against the tight-packed mob and roared out, ''Move aside, he's war-trained!'' Someone caught hold of his leg; Dom slapped the hand aside with the flat of his dagger and Gabriel swung around, teeth bared. The fight went out of the crowd at once. ''Be still, all of you, your Prince is here!''

''Get buckets and put that fire out!'' Conrad shouted. Men turned to stare at him defiantly. These were older men, hard men who'd fought with the old King. He held Parsifal steady. Retreating would be the greatest mistake he could make. ''Put it out, I say!'' He looked down and found a familiar face. ''You, Hildebrand! Is there not a well nearby? Get that fire doused, at once!'' The man eyed him sullenly from under the brim of his hat but moved, and those nearest him followed.

He was afraid to move, afraid to trust his voice again. But there was no more overt defiance, and moments later, Count Ernst Gustav von Elbe, his two sons and several men in von Elbe colors came down the street afoot. The Count stopped by Conrad's horse. ''Your Highness, you should not be here.''

''There are women in there somewhere, Count. These men thought one of them a witch.''

''Impossible; I know those women, there's no witch in the von Mencken household. Wait here, Highness.'' Conrad went white and only the hand wrapped in Parsifal's mane kept him from falling. That name—her house! But she had not been one of those women!

The Count was already at the front door. Conrad drew a steadying breath and slid from his gray's back. It was hot on the steps, and smoke was beginning to slide across the sill. ''Lady Beatrix, it is Ernst Gustav! Come out, I will see to your safety!'' Someone in the crowd laughed harshly; the Count's eldest son snarled him down. ''We know you are the widow of Leopold's Armsmaster and no witch! And your daughters are not witches, nor your servants! Come out while you can, Lady Beatrix, the house is aflame!'' Beatrix's voice was muffled by the door; it opened, suddenly, and men fell back, but nothing could be seen of the women. ''Lady, I cannot hear you!''

''You swear we will be safe?'' Beatrix shouted. ''Myself, Isabelle and Johanna?''

''I swear it by my own daughters!'' the Count shouted back.

''And I swear it!'' Conrad added loudly. ''I, Conrad! No one will die here, Lady!''

Momentary silence. Then: ''There is no witch in this house, I swear that before God. Only myself and my blood daughters!'' Less than a breath later, Isabelle stood on the threshold, coughing and gasping for air, her pale hair loose on her shoulders and her feet bare. A hand pushed her down the steps and she stumbled, fell into the Count's outstretched arms. Ernst Gustav pulled a handkerchief from his sleeve, stuffed it into her fingers, and put her aside. Isabelle stumbled and the Count's son caught her and held her.

Johanna stood there now, her face smudged, tears running down her face, two small, squirming dogs in her arms. Beatrix, kerchief to her nose, was at her shoulder. Johanna went unwillingly down to the street, only Beatrix's hand on her sleeve holding her steady. She was dead white and visibly terrified. Her gaze darted from one man to another, back again; her eyes momentarily fastened on the Prince, went beyond him to stare into the dark. One of the dogs slipped from her arms and ran under her legs, back into the house; the other followed.

''No—no, babies!'' she screamed; Beatrix, startled, lost her grasp on the girl's gown. Johanna turned on her heel and fled back into the hallway.

''Johanna, come back!'' Beatrix's voice rose in anguish; she cast one terrified look at Isabelle, another at the upper floor, and plunged back through the open door. Conrad and Ernst Gustav leaped up the steps together, but as they started through the door there came a terrible, rending crash. The stairs fell, bringing down the landing; flames bloomed in the lower hall and flared out into the street.

Men grabbed Conrad, who in turn wrapped his arms around the Count and pulled him away. Other men beat at Conrad's smoldering sleeve, and the older man's breeches, and someone poured a bucket of water over them both.

Conrad staggered to his feet. Once he was certain he could walk without swaying, he walked back to his horse. Von Elbe wordlessly held out cupped hands to help him mount, then stood looking up at him. Conrad shook his head. "See the fire is put out."

"Your Highness, we shall." Count Ernst Gustav looked as though he would have said something more, then shrugged, inclined his head and went back to shout orders at the line of men passing leather buckets. "And I'll see the young lady cared for."

"Young lady?"

"The Lady Isabelle."

Conrad glanced at Isabelle, who stared at the burning house in a most unnatural silence. What did he care for Isabelle—for any young lady save one? And it was not her well-being he cared about. "Thank you," he said finally.

The destruction of the Armsmaster's house had a strong dampening effect on the violence; there was silence here, silence all about them. Not far away, the great clock tolled three; men went into the garden and came out with two elderly folk—servants, perhaps. Men watched in silence as the old man's leg was braced and wrapped—he'd somehow broken it—and the dazed old woman was bundled unconscious into someone's cloak.

"Conrad." Dominic touched his hand, and he winced; he'd burned his fingers dragging Count Ernst Gustav away from the fire. "It is enough. Come back to the palace." And, with the flat matter-of-factness that was Dom: "You won't find her here."

"No." Conrad turned Parsifal toward the palace and kept him to a walk. "But I will find her, Dom; I swear that. And I'll kill her."

Dominic merely nodded. The fire was warm on their backs.

He was dreaming—Gustave caught himself on the edge of a pit of sleep and woke with a gasp. He blinked, stared for some moments at the dark canopy overhead, the heavy curtains drawn on three sides of his bed. Footsteps in the doorway; he let his eyes close and slowed his breathing. *Augustine*, he thought. The slight shuffle that was not quite a limp sounded like Augustine, but he was not about to open his eyes and see. He wanted speech with no man at this moment. Whoever was there, Augustine or another, came across to the bed with a shielded light that made a ruddy glow on his closed lids. Silence. The light and footsteps retreated, the door brushed against its jamb and he was alone again.

He didn't want to think, either, but it was absolutely essential, no matter how humiliating. The Prince no doubt wanted his head at the moment. The Queen might. Of course, Queen Henriette was not a combative person; she'd never say or do anything against her dead husband's favorite sorcerer. Conrad was another matter, particularly if he knew what Gustave had intended. Somehow, Gustave was afraid Conrad might know—Gustave's certainty of Ilse's arrival, his intention to wait until the witch had entered the ballroom and only then expose her and save the Prince from harm.

Nothing, *nothing*, had gone as he'd wanted! It could not have been worse; Conrad might not know but he'd suspect. He *wanted* to find bad faith in anything Gustave did. The old sorcerer bit his lip to contain his vexation. Arrogant brat, who did he think he was? Did they not teach respect to the young any more?

Well, snotty brat or no, he *was* Leopold's heir, and the only heir—unless Saxe-Baden went through a rather ugly succession war. Gustave would lose too much by that alternative. Like it or not, he would have to butter up the Prince, somehow gain his confidence, as he once had Leopold's. It must be this Paris education that made them so suspicious, though old Leo had never been as impossible to deal with as Conrad presently was.

Gustave cast a thoughtful glance at the closed door to his chamber, closed his eyes and *reached*. No one in the outer chamber, or in the hallway—Augustine was the only one who could shield against discovery, but not against his own master. For all practical purposes, Gustave had this wing alone for the moment. Good.

He pushed the covers aside and got to his feet, swayed and grabbed for the bedpost. Damn his assistant for dosing his wine; he absolutely did not need soporific in his blood just now! He'd have to operate around it, somehow. He waited until the room steadied, walked to the door and peered into the next room. Empty, as he'd thought. He padded barefoot across to the main door to the hallway and shoved the bolt to, absently lighting candles with a snap of his fingers as he came back. He had enough things here, he thought; enough that he wouldn't need to go down the hallway to reach his laboratory. Better if he could avoid household *and* family tonight. Tempers might be more even in the morning.

The large chest was full and it took time for him to work down through books, scrolls, rolled hides, bottles and boxes to reach the box he needed: an ancient thing, carved and bound in copper. He set it aside, replaced the other things, shut the large chest and took the small one back to his bed, locking that door behind him also. Now only Augustine could come in to bother him. But Augustine would know what he did and leave him alone.

He extinguished the outer-room candles with a word, lit two near his bed and stuffed his cold feet back under the covers as he opened the small chest and took out a smaller box of blue powder, a stoppered, hollow antler full of liquid, and a shield-shaped bit of polished copper with several symbols scratched on its reverse. He needed to read the symbols through twice; it had been some time since he'd attempted anything like this. But his need to know was strong and this was the only way to do it. There *must* be a clue to the situation, must be a way for him to gain control of it once more. Or at least control of Conrad.

He set the copper lozenge back in the box, slipped the stopper from the horn and dabbed clear, odorless liquid on his temples and wrists; set it aside and moistened one finger on his tongue, set it in the powder and sucked what clung to it. It tasted like bread mold, rather musty and unpleasant. He ignored that with ease of long practice: A sorcerer couldn't be choosy about how things tasted.

He closed the chest and locked it, plumped pillows and lay back among them, eyes shut, and *reached*, leaving his body behind on the bed. He had one brief, disconcerting vision of it: an aging body, his skin loose on his bare, skinny arms, crepe-y on his throat, lined around his eyes and deeply folded around his tight-set mouth. His smoothly bald head and wrinkled brow; the wig, forgotten, caught between pillow and shoulder, looking like a long-dead rodent. *Am I really so old as that?*

He set that aside then. The Queen—she lay in among her comforters and soft sheets. Several of her ladies sat nearby; two slept on couches near the windows and one on a trundle. The Queen was not asleep, Gustave knew. She was worried about Conrad, and that drove out any other concern she might have, including any about Gustave. He withdrew carefully, wary lest anyone sense his presence. One or two of her ladies were sensitive.

Conrad. He was not in the palace or anywhere on the grounds.

Gustave expected a long and hard search for him, and was rather surprised to come upon him almost at once, before old Ladislaus von Mencken's town house. The part of him that went out stood upon the wall opposite and watched—with growing approval— as Conrad subdued the witch-hunters. The Prince had the right kind of strength in there, somewhere; he wasn't all spoiled and indulged child.

He was about to withdraw and begin a final search—not without trepidation—when he sensed the object of that search almost at his feet: Ilse, under a Green spell for invisibility, Sofia in her grasp and under the double spell of invisibility and obedience. The witch was watching the house burn, aware of Sofia's horror, enjoying both.

Gustave had never cared much for the Armsmaster's second wife. Or his first one, for that matter. Women were an annoyance, a drain upon a man's financial and spiritual resources, a block for any who wanted to seek Answers. Women were cards to play in whatever game a man played, or coin in exchange as Henriette had been. He watched Johanna follow her dogs back into the house, sealing her own fate and her mother's. Watched the Prince leave, and Count Ernst Gustav's son lose control of Isabelle, who tore free of him to flee wailing into the night.

Ilse was not aware of *him*. Of course, he was not there in Body, and she would need more wizardly skill than she had gleaned to detect what was there.

Gustave sighed, silently from his perch on the wall, deeply in his bed. He so seldom left his corridor in the palace these days, let alone went out into the City! He'd have to do that much; he was afraid he'd have to do more, to secure the Prince to him.

And he *would* have to secure Conrad; his future and his very life depended on that. He had no place to go, if Conrad took away his title. He had worked too hard for too many years making himself indispensable to Saxe-Baden's King; he didn't want to give up what was his.

He was tiring; sending his Being out of Body was an exhausting thing. But he waited until the Prince and his dandified French friend were back in the palace grounds before returning to himself. Until Ilse slipped past the scattering crowd before the now gutted Armsmaster's house, dragging Sofia through the side gate and into the garden. She was prepared for a confrontation, he thought. Not with him.

He wouldn't force one with her, not just yet; not until he was certain he was strong enough to fight the residual effect of her original holding spell.

No, Ilse was waiting for Conrad. Gustave smiled as he withdrew Being and returned to his Body. He thought he knew, now, how to deal with the Prince.

"To render invisible—hazelnuts, ground to fine powder, a pinch of seed from the first scythe of grain, a measure of water. Cool to a paste, dry and grind to a dust. When it is touched upon palms and ears, [the witch] becomes invisible."

An Oral Grammarie

9.

Ilse sat on the stone bench at the end of Magdalena's rose garden and divided her attention between the dying fire and her companion.

She was tired; tireder than she had any right to be, and there were still long hours before they could leave Neustadt.

And much to do.

She smiled as she thought of Count Ernst Gustav gathering his older sons to him, the three men walking back toward the palace. *Hope all you want, old man,* her thought jeered him. *The boy is dead, and nothing will bring him back! One son yet to die—Ernst Gustav!* The eldest alone had not gone on that witch-hunt. Perhaps she would not allow that to matter; it would all depend upon how she felt once she'd found a way to kill the Count's next eldest son, Alphonse.

Sofia huddled on the bench next to her, eyes closed. She was giving no trouble, but then, Ilse expected none: The poor, simple thing had thought to use *her*, Ilse! The child learned, and she would learn more in the days to come, she and that young Prince both. She would learn more in the next hours.

There was no one to oppose her now, and so very much to look forward to.

Sofia blinked. Roses—her mother's roses. But over all was the dreadful odor of burned wood and fabric, wet ash. She couldn't

think; she had not thought for hours. It was too much effort just
now; it hurt too much. She drew both slippered feet under her
and tucked the skirts over them. Ilse ignored her; she supposed
she must be grateful for that, but the change in the woman terrified her.

How had it gone wrong? She didn't understand. She was afraid
to try and find out, and Ilse—she couldn't ask Ilse.

She was sweating, despite the cool night air; the white and
gold gown was ruined. The witch had dragged her from the
ballroom, through fire and a pack of wild men. They'd dodged
mobs through the streets for what seemed forever—and then to
come here, and see . . . She couldn't mourn for Beatrix, not
even for poor, silly Johanna. Risking her life, losing it, for those
dogs. At least Drusilla and Otto had somehow escaped. At least
she did not have their deaths to blame on herself.

Witch. Was it her fault two women were dead for certain, and
how many others in that ballroom?

She couldn't bear it any longer, suddenly. "What are we doing?"

"Keep silent," Ilse hissed, and gave her such a look Sofia
pressed herself back against the vines and was still. But the
witch finally stirred and began talking. "I tried to control too
many people tonight, and I lost sight of what I wanted most.
That was foolish. I won't do that again. Gustave still lives, unfortunately. But for the rest—no, I can salvage what is left. It
will work, and better than the other." She seemed to suddenly
realize she was talking out loud. "Do you not understand?" She
smiled faintly, unpleasantly. "Shall I explain to you? I shall; it
will give me pleasure. Your father was the King's Armsmaster.
He must also have been a close-mouthed old man, for I gave
you my true name and you did not know it. Ilse." She paused.
"Daughter to Gerthe, who was Tannen's Green Witch—"

"Oh, *God*."

"God will not help you; no one else will. Not after what you
have done. Listen. I called down a curse upon three men that
day, but three deaths are not enough; my mother does not yet
sleep. I know; I see her in my dreams, she tells me. And so—
but I did not wish simply to again poison or bespell my enemies.
Any witch might do that. But in the end, I had no need to plan,
for the old King's Will gave me the answer. And *you* gave me
entry. I could not have done what I did without you, Sofia. Are
you not proud?"

"Are you mad?" Sofia whispered, aghast.

"I am not mad," Ilse replied evenly. "Do not say that, ever, to me! And you are a fool, for who but a fool would commit treason to steal the heart of a Prince?"

"I did not mean—!"

"She did not mean—who will care what you meant?"

"I was a fool, to listen to you," Sofia replied bitterly. "He liked me!" Ilse's laughter drowned the rest of her words.

"Liked you! He loved you, wretched girl, and it was all my doing! He would never have looked at you but for me! You were cringing in your grubby little room behind a locked door—and had you somehow gotten out, what then? They would have laughed you out of the ballroom!" Silence. Sofia looked at her, not trusting her voice, but there was still defiance in her eyes.

"He liked me," she said finally, but her shoulders drooped.

"He will hate you now," Ilse retorted. "After what you did to him. That was not love in his eyes when I pulled your throat away from his hand, was it?"

No answer. Ilse went back to silent contemplation of the smoking house, and Sofia let her head drop to her knees. He must loathe her. But that was the least of her worries just now. What she had said to Conrad was true; she'd intended harm to no one. She'd willingly accepted Ilse's help, but she would have held up a wife's honest bargain had she married him.

He wouldn't believe it, of course. She wouldn't either, in his place.

But for the witch's whim, they would have died tonight. *She'll kill me, and him—if I let her.* Words. They couldn't touch her just now. Finally she sat up and stared across the ruined, trampled garden, stared at the ruin that had been her home for all her life.

"There is no shame in using specific powders to focus thought or complete a spell, though many a sorcerer or alchemyst believe it to be so."

Green & Gold Magyk

10.

Conrad and Dom returned the horses to the stables and found a rather harassed Second Armsmaster Eino Trompe about to come in search of them.

"There is to be a search of all the houses, beginning at dawn. The Queen suggests you go and sleep. But if you can recognize these women—"

"I'll come."

There was a silver rose tucked in his belt. He'd found it when he'd rid himself of the ruined white and gold; it was hooked on his falling lace. Hers. He'd keep it to know her by. Perhaps she'd still be wearing the other one when he found her.

There were forty of them to search an entire city; there would be more, if needed. The City gates would remain closed to anyone seeking to leave.

The city clock tolled five times. There were signs of burning and destruction everywhere. Merchants moved through the streets, but few women, no nobles.

Who would harbor a witch? The burghers mistrusted witches, though they liked sorcerers no better. But there might be constraint, or they might be disguised. Anything was possible. They might well be gone. But that—no. Somehow, Conrad did not believe that.

Time went by slowly; the Prince took five men of his own,

including Dom, and went doggedly from house to house along the main street. The clock struck ten before they reached the last dwelling before the market; Eino Trompe had thirty men quartering the market.

He had been called away to look at women in other parts of the City; none was the witch Ilse, none Sofia.

It was enough; he looked and felt gray. He sent most of the men back to the barracks.

He shifted uncomfortably in his saddle. Something—like a hand, touching his back or his shoulder to get his attention. There was nothing unusual to see here, though—except Dominic, hunched over his pommel, cradling his burned forearm.

"Dom, you look terrible."

"I feel it."

"Go get some sleep, you need it."

"And you do not?" Dom snorted, an almost-laugh. "I know you; where do you mean to go without me?"

"I won't be long behind you, it's all right, go on. I—want to look at the von Mencken house again."

Dom's nose crinkled. "If that is all, if you are certain—" Conrad nodded. "I have had enough to do with burning and all that. Why, though? There is no one hiding in that house. But as you please. Remember only that the Queen will have my head if you do not come soon, will you?"

"I'll remember." Conrad shifted in his saddle as Dom turned and let Gabriel walk up the street. Like an itch he couldn't scratch. Perhaps he imagined it; exhaustion did funny things to a man's perceptions. But he nudged Parsifal on.

The day was still and already warm, the house no different than it had been an hour before. He let his eyes close briefly, shook himself and dismounted. He could not remember having ever been so tired, but it wasn't that that was sapping him. He felt unspeakably fouled, his mind, his heart—his very soul— tampered with. He'd thought—he wouldn't try to remember what he had thought. He could kill her for what she had done; he *would* kill her.

The clock bell struck the quarter.

They were there; somehow he knew. Witch—two witches, whatever his mother said.

She might kill him, Ilse might; she'd killed his father. He didn't care; danger or no, to have one chance to see her again, perhaps to find her black heart with his dagger, to kill them both. . . . He squared his jaw, loosened the rapier and the slender daggers in their sheaths, shoved the garden door aside and slipped through the opening into shadow.

The smell of fire clung to him; it seemed he'd breathed nothing else all his life. Incongruously, he could also smell roses: There was a white damask touching his left shoulder. He moved jerkily away. *I shall never again deliberately smell roses.* His throat tightened, relaxed a little as he swallowed. He stepped gingerly across the fallen boards and loose stone, skirted a row of ash-dusted cabbages, moved through a thicket of rosemary and lavender edging a sanded path. His breeches rubbed the herbs, releasing a light fragrance.

Roses were everywhere, planted thick beyond the chamomile and sage; Spanish roses, the heady deep purple named for the French Cardinal Richelieu, the almost unbearably sweet Queen's Silver, and half a dozen of the creamy, pink-edged Rose d'Alba. He knew them all; he'd gathered them for Marguerite in the Queen's gardens near Orleans. And the night before, he'd breathed nothing else until the smell of burned wood and smoldering curtains replaced it. He bared his teeth, expelled a held breath, and pushed his way through Magdalena's roses.

They were there, both of them. Ilse was tall and golden, her skin like cream against the midnight blue of her gown. She looked somehow regal, supremely confident. *Why did I come alone?* Conrad wondered; but he wasn't afraid; he hadn't felt fear in hours.

He turned away from her deliberately to look at her companion. Sofia sat in a huddle on the stone bench, morning sun touching her dark hair. She felt his eyes on her, for she glanced up swiftly, back down again. Her shoulders sagged; she would not look at him again. She looked so small, so terribly vulnerable, and despite himself, Conrad wanted to reach out, touch her, assure her—*Assure her what, you fool? That she is free to bewitch you again, if that is her desire? Has she not done enough?* He gritted his teeth, drew out the dagger and balanced the point between thumb and forefinger.

"You may as well put that away, young Prince," Ilse said stonily. "No one here will be killed just yet."

"No?" He looked at Sofia again. "Why not?"

"You can kill her later—perhaps. I am Ilse—but you know that, just as you know your father murdered my mother."

"I know it. But why me? Why her?"

"Why not?"

"I did you no harm—"

"That is not for you to say! Your father—your family, her family—they did!"

Conrad shuddered. The woman was not only dangerous, she was mad. "Killing the entire royal family and half the nobles of Saxe-Baden will not bring your mother back to life," he said finally. "It changes nothing."

"That is not for you to say," Ilse said again. "Two more deaths—three, five—how will you stop me?"

"I will. If you kill me, someone else will."

"Perhaps not. But we are straying from the point. This child—would you like her?"

"No!" It tore at his throat; Sofia closed her eyes.

"But I thought," Ilse said in a silken voice, "that you cared for sweet Sofie. You danced so well together, this past night, you and she. She is a pretty thing, isn't she? All dusky Spanish skin and hair, white and gold gowning. But then, you never saw her before I wove the spell around her that ensured you would want her, did you? Would you like to see what she *really* is?"

He'd thought her pale before; she looked suddenly like death. "Oh, no," the girl whispered. "Please, no. I never meant—" She huddled back on the hard stone seat, pressing herself into shadow, edging away from him.

Ilse's spell left her reft and shaking. Reddened hands plucked at a shabby, plain apron, pulled the heavy gray skirts down over bare little feet and hid themselves in the folds of fabric. The witch had not even left her the least bit of her own finery, her own attempts to smooth her skin or hair; she looked as much a scullery maid as she had the morning the invitation to the Prince's ball had arrived. She turned her head away, let her wildly loose black hair fall around her face, and closed her eyes. A wave of color and heat washed over her face and throat.

Prince Conrad's eyes went wide in shock. This—she looked like a drudge! Her hands were a peasant's, all rough and dreadful, her hair loose and snarled, her feet bare and filthy, her gown rough and patched! He had danced with—with this? Ilse laughed delightedly.

"How lovely; she weeps because I show you what she is; and you retch at the very sight of her! Is this not true love? You would kill her now, if I let you, wouldn't you? Only look at his eyes, Sofia; see how he wants you—for his sword. No. Not here. If you want her, you must come for her.''

''Where?''

''Patience, and I will tell you.'' Ilse snapped her fingers; Conrad jumped; Sofia cried out and came unwillingly to her feet. Ilse caught her arm and dragged her close. ''In the woods, in the meadows, in the mountains—who can say? Somewhere beyond cold stone and chill walls and gardens where man sets his will upon the plants. Within the boundaries of Saxe-Baden. But I wonder, sweet Prince, what you will do when you find us—do you think an iron dagger will ward off *my* magic?''

''If there is a thing that will find your heart, I will use it,'' he replied grimly. ''Somehow, I will find you. And you will both die.''

At that, Sofia's head came up, and her eyes met his. One silver rose shone through a mass of loose hair and caught the morning sun. And they were gone.

He blinked. The smell of roses was all around him. ''Ah, *God*.'' A faint creak behind him brought him around, dagger concealed against his arm. The weapon fell to his feet, his jaw dropped. For down the sanded stone walkway came the last man he would ever have expected—Gustave.

The old man looked terrible in full sunlight, and Conrad could not remember having ever seen him so exposed before. His robes looked slept in, and a broad-brimmed hat was crammed down nearly to his brows; the wig was missing. His eyes under that shaded brim were black hollows; his mouth sagged at the corners. He stopped before the sundial in the midst of lavender and low mint, and one hand came out, ostensibly to touch the bronze face. Conrad thought he was holding himself erect only by his grip on the thing.

''What are you doing here?'' The words came out, flat and rude; Conrad didn't much care at the moment, and Gustave for once seemed impervious to insult.

''I *saw* things. I knew she would be here and she would see that you found her. I felt her leave as I arrived. She is truly gone, not merely unseen; she has left behind no spells to inform upon you, though I doubt even she could do so much as that, after this past night.'' Conrad opened his mouth, shut it again. Somehow, all the things he had to throw at the old sorcerer wouldn't come out. ''You should not have faced the woman alone, Prince. She is a dangerous foe.'' Gustave's mouth quirked, the least bit. ''I know. I underestimated her.''

Is he trying to invite a confidence? Does he think I should trust him or does he simply want to use me? Was everyone ready to use him? It should have infuriated him; at the moment it simply made him tired. ''Riddles,'' he snarled. ''Riddles, old man. Speak straight for once.''

''What, a sorcerer speak straight? Riddles are the very matter of my *philosophie*,'' Gustave replied dryly, and in spite of himself, Conrad was amused. ''The Queen sends a message for you. She says your mind will function better after sleep and food. She hopes you will dispose of all thought of no food and no sleep before she sees you, so that she does not have to make the arguments.''

''She trusts you with messages for me?''

''No,'' Gustave admitted. ''The steward was about to send his first assistant in the direction your young French friend said you had gone. I merely intercepted him, and said I would go in his place.''

''Oh.'' Sleep and food were a good idea, Conrad decided; he needed to be much more alert than he was to cope with Gustave. The man was entirely too friendly. ''All right, then. I'll go.''

''Wait.'' Gustave traced the raised pattern on the edge of the sundial. He stepped away from it, swaying slightly without the support, and stood still in the path, his shadowed face turned toward the far wall of the garden with its stone bench. He closed his eyes momentarily, then caught at Conrad's wrist and drew him toward it. Conrad would have resisted, but the old man's fingers dug in, hard. He stood there a moment, silent, his head cocked as though listening. Finally he nodded. ''She sat here, the little one.''

''How do *you* know?'' Conrad demanded. Gustave looked at him and sighed heavily, tiredly.

''Give me the credit of knowing certain things, my Prince! I learned such simple spells when *you* were a mote in your father's loins! I can sense her, of course. I can sense the witch Ilse. And also—'' He pointed. Conrad went down onto one knee and gazed under the edge of the bench. Back still in shadow, nearly invisible, were slippers. Tiny slippers, light-colored velvet. A faint odor of roses touched his nostrils. The Prince reached, stopped as Gustave touched his shoulder. ''Wait. When you touch them, they will unmake. They should have unmade when the other

garments unmade. A rose spell is one of the most difficult, and
beyond most witches. Even so, it is fragile. They should have
fallen apart at once. Wait. They might be useful.''

Gustave brought out a small box from one of his inner pockets, searched through it until he found an even smaller box made
from a nut shell, sealed with a bit of silver paper. He prised off
the paper, shook half a dozen grains of some substance into his
palm, recapped the nut carefully and restored it to the box. He
then carefully divided the powder equally between both hands
and opened them over the slippers. ''She wore them; her essence
will stay with them, made or no; perhaps you can use them to
find her, or to find the witch who made them. Find one and you
find both.'' He sat back on his heels. ''They will also be useful,
when you have the girl, as a test. Two tests. They will unmake
as soon as we remove them from the bench; they will remake
only on *her* feet, so that she or Ilse cannot somehow present us
with a substitute. But they will remake only if she is a witch
herself.'' His slightly protuberant brown eyes met Conrad's
briefly, then fell. He reached out to touch Conrad's belt. ''But
you have a better guide than a bundle of rose petals. The girl's
earring will show you the true Sofia beyond doubt, and will
perhaps help you find her—if she still has the other. But it is not
precisely safe; Ilse may have bespelled it to harm you.'' He held
up a hand. ''I know her plans, but why should she not use the
bauble to cause you pain? Mmmm? Let me see it.''

Conrad eyed Gustave measuringly, finally handed the earring
over. Gustave held it to the sun, touched it against the sundial,
hummed tunelessly. Conrad ground his teeth and turned away.
''It seems safe. One last test will make certain, but I have none
of the liquid with me.'' He handed it back and went to look at
the slippers. ''Do you see now why I advocate the repression of
Green Magic and its adherents?''

Conrad turned away. ''I won't argue that with you until I've
slept, Gustave; I haven't the patience just now, and I've more
important things to worry about than that.'' He sensed Gustave
at his back marshalling arguments, felt purpose leave the man
as suddenly.

''As you wish, Prince. Let us finish our business here, then.
Take up the slippers . . . so . . . carefully!'' The sorcerer
stripped off his short cloak and spread it on the ground before
the stone bench. ''Set them here—quickly!'' Conrad nearly
dropped them; a silvery-lavender rose petal caught on his ring;

the slippers dissolved into a spray of petals. Gustave folded them carefully into the dark green wool and set it in Conrad's hands. "Another cloth might have done better for them. It is too late now. Do not open this. Keep it safe. There was magic used on these roses, and the girl involved. And so were you. They came into your hands whole, however, and that must mean something. But you do not waste magic. Ever."

Conrad held the bundle close as they left the garden: Queen's Silver by the color and sweet smell. *Roses. Ah, God, will I never again be free of roses?* He followed the sorcerer back into the street. Gustave's ancient wooden cart stood there, one of his young apprentices crouched patiently on the seat. Gustave climbed into the back of the thing. He seldom traveled, but when he did, he never rode horseback, never walked. Even for a rare, short journey to the city gates, it was always this cart. So far as Conrad could recall, he had never seen Gustave on horseback.

He'd never seen inside the cart either, but he'd heard rumors and tales. The cart was said to be a wonder. It contained a comfortable chair, a bed, decent wine and good food, books and boxes of spells, bottles, salves, powders—everything a sorcerer needed for comfort away from home. There was even a small brazier for the rare times he must travel in winter.

Conrad stared after the cart as the driver brought it around the fountain and started slowly back toward the palace. Gustave had been decent—too decent. He must truly fear for his neck, to be so—well, he had been polite for Gustave. And useful; those slippers.

Whatever the slippers might mean; he had only Gustave's words for anything, and few of them made sense. Riddles. He was simply too tired to draw any real conclusions at the moment. He mounted and pulled the bundle tight against his ribs while he guided Parsifal one-handed back up the broad street.

"Words are the mainstay of sorcerers, and not only for their magycs . . ."

Green & Gold Magyk

11.

A late afternoon sun slanted through high windows, warming the Queen's study. The long doors with their numerous tiny glass panes stood open, braced against potted fruit trees. A light breeze kept the room from becoming too stuffy: It was not suited for such a large group of men, and certain of them—Gustave seated well back in shadow on a fine-legged French chair in one corner, the Second Armsmaster with his broad shoulders and battlefield voice—looked quite out of place.

It suited an important requirement, however: It was upwind of the reeking, blackened ballroom. Even the flattened lawns and topiary of the surrounding gardens could not be seen from Henriette's present vantage.

They were seven, all told: Conrad, his eyes red-rimmed and puffy from the long, sleepless night and morning, followed by a long, hard sleep from which he'd wakened in the late afternoon heat; the Queen, her needlework covering her lap but momentarily untouched and indeed forgotten; Gustave, who sat still and watchful in his corner with his chief apprentice Augustine; Eino Trompe; Nicholas de la Mare; and Dominic de Valois. The latter alone stood, one shoulder against the wall, just behind Conrad. He was hardly visible and nearly unrecognizable in plain dark riding leathers. Only his weapons—dual rapiers, daggers, two English pistols—marked him as Frenchman and noble.

He nodded faintly as Conrad looked up at him, and Conrad

felt himself relax a little. This meeting was not likely to go as he wished, but Dom's little nod said volumes: *Patience*, it said. *We know, you and I, how to subvert authority.* How to avoid it, at least. He and Dom had managed in the face of rules and orders before.

It was quiet, save for the sounds of workmen laboring to pull down the hazardous remains of the ballroom, and Gustave's occasional, irritating sighs. *We could wait forever like this*, Conrad thought vexedly. He stirred; eyes focused on him.

"They are not in the City," he said. "The last houses were searched hours ago. We are wasting time."

"The woman threatened you again this morning," Henriette said quietly. "We cannot simply act without forethought. She might yet be within the walls."

"She is gone, I know it."

"Green Witches do not wield well in cities," Augustine said.

"She wielded quite well last night," Eino Trompe replied pointedly, and Gustave sank further into his corner.

"They—" Augustine began. Henriette held up a hand for silence. She was visibly distressed.

"Sofia Magdalena von Mencken is not a Green Witch—or the willing accomplice of one!" Her dark eyes touched on each of the men in the small chamber, resting last on Gustave, who looked very uncomfortable. "The Supreme Sorcerer will certainly agree with me, will he not?"

Gustave's mouth was a thin line, his color high, and he had the look of a man who wanted to admit nothing of the sort. The Queen waited him out; his shoulders sagged. "The woman Ilse has trifled beyond her class and station. I first heard of her a year or more ago, when word came down from villages on the Scarp that a witch had used fire as a weapon. That is forbidden. She is no longer witch. But she is not sorcerer, either—she could never be that."

"The lady," Eino Trompe prompted him. "You are straying."

"The lady—eh," Gustave replied sourly. "She is no witch. Who could think it?"

"Rubbish!" Conrad was on his feet. He subsided as Henriette touched his hand.

"It is not rubbish," she said crisply. "Listen to me. Sofia was my Lady for two years."

"You *said* that, Mother—"

"I will say it again, since you do not listen. I know that child as well as I'd know a daughter of my own. And I blame myself that she was driven to such an action." Conrad shook his head. "Never mind, that is not important now. But I fear for the girl. Ilse may already have murdered her."

"No. She is not dead," Conrad assured her grimly. "Not yet."

Henriette determinedly took up her needlework and set several stitches; she let the needle fall to her lap. "Something must be done. Why do you all watch me, and wait for each other to speak? Does no one know anything? How could this Ilse vanish into thin air? Commander Trompe, the villagers of Tannen, might they not know?"

Trompe shrugged gloomily. "Your Majesty, believe me, we have searched for that woman since she first uttered her curse against the King. If Tannen knows where Ilse is, no one will say. No man of us got anything; by that, I can only believe they fear her more than any King's man."

"Then she cannot be far away; is that not sense? Why should they fear her if she is gone? Try again, send common men; the villagers might trust them. And prepare a search!"

"There will be one, as soon as it is light tomorrow."

Henriette folded her needlework and set it aside. "The hunting and persecution of these Green Witches must cease. I have always said so; this to me is proof of it." Gustave stared at her in astonishment. "All of this because an old woman was burned to death—and what was *her* crime? She wove love charms, cast good-luck bundles on the fields to ensure good harvest, or brewed medicines for sick children and ill herdsmen!"

Gustave opened his mouth. No sound came. He tried again. "Your Majesty, no! Those young men sought Ilse, it was only a mistake—"

"Only a mistake," Henriette mocked gently, and the sorcerer flushed. "There would have been no 'mistake' if we did not encourage this witch hysteria. Are we barbarians like the Spanish?"

"Is not Ilse proof enough?" Gustave shouted.

"Of what? You yourself admit she is no village witch. Green Witches have a place here, they serve useful purpose and cause no harm. We need them; the village folk need them."

Conrad jumped to his feet again. "What foolishness is this? A woman uses magic against us and we argue the worth of Green

Witches? I do not *care* about Green Witches! I only want those women found!''

"Witches," Gustave spat, "are an abomination!"

"They are not the only abominations in Saxe-Baden," Conrad snapped. Henriette clapped her hands together; the report silenced both men.

"What now is this? I will not countenance such squabblings here! I am aware you two do not like each other, but you will behave civilly *here*! Have we decided—yes, several things already. A search of Tannen and its lands.''

"I ride with that search," Conrad said flatly.

"No. I forbid it."

"You dare not, Mother. Wager me what all the gossip is this afternoon in the marketplace. If I do nothing, men will believe I am still under the woman's spell—even that I connived with her! I am part of that search.''

Dominic de Valois cleared his throat. "Your point is valid, my friend, but to speak bluntly, you were bespelled last night. Is it safe for you to hunt the very women who entranced you? Is it not true that one betwitching makes a second easier?''

Color flooded Conrad's face. "My thought is my own; leave be, Dom.''

Henriette stirred indignantly. "I am head of the Regency, Conrad, and I will not agree to this! Not if you ride from the City with that look to you and the purpose it bodes. Whatever your feelings, you cannot murder either of those women without trial—that is what your father did, and look what it brought upon him!''

"Mother—"

"Be still! I am not finished! Do you really believe Sofia knew what that woman planned? My honor she did not.''

"Honor," Conrad said bitterly.

Dominic touched his arm. "This takes us nowhere. If we could make some compromise. Madame, if you permitted the Prince to ride tomorrow, and Conrad, if you swore no harm to those women, to return them for trial, would that serve?'' Conrad hesitated; he looked as if he might refuse, but he finally nodded.

"Let me think," Henriette said. "There is also the matter of your safety, Prince Conrad. Your present mood scarcely reassures me.'' It was a stinging reproof from his normally softspoken mother. "We must also draft a proclamation to counter rumor; have it cried in the towns and villages that Prince Conrad and I are unharmed, the palace still stands, the witch Ilse is not to be given shelter or food since she is held traitor."

Eino Trompe shook his head. "Mention the word 'witch' and there will be mobs and burnings all across Saxe-Baden. When the guard rides out, they will spread the word also. No one will aid the woman when she is named traitor."

Henriette tugged on the rope hanging by her arm, sent the servant for her secretary. Conrad cleared his throat. "Madame, I gave you my word. Do I ride in the morning, or no?" He would, with or without permission. The Queen hesitated, and Gustave came unexpectedly to his assistance.

"The Prince must go," he said. "Ilse wants him; might she not reveal herself to him tomorrow? And if he bears certain things with which to bind her power—" He sighed and looked around the room complacently. "It is a great pity I am not fitted to such a ride, but Augustine shall go with him. And I myself shall see to the spells and charms they need."

"And if the Prince should be killed?" Trompe demanded harshly.

"He will not be."

As the King was not. Trompe did not say it, but he might as well have. Gustave shook his head. "I made mistakes, I admit it. I underestimated her, but I was not alone in that, was I?" The others in the small room simply stared at him; there was no possible answer to such an outrageous remark. "I shall go at once; it will be a long task."

"I will be ready," Conrad began. Henriette and Eino Trompe overrode him in chorus.

"It is not safe!"

"You are Leo's only heir!"

"I was not safe in the palace last night. Think not only of the gossip, but what may come of it! Mother, there may be nothing to inherit if she gets away with this. And you remind me, Trompe, I am father's heir. How will the army ever respect me if I remain behind the Queen's skirts? Mother, you know I cannot stay behind. After all, I will not ride alone, will I?" *Yet,* he thought grimly. If a thundering pack of horsemen did not flush those women from hiding, that was just what he would do.

They were gone at last, leaving him alone with the Queen. Henriette watched him with troubled eyes; Conrad was nodding where he sat. "Go and sleep again, please, Conrad." Conrad shook his head. "You look like death."

"I feel it just now. But I cannot sleep."

"Then be sensible and take some of my drops in a cup of wine. You were awake all night, and do not think I don't know about that bandage under your glove. What use are you right now?" Henriette went back to her pettipoint. "And since I could not persuade you to reason, you will have a dreadful ride tomorrow—I have listened to your father complain of them often enough. Think how shamed you will be if you cannot stay the course."

"I know. I'm sorry. I—I am not thinking clearly—"

"I am unhappily aware of that, my son. Let Augustine prepare you a sleeping mixture, take a plate of cold soup, go to sleep. That is sense." Silence. "You will not, will you?"

"No," he mumbled. Henriette looked at the bowed head, half in frustration and anger, half in pity. "Mother, I'm sorry. About tomorrow—let's not talk about it, please."

"As you wish." She could have shaken him. He and young Dom would have gone alone this afternoon if she had not forestalled them. Thank the good God her steward had caught them and sent them here; and that de Valois at least had shown a little sense in trying to ease tempers. She knew Conrad was not reconciled; he would have to be watched closely until this mood passed. Perhaps tomorrow might end the matter; she could only hope and pray it did.

Conrad swayed back into the wall, folded neatly at the knees, and slumped to the floor. She let her needlework fall, dragged on the bell. "I *told* you," she murmured crossly as servants hurried in. "Get him into his bed, and send for Augustine; he needs valerian."

"No," Conrad whispered vexedly, but there was no strength in him, body or voice. Everything faded; he was barely aware of being carried up the broad stairs and down the carpeted hallway to his rooms, of one of his men applying cool, damply scented cloths to his forehead and cheeks. He could taste the slightly bitter edge to the wine someone held to his lips, and he thought he saw Augustine there. The circle of worried faces blurred, was gone. He slept.

"To cause obedience, a piece of old cane from a white Damask Rose, ground to powder with a part of valerian seed and put into a measure of water. Let a blossom of any kind stand therein a night and a day until all the water is drawn within, and whoso takes that flower from you will surely do all your bidding without question, but for only a night and a day."

An Oral Grammarie

12.

Sofia's throat was tight with unshed tears; her head ached dreadfully. Everything else hurt, to some degree or other: Her bare feet and her legs below the kirtled-up skirts were scratched; her calves ached from the pace Ilse set; and she'd scraped the ends of her toes on cobbles. Now they walked in open woodland, and the dry pine needles pricked her instep.

It was mid-afternoon before the witch came to a place she seemed to consider safe enough to allow them a rest. There was water somewhere; Sofia heard it above the shrill of birdcall and the throbbing in her ears. She was thirsty and there was a grinding pain in her stomach, but she scarcely cared at first. Simply not to walk another step was bliss.

She dropped to her knees, heavily, slumped to one side against a smooth tree bole while Ilse mumbled and muttered over her head somewhere. The birdsong was muted, the air seemed heavier and the glade was a little darker. *Magic, a concealing spell.* Sofia closed her eyes and tried not to think about it. Everything faded for a long moment; she jerked and cried out as Ilse nudged her thigh with her hard hide slipper.

"Drink this, and eat. You need both; I cannot carry you and we have not gone nearly as far as we must before dark."

Sofia drained the rough wooden cup at a long swallow, bit into the thick bite of bread. It was spread with a slightly sour, white and crumbly cheese, and the bread was dry and coarse.

Not really much worse than some of the things Beatrix had fed her. Ilse refilled her cup from the stream behind her, ate her own bread and cheese and watched her companion. Sofia drank the second cup of water more slowly, using it to wash down the bread. It cleared her mind of the hopeless fog that had filled it for so long.

She looked up to see Ilse's narrowed gaze and the small smile she was beginning to hate. She set aside her cup, picked the cheese off the last of the bread, ate it separately and stuffed the bit of bread in her pocket. "I go no farther. What you did last night was unspeakable! You *used* me to ensnare the Prince! You used a love spell to make him care, knowing how he would hate that—*and* me, once he knew! And then you made certain he did know!"

Ilse's eyes had gone cold and it was all Sofia could do not to turn away. "Of course I used you, you stupid girl! I will continue to use you and there is nothing—not one single thing!—you can do to stop me. Nothing you can say. You will go where I tell you, when I tell you, you will do whatever I wish you to do. Because if you do not freely, you will do so under constraint, and in pain. Do you understand me?"

"I will not!"

"You will! You are part of the magic, like it or not, until Prince Conrad comes to find you, and kills you. Then you will die, and so will he. Do you understand me?" Sofia's gaze faltered, fell to the ground in front of her bare, filthy feet. She felt sick. "It was so delightful to watch, you and he, the fairy-tale prince and princess. For three hours, he thought he had found True Love. What a pity it was all a sham. Caused by *your* touch." Ilse laughed, Sofia shuddered. "He hates you for that; did you watch his eyes in the garden, whenever he looked at you? And so you are bait in a very special trap."

"No." It was less than a whisper, but Ilse heard. She caught Sofia's near shoulder, dragged her around and slapped her hard.

"I warn you now; do not *dare* say no to anything I tell you!" she snarled. "One way or another you will obey me. Did you learn nothing after so many years under Lady Beatrix?" Her fingers gripped the girl's jaw, brought her head around and up so she could stare down into Sofia's wide, blank eyes. "You are no one and nothing; you are bait in a trap, and then you are dead. Do you understand me?" Silence. "Do—you—understand—me?"

"I understand you," Sofia said flatly. Ilse released her and she slumped back against her tree.

"Good. Remember what I said."

"I shall."

Ilse studied her closely, searching for sarcasm in the two words, but she finally turned away and settled her back against a tree. "Sleep. We have a long way to go. Do not try to sneak away, I will know if you do, and you will not like what I will do to you. Do you understand me?"

"Yes." It was very quiet all around them. Sofia let her eyes close. Bait—no. She had done enough harm; she would do no more. But she was too exhausted and miserable to think.

It was late afternoon when Ilse woke and dismantled her spell. Before they went on, she gave Sofia shoes similar to hers: plainly constructed, with hardened, curved leather soles. They were too large and very ugly, but Sofia scarcely cared. Her feet were swollen and cut; the leather would keep splinters and needles out of her toes. She cried out when she stood; her calves were so tight she could not force her heels to the ground. But Ilse would not wait; she limped for some time on the balls of her feet, until cramping muscles and tendons loosened.

Fortunately, the first hour or so of their journey lay over open forest floor: Deeply carpeted in leaves and pine needles, it was soft, mostly flat, shaded and cool. And Ilse held to a reasonable pace; she seemed to have no fear of being followed.

They made another stop while it was still daylight. Ilse gave Sofia a small, hard apple, let her drink from the stream, and dragged her across the water and on north before the girl could properly catch her breath.

Sofia remembered little of the journey, that night or in later years, save that almost at once the land changed: There were deep, sheer-sided ravines cutting across the land, and the ground itself began to slope up; trees grew closer together in places. There was undergrowth to force through or—where it was a thicket of bramble and berry bush—to find a way around. There were bogs and mud, mud and grass-slimed rock in the low places, insects that swarmed in thick clouds around her eyes and mouth, mosquitoes that left enormous welts on her bare arms and her throat. Once there was a high, crumbling ledge that Ilse dragged her across, cursing her for a coward as stone slid from under her feet to slither and crash down a near-perpendicular slope and splash into deep water a long way down.

This was the Scarp: that long, steep ledge that rose like the very edge of the world, cutting Saxe-Baden nearly in half, east to west. Scarp—she knew the tales: wild beasts and bears who ate men; kobolds in the deep woods and fairies in the meadow, both hating men and working evil on any they encountered. Dreadful heights and spills of rock where folk fell and died, their bodies smashed to pulpy blobs. Terror slowed her steps, froze her thoughts; Ilse finally had to drag her along when she simply could no longer force herself to move.

By the time the moon rose, a thin and late shard, she had become a compliant creature, following where Ilse led so long as the witch kept a hand in hers or on her arm. Ilse no longer cursed her; it took breath she did not have to spare, and clearly it did no good since the girl either did not hear her or did not care what she heard.

Sofia's first conscious memory in hours was moonlight and the faint smell of woodfire. A brooding black forest stood on three sides of them, a steep, shelving ledge on the fourth and at its foot, a village. Most of the huts were black, regular shadows in the deep tree-shade, here and there a blue-white wall or bit of fence stood out. In one hut, well back in the trees, there was a light. Ilse sighed in relief. She had not realized how worn she was, how much she had counted on Aunt Hel being *here*, being awake at this hour. She tugged on Sofia's wrist and started down the trail worn into the ledge by countless generations of hunters and herders, pigs and sheep.

The old woman was weaving straw into a door protection spell when they came into the hut's single room, and Ilse caught her breath. Gerthe had been weaving straw almost the last she'd seen of her mother—the room swam, briefly. Sofia, released and forgotten, sank to the floor and leaned back against the wall near the stone fireplace, eyes closed.

Hel finished the shape and bound the ends into place before she looked up. "Niece. What is this?"

"Trouble, Aunt. But no great trouble—"

"No?" The older woman's mouth twisted in a wry grin but her dark eyes remained expressionless. "And since when is there trouble with you and it is not great, young Ilse?" Silence. "The girl. Who is she, and why here?"

"A favor, Aunt. Keep her for me—"

"Why?"

"Until I can ready a certain place—"

The older woman held up a hand, and Ilse closed her mouth. She could not afford to anger her aunt, not just now. Hel pushed slowly to her feet, walked the two paces from table to fire and shoved two sticks in among the coals, then pushed a pot of water through the ashes to rest against the coals. She glanced at Sofia only once, then squatted down, back to the girl, to wait. When the water steamed, she took a cloth bag from a box next to the fireplace and tossed it in the pot. A pleasant fragrance floated on the steam. Hel dipped a wooden cup in the pot, handed it to her niece, filled a second and slewed around to sit with her faded black skirts touching Sofia's. "One day I must have another cup made; the girl and I will share. Tell me." She sipped, nodded, and leaned over to press the rim against Sofia's lower lip.

Sofia came a little awake at that, and at the sweet-sharp scent. Where was she? Through half-closed eyes, she could see a tiny one-room hut, overwarm after the cool of middle night in high places. The ceiling was low, made lower by the bundles of herbs and sausage hanging from the rafters, and the scent of the air reminded her of the hut in her mother's garden, where she dried herbs and flowers. The woman who had pressed her to drink was old—her hair might have been gold or white, hard to tell by the light of a fading fire, but her face was deeply lined. She wore a heavy ring in one ear. Black intense eyes met hers; Sofia let her lids shut again.

"She's the Armsmaster's daughter, Aunt," Ilse said calmly. The tea seemed to have revived her; Sofia wanted only to sleep but another part of her held her awake. *Listen. Learn where you are. Escape*—no, do not dare think that, the witch would know, she would hear the thought. *Listen*—

"The daughter of old Ladislaus, is she? And why here?"

"I need you to keep her for me, Aunt. Please."

"That's no answer, niece," Hel snapped.

"No. All right. To complete what I started, for—on account of Mother."

Sofia's eyes snapped open as Hel began to laugh. It was a high, unpleasant sound, like nailed shoes across a stone floor. "Vengeance again? Or vengeance still? And is it for Gerthe or for yourself? Ilse, by all the great and little ones of the woods, you are mad!" Ilse shouted out something but Hel's laugh drowned it. The laugh died away finally. Hel finished her tea and dipped another cup. "Do you think Gerthe sits at God's hand and asks this?"

"Aunt—!"

"Ah, never mind."

"If you had seen," Ilse began.

"Do not dare say another word, I will hear none of them! I have wit enough to know that is no use to me, or to Gerthe! But I was not the one tampering with things forbidden a Green Witch, by law *and* by common sense. I was not the one they were seeking when they found poor old Gerthe instead and burned her." Silence, save for the settling of the fire and a night-bird somewhere beyond the unglassed window. "Think on this, girl. Gerthe was my sister. I knew how she felt about your fiddlings. But she died thinking she'd saved you. She did that of her own choice, will you make nothing of what she did?" Ilse stirred impatiently.

"If *you* won't help me—"

"Oh." Hel took another stick from her pile and stirred the coals of her fire. "I never said that. You want the lass kept, I'll keep her. You're family, Ilse. I feel that no less than your mother did. How long?"

"Tonight, tomorrow night. I'll sleep here tonight, a few hours, I'll be gone before the sun comes up or the herders go, the village won't know I've been."

"They don't like what you've done," Hel said simply. "It's not my doing, it's how they are."

"I know. Stupid peasants."

"They only know what is theirs, girl. They dislike sudden change. You can't fault them for being what they are. Two nights, then."

"And then I'll come for her. Keep her hidden."

"No one comes in here save my apprentices, and they're away gathering nightshade and fairy-caps for old Hulgen. His eyes don't work as well as they used to." Hel laughed shortly. "If they saw her, they'd never say to outsiders, anyway. You know that."

"I know." Sofia's eyelids had long since drifted shut again and she floated on the edge of sleep but her legs felt so odd, not being walked on after so many hours, she could not quite drop off. She was aware of Ilse standing close, looking down at her, of the old woman Hel crouched by her side, the soothing smell of that herb tea, the faint, left-over taste of it in her mouth. "She will give you no trouble. I took the spine from her. But if she—"

"*I* can manage a slip of a girl, thank you!" Hel snapped. She moved away briefly. Sofia felt scratchy warmth across her shoulders as Hel tucked a rough woolen blanket under her chin. She sighed and snuggled down into it, moved unresisting as the old woman pressed her down onto the floor. There was something under her ear that rustled and smelled like grass or straw. Someone pulled the hard shoes from her feet and tucked the blanket around her toes. She drew a deep breath, let it out as a long sigh, and slept.

"Though a witch might have knowledge of the stars, as they relate to her gathering of plants and flowers, true understanding of the paths of the stars, and how they control destinies, is a matter for the study of sorcerers."

Green & Gold Magyk

13.

It was cool in Neustadt, the streets slightly damp from a pre-dawn rain. The palace lawns and shrubs sparkled in first light. The air was still and smelled faintly of smoke. A single file of horsemen rode down the cobbles and out the double gates, vanishing into early mist rising from the road.

They returned well after dark, a sorry little line of tired men leading exhausted horses, shadowy figures skirting the edge of the sanded palace carriage area—almost furtively, as if they were somehow ashamed.

The Queen had been waiting for them for hours, and Conrad came to her even before he shed his gloves. His appearance shocked her: He was drawn, gray-faced, and his eyes weren't properly focused. She sat, locked her fright behind set lips, and waited as he drank the wine she'd had warmed for him.

He relaxed, so suddenly he sagged against the chair; he fumbled for the table at his elbow, set the empty glass on it.

"Nothing?" she asked finally. He shook his head. "At all?"

"Nothing." He ran a bandaged hand through his hair. "All I could think that last hour was, if that Ilse lied to me—if it was all a lie they could be across the Rhine already. They could be anywhere." He let his eyes close. "We rode everywhere, I think—nearly as far north as the Scarp at one point." A servant refilled his cup and retired to her place against the wall.

The Queen pressed the cup into his hand. "Drink. Marie,

send for something—cold meat, bread, whatever the kitchen has at hand. Go, quickly. Conrad, did you eat nothing today?''

"Mmmm? Food—oh. Yes. I think so. Hours ago.''

"You cannot aid her if you starve yourself and render what brains you possess to uselessness.''

"Aid her. Aid *her*?'' Conrad laughed sourly. "Mother, do you think that night was real? You know why I went.''

"All right. That night was not real,'' Henriette said. "And so you smart from bruised pride. How must she feel, do you think?''

"Why should I care?''

Silence. The door opened and a footman came in with a tray: a bowl of thick, hot soup, a small round loaf of bread, cheese and an apple. Henriette waited until the man left. "Put pride back in its place and think—eat first; you cannot think when your stomach is growling.'' Conrad scowled and applied himself to his food.

It did help. At least the hollow feeling, the high, ringing scree in his ears, the impatience and anger all faded as he emptied the bowl, cleaning up the last drops of broth with a chunk of the bread. "I—Mother, I'm sorry.''

"Do not apologize to me. I think perhaps I know how you must feel.''

"Do you think so?''

She smiled faintly. "Hardly of my own experience! My life has been quite placid and ordinary, and believe me, I am not sorry for that! Your father and I were wed because two stuffy and not so friendly governments thought it a wise course, to seal a temporary peace between them, and because your one grandfather wanted a pretty Frenchwoman to settle his son, and your other grandfather saw marriage to any King as a fine increase in his own social status. I was afraid of Leopold when I first saw him: He was so stern-faced, so large, so very German. And for many days after that first meeting, I had no opportunity to say more to him than 'Good day.' We actually had little in common, you know; but for all that, we found we liked each other, quite a lot. And I think he respected me in his own way, as much as I respected him. A very *pratique* relationship, with little or no fire to it. So of my own experience, no. But I was young once; I listened to the bards and the opera; I read the works of the young men who filled the Courts of Love and I wept over them.''

Silence. "She was so lovely, how could you have failed to love her? In all honesty?"

"I didn't—" He stopped. In all honesty—before it began, when he first saw her, his heart had stopped. He let his eyes close. "No. Mother, don't ask that of me, please. I—I already promised you I won't hurt her. She can clear or convict herself from her own lips. Isn't that enough?" He began peeling an apple, scowling moodily at the curl of peel and the knife, his eyes dark and the muscles bunched at the corners of his mouth.

Henriette thought of five things to say and said none of them. She knew that stubborn look. At least she had his promise. "Where will you go tomorrow?" she asked finally.

"Trompe thought further east and north." He had expected difficulties and was a little surprised to find none. Of course, if she knew what he really planned, he and Dom. . . . There was no sense to fifty men searching for them. Two men, perhaps . . . and two men it would be.

He looked up to find her watching him rather thoughtfully and for one cold moment he thought she might have guessed, but she only smiled and asked, "Better, a little?" He smiled faintly, nodded. "I hope you intend to sleep *after* you reach your bed tonight and not before."

"Mother!"

"Before you do, go and see your astrologer. He sent word an hour ago that he needs to speak with you."

"Nicholas? All right." Conrad stood, leaned down to kiss her cheek. "Thank you, Mother."

"For what? A little food?"

He shrugged, smiled. "A little food, a little common sense. I'm sorry to be so tiresome."

"You are tiresome, just now," Henriette said calmly. "But I would perhaps be tiresome in your place. You at least do not shout as loudly as your father did when he was being stubborn and tiresome, and you have cause."

"Ah. Then—goodnight, Mother. I'll go and see Nicholas at once. I will speak with you in the morning." He left before she could possibly catch the lie: By the time the Queen was awake the next morning, he and Dominic would be an hour gone.

There was a set of rooms with a glass-roofed observatory not far from Conrad's suite of rooms; they had stood empty for years, since Gustave seldom dealt with the stars. Conrad had appropriated them for Nicholas de la Mare and his assistant.

Prince Conrad went up the near perpendicular, circular wrought iron stair headlong, and only by good luck did not slip until the top step. He swore as he cracked his shin, just above the protective leather of his right boot, and the astrologer looked up in alarm.

"My Prince, I beg of you to use care. Events hang on threads and the least thing might cause them to go awry!"

"Mother said you needed to speak with me. Can you tell me how to find—that is—" He stopped as the old man held up an admonishing hand.

"I have spent entirely too many hours last night, today, this night searching for answers. A man my age misses his sleep, my Prince. I—what was I saying? Oh. Sorry." He smothered a yawn with the back of his ink-stained hand; Conrad's jaws twitched with the effort of not yawning with him. "I spent hours reading not only the path taken by your stars but those of others. It is most fortunate the records kept by your father's tax-gatherers are so accurate, and the birthdate of the von Mencken girl was available." He shuffled through an unstable pile of paper, fished out several individual sheets and set them aside; Conrad leaped forward to grab them as they slid off the table and the rest of the stack slipped sideways. The astrologer dropped a heavy brass protractor on it, and rested his elbows on the flattened and stabilized mass.

Conrad dragged a stool across, collapsed onto it and looked at the loose pages in his hands. "Whose horoscopes are these? Nicholas, you know I cannot read your writing, let alone these charts."

De la Mare tapped the top page. "That is yours, of course, just finished moments ago. The girl's beneath it, see? It also bears the sign of the Archer. And that of your *cher ami* de Valois."

"Dom?" Conrad stopped rubbing his bruised shin. "Why should you make a horoscope for Dominic?"

The old man yawned again; Conrad clamped his teeth together hard and looked away. "Listen, my Prince, I explain all at once, piecemeal is too confusing. The Queen tells me there will be another armed company that rides tomorrow, to search for the two women. Not so?" He glanced up; Conrad started, nearly blurted out the truth, finally nodded. He would have sworn there was a gleam of amusement in de la Mare's eye as he went back to the horoscopes; but if he knew Conrad's true intention he didn't say. "So. By the conjunction here—you see?—on your chart, and just—here—" He pulled both sheets onto the floor between them, repositioned his lamp and bent down to point. "You and she will come together three days hence."

"But—"

"All at once, I said," Nicholas interrupted in turn, rather sternly. Conrad subsided on his stool. "Three days. You and she, Dominic de Valois, another who is perhaps the woman Ilse; I sense power involved and so she is most likely. Whatever is intended for your ride tomorrow, add to it that knowledge: Three days, not one. Prepare for that."

"I shall," Conrad promised; inwardly he felt uncertain for the first time all evening. He and Dom could easily sneak away for a day, there'd be fuss when he returned, nothing he couldn't handle. Three days, though—even more fuss, and the matter of food, food for the horses, blankets . . . "If we did nothing until the third day?" he asked tentatively. The astrologer shook his head.

"Three days. Now, attend! There will be difficulties, less of the land you ride, food and shelter, more in your dealings with the people you encounter. There is much ill feeling in the villages brought on long since by this conflict of magics; now there is even more conflict, between witch and witch, between villagers and wielders."

"Where do you see that?"

De la Mare smiled fleetingly. "I speak to people; Raul my servant speaks to the household and tells me what he learns that might be of use to me. As regards yourself, this"—he pointed—"shows discomfort and conflict. I suggest, my Prince, that you listen with both ears, your mind and your heart all together, should any of your people speak to you during these next days. Listen, and think carefully before ever you speak."

"Or—?"

"There is no 'or,' nothing in specific; only that feeling I have."

Conrad studied the chart in silence for some time. All those lines, marks, stars and sketched-in constellations: It made less sense than the Oriental characters they'd shown him in Paris. Still—"I trust your feelings, Nicholas. They haven't failed me yet. Ilse, though—could this mean the peasants would betray her?''

"All I have learned says they fear her. No one has said anyone accepts what she has done. A last thing. The Queen tells me you are still angry with the von Mencken lass.''

"I—'' Conrad shut his mouth and let a heavy sigh out his nostrils; he could feel the blood prickling at his cheekbones. Was nothing private allowed him?

"It is important you not harm her.''

"Why?''

"Because I say it is,'' the astrologer replied sternly. "And before you breathe fire at me, no, it has nothing to do with Madame. You do not study the stars; I do, and have most of my life. I say it is important; whatever your feelings, bury them like a wise Prince, and bring the lady safely back to Neustadt.''

"I—''

"Swear it,'' Nicholas de la Mare said evenly, "or I shall betray your plans for tomorrow.''

"You wouldn't dare,'' Conrad began hotly, but stopped at that. Nicholas would, if he thought it that important. He managed a faint grin. "You did know, didn't you?''

"I know you,'' the old man replied complacently. "Also, it was clear from what I saw, here and here, that you would not be in the company of many men. Take the advice of an old man, my Prince; Raul has already been accepted among the household here. Let him seek out someone discreet to prepare food and bedding for you; let me ask him to find you a companion.''

"Nicholas—thank you. But I can't chance that.''

"And how well do you know the lands around Neustadt? Or Saxe-Baden beyond the main roads?'' Nicholas shook his head. "Or this Scarp and the lands above it? Discreet, I said and meant. Continue to trust me, please.'' Conrad finally nodded. "Good. Go and sleep then; the next days will not be easy ones for you: Physical strain and hard thought will be yours in heavy measure. You will need to think like a King, to continue as you began in the streets of Neustadt. That, I think, will be the most difficult thing of all. There is magic, all kinds of magic, embedded in everything in your horoscope. Against it—if it is against you—you will have amulets, a talisman, herbs and certain words. Augustine will see to that.''

"Gustave still avoids me, then.''

"Yes, and so would any man in Gustave's boots," Nicholas retorted. "The man has lost face."

"Does he think to restore it then by supporting me as he did yesterday?" Conrad demanded. The astrologer merely shrugged.

"Anything is possible; I have done no charts for Gustave and I do not see him personally touching your path. It is not easy to separate kinds of magic in a horoscope, however. Never mind. Keep careful track of the protections supplied you—keep careful track of your blades, watch where your horse places his feet, and this above all: When you feel certain beyond all possible doubt that you have found the right path, the way that will lead to your goal, question your sudden certainty. Fear it. And do not go that way. Ilse will surely try to use the hold she had on you, through Sofia. If you follow the sure direction, you will die of it."

"I'll remember. But—" Conrad set the horoscopes back on the small table, stood and began to pace the small observatory. "Could Ilse bespell me at a distance, because she bespelled me before?"

"I fear she could. Magic ordinarily needs contact for true control, but not always; act on the assumption therefore that she could do so. If you go forewarned of the chance, if you wear your protections, you should be safe from the dangers I see. The second danger is this: your friend Dominic de Valois. I see in his stars a resentment so slight even he is not aware of it, yet if it were manipulated in certain ways it could explode like a pitch-fire into full-fledged fury—against you."

Conrad stopped and stared at him. "*Dominic?* Dom's my best friend. He'd never hurt me!"

"Not of his own choice, no. And I would say to you to leave him behind, if you would listen, but I know you will not. And this one small concern of mine aside, yes, you need him, and he should be with you."

"I can't—Dom would never . . ." Conrad sighed, shook his head and leaned against rough stone and plain curtain to stare out across the darkened city. "And yet—perhaps he does have cause to resent me. You know about his duel, of course. The Duc de Merier's heir taunted him, Dom took offense and challenged poor stupid Henri, they went out on one of the balconies—it was hardly a duel at all; de Merier was drunk, Dom furious, the whole thing was over before anyone could find a way to intervene. The Duc's heir was dead in an illegal duel, and Dom would have been imprisoned at the very least if he were not a Valois—even a distant cousin to a King has rights an ordinary nobleman hasn't.''

"And so, a quiet exile disguised as a journey with his good friend Prince Conrad of Saxe-Baden, a few years away from Court while de Merier is somehow appeased. And then young de Valois quietly reemerges in Hotel society—a few *sous* poorer for the bribes, his clothing and speech out of the fashion. Perhaps he does have the seed of a resentment in all that. And so I tell you again, watch him carefully!''

"But he'd never—!''

"I have seen the *chance*, I tell you,'' the astrologer thundered. Conrad turned back and stared at him, stunned into silence. "That does not make it graven in stone, merely a thing that may come to pass if other things come to pass! I have served you two years now; surely you understand that much of my work?''

"I—I'm sorry, Nicholas. I didn't mean—'' He spread his hands, let them fall back to his sides. "I will watch him. Though what I am to do, if Ilse turns him against me, I do not know. I fence; I do not duel, and I have never killed anyone.''

"Simple enough,'' Nicholas said tartly. "If he begins to act in an odd manner, leave him. He is a French master swordsman, not a horseman. Leave him, and that quickly. Swear you will.''

"I swear it.''

"He has protections also; Augustine said he would make an additional talisman and have it left in Dominic's rooms. See that he attaches it to his clothing and keeps it there at all times.''

"I will.''

"Good. You reassure me. Go now; there is little enough left of this night, and a sensible young man would take what sleep he can.'' Conrad opened his mouth, shut it again. He was shifting from foot to foot and color stood in two ruddy spots on his cheekbones. "Well?''

"Suh—Sofia.'' It came out awkwardly, stiffly. "What—what can you see in her horoscope? Be-besides what you said?''

The astrologer shrugged. "She lives. She is a distance from here, but you knew that, I think.'' He shoved the brass protractor to the floor and rummaged through his stack of papers. "Here it is. Remember something; I saw her at the ball. She is tiny, she is young, and by this and this—and by what certain others have said to me—she has the look of a lady soft, weak and helpless. And yet there is steel in her. Do not make the mistake of looking upon her as a counter in some game, with you and Ilse as the only players. I have done her horoscope, Prince Conrad. Sofia von Mencken is also a player.''

Conrad gazed at him, then turned and walked toward the stairs. He stopped with a hand on the railing. "But a player on whose side, Nicholas?''

"Perhaps her own?'' the astrologer suggested quietly, but Conrad was already on his way down the metal stairs. Nicholas turned down his lamp and gazed out the window. The moon neared half; already it was bright enough that he could have written by it. The Hunter was hiding, not the best of omens, but Draco crouched low in the southern sky, at the jagged line of mountains, and watched as Pegasus approached ruddy Mars. That might balance matters. Perhaps. A man cast horoscopes and interpreted the paths of the stars, and when all else failed, he prayed.

It was chill, windy and still pitch black when the French doors on the second-floor balcony of the Prince's sitting room opened, a little. The shadows that were two men moved along the wall and down the thick vines growing there. Two shadowy figures clad in dark, heavy clothing carefully avoided the graveled paths, stayed on grass and in the deeper shade under trees wherever possible, and made their way from the palace to the stables. There was no light behind them, no alarm raised.

The stables were deserted at this hour; the night watch had gone through at midnight, the grooms would not arrive until the gray hour before sunrise. Conrad and Dominic took no chances, however; they skirted the entire building before checking the bolt on a small side door—it had already been opened—and entering.

Raul was there, heavily cloaked, shivering a little and trying hard not to sneeze from all the hay and horse smell. He had two packs for them. He waited in silence while they saddled and bridled the horses and tied the packs on, then gave them a last whispered message: Two men waited for them by the burned-out shell of the old Armsmaster's house, cousins of the cook's assistant who had put up the bread and meat. "Jussl is a forester; he knows the lands beyond Tannen. Hans trained as a pikeman and crossbowman. Discreet and good men.''

Conrad merely nodded; he was too nervous to trust his whisper staying under the control Raul had, and he was in an agony to be gone before someone caught them. That would be too humiliating to bear. He cast a sidelong glance at Dominic, who had leaned across Gabriel's neck to thank the man and slip a coin into his hand. Dom had never been one to worry about getting caught; he was superbly, irritatingly relaxed.

They rode down the grassy verge of the road, waited until the gate guard went back into the small hut just within the wall, dismounted and slipped out past him. Conrad felt a twinge of guilt as they moved into shadow beside the palace outer walls: The poor man couldn't be expected to guard against someone from inside sneaking out; all the same, he'd probably catch a hard lecture from Eino Trompe when it was discovered the Prince and his friend had gone.

They only had to wait a moment or so until a wagon went by; the clatter of wheels on the uneven stone paving effectively drowned the sound of horses. By the time the wagon was gone they were far enough from the walls and the gate guard that the noise they made no longer mattered. The guides were waiting just where Raul had said. Conrad could not make out more than general build—both men were short and dark—but he saw the gleam of a pike and boar spears above one saddle. Jussl came forward to identify himself then and the four men rode down to the city gate, waited until the gate guard let two wagons and a hand cart in for market. They rode out unchallenged and almost unnoted, as Conrad had hoped: During time of peace, during market days, even entry to the city was seldom questioned, and no one cared who left.

"Too easy," Dominic mumbled. He hated mornings and was beginning to feel the hour now that the excitement of evading authority was fading. Conrad grinned at him but didn't bother to comment. Dom really wouldn't be much company until the sun was up several hours. The grin faded as they started down the main road toward Tannen at a leisurely trot. It had been easy, hadn't it? But who would have suspected—?

Once beyond the City, Jussl spoke just enough to suggest the starting point and a direction. Conrad, fresh from an hour of staring at maps, nodded. Back into the hills north of Tannen—rough country; they had avoided that area the day before. Straight back in, there were villages, and high on the Scarp more villages and a connecting cart track.

If anyone came after them now, they'd be unlikely to try near

Tannen, particularly if the four men reached that trail before any of Tannen's peasants saw them.

His mother would be utterly furious when she found the letter he'd left her. He hoped she would understand. But she knew how he felt, and Nicholas not only understood those reasons, he had horoscopes to back up the Prince's reasoning. Nicholas would make the Queen see reason, and she in turn could surely convince the Council.

Not that the Council mattered so much. What could they do to the King's heir? Slap his fingers, confine him to his rooms without supper? All the same—there was a small kernel of dread, or something very like it, lodged in his throat as they rode toward the west with the sky growing gradually lighter behind them and the last stars fading before them. Something in what Dom had said; somehow, it wasn't going to go the way he planned.

It wasn't until they passed Tannen and came to Jussl's trail that Conrad's fear took on real form and substance. The form was that of a wagon, pale wooden walls and a sloped roof, two horses standing in the traces, heads down and grazing. The substance sat in the canvas-curtained doorway, feet tracing patterns in the dusty road. Gustave was waiting for them.

Waiting. Conrad felt the blood mount in his face, and his fingers were twitching. He wanted to murder the man; wanted to draw his sword and spur Parsifal forward, to take off his head at the shoulders with one smooth swipe; he'd practiced that often enough. Gustave's head would split just like those melons he'd halved. . . . Dominic, ever sensitive to his moods, rode near and touched his arm.

"Easy. This is not a man to sit and wait for you to kill him, Conrad."

"No," Conrad choked out finally. "I'm all right," he managed, but he could hear the anger vibrating his voice, and so could Dom.

"You are all right, but things are not. What does this buffoon mean?" Dominic demanded.

"God knows, and I fear we shall find out momentarily," Conrad said grimly, and then he did spur Parsifal on. Gustave remained where he was, seated on the steps of his caravan. He was playing with the enormous, slightly tarnished silver and ruby watch that dangled from a long silver neck chain. Dominic, his

Gabriel keeping pace with Parsifal, touched Conrad's arm once more. A warning glance at the sorcerer's watch. But Conrad knew better than to let the thing hold his eyes; sorcerers and witches bound men and women so, but Gustave would not take him by such a trick.

Gustave waited until Conrad leaped from the saddle and strode forward, stopping only short of the old man's much out-of-date pointed slippers. "My Prince," he said quietly, and inclined his head with deference. But there was complacence in his voice.

Conrad bared his teeth and narrowed his eyes. "This grows boring, Gustave. Whatever you think to prove or do here, I want no part of it!" The faint smile left Gustave's face; his eyes were almost as narrowed as the Prince's. "Go back to the palace, back to the Council, and stay away from me, I warn you. Sorcerers can die like other men."

Gustave leaned back against the door frame, slipped the watch into an inner pocket and folded his arms. His eyes remained dark slits and despite his scruffy and ancient garb, the disgusting wig, the sloppy shoes that should have made him look comic, he was not at all an amusing sight. "Threats again? And shall I counter with threats of my own? All right. Let us be honest with each other, if that is how you want it."

"What I want is you gone," Conrad growled through clenched teeth. "Now."

"Or what?" Gustave demanded. "Sorcerers can die, yes; but not as easily as other men. Besides, you don't dare kill me, even if you could. Do you?" Conrad opened his mouth and shut it again without saying anything. "Of course you don't dare. So what you want scarcely matters, does it? And what I want—but I am willing to make a bargain with you so that you and I each get a portion of what we want. Are you interested?"

Dominic caught hold of Conrad's near arm and pulled him back a pace, whispered against his ear, then spoke to the sorcerer directly when it became clear the Prince was momentarily too furious to speak. "That, sir, depends upon what you think Prince Conrad wants, and how much of that you are willing to grant him. If you can."

"Bargained like a Frenchman," Gustave retorted sourly. "You want the witch dead, and so do I. Let us be frank with one another, Prince. You lost as much face as I did in that ballroom. Oh, in your case men pity you and in mine they jeer and tell stupid jokes behind my back. Is pity better than laughter? You want the woman dead, so do I. You are clever enough to realize Ilse will never be taken by companies of mounted armsmen quartering the woods, she will never be taken tamely to stand trial for treason. You know from her own words what her intentions are.''

"Why do you think we are here?" Conrad snapped.

"Why do you think *I* am here?" Gustave countered. "Because I knew you would defy all sensible cautions and do what must be done. What you are now doing. Do not look at me that way, I said must be done. Your father's councilors are old men with the caution of old men. And you are their only Prince, so they have a right to their caution. This is no time for caution, though. Is it? Would you let Saxe-Baden and her neighbors know that Ilse has wrought against you and gotten away with it?''

"Do you really need my answer to that?"

"Not really, no," Gustave replied. He sounded almost cheerful at the moment. "And so, a bargain. You and your noble friend, and these two companions, you will be no match alone against that woman. The charms you bear may be full protection, but that is only defense, no aid in hunting her down and overcoming her. With my aid, you will be able to do that.''

Conrad snorted. "Your aid. Why should I trust you?"

"That was extremely rude, but I shall ignore it because I understand you are in a temper. Not only are your plans discovered, but discovered by me, of all men, mmmm? You will trust me, Prince, because you have no choice: You accept my aid and my advice because otherwise I shall see to it that your efforts in sneaking from the palace this morning are quite in vain. Do you doubt I can do that? Mmmm?" Silence. "And so, we do understand each other, don't we?" Conrad's eyes were all black and his color high.

"That's bluff, Gustave."

"Is it?" Gustave smiled. "And will you call the bluff, then? I doubt you will, young Prince."

Conrad shook his head. "There isn't time for this, damn you, Gustave!"

"Then stop raising fool's arguments!" the old man growled.

"Talk," Conrad snapped back. "I'll listen—for the moment, anyway. No more riddles!"

"You show sense." He looked beyond Conrad and Dom to the other two men for the first time. "You chose wisely. I know this man, Jussl. He will take you down that trail when you leave me. It leads up into the high country; Jussl, mind you hold to the right-hand trail whenever it branches." The forester nodded once. "You know the land; I am speaking now for the benefit of the Prince, who does not.

"There are three villages on the western end of the Scarp, one surrounded by woods and rock ledge. I can give you no other description—Jussl, you know it? Good. There is a woman called Hel, a village witch. She is related to the woman Gerthe who was burned last fall. I saw her speaking with Ilse late at night. The girl was still with Ilse then, but Ilse had gone and Sofia remained in the village. Where Ilse has gone, I could not discover; she has enough true magic to conceal herself from me."

"That's all?"

"It is more than you had moments ago, is it not?" Gustave demanded. Conrad scowled, finally nodded. "So I am of use to you; even if I cannot reliably find Ilse, I can find the girl, and Ilse is not yet done with her. Sofia is very important to her plans. Find one, and you have them both."

"Perhaps."

"Perhaps," Gustave mocked, and Conrad flushed. "But I am more use than that, young Prince. I have left word of my own for the Queen and the Council that you, your friend and your guides are under my protection, and Augustine's. They will not be pleased but less displeased than by your message—which I burned, by the way. No one will come to find you and take you home. One last thing. When Ilse decides to kill you, I will see that she does not."

"If that's all," Dominic said flatly and in patent disbelief. Gustave shrugged and pursed his mouth irritatedly, but his own color had gone high.

"That is more than enough, I think. It is more than anyone else could offer you—or would. But perhaps Prince Conrad finds it easier to nurse a long-standing child's hatred of me than to strike an unpleasant but necessary bargain—as a grown man would." Dominic flushed a dark red under his tan, but it was Conrad this time who held him back.

"No. Wait, Dom." The Frenchman withdrew a pace or two, swearing under his breath. "That was scarcely flattering, and I am more than repaid for my rudeness. But I see the sense of your words.''

''I thought you might,'' Gustave said. ''You do not like me; I do not like you. All the same—''

''All the same, there are times for alliances that might otherwise not exist.'' *Like Ilse and Sofia?* He shoved the thought aside, unanswered. Better so; questioning blind hatred was confusing, it slowed one's reactions. This with Gustave proved that. This with Gustave was enough. He hesitated, finally extended his right hand. Gustave gripped it briefly with his own; then he was all brisk business.

''The astrologer's horoscope, Prince Conrad. Did you bring it, and will you let me see it?'' For answer, Conrad turned away to rummage in his pack and handed over the folded sheet of thick paper. Gustave muttered as he opened it, held it close, then at arm's length, finally set it on the bottom step and leaned away from it. He nodded finally. ''My French is poor; fortunately he uses more Latin. And his writing—well. So.'' He bent down to pick up the horoscope, refolded it carefully, then sat back, eyes hooded. He was humming tunelessly to himself. Conrad ground his teeth together, closed his eyes and prayed for patience.

Gustave stirred finally. ''You know what the horoscope contains? Your man told you?'' Conrad nodded. ''Good. Now. Tonight you will be well into the high country. Find shelter with a roof; Jussl will know one. Stop before sunset. Build a fire immediately; there must be a strong fire when the first stars come out. When the sky is blue, not yet black, and there is no edge of sunset to be seen, you will seat yourself on the north side of the fire. You will take the pouch of seeds and the silver bird I shall give you presently. You will sprinkle exactly five seeds on a flat rock so near the fire that you cannot touch it; you will set the bird down on the seeds just as they begin to smoke. I will be able to speak with you then.''

''That's all?''

''It should be enough. By this horoscope''—he handed it back to Conrad, who pocketed it—''you will need nothing but advice until the third day from today.''

''All right,'' Conrad said. His face was unreadable, his voice level. Gustave laughed shortly and slewed around to lift the canvas flap.

''Augustine, fetch for me the blue enameled box—no, the

next shelf up, the smaller one.'' He turned back and held that out. ''Use this please only as I have said; it is a simple spell, but even the simplest of them can go wrong if misused. Do not take off that talisman you wear, even to sleep, but particularly not when you use this box tonight. The charm should hide you from search; it will protect us both from discovery when you begin the spell.''

Conrad nodded. ''Is that all?''

''Enough. Go now, before the day begins! Dawn and dusk are times of strength; it were best you were hidden among the trees before dawn comes.'' Conrad merely nodded, turned away to mount Parsifal. Dominic followed him; Jussl moved out to lead and Hans dropped to the rear. Gustave watched in silence as they vanished into the woods. He sighed then and shook his head.

''Well?'' Augustine stood just behind him, framed in the doorway. Gustave merely nodded his head toward the departed riders. ''Was he convinced?''

Gustave was still watching the woods. ''I doubt it, I very much doubt it. But events are shaping themselves despite what the Prince thinks—despite what he wants. Despite what any of us want. And so I shall begin the purification while we go on. We must be in place along the north road long before Conrad uses that box; you know how long the safeguards will take, and you must purify the wagon by yourself tonight. I will not be able to back you.''

''But will the Prince use that box?''

''He will. Whether out of—mmm—curiosity or need does not matter. He will use it; I must be ready.'' Gustave turned and mounted the steps and pushed past the curtain; Augustine was on his heels. The interior of the wagon was warm, comfortably furnished with a deep chair, a pile of cushions, a narrow cot. The floor was covered in thick rugs. The walls were lined with cupboards, and a shelf holding three ancient handwritten books and a more recent printed one. There was a copper bowl balanced over a brazier mounted in turn on a tripod; tongs and charcoal; there were lanterns and glass-encased candles, candles on wall sconces, a box of squat candles near the entrance. There were no windows.

One light burned, enough to show the bed was occupied. Gustave stood beside it and gazed down at Isabelle, who lay shivering despite the warmth and the cover pulled up to her chin. Her eyes were open but saw nothing, even when Gustave passed his hand back and forth almost at her nose.

"You cannot spare me or Fritz," Augustine said quietly. "But even you dare not take her with us—that would surely endanger everything. Is one girl worth that?"

"Worth—she has potential worth. But she will not come with us, Augustine." Gustave set a light hand on the girl's forehead, withdrew it as she shuddered. "How odd. I saw her that night, you know. But I forgot about her, the same as everyone else did. Poor Isabelle." He sounded detached, scarcely interested. "Watch the market-bound villagers as we go our way, please. Find folk who will take this young woman to the City; I dare not leave her here, either. Queen Henriette will see she is cared for. And that would be convenient, if she were in the palace; I will have a use for her, if certain things do not go as I wish them to."

Augustine shrugged finally. "All right. I will."

"And hurry," Gustave said as he turned away to rummage through one of his cupboards for a box of ointment. "We cannot afford much time, and I would not have worry about this young woman's fate to disturb my ritual. Would you?"

The look on the apprentice's face clearly said he thought it impossible that any woman's fate should disturb his master's preparations—or at least astonishing. But he turned and left without further comment, and Gustave barely had time to kneel beside the cot before the wagon lurched forward. He had to hold himself in place with both hands as it turned on the narrow road and headed back toward the City. Isabelle stirred slightly as he rubbed the fragrant ointment into her fingers and smoothed it into the line of her jaw.

He waited until Fritz brought the wagon to a halt minutes later before attempting to reach her thought, but she was still too near hysteria for him to control, even if he could bring her conscious again. It didn't matter, though; he would deal with her later if he must. If the Prince proved himself, it would not be necessary.

Augustine's voice brought him out onto the back step: A rough cart had stopped; a white-haired man and his wife sat on the seat side by side and stared as the sorcerer came into sight. Dumb and stupid both, he thought impatiently, but the woman's face softened when the servant brought Isabelle out, and she bundled the girl into her own heavy cloak. The man agreed to take her to the palace, to pass Gustave's message on. He repeated it twice before the sorcerer was satisfied it would get through as he wished.

He thought about a charm for her, but decided not to—the peasants would fear it; they clearly feared *him*. There was no need, so near Neustadt anyway. He watched the man urge his horses forward, the wicker cages of young pigs shifting in the back, the near invisible bundle next to them. She'd die of shame if she knew.

Augustine came back to urge him into the cart; he was practically shaking with impatience, and Gustave smiled faintly. "Don't worry so much, Augustine. We are in control of matters this time." Augustine cast his eyes heavenward and went back around the wagon. Gustave settled into his cot and closed his eyes. Already Conrad was wavering. Perhaps it was not too late to mold the boy after all, now that he had a better sense of him.

The wagon followed the farmer's cart part way toward Neustadt but turned aside well short of the city gates, taking a narrow cart track Fritz knew. It would save them at least an hour, and each of them knew Gustave and the wagon must be in place along the north road well before sundown.

No sooner had the sorcerer's wagon turned left than the farmer's cart turned right, into a dry bog, and stopped. The man and his wife stared blankly ahead, and the man's fingers slipped from the reins. Ilse stepped from the trees and gazed into the back of the cart in satisfaction. It had taken no effort at all to pull these stupid peasants in and yoke them to her will; they'd remember nothing once she sent them on again. And Gustave—why, he might have sent the girl to her, on purpose!

He had underestimated her once again. And he'd given her a weapon—not a weapon she wished to use, since it would only be worked if she was dead. But if she died, Isabelle would be one final blow, the unexpected answer from beyond the grave or the fire.

Otto or Drusilla would have done; they were, after all, quartered among the palace servants. But Otto's broken leg made things difficult, and the old woman was nearly mad. This was better.

Isabelle, though: scarcely stable, far from mad. And it was such a nice touch. Ilse was smiling as she pulled herself up onto the back of the cart.

"Take a broom, and let its stalk be an ash, its bristles of birch tied with osier, and let a witch of full strength and proper skill mount it; it shall carry her whereso upon the air she wisheth to go. If she have great power, and if there be no such broom, she may fashion a horse by this manner: a bundle of ragwort or a bundle of hay, lashed about with cinquefoil if there be any, or dusted with powder of osier; and this shall become a dark horse which shall carry her whereso she will go, upon the earth or through the air."

An Oral Grammarie

14.

Sofia started from a deep, dreamless sleep as chill, hard fingers gripped her shoulder. "Sst! Girl, wake if you'd have your food hot!"

Hel. She was surprised to find she remembered the witch's name, rather surprised she remembered anything. That ghastly walk from Neustadt to this place with its thin mountain air and bone-chilling nights, her aching legs and cramped feet, the knot in her stomach that was not enough food and dread combined. Ilse and Hel had argued furiously over her that first night, and when she woke late the next afternoon she found Ilse gone and the old woman's pale eye fixed on her. The woman had given her stale bread and a little hot broth; she'd slept again almost at once and was uncertain whether she'd heard Ilse return, or if that was dream. The fight later still had brought her awake. That had ended moments later with Ilse storming from the hut, the old woman throwing a heavy pot after her.

Hel crouched beside Sofia, a steaming kettle and clay cup on the floor next to her. Sofia tried to smile; the old woman simply looked at her. *She resents me,* Sofia realized. Ilse had foisted something on her she would have avoided of her own choice. Hel would never like her, but at least she had been good about food. She'd let Sofia wash, and when her unwanted and unwilling houseguest sat shivering by the fire, Hel had put a pair of heavy stockings in her hand and draped a thick shawl across her shoulders. But she met all friendly efforts on Sofia's part, all politenesses, with that same resentful stare.

Hel pushed a hand-chipped wooden bowl into her hands. The stuff in it was gluey, Sofia knew from the prior morning's experience, but it was hot and filling. And sweet; Hel had a taste for sugar, and the village indulged it. "Thank you, goodwife."

"You're a polite lass, I'll say that of you," Hel said grudgingly. She dipped tea into the single cup and took the first swallow. She became suddenly quite talkative, though the hard edge stayed in her voice. "There. That's because I'm old, and so you'll see there's nothing in the pot save good herb, eh?"

"Oh." She hadn't thought of *that*. Hel chuckled as Sofia stared at her apprehensively. "You wouldn't—you wouldn't—" She drank tea too hastily and choked on it. Hel slapped her hard between the shoulder blades. She was still laughing.

"The look on your face. Wouldn't poison you? Haven't yet, have I? Besides, I was the one brought it up, wasn't I? Poisoning the pot?" Hel took the cup from Sofia's limp fingers and drained it. "I could, of course; I could find twenty plants within this clearing to poison tea, half of them you'd never taste at all. I took a vow, though, when I apprenticed to Hansa, God rest her, to nurture, not kill. *I* hold to that. Those who tread the Green Way all do." Hel shook her head. "Ilse is my sister's child and she took that vow from my lips. A mother never knows what her children'll grow to be, does she? No more than a witch knows when her 'prentice will go wrong, though few of them do." She pulled a loaf from the hot bricks next to the fire and a knife from its place wedged in the stones of the fireplace. "Here, have a bit of the loaf, you're all bones and eyes. I've no dripping for it, but there'll be meat for noon; headman's wife promised me." Sofia tore a small bite from the rather tough slice and began to chew it. Hel tore hers in half, stuffed a half in her cheek, dipped the other piece in the teakettle, and went on talking.

"To bring you here as Ilse's done—" Hel shook her head, swallowed and pushed the tea-soaked bit of bread into her mouth. "Eat," she mumbled. "The bread's going cold on you. The village will suffer for what Ilse has done." She chewed steadily, scowled at her companion.

Sofia broke off another bit of bread and obediently ate it, then gathered her tattered courage along with a deep breath. "Hel. I didn't want to come here. I wish no ill on your village or you."

"Fine lot of aid that is when the old King's army comes and finds you here," Hel snapped.

"Ilse might take me away first. If she does—she will kill me."

The old woman stopped chewing; old, pale blue eyes stared into young dark ones unblinkingly. "So? I know what she plans; hasn't she told me enough these past two nights? But what is it to me? Trouble, that's what you are. As much as Ilse. More."

"I'm sorry. But, Hel, if I'm gone before they come, then who will know I was here? Do your villagers even know? Or would they say?"

Hel turned away, muttering angrily to herself. "Do that, and I have crossed my niece. What do you think she'll do to me—and this village—if I simply let you go?"

"Ilse is already angry with you. But you are her mother's sister; she won't harm you. With me gone, at least your village is not in danger when the army comes."

Hel considered this, finally shook her head firmly. "I dare not."

"You must! Please, Hel, it is not only me who will die. She will kill Prince Conrad also." Tears tightened her throat, stopping further speech, but the sudden attack of misery was gone as quickly as it came, replaced by anger. Hel was laughing.

"Why should a peasant care whose foot is on her neck? One noble boot is much like another, when all one sees is the sole."

Sofia leaped to her feet and glared down at the old witch. "That isn't true! The old King was a hard man but his father was harder, and his father before was a tyrant! Across the river, in Saaren, they have burned a hundred witches this past year, and in Upper Hesse people are starving because their King puts such high taxes on them. You have a roof, food, your people live their lives much as they please—"

"Enough," Hel growled. Sofia leaned back against the wall. Her face was tingling, her breath coming fast. "So it matters to you, anyway, whether this Prince lives, eh?" Hel smirked up at her, eyes bright with curiosity. "Perhaps Ilse was right about that."

Sofia dropped to her knees and glared at the old witch. "Right. How right?"

But Hel would not be drawn. "I know what Ilse plans; she told me. She still thinks I'll help her." The witch looked up again. "And so I am, despite everything I said to her, by holding you for her. It's a bad business.'' Sofia just looked at her. Hel turned away to cut another slice of the bread, wedged the knife back between two stones. She tore the slice in half, concentrating her gaze and most of her attention on the trivial task, held out one piece without looking up from her own. "Ilse went aloft just before dawn; she cannot return until dusk. After midday food, I must return a pot to the headman's wife. There is no block upon my door." She held up a silencing hand as Sofia cleared her throat. "Wait. If anyone were here when I left and not here when I returned, I would not know where they had gone.''

"Thank you,'' Sofia whispered.

"Don't thank me. Just go from here, go quickly and far. The great river is that direction''—she pointed—"and the King's City that way. Stay under the trees, when you can. Ilse cannot both fly and search for long at a time, and the woods are vast.'' Hel braced heavily corded hands on her knees, pushed to her feet and stood staring down at the girl. "Wait. What is in your pocket? There.'' She pointed at Sofia's apron. "Something—I feel Gerthe's magic there, but Ilse's power overall; she will find you by it. Give it here.''

"There's nothing there—" But she felt gingerly in the pocket. Something tiny and cold. She drew her hand out and uncurled the fingers to reveal a silver rose earring. Hel picked it from her palm. "It was my mother's,'' Sofia said steadily. Her throat still hurt but the urge to weep was gone. There was no time for such a weakness, not now.

"It was once a rose petal,'' Hel said to her absently. "How curious; that's neither Green nor Gold Magic.''

"No—it's Spanish.''

"Ah. I remember now. Gerthe cleansed it.'' Hel turned away, mumbling vexedly under her breath. Sofia pulled the blanket around her shoulders, edged nearer the fire and watched. Hel went to the table with its high pile of bottles, boxes, green and dry herbs, straw braid and a length of red ribbon for binding it, shoved things back and forth. After several minutes of this, she swore and walked back across to the narrow bunk built into the wall. There was a cupboard under the bed, a hamper in that, and in the hamper she finally found what she wanted—a small red bottle.

"Come here, girl,'' she ordered. "Hold out your hand.'' Sofia held it out; Hel pounced, caught her wrist and jabbed her index finger with a pin, squeezing until a drop of blood pooled and quivered. Just before it fell, she dipped the silver rose in it. She unstoppered the red bottle and dipped her finger in it, swabbed the damp finger across Sofia's finger. "Yarrow; that's to stop the bleeding."

"I know. My mother taught me." She clutched her throbbing finger in her other hand; it had already stopped bleeding.

Hel's lips moved soundlessly. She cupped the rose in both palms, then caught it between thumb and forefinger and ordered once more, "Hold out your hand." Sofia bit her lower lip and held out her hand, but Hel merely dropped the earring back in her palm. It was oddly cool. "Ilse did something of her own to it, recently, but your blood erased her work. She cannot find you by this. But someone else might, by its mate." She hadn't missed the mate until now; cold certainty told her who had it. Hel's eyes narrowed. "I will destroy this, if you prefer."

"No." Her fingers curled around it protectively. "It's—well. It—was Mother's. Everything is gone now; it's all I have to remember her by—and to remember the ball. Some of it was pleasant."

Hel snorted impatiently. "Your life is not over yet, girl. You young, to you everything is all this or all that, and you will die if it is not the other way! And I will tell you two things: The earring is again bound with Green magic. And Green Magic is stronger than Ilse believes it or than the sorcerers think. Another thing: Rose Magic is strong stuff. Lovers' magic." She laughed. "Those who use Rose Magic sometimes find the spell takes a direction and a pattern *it* chooses."

Sofia shook her head. "I—I'm sorry. I don't understand you."

"Of course you do not. Why should you? Keep that earring safe." Hel dropped the red bottle in the midst of her high-piled table and pulled her shawl from the single stool. At the door she turned back. "I am going to milk my goat, nothing else. Stay where you are; it is hours until midday."

Sofia nodded. She walked across to the fire. The air in the hut was chill with the door ajar, the stones of the hearth too hot to stand on for long. She warmed her feet thoroughly, then tucked them back in the thick woolen blankets, wrapped the shawl around her shoulders and lay back down.

She would not think about it; she did not dare. Ilse might return early, whatever Hel said. Hel might change her mind. But if somehow she found herself beyond this village—if the bears did not find her in the long night hours, if she did not stumble unwitting into a fairy circle, where would she go? Ilse would hunt her, Prince Conrad and his father's armies doubtless already did hunt her. She would not dare the villages, even if she came near any: The villagers would fear her, they'd kill her, or hold her for Ilse or the Prince. Noble landholders, townfolk—they would be more of a danger than villagers.

There was no one she could trust. No one—except possibly the Queen. Queen Henriette knew her; she had liked her once. And she was Regent, head of the Regent's Council—she was a just woman. However she personally felt about Sofia, she would listen.

The Queen, then. One had to have a goal of some kind, even if she were certain she would never reach it.

The stew had been excellently prepared, the meat fresh, the vegetables new-picked, the bread still warm from baking, dark brown and slightly sweet, but Sofia had had to force herself to eat, and the little she'd been able to swallow sat like a lump of ice in her stomach. She was not certain which frightened her more: thought of Ilse finding her after she'd attempted this escape, thought that Hel might change her mind, or that a mob of young witch-hunters might find her. . . . Her skin felt cold and hot at the same time, painfully sensitive to the least current of air or touch of her shawl, her companion's hand—as though she had fever. *I am not made for courage, or for courageous acts,* she thought in some despair. Faced with death unless she acted and if she acted, her only desire was to find a dark hole and cower in it like some timid beast. *Have I none of Father's blood at all?*

But death was a certainty if she waited here. There was the least of chances for her otherwise, and that would have to do.

Hel scarcely looked at her unwanted guest when she left; she hung the empty stew pot on one arm, cradled the door charm in the crook of her other elbow and strode from the house. Sofia sat at the table, hands clutching each other, and watched the witch push the gate closed behind her and turn left, toward the sounds of village.

Well. She took a deep breath, a second, and got resolutely to her feet. She spread the shawl out on the floor next to the fire, set the remainder of the noon loaf on it. There was a bundle of dried meat strips hanging to one side of the fire. Hel had not offered that, but she took it and the knife Hel had used to cut the bread. That thick blade must be good steel, since no true witch could use iron; it was fairly sharp, not very long. Better than no weapon at all. She folded the shawl around the things; then, on impulse, she went to the table and found the bottle of yarrow. Hel could easily distill more; Sofia might need it. There was a length of thick rope also, long enough to tie about her waist. She knotted it in place, thrust the knife between it and her tattered gown, and then knotted the shawl and tied it to the rope, leaving her hands free.

Time. She was wasting it, dithering. "Afraid?" she whispered derisively. She was, but that got her to the doorway, through it and then through the gate.

Hel's cottage stood alone, a short distance east of the village. It was small, a few grayed log huts, stables and brush fences, chickens and geese wandering loose in the road. To the south, the black shale ledge she and Ilse had come across, trees and more trees sloping up beyond it to a rugged scarp and mountains beyond that. North it was much the same with meadow and the bright green of bog and stream in place of the shale. East, dry meadow, tall with grass, purple and white flowers, woods beyond that.

The road came out of the woods to the southeast and vanished westward through the village. It must run down the Scarp and it would connect somewhere with one of the main roads to Neustadt. Ilse would suspect the road at once. But Sofia could not simply strike off southward; the Scarp was completely impassable in places, and it would be too easy for her to become lost.

She walked quickly through the meadow. Her legs wanted to shake; she had to fight herself not to keep looking over her shoulder for Ilse or even Hel. Or perhaps Ilse was in the woods, watching her, waiting. . . . The woods were almost worse than open land. She could not see very far, trees and brush everywhere blocked her view, anyone could be there. . . .

"Stop it," she told herself sharply, and, pulling her skirts and the bundled shawl close, she edged through a small clump of trees, leaped over a small stream, and began working her way around toward the road.

It took time, and when she could finally see the clearing in the trees that marked the road, she was hot and sticky; her hems clung to her ankles where she'd stepped into a boggy place. Bad beginning; perhaps it was an omen. But omens could cut either way. She caught her skirts up to one side, knotted them at her knee and began walking again.

It wasn't too difficult at first, keeping the road just in sight; then there was a steep drop. Sofia scrambled back and forth through the trees, searching for a better way down, before she decided she had better chance the road.

It was narrow here; narrow and hard, a soft dust covering granite. It ran in a shaded notch through weeping stone walls and high fir, then through trees only and finally out into the open. Sofia stopped while she was still hidden by tree shade and stared.

It seemed the whole of Saxe-Baden was laid out below her: woods and more woods, dark green fir with bands of pale green aspen and birch marking hidden streams, a paler tan ribbon of road. Small lakes, a fair-sized river and waterfalls. The sky was a cloudless blue bowl over all; nubs of mountains, small and purple with distance, rimmed what she could see. Smoke here and there that marked villages buried in the forests. And a gleam that might be sun on water, but could, just perhaps, be sun on the metal of Neustadt's tall clock tower. So far away!

The road wound down the ledge where she stood, now and again hidden by rock and tree, more often exposed to all the world below—or above. Sofia stared until her eyes watered: There were birds everywhere, an eagle high above her heading toward its nest on the crags, a flock of sparrows below her. Nothing that was a witch in flight—

She flinched as sun touched her face and shoulder, and practically ran to the next patch of shade, two turns down the road; she had to rest a few moments, then, to get her breath back. She was lower than Hel's village, but the air was still too thin.

Another two turns of the road brought her into a stretch of oak and not far beyond that, she left the road and plunged back into the woods. It was still a clamber and the sun was making long shadows by the time she reached level ground. Time to begin thinking of the night.

She knew there were huts in the woods; when she had ridden her father's northern estate there had been shelters. Some were only a wall propped on branches, some four low walls and a roof of woven stick and straw; others three-sided log buildings for hunters or those who rode the woods in summer. But even if she could find one, she wouldn't dare use it, more than she'd dare approach a village. Ilse would try villages first, but she'd doubtless search whatever huts she knew between Hel's village and Neustadt after that.

She was hungry and thirsty, but the bread might have to last her a while. She finally fished a stick of the dried meat from her makeshift pack and made it last as long as she could: It was terribly salty and the meat itself had a gamey flavor—bear or something else that lived on other meat. There was plenty of water, at least; she drank and washed her face at a stream just before the sun left the ground and began climbing up the trees.

Late. Time to find a place to hide. It was getting dark down here in the woods, dark and cool; she moved away from the stream when she startled a red deer and her fawns. Beasts came down to drink in the gray hour, not only deer but wolves and bears.

When she could no longer hear the sound of running water, she stopped and looked around. A tree? Most of those around her were fir, sticky of trunk, spiny-needled, branches too near together to be of use. Most of the oak didn't branch until well over her head. The birch and aspen were too small.

She knew, suddenly, that she could not face the night on the forest floor. Whether she could sleep in a tree, whether she still remembered how to climb a tree, was another matter.

Beyond a small clearing, she finally found an oak that might do: The branches were low but not too low, and a boulder leaned against it. Once she found a way up the rock, she could just reach one of the branches, and with her skirts tucked up above her knees she swarmed up it like a boy. Well above ground—high enough that she was hidden by leaves, not so high she'd break her neck if she fell—she wedged herself into a crotch formed by the main trunk, a secondary trunk and two thick branches.

She shivered. It was much cooler than it had been, and it wasn't easy sorting herself out so she could free the shawl from her rope belt, undo the knot in her skirt—it had worked its way under her knees and she had quite a job of getting her hands on it and pulling the skirts free. She tucked her feet up in the skirts. At least the hems had dried.

The shawl was a business; getting the knots and folds out of it and refolding it, getting herself moved around to get it behind

her back and over her shoulders, across her breast. Her feet
needed retucking by the time she was done. She pulled her hands
up inside the folds of the shawl, leaned back against the tree and
closed her eyes. Later she might come awake from cold or fear—
or both—and start at every noise, at the tickling at the back of
her neck that she could only hope was moss and not some spi-
ders living in the moss. Later she would doubtless lie awake in
her hard nest and feel her heart thump at every cracked twig,
every least noise, certain that Ilse had found her. Just now she
was too tired to care.

There was a faint music all around her: reed pipes and strings,
swirling like a soft summer wind. It blew leaves in little circles,
bent branches and made black shadows. Night, but with such a
moon that where there was light it hurt the eyes; the shade was
too sooty to see. There were clouds, but they were few and only
served to show the moon racing across the sky at dizzying speed.
Sofia stood still. Trees were all around her, enormous oaks, but
spaced formally as though in a park, and they seemed to have
been shaped by man. The turf beneath her feet was close-cropped
and neat—no fallen leaves touched it, there were no barren
patches of dirt. She let her head fall back to watch the moon
slide through bare branches, past leafy ones, across the pointed
tips of conifers.

She wore white and gold, silver roses weighted her earlobes.
But her feet were bare, and around her wrists and ankles she felt
bruises. As though there had been chains and manacles holding
her, chains that had only just fallen away. *Dream.* The word
skirled around her, like the music, like the wind, then was gone.
It made no sense anyway.

I'm free. Everything fell into place then, so very neatly. Free
of everything: no Father, no Beatrix; no Queen Henriette to
bind her with love and pity; no Prince to bind her with his
handsome face and warm hands, or with his chill eyes and
vows of death. No witch—no witch. She flung her arms wide,
tilted back her head and laughed as the moon sailed behind a
cloud and the woods were mysterious and magical, all silver
and velvet blue.

She ran light-footed, her gown rustling softly, making less
sound than the trees and the wind. Down a low slope, down a
broad lane between massive oaks, grass that was soft and cool

beneath her toes. Free. She owed nothing to anyone but Sofia; there was no one but Sofia now.

On a sudden urge, she gathered her skirts in both hands and ran down a narrow lane that slowly grew wider. It was the lane to the palace—*No!* she thought in sudden panic. *I must not go there, the Queen will hold me, the Prince will kill me!* But the woods were thick, the trees too tall to be the Queen's French-pruned fripperies. The music was gone; dead silence save for the rustle of her taffeta underskirts. And the lane was narrower, halved again—it was gone. Fir needles pricked at her insteps, something sticky caught on one heel, pasting a leathery oak leaf to her foot. She stopped, leaned against a tree and stood on one foot to try and work it free.

It was so still she could hear her heart beating, double time. Or—she let her foot down, swung around to put the tree against her back: Her heart, or hers and another? There was a shadow there—what, she couldn't tell, save that it moved. With a little cry of terror, she caught up her skirts—harsh woolen skirts— and ran back the way she had come. The shadow moved from under the trees and came with her.

She could see nothing save darkness and something enough darker to tell it from night and shadow. She dragged the awkward skirts to one side and clutched them one-handed, held the other hand before her. She dared not run here; even fear of what came after her could not counter the fear of running blindly into a tree—or into something else that might stand there, waiting. She cried out and snatched her hand back as something soft wrapped over her fingers. Trees everywhere. She tried to turn, to go the way she had just come, but they were behind her too, huge trunks where no trees had been, with no room between them, nowhere for her to go. And her hand was being pressed back, her elbow touched her stomach, her back was hard against a tree bole, they were so near now she could not breathe—with another cry, Sofia woke.

It was dark in her tree. A little fog lay on the ground, what seemed at once too far below and not far enough. She shuddered. It was dead silent; so silent her ears rang. Never in her life had she been anywhere so still. Not even the faintest of breezes moved the trees; no animals moved through the bushes down there. "One can dream anything," Sofia told herself firmly. She stared into darkness for a while, finally fished a bit of bread out of her pocket and ate it. The nightmare was losing its hold; her heart was beating almost normally, her hands no longer shook. Hel's shawl was warm and soft. She snugged it around her shoulders and settled against the main trunk. Though she had not intended or expected it, she fell asleep again. This time—so far as she recalled—she did not dream.

"Great skill and strength are needed to project Being from Body. Seven times must a man speak the seven words, seven times each repeat the seven psalms, and seven times must he contemplate his own seven criteria. Then and only then may he send forth that of him which cannot be seen, in the certainty that it will return to him."

Notes on the Key of Solomon; Green & Gold Magyk

15.

"God above, Conrad, have you lost your wit?" Dominic was barely able to contain himself until they were out of sight and earshot of the sorcerer's wagon. Conrad reined Parsifal back and glared at him.

"What do *you* think? I told the old fool what he wanted to hear, Dom!"

"Then get rid of that stuff he gave you, Conrad. Do you want him coming after us?"

"Dom, really! You've seen him and that wagon of his; he can't follow us." Conrad frowned, and when he next spoke his voice was wary. "Do you think that's what the stuff is? Something to trace us?"

"I think you have told me enough times how you trust the man—not at all. That box could be anything from a means to trace us to—who knows? Sorcerers are so devious; how could a normal man reason their thoughts? Get rid of it!"

"I can't, Dom—no, wait, save your air for the ride ahead. I don't trust him. But this stuff—I think it's what he said. What if we need that?"

"Need that old man's sorcery? You *must* have lost your wit."

"Possibly. I can reason this far, though: Gustave has no choice but me, however that galls him." He smiled grimly. "He must do everything he can to ensure I do not feed him to the wolves or send him packing to Saaren once I am permitted to do so."

"He might think no Prince better than a Prince who loathes him." Dominic glanced over his shoulder, saw Hans there and impatiently motioned him ahead.

"I doubt it. My nearest relations are Mother's French uncles and two cousins of Father's—and this is Saxe-Baden, not France. There would be a war for succession if I do not succeed Father. Gustave is an old man; he's done nothing of worth in years. Who would want him? He knows that, Dom; why do you think he played out that little farce back there?"

"Hah. Ask such a thing of me," Dominic growled.

"Remember, our Swiss strategy masters told us to use any weapon that presents itself in need. They did not say one must like the weapon."

Dominic shrugged and fell silent; he needed all his concentration for the trail, which had suddenly taken a sharp turn upward. Conrad brooded: He must walk cautiously. Too many things happened all at once.

How had his father really felt about Gustave? Conrad wondered. Had Leopold really been fond of the sorcerer, or had he simply taken the easiest path to using the old fool? Had Gustave used him? Had each used the other? In which case, who was the greater fool?

Conrad shifted his weight forward as the trail took another turn upward and boulders and large rock cluttered the narrow, gravelly way.

How had Leopold felt about witches, or could he have separated what he felt from what Gustave told him? *What do I feel about magic and witches myself?* Magic: He'd had little to do with it; he had avoided Gustave and Gustave's apprentices; in Paris he'd had no reason to seek out sorcerers except Ordnance Sorcerers—and astrologers, of course. Witches—until Ilse, he was certain he had never seen a witch in his life.

Ilse: Even Gustave said she was not a true Green Witch. If they did what his mother said, how could he fault them? Arrogance and ambition were not failings limited to one kind of folk or other. Any more than treason came from only one class.

He shook his head to clear it; he was solving nothing and the trail demanded all his attention. He glanced back at Dom; Dom's jaw was set, his eyes fixed on the ground just in front of Gabriel's nose. The trail was unstable, rough-cut, steep.

Nothing but a walking pace would do here. A horse could break his leg, the horseman would see nothing until too late. Or the horseman could break his own leg and have a hell's journey back to civilization.

The trail leveled out briefly, wound through brush and scattered oak, forded a wide creekbed with only a ribbon of water running down one side, and started up a grassy slope toward thicker woods.

Here, there were innumerable animal burrows and thick brush; trees clustered closely. Conrad stifled an oath against his sleeve and swung to the ground to lead the gray. Dominic followed his lead. Jussl was already afoot, a distance ahead.

They were still climbing, but not as steeply. The trees came closer together, blocking all view of the overcast sky; there was little undergrowth here but fallen branches were everywhere. The woods were hushed; a squirrel chattering like a saw some distance away made Hans jump, and his horse shied nervously. He patted its neck, soothed it, caught up with the others as they came out on a rock ledge. It was flat, wide, surrounded by low bushes and curled yellow wildflowers. Flowering ash rose behind them, and behind the ash, dark conifers. They could see nothing in any direction save a patch of overcast sky far overhead, flowers, bushes and trees. Jussl turned a little to his left and led on again.

The ground leveled here; conifers, spaced as if planted, were everywhere; the horses walked on a thick pad of pine needles. An hour or so of this slow travel brought them to another upslope. Here even Hans dismounted as the way became treacherously steep; there were slides of shale everywhere.

The climb ended abruptly. Conrad caught his breath as he came up last onto another wide stone ledge—from this one, he could see out across forest, could see mountains and betwen forest and mountains, a shining ribbon that must be the Rhine. The sun had broken up the morning mist, and aside from a few fat clouds on the western horizon, the sky was clear, the breeze warm.

"Rest the horses." It was the first thing Jussl had said in hours. Conrad cast an eye up and raised his eyebrows in surprise. It was nearly four hours past sunrise; no wonder his legs ached! He dropped Parsifal's reins over a low branch, left the horse nibbling yellow flowers and went to sit in the sun.

Dominic handed Gabriel over to Hans, pulled his water bottle free of the saddle and went to join Conrad, who was now staring morosely out across the expanse of treetops. He started violently when the Frenchman touched his shoulder, subsided on his out-crop of rock with a rueful smile and took the proffered bottle. The smile faded as he fiddled with the cork; his hands fell to his lap, taking the forgotten bottle with them. He suddenly felt depressed, tired beyond his years.

"Look at that, Dom. They could be anywhere."

"But the witch intends you to find her; you said so."

"She *said*." He let Dom have the bottle, crossed his arms on his knees and rested his chin on them.

"And Nicholas agrees, doesn't he?" Silence. Conrad shrugged moodily. "Well, then?"

"I'm sorry. I'm hard to live with, aren't I?"

"Not so hard as some, which is one reason I ride with you. But you knew that already." Dom spread his hands in a wide French shrug. "But the good God knows you have cause to stage scenes and throw tantrums. Since you do not, we can all be grateful that you sulk in silence and curse at a point between your horse's ears instead of at us. So, then." He drank, restop-pered his bottle. "There is bread and a little fruit for now; Hans says no hot food until tonight."

"Fine," Conrad replied absently. He was staring out toward the Rhine. He shivered, looked up. "What was that?"

"I don't know; I saw nothing."

"Nor I." Conrad was staring up, hand shielding his eyes. There was an expanse of blue sky, a few small birds nearby, nothing else. "I felt something, though."

Dom shrugged. "Wind against your sweaty hide, most likely." Odd, though. He had felt something: A bird of prey far overhead or just an unpleasant thought? A goose crossing his grave?

Witch? Dominic disliked magic; given his own choice, he'd take none of it. After all, a man had a right to set the course of his own life, hadn't he? And to win his way by the strength of his hands and not the strength of his wizards! But there was little he could do just now to avoid them: He had set the course of his own life right into exile—and Conrad needed him.

Dominic took the pack from his saddlebags and got out bread and two leather cups, a bottle of red wine. He settled down next to Conrad again, cut the bread in half with one of his daggers, poured wine and stuffed bread and cup into his friend's hands, setting himself to being amusing until Conrad laughed. Then he shook his head and began to eat and drink. He might be indifferent on a horse but he could handle Conrad, in any of his moods—even this worst of all moods ever.

They went on shortly after; Dom stayed afoot from the first, having seen the trail from that height, and he was glad he had: The down-slope was a steep one and Gabriel had difficulties with his footing at that angle. Dom swore continuously, in every language he knew.

Conrad stayed on Parsifal, but his thighs ached from clamping the saddle, from not squeezing Parsifal's barrel at the same time. The air was thick with dust the horses kicked up, still and heavy under the trees. Down here, there was no wind. His old hunting leathers were too warm; the linen under them stuck to his body unpleasantly. He was beginning to think he must fall off the horse and die where he was when Jussl called a short halt to check straps.

Jussl remounted and led them into thick woods. Conrad sighed. He was tired from so much riding, tired from not enough sleep, tired and despondent—how could he have believed that woman? How could he have believed a man who claimed to know the stars, another who was so poor a wizard he could not even properly protect the palace? Maybe they would just go on like this, day after day, riding, up and down hills, on trails where even surefooted Parsifal stumbled on loose rock; maybe he was bespelled again and this was all there would ever be, time unending. . . .

He came back to himself with a little start and ducked under a low branch, turned aside as Jussl had to cross a deep, narrow brook and stop on its far side to water the horses and refill the bottles. There was sun where they stood, almost too warm after so long in the shade.

Magic; everything came back to magic. His father had persecuted and burned Green Witches, but his father was dead now; his mother claimed they were necessary and loathed persecution. Gustave openly hated Green Magic, but he no longer had the King's ear. The city folk feared Green and Gold Magic equally; the commons went in terror of sorcerers.

Who was right? Was anyone? If either or both were outlawed, would they then vanish from the face of the earth? "Why are there no simple answers?"

"No what?" a voice demanded against his ear. Conrad started. While he had ridden blindly behind Jussl, the way had widened; there was a track for carts, room for two men abreast, and Dominic now rode beside him. "My poor friend, you look so serious, as though your stomach hurt or you solved all the problems of your realm in one afternoon! Save King's worries for *after* your coronation; they do not pay you a King's allotment yet!"

Conrad laughed. "No. But the problems will not go away until Father's Council is ready to see me crowned, will they?"

"Nor will they change because you knot your guts over them."

"Point taken, my friend," Conrad said.

"Good. It is too bad you will fret them anyhow, but that is how you are. Enough. Talk with me a while. I grow bored with this—this not-hotel society, not-party, not-game of chance. Amuse me! Tell me again how I decided to come with you of my own free will; how I told you so and you never realized I had suddenly gone mad!" Conrad grinned, shook his head. Dominic tilted his head to one side and eyed him thoughtfully. "And now he thinks, 'Why *did* I agree to take this buffoon with me?' Well, clearly it is because you wanted someone upon whom to spill your guts, my Prince. Tell me something of this pretty little girl from the ball, besides your intention to murder her."

He would have refused, but Dom spread his hands in a careless shrug and nearly fell from his horse. Conrad laughed and felt better for it. "I—damn you, anyway, Dom."

"God may do that yet, my friend, and for no more than the sins I have committed so far. I know, you wanted to sulk over her, not talk and feel better."

Conrad gripped his wrist. "You know me too well. Dom, I'm sorry."

The Frenchman scowled at him. "Do not *dare* apologize! I am nosy, I admit it. But you are entirely too self-contained; it is not good for you. Talk. I will listen."

He talked, and after a while the tightness in his chest eased a little. "If I only knew why she thought she would need magic! Why a—why bespell me?"

Dominic shrugged. "I cannot say. Ask her, when you find her. Listen to what she tells you."

"You make it sound so simple! It's not—"

"Things are."

"How can I trust her, trust anything she says?"

"How can any man trust any woman?" Dominic demanded reasonably. "Or, any woman trust any man? Who would be so mad as to do that?" Dom pulled Gabriel back behind Parsifal as the cart track turned one way, and Jussl led another, dcwn a rapidly narrowing path. He watched Conrad's back thoughtfully, and as hour followed hour, his eyes narrowed, his gaze became cool, appraising, and not altogether friendly.

Jussl brought them to a small woodcutter's cabin not long before sunset—or what would have been sunset, if they could have seen it for the thickness of the surrounding trees. By the time they reached the ugly slash of cut forest, Conrad was slumping in his saddle and Dominic was remaining upright only by grim determination not to make a fool of himself before two German commoners.

They pushed through tall bracken to ford a small, stony, meandering stream, and rode across the clearing. Dominic got himself down without loss of face and limped over to help the Prince; Conrad was too tired to push him aside as he ordinarily would have. Dom waited until Hans led the horses away and Jussl vanished into the hut before he tried to walk; the muscles and tendons down the backs of his legs had stiffened terribly over the afternoon.

He managed to walk into the cabin and to sit next to the firepit without falling. Hans came in with the food pack and an armful of wood. Jussl had an encouraging fire started with a pile of needles and twigs and was cautiously feeding it slender branches. Conrad was staring blankly at the fire, blindly working one boot off with the toe of the other.

"Is that a wise idea? You'll never get them on again."

Conrad considered this, then went back to work. "I'll chance it. I have to soak them in cold water; I think I'll die if I don't."

Dominic shuddered. "*Dieu!* But the hour—?"

"I know." Conrad bent down to try to see sky through the open wall of the hut. "I haven't decided yet. Maybe I don't want Gustave to know where we are." He dropped his boots away from the fire and began rubbing blood back into his feet. "But what can he do at such a distance?"

"I thought you had decided all of this."

"Maybe I'm deciding again." Conrad sighed, let go his foot and leaned forward to stretch out his back muscles. "I think I will. All available weapons, remember?"

"And not being too proud to use any necessary weapons," Dominic said. "I know very little of magic; still, more than I wish to know. Consider that Gustave must do certain things to work this spell, things which cost him time, strength—whatever it costs him, it means less time or strength to make mischief for you.''

Conrad frowned, shook his head. ''You were always rotten at Greek logic. I don't know,'' he went on, more to himself than anyone else. ''I think we should. It's just possible he might have learned something important.'' He brooded, drew lines in the dusty floor, nodded finally. ''We'll do it. Jussl, what's the hour?''

Neither of their guides would stay inside the cabin once Conrad told them what he planned. Jussl built up the fire and left, his fingers wrapped around some charm under his shirt.

Dominic sat cross-legged before the fire; he had drawn out three of his four daggers and now laid them in a neat row just in front of his knees. ''Just in case,'' he said. ''Is it time?''

''Just, by the look of it.'' Conrad gripped his hand. ''Luck?''

''Luck,'' Dom said.

Gustave sat on the small white carpet in the midst of his wagon. The carpet was his work from inception: He had bought the sheep as a lamb, raised it himself, sheared and spun and wove the raw wool himself—everything by his own hands as the books said. His back ached, or it would if he let himself feel it—he had sat here, not moving, for long hours, performing the ritual of purification. He had removed his shoes and replaced them with the thin white leather boots whose soles had never touched the ground; he had checked carefully to make certain there was no knot, no bow, no buckle, button or other fastening anywhere about his person, his clothing, anywhere within the ambit of the white carpet.

Five rowan branches surrounded him, just beyond arm's reach—rowan, to protect from witches. Candles dipped by his own hand, the wax heavily laced with oil of rosemary, stood between the tips of the branches. Rowan and rosemary both protected from witches; ordinarily either would be sufficient but Gustave was not about to take chances. Not now. Ilse could tear the life from him in a most hellish manner if she caught him out of Body. Worse: She could imprison him apart, Body and Being. And so, both protections.

Outside the wagon, Augustine was going through a purification of the entire wagon; he had himself forged the knife with which he would draw the circle and triangle; had woven the slender seven-foot, seven-ply rope bound to the knife's handle.

There were rosemary candles set around the circle that would protect Gustave's Body from harm; there could be no such protection around the triangle, since he must project Being outward. Unfortunate, but there was always some risk involved in such things.

Unfortunate he could not simply have managed all of this from his chambers. His rooms were protected already; full purification hadn't been necessary in so long he'd had to think long and hard to remember the words to those psalms. But there it was: He must be prepared to be on the Scarp by the next night. It would be exhausting enough from this far along the road.

Chanting completed, protections finished, he merely sat. Doubts pressed at him; he forced them aside and cleared his mind just as the familiar tug came.

It was full dark when Jussl came warily back into the hut—as though he expected the old sorcerer to leap out of the shadows. Conrad and Dominic were arguing; Hans was cutting bread and heating water; a pleasant fragrance was rising from a second, larger pot into which he'd poured the contents of his soup bag: dried peas, beans and strip meat that had soaked all day in herbed water.

"He wasn't really much use," Dom said mildly.

Conrad shrugged. "You didn't expect him to be, remember?"

"A man can always hope, can't he?" Dom took a wooden cup from Hans, sniffed happily and drank. "Another long ride tomorrow, I take it?"

"Afraid it is; at least we're on the Scarp now. There won't be any more climbing like today."

Conrad went out to wash and stand in the stream long enough to get his feet back into his boots; he came back to find his blankets laid out between the back wall and the firepit. Dom was already asleep. Jussl had not suggested setting a watch, but he and Hans had settled in at the open side of the hut. Conrad loosened his trousers and pulled the light cloak over his shoulders.

He woke hours later. At first, he couldn't remember where he was, or why: The unfamiliar smell of woodfire and dust reminded him of the journey from France, but this was no fine pavilion, no pile of silk and wool cushions, and where there should have been the soft glow of a shielded candle there was the sullen glow of coals. He'd dreamed—something odd, he couldn't remember what. But now, having come so sharply awake, he couldn't fall back to sleep.

He shifted; he was reasonably warm, there were no stones under hip or elbow. The ground was considerably harder than anything he ordinarily slept on, though, and dusty besides. His nose twitched and he fought a sneeze, finally shifted around and edged the blanket up under him to cover more of the ground around his head. Now his legs were in the dirt, but they didn't matter so much.

He closed his eyes resolutely, practiced breathing deeply and slowly, tried to remember all the words to one of the longer love songs popular in Hotel society just now—that could usually put him to sleep—but it was no good. He felt painfully, unnaturally awake, his skin prickling faintly, his heart thudding heavily and rapidly in his ears, and the meat and bread sat like a lump in his stomach; the least noise, from someone's soft snore to the fire settling, to a branch rubbing against the roof or one of the horses shifting beyond the connecting wall, made him jump. His whole body was tense, his jaw muscles too tight. He forced them to relax, but a few breaths later, his teeth were grinding together again. His eyes would not stay shut, but he was too worn to keep them open, and they felt dry and full of sand. There was an unpleasant taste in his mouth; he wanted water. There was a wooden jug of it on the stone shelf near the fire; he thought of sitting up and reaching for it but couldn't gather the energy to do so and the air on his face felt cold; he didn't want that on his shoulders just now. He rolled from his side to his back, to his other side; the fire was too warm against his face, too bright for sleep. He rolled onto his back, could find no comfortable place for his arms; the small of his back protested until he brought one knee up. His foot slipped on the blanket and the leg went flat again. Conrad bit back a sigh and rolled away from the fire again, got the cloak straightened over his shoulders and around his feet once again, wrapped his arms across his chest and tried to relax. His heart was thudding in the ear pressed against the pack; he moved his head a little and bit back another sigh. Not far away, Dominic mumbled something in his sleep. Conrad lifted his head again, glared at his friend and lay back down once more. How he could sleep so comfortably!

He ached from the long ride and wondered how Dom had held up to the extent of keeping his famous temper in check.

The Frenchman was not much of a rider at best. That had been a distance indeed since dawn, across country and onto the Scarp.

The tension went from him all at once. He rolled onto his back once more, rearranged the pack under his head and let his eyes close. But it seemed forever that he heard the quiet, regular breathing of the other men before his own slowed and sleep claimed him.

It was darker on the ballroom steps than it should have been, though the sconces were full of burning candles, the chandeliers fully lit. Perhaps it was the air itself that was dark, perhaps his eyes were not seeing properly. He stood by himself in the very midst of the second stair and the brightly clad nobility of Saxe-Baden came through the great double doors and bowed or curtseyed before him. Odd; the girls and the women were courteous, formally polite. But distant, as he'd wished them to be then; no one blushed or giggled; he kissed no hands. It was as though there were a glass between them and him; a slightly fogged glass that made them a little distant, their faces a blur. He recognized no one, though the entire nobility of the land must have passed before him.

Music played and people danced. He heard the light, pleasant laughter of women, the rumbling laughter of men. But none of it was for him, none of it included him, and none of it touched him. A galliard was playing; slippers and soft boots whispered across the floor, skirts rustled and hissed as fabric brushed fabric. He stood with his back to it all, eyes fixed on the doors.

Ladislaus von Mencken came through them, his ruddy face and great thatch of graying hair and the dress uniform identifying him to a Prince who had not seen him in many years; the von Mencken crest and the Orders of King and Country decorated his chest, the sashed medal of Armsmaster hung from his throat and decorated the empty dress scabbard.

He was surrounded by women: On his right, a woman as tall as he, gaunt and unnaturally dark-haired, clad in deep violet. *Beatrix, Countess von Mencken.* And beyond her, her daughters, modestly clad in lavender and pale pink. They were presented, they curtseyed gravely and moved on. Ladislaus turned slightly to present his daughter. Conrad's breath caught in his throat. Sofia wore unrelieved black; she looked infinitely tiny, like a jewel in a velvet case, and he held out his hands to her. She took them, met his eyes as she came up from her curtsey.

But he scarcely felt her touch, and there was nothing in her face save a grave courtesy and a mild curiosity. He let go her hands, turned to watch as her father handed her down into the ballroom.

He wanted her, ah, before God, he did! But the light faded, was gone—and so was the dream.

Dream. He shifted in his sleep, pulled the cloak more snugly around his throat. His breathing deepened. . . .

The ballroom was brilliantly lit, so bright he could not look at the white walls or the mirrors. They were all there, behind him, dancing, laughing, drinking and eating. This time he was not alone; Queen Henriette stood at his right, King Leopold I at his left, both brilliant in red and gold; the Prince wore his hunting leathers and felt like a sparrow between them. He looked up as movement at the doors alerted him, his breath coming quickly in anticipation: Ladislaus, flanked again by two women. Sofia on his right hand, again in black, and on his left Magdalena, glorious in black that matched her daughter's. They bowed and curtseyed from the top step, moved across, down into the ballroom. Sofia had scarcely glanced at him.

Conrad started and would have followed her, but the King's hand was about his shoulders, the Queen's on his arm, and when he twisted to free himself, the King's grip tightened painfully. And then everything was gone, save the music. It was solemn, but the high sweet melody of the flutes gave it a gaiety that lifted his spirits. There was a pool of light, faint and yellowish. He walked toward it, his boots clicking on the tiled floor of the ballroom, echoing as though the room were empty of all save himself.

He could hear laughter, faintly, under the pavane. Light touched him, warmed his hands and sparked his rings, and he could see himself, suddenly, from a long distance: a slender, rather forlorn figure in white and gold. And then he was himself again, staring into the darkness. He drew a deep breath. Roses.

She was there, a faintly shining thing in the gloom, and then Sofia in white and gold, her small hands in his, her face upturned to his and her smile radiant. She said nothing, he said nothing; the music surrounded them as he led her in the dance. He was scarcely aware when it began to fade—music, scent and light alike—and he was alone in a darkened ballroom.

There was a light. He moved toward it. He heard no sound as he mounted the steps and stood in a reception line composed of himself, his mother, two royal cousins and the Senior Steward, all grave courtesy without, all intense embarrassment within as the noblewomen of Saxe-Baden passed before him, simpering and smirking. Their faces were darkened, as though the light did not fall on them properly; they looked sly. Beatrix came with her daughters in dreadful La Mode gowns. Sofia, somehow dull and pale beside them, was caught firmly in Beatrix's large right hand, as though she had been dragged to the ball perforce. He reached for her, but she was gone, somehow evading Beatrix's grip and his fingers, and his feet would not obey him when he tried to follow her.

He stood in the same line. The music had not changed; Beatrix and her daughters again passed him, Sofia imprisoned in her grip, but now in ragged skirts and bare feet, her hair wildly loose about her shoulders. Her eyes were black with horror as they met Conrad's; she twisted free and went running like a deer through the double doors.

She was there again, between Johanna and Isabelle, clad in Beatrix's violet, and all three girls simpered at him; now she came in rags, and then with the witch and both of them in rags. Conrad thrashed in his sleep, rucking the blanket around his hips and twisting the cloak half under his side. *Sofia*. His lips moved, no sound came.

Sofia! It was dark where he stood, dark and cold. A wind ruffled his hair and cut through the thin white jacket and shirt; he felt pebbles through the soles of his white boots. She was there, somewhere, and he could not see her— Fingers closed on his, small, warm and somehow reassuring, but when he tried to move closer to her, they were gone. *Ah—!* With a sudden start, he woke.

"Command of all living things is the goal of a Green Witch; this is first learned by command of self."

An Oral Grammarie, Green & Gold Magyk

16.

There was fog in the predawn hour, softening the outline of Hel's house and turning the light of her single lantern to a faint ruddy glow, like the light of a burned-down fire. Ilse set her jaw and turned her back on the house, squatted down to gather her handful of branches. She'd lost some of her osier lashings earlier, when the horse unmade. They were somewhere on the ground and couldn't have gone far; there'd been no wind. She would not go back into that hut and ask Hel for light.

She was acutely conscious of the old woman's tight-lipped anger. It filled the cottage and spilled out, eddying through the fog. It refueled Ilse's own anger, but that quickly faded: She hadn't time for anger, nor for the guilt that tried to edge it aside. The things she'd said to her dead mother's sister—well, Hel had deserved many of them, and Hel herself hadn't spared Ilse during their long hours of argument, had she? Ilse scrabbled over the ground with her right hand, finally found the osier and began wrapping the stringy vegetation around her bundle of branches. Concentration: She needed that; the horse must be made before any light separated the trees from the darkness beyond them. And Hel had been right about one thing—she had best be gone before daylight anyway; their shouting match must have been heard clear in the other end of the village, and the headman might well come to make certain their witch was all right.

He would not personally do anything to her, of course—he

could not, even if he tried. But Ilse would prefer he not know of her presence. She must take Hel's word that no one did, and none knew that Sofia had been there.

The anger threatened to choke her. How *dare* Hel? And how dare that girl defy her? She would not do such a thing again, Ilse vowed grimly; she would not even think it without weeping. She shook her head to clear it once again and concentrated on her spell. Horse. She could vent her fury on the air; for all Hel had noticed or cared, she might as well have vented it all there to begin with. Better, she'd save it for that wretched black-haired girl. . . .

She shivered as the horse came to life under her fingers. It would be cold aloft this morning. She wrapped the heavy shawl around her shoulders over her cloak before she mounted and pulled the cloak closer as the coal-black beast padded across Hel's foreyard on soundless feet and rose into the air.

Sofia woke chilled to her bones and so stiff she did not immediately dare attempt to reach the ground. It was the blue-gray hour; fog hung in the upper branches and was thick just above the ground. Droplets clung to the hair around her face and her shoulders were damp. Something crunched its way through the brush, too far away to see, not far enough for her peace of mind. Beast on its way to water; bear? She closed her eyes and bit her lip not to cry out, then bent forward to stretch her aching back and to begin massaging her calves and feet.

Everything ached, including her stomach, but she could not face the dried meat; the smell of it threatened to make her ill. The bread was hard-crusted all around but where she cut some from the loaf it was still soft in the center. She chewed and rubbed, rubbed and chewed until the fog began to lift and she could see the least edge of pale blue sky high above.

Birds chattered in the upper branches and birds under her tree fought for fallen breadcrumbs. They scattered in a clatter of wings when she began working her way down to the boulder and then to the ground. There was no other sound save birds.

The sun was not yet up; from so far down in the woods, Sofia could not tell if she would see it when it did rise. There seemed to be considerable fog or cloud, up there. The ground was wet; wet grass soaked through her shoes almost immediately and damped her skirts and the stockings. The latter being woolen, her ankles stayed warm, but the wet skirts rubbed her legs.

She went to the stream first, washed face and hands and drank, then sat on a flat rock a few moments to eat another piece of the bread and try to do something with her hair. She had no pins, no ribbon, no scarf to restrain it; it had been wildly loose when Ilse dragged her from Neustadt and now, after that flight and this one, it was horribly draggled and snarled. She finally gave it up, twisted it into a hard knot at the base of her neck and pulled the knot through itself to keep it at least out of her face. She would look dreadful with the hair skinned from her face like that, but who would see her, and who would care? But she did not look at her reflection in the water as she dipped bread into the stream to soften it.

Finally she went on. The bread had not made a proper meal, but she dared not eat all of it, and the thought of the meat still made her queasy. She looked longingly at a few small red berries, but the leaves on the bushes weren't familiar; she did not dare eat them.

Direction . . . the City was that way—was it not? She could not see far at all; she hadn't been able to see any distance from the tree she'd spent the night in. And if she wasn't certain of that direction, it would do her no good to try to find the ledge, would it? She turned back to the stream, indecisive, stood still and thought carefully. "No. The stream was to my left, the ledge and the road behind me, Neustadt before and somewhat to the right. So, if I continue this way, following the water, I will certainly not cross back toward the Scarp, will I?" She considered this, nodded once and set out again.

The ground began to dry out as she walked; the air warmed and dried her hems. It was still quite cool in the woods, everything still shade. She stayed as near the running water as possible, though often it was necessary for her to skirt boggy areas and several times the brush was so thick she had to go far enough afield she could no longer hear it. That terrified her; to lose her only guide—! But each time, she came back to it.

There was, finally, a narrow clearing: a woodcutter's hut that was scarcely more than a leaning wall braced against two waist-high upright logs over a platform for sleeping, a stack of felled trees and two heaps of smaller branches, an ugly collection of jagged trunks. But there was sun here, and Sofia realized with amazement that the sun was almost directly overhead. Midday—no wonder her stomach hurt so!

There were no clouds in sight, though in truth she could see little from here; ancient fir ringed the clearing thickly, leaving sky only as a blue slash far overhead. It was enough.

She found a place to sit on the far side of the clearing, near the edge of the trees so she could flee into whatever protection they might offer, if she must. She had heard no sound of any woodcutter all morning, near or far, and though she had no forest craft it seemed to her the cuts were sufficiently grayed as to be weeks old. But men might come to take the wood away, and they would not necessarily make much noise. And the others, the ones who were looking for her—hunters would make little or no noise.

That brought a lump into her throat, and she nearly retreated into the shade of the woods and the sense of protection they offered. The warmth of the sun lured her back out, though; she sat still for some moments, letting it touch her face and closed eyelids, let the shawl fall away from her arms. She finally roused herself to shed her shoes in hopes they would dry at least a little while she ate.

There was fresh water: a small spill in the swift-moving current. She drank from that, held bread under it in both hands and ate, then resolutely pulled out a stick of the meat and began chewing. It was still much too salty but now she was hungry enough that the taste didn't much matter. It made her jaws ache, chewing it; she drank more water, stretched long and hard as she stood and started back across the clearing.

Direction—perhaps she could conjure it better from here. Sofia tilted her head back and gazed at the sun. It had moved—so. Which meant that Neustadt was—

She swung around, a considerable angle off the way she'd been walking all morning. It *had* to be that way, didn't it? But the stream—"Ah, sweet Mary, have I been following water that's bent north? All the morning?" It chilled her; she wrapped arms around herself and hugged, hard. Not only wasting time; she'd wear herself out to no good cause, the bread would not last her past tomorrow morning.

"No. It's all right, a little time and distance only; don't worry it." Her voice sounded much too loud here. She cast another glance at the sky. She had long hours yet to walk; she had better be gone.

She started toward her few things, froze. A shadow moved under the trees and came into the open: an enormous horse, all black and without saddle or bridle. He moved with a delicate grace for all his bulk and his hooves made no sound on the dry branches that should have broken and crackled underfoot. *That is no true horse,* she realized in a sudden panic: She could see forest, hazy and diffused, through his neck. Sofia let the meat fall from her hand and began edging away from him, one slow, cautious sideways step at a time. The horse stopped and turned to face her.

A step—another. "Shoes and shawl, there, hurry," she whispered. One more step. The horse stood like a sooty statue, only his head turning so he could watch her. Her eyes fixed on him, she bent to fit the shoes on her feet. They were still wet and so were the stockings; they didn't want to go. She swore, brushed tears of fear and frustration aside angrily, gathered them up and reached for the shawl-bag. A shadow crossed hers.

"Where were you going?" Ilse's voice hit her like a blow; Ilse's hand clamped her right wrist to the ground.

Sofia drew her breath on a sharp little terrified cry; it broke as Ilse dragged her upright and fastened one hand on the throat of her bodice. The witch's face was white, her eyes black fires, her teeth bared. Sofia tried to twist away. Ilse dragged her around and smacked her open-handed. White light exploded behind her eyes; she felt her bodice rip from the witch's fingers as Ilse's open backhand caught the other side of her face and she reeled away and fell. Everything went briefly dark.

A loud crack and pain like fire across her shoulders brought her back; her eyes snapped open as Ilse brought a long green branch down across her back again. Sofia shrieked and hid her face under her arm, tried to scuttle away on hands and knees but the witch was there, wherever she went. Her back was afire, her arm cut and bleeding from a blow aimed at her face. She finally stuffed the shawl between her teeth and curled in on herself. The pain was all-consuming; it turned the inside of her eyelids to blood and then to night.

Ilse threw the tattered remnant of branch aside and gazed down. The wretched girl would remember that! She'd feel it as long as she was still alive to feel anything, and she'd know better than to attempt another such escape. All the same—

All the same, she had looked like a squashed bug before, hadn't she? Ilse squatted on her haunches, took her knife and cut Sofia's muddied hems into strips, wound cloth around Sofia's wrists and knotted them snugly before her. She sat back on her heels then, caught up another branch and prodded the girl with it. "Get up, you stupid creature," she snapped. Sofia winced as the stick touched bruised skin. "There's more of that for you unless you do exactly as I say. Do you understand me?"

"Yes." It was barely a whisper. She gasped as Ilse grabbed her shoulder and yanked her upright.

"I did not hear that," she said crisply.

Sofia's gaze fell, a wave of red colored her face and throat. "I understand you." It still wasn't much above a whisper, but Ilse was satisfied, with that and with the look of her prisoner. She heaved herself to her feet, pulling Sofia with her.

"Go to the horse. I am immediately behind you; do not think of going anywhere but that horse. Do you understand me?"

"I understand you," Sofia said. Ilse let go of her and she staggered, lightheaded and off balance. She didn't fall, somehow—Ilse might take that wrong, God knew, and beat her for it.

Getting mounted was a terrible task; she simply could not use her arms to pull herself up, her shoulders hurt too much, and the shock of Ilse's sudden appearance had drained nearly as much strength from her as the beating had. Ilse fumed at her and nearly beat her again. There was no saddle, no bridle; she wrapped her fingers in the long mane and edged forward as far as she could. Ilse got up behind her, and spoke; the horse moved smoothly across the meadow. Sofia set her teeth as the witch gripped her arm, and closed her eyes. Tears ran silently down her face.

The horse moved through the woods for the next hour; Sofia slipped in and out of a daze and remembered little save trees and the misery of the rough-woven bodice against her aching shoulders, Ilse's grip on her bruised arms. Her stockings rubbed against the horse's barrel, rubbing her legs in turn. There was a growing ache in her hip joints from riding astride, something she had only done when she was very young. She finally let her eyes close and drifted in and out of consciousness as the spell-horse traveled through woods, across small streams and bogs, on and on, deeper and deeper into the forest until she lost all sense of direction. If she had had any that day at all. She couldn't make herself care, just now. Nothing mattered.

She stirred when the horse stopped, and Ilse leaped down. The witch looked up at her. "Do not move, not the least bit. Do you understand me?"

Beatrix's favorite question. "I understand you," Sofia whispered. Ilse let go of her leg and walked on past the horse.

There was a broad meadow, the pale green of bogs and a few dead firs, some large boulders scattered as though by a giant's hand. She heard bells and the high trilling *baa* of sheep off through the trees to her left, somewhere in the meadow no doubt, but not visible from this vantage. The Scarp was visible, though: It was directly before them, just beyond the meadow, rising in black and gray sheets of impassable stone. Sofia let her head fall back, bit back a cry as her loosened hair fell across her shoulders; far overhead, she could see a line of rock and tree that marked the upper ledge. This must be one of its tallest points.

Ilse must have misjudged the way, Sofia thought. But she did not look as though she had gotten lost. She drew a small bundle of powdery-looking twigs from a bag under her shawl, divided them into two bundles, bound them with a length of grayish, stringy herb, mumbling to herself continuously as she knotted the bundles to a length of pale hay braid. Still muttering under her breath, she draped the result over the horse's neck just in front of Sofia's fingers. "Do not touch that. Do not touch any part of it."

"I will not touch it." Ilse gazed at her, eyes narrowed, then nodded, tucked the bag back under her shawl and remounted behind her prisoner. Sofia set her jaw to not cry out; Ilse's fingers dug into her arm, her shawl rubbed against the girl's shoulders as she leaned forward to speak against Sofia's ear.

"Now. I warn you, for your own sake, do not move! Not so much as a hair! At best, I will simply let go of you."

"I will not move," Sofia responded dully as Ilse paused for a response. And a breath later, the horse stepped up onto the air. It moved upward at a steady, smooth walk for several more paces, then simply lifted into the air, angling toward the upper ledge. Sofia swallowed and resolutely closed her eyes, but after a moment she opened them again and fixed them on that black-shadowed row of trees and rock. Better to at least see where she *went*; but she could not make herself look to see where she had been.

Ilse's chuckle startled her and she nearly fainted with terror as her weight shifted; she found herself grateful for that painful grip on her upper arm. "Fewer would attempt this than would dare Rose Magic. Do you know that, Sofia von Mencken?'' Silence. ''Do you?''

''Fuh—flying?'' The word came out an octave higher than her normal pitch.

''Ah, that.'' She felt the witch shrug. ''Flight is nothing; any witch beyond 'prenticing can fly. Even the horse is not terribly difficult, but to send the horse aloft while it carries a non-witch—'' She chuckled again, a muted, nasty laugh behind closed lips. ''You thought you could evade me, did you? You are more of a fool than I thought when I first came into your shabby little chamber and convinced you to help me bespell Prince Conrad. Aren't you?''

There was no answer to that. None she could safely voice. *A fool—I suppose I am.* The upper ledge was coming nearer, the meadow below a terrifyingly distant blotch of pale green. She closed her eyes resolutely.

The horse finally stepped onto solid ground and began picking its way between boulders, slabbed stone, fallen piles of shattered rock and broken trees, and into bushes, brush and open woods. They went only a short distance before the forest changed: Tall, thick-boled fir and cedar crowded out oak and ash; no sun reached the ground, there were no low branches, no grass or flowers. Trees pressed like pillars against them on all sides, reminding her of her nightmare. *No!* she told herself fiercely. That had been nothing; what she had was worse than any nightmare.

It was late afternoon when they finally came into the open. Here was rock, with a little green where plants had rooted in shallow basins or between expanses of stone. It was hot here; no breeze, no shade. But the horse turned aside after a few minutes and shortly came to a thread of brook, a stretch of aspen woods scarcely taller than the combination of woman and horse. Beyond that, black stone and a bridge across a deep, shadowed defile. Sofia could hear water roaring below them. The horse showed no distress at either ravine or bridge; his hooves made no sound on the wooden planks.

They were in forest almost at once: thick brush and oak, ash and maple, then aspen and willow surrounding a deep, clear and sun-soaked pool. Sofia gazed at it longingly as they rode past. Beyond it was a trail, leading up and into woods again, this time fir and cedar. The air was dry, cool and fragrant. They crested a knoll and went down its other side, and here the trees were enormous and ancient: Cedars a man could not have reached halfway around. They were so neatly spaced, the ground beneath them so free of obstacle, it looked as though someone had planted them. A giant's garden, Sofia thought.

They rode toward sunlight, through trees and then purple and yellow flowers, grass and wild red strawberries. Before them was a rock ledge, and Sofia sighed tiredly; her entire body ached and her left leg had long since gone numb from the pain in her hip. But the horse did not climb the ledge as she expected; it turned aside, found a way that looked almost swept and walked between two long piles of rubble.

There were caves here, hidden by afternoon shade. They passed two that were mere shallows in stone, a third at eye level that looked deep but had no height to the opening. Ilse dismounted as the black horse stopped in shadow. ''Get down.'' It was the first thing the witch had said to her in hours. Ilse waited impatiently while her prisoner awkwardly maneuvered one leg back over the horse's withers, slid down; her legs folded and she sat, hard. ''Do not move, girl.''

It was an unnecessary order; Sofia did not think she would ever move again. The witch was muttering to herself and suddenly there was a cave, its entrance as wide as her arms might reach, the height well above a tall man's head. Ilse pulled her to her feet and dragged her inside, left her sitting just inside the entrance; she returned with a bit of dark, sour bread and a small cup of ale. ''Eat, drink—do it!''

It was hard, forcing herself to chew the tough bread with Ilse's unfriendly gaze on her; she choked down the last of it and washed it down with warm, flat ale. Ilse untied the woolen bindings on her wrists, stepped behind her and rebound them at her back. She cut another strip from the girl's skirts, knotted her ankles together with that.

''I have business with Prince Conrad. You will remain here. There are safeguards on that entry, so do not dare think of escaping me again. The bonds will keep you from mischief you still might contemplate. The alternative is to give you a drug. But I need you alert when I return; there is magic to work and you are part of it.'' She turned and walked from the cave, mounted and was gone. Sofia closed her eyes and drew her breath on a sob. Everything hurt. Worse, Ilse's sudden and violent appearance had completely sapped her. She edged down on her left elbow and cautiously eased onto her side, curled up on the hard, cold stone.

She slept so deeply it took her a long time to come fully awake and at first she could not recall why she ached so, why she was so chilled, why the surface under her was so cold. She cautiously eased herself up, causing no more than an occasional twinge in her shoulders, and edged over to the near wall of the cave. It was difficult, finding a place to lean where she did not press bruised skin.

Her shoulders were a mass of swollen and purpled weals; her head pounded when she turned it to inspect them. Even Beatrix had never beaten her; it hurt and humiliated her to remember cowering away from Ilse's white and furious face, from that branch—a deep, chill anger settled in her stomach. *I could kill her for this!*

The thought was like cold water on her neck. *Could I, really?* In anger, perhaps; by deliberate plan—she tried to picture herself with an iron blade, a steel blade, herself with a flaming branch setting the woman afire, and she knew she could not. But Prince Conrad could.

Or, he could if somehow the witch's plans were undone, turned against her, if he were his own man and armed when he confronted Ilse.

Direct action had never been Sofia's way. But she had survived Beatrix. And while Ilse was powerful, she was vulnerable: She was arrogant, and she still tried to manipulate too many people and events. That had nearly cost her everything in the ballroom; she spoke of caution, but she had not changed.

"I must keep her from using drugs to make me sleep," Sofia whispered. "I must watch her, learn what she intends, find any flaw in her plans." She must use all the wits and all the cunning she had used against Beatrix; Ilse must think her defeated. She must be patient—she had gone headlong and unthinking since the night Ilse had come to her room.

She might even survive *this* if she worked from her known strengths; the Prince might, if he did not simply let humiliation and anger blind him.

"Enough," she told herself, and let it go. Worry solved nothing. And it would be better to study the cave while Ilse was gone. She resettled her shoulders cautiously, tested the bonds on her wrists. They were too snug to manipulate but not tight enough to stop circulation; her shoulder and elbow joints were beginning to feel the strain, though, and her hips ached from riding astride. They would be worse in the morning.

The cave was not deep, not much larger in fact than Hel's cottage. There was a flickering, chill blue light near the back wall and the table under it was littered with bottles and boxes and piles of dry herb. A wooden cupboard had been fitted into a niche in the wall. There was a firepit and stacked wood. A little light came in through the chimney hole high above to fall on a kettle, loose ash and burned wood. Back among rock and shadow, there might have been another hole leading into darkness.

She did not turn her head to look outdoors. The way out was sealed against her. But she could see nothing useful in Ilse's cave. The next move must depend on the witch.

"Even charms, spells and amulets concocted by a master sorcerer are not proof against determined opposition. Possession can be managed despite such protections if the one to be possessed is sufficiently weak-willed. Or if the protections are taken away . . ."

Green & Gold Magyk

17.

They had left the woodcutter's clearing at dawn; Conrad lost track of time after that. There had been villages, suspicious and silent villagers. Conrad had felt nearly as uncomfortable as the peasants had looked; he had hardly ever spoken to his commons, and now he must ask them to betray one of their own—or so it clearly seemed to them. Suspicion had deepened to fear; most of his questions or Jussl's had met silence.

Midday, another village. A half-blind old man named Hulgen had cursed Ilse at length and finally directed them to a village south and west, to the woman Hel. But there were few people about when they reached that village, and Hel's hut was empty and cold. There had been loud arguing, three nights in a row; no one would say anything else. Conrad and Dominic had searched the Green Witch's hut but found nothing to indicate Sofia had ever been there.

All the same, Conrad was certain. The silver earring which he now wore on the inside of his collar was pulsing gently. It had gone chill on him earlier, so briefly he might have imagined it, but now the thing left no doubt. And he would have sworn he could smell the faintest hint of roses near the fire.

They ate next to a shallow, gravelly stream that paralleled the road—here merely two ruts worn by cart tracks through thick woods. Dominic greeted it with a whoop, leaped from his horse and swore as his legs touched ground. He hobbled across to the water, sat to strip off his boots and waded out to stand ankle-deep, bent over to scoop up water with his battered hat and poured it over his head, gasped and spluttered, and took two gingerly steps into full sun.

Conrad sat on a flat rock to shed his boots. Dom grinned, flicked water drops at him, waited for him mid-stream, clapped him on the shoulder as he came out into the water. "That's the proper stuff, isn't it?"

"Beloved God, it's cold," Conrad said feelingly.

"Of course it is. Your face is nearly black with dust; you look like one of Marie's little pages, without the green parasol."

"I know I'm grubby, I can feel it. My very teeth are gritty. Lend me your hat, it's already wet."

"Get your own hat wet; you can afford another better than I can," Dom said rudely, but he was still grinning.

"You can't tell me you haven't doubled the money you brought with you," the Prince retorted. "I've already heard complaints about the gambling down in barracks, and the saints know there was enough of it on our ride from Paris." Dominic handed over the wet hat with a flourish.

"A de Valois has a certain lifestyle and a reputation to maintain! And once I return home, my expenses simply in renewing my sadly dated wardrobe—ruinous, I assure you!"

"I see I shall have to find you a position, to save my army from being impoverished. Since, after all, it is partly on my account you are here." Dominic laughed and waved his hands in cheerful denial. "No, listen, Dom, I have thought about it and I would like to. Some post of importance, a stipend to go with it." They stood mid-stream looking at each other. Dominic's face had gone still, the expression wiped from it, and Conrad felt his pulse speed—he wasn't certain what he had said, but he had said something wrong. The moment was broken a breath later as the Frenchman shook his head and began laughing.

"My dear sweet Prince, you shame me!"

"I do nothing of the sort," Conrad replied tartly. "And do not dare call me that! Or I shall find a worse thing to call you! The ribbing I took for that in Paris! 'Sweet Prince' indeed!"

"Your Royal Highness," Dominic began formally; the corners of his mouth twitched and he was laughing again. Conrad bent down, filled Dom's hat and solemnly emptied it over his friend's head; Dominic retrieved the hat from Conrad's fingers and gently settled it on his friend's brow. Conrad wiped water out of his eyes, grinned, and was laughing as hard as Dominic when Jussl came for them. Dominic's hat was soaked, the brim sloppy and shapeless, the single plume—which had been a disreputable, ragged gray thing anyway—now a sodden mess plastered across band and brim.

The afternoon was warm, the air still, the road dust a cloud all around them. Dom passed Conrad his water bottle and took a drink of the flat ale himself. "You look too tired, my friend Conrad; I warned you about your dissolute lifestyle before this, did I not? I thought you were an accomplished rider; you look like I feel."

Conrad smirked, turned away to spit water. "How very quaint, coming from you," he retorted. "Dissolute!"

"Dissolute, I say. You rode too much with my sister or my mother, not enough to build your strength at it."

"Listen to the man talk," Conrad said mockingly.

"I am not a Crown Prince; it is not necessary that I ride across country like this with an army at my back."

"I know. It—" Conrad shrugged. "Who would have thought of this, though? Or all this talking to commons? I wager Father never did!"

Dominic sighed heavily. "You talk quite well, but I swear you will turn my hair white with this habit of leaping from your horse into situations! It is wise to keep a horse between you and them, I can tell you that!"

"Parsifal isn't war-trained—"

"No man of them knows that."

"Be still, Dom. Let me finish. And it was only after I dismounted to talk to the headman in that village that he brought the old witch Hulgen out."

"Yes," Dom agreed sourly, "you disarm them with your approach, all innocence and charm. How can they resist you, peasant and noble alike? And when you come upon one who is not disarmed so, you will be a very dead Prince before anyone can save you."

"Bah," Conrad retorted cheerfully.

"And bah to you, my friend," Dominic replied. He shifted and eased his right leg over the pommel to massage his calf. "Conrad. Do you mean to call up Gustave tonight?"

"I cannot think why we should."

"Nor I. You looked like a man handling unclean things, last night."

"I felt that way," Conrad said. "Odd—I thought magic would be—well, exciting." He shrugged again. "It didn't feel evil, particularly. It just felt wrong. I didn't care for it."

"That will please Jussl," Dominic said. "I did not feel anything myself, but I sensed nothing whatever in the ballroom. I am not particularly sensitive to magic, I suppose." He rubbed the side of his knee and swore as fingers pressed on tight muscle. "I only regret the time, since now there is no reason to stop before dark."

Conrad shifted and stretched in his stirrups. His back was tired and his hip joints tight, his left knee ached abominably. "We may as well stop early anyway. Give Hans the opportunity to fix a decent meal. I'll go and tell Jussl." He dropped back into the saddle and tightened his knees. But Parsifal stood on his hind legs and spun around; Conrad dropped forward and gripped the horse's mane, hanging on for dear life as the gray reared again. Dominic's Gabriel was dancing nervously sideways; Dom cursed him fluently as he worked his freed leg back across the saddle and into the stirrup. Some distance ahead, Jussl had turned back to bellow out a warning. His mount screamed and would have bolted; Hans's horse and the pack horse fled into the woods north of the road.

Conrad overbalanced as Parsifal came down and braced himself hard in the middle of the road; Dominic swung an arm and slammed him back into the saddle. A brown bear crashed through the brush just in front of them and came to a halt in the middle of the trail, between them and Jussl. The guide was shouting, but neither of the younger men could understand him. Dom could not have heard him anyway; he was screaming and cursing in wild French until Gabriel came back under control and stood, rock steady, in the middle of the road. Parsifal pranced away, eye fixed on the bear. Conrad pulled him further back and rather doubtfully drew his sword—his crossbow was under his food pack and not armed. But Dom had brought out one of his new English flintlock pistols and was coolly checking the powder pan.

Conrad turned back to stare at the bear, fascinated and horrified both, as the beast came up onto two legs and stood swaying in the road, beady little eyes nearly on a level with Conrad's. He nearly fell from his saddle as Dom's pistol went off and the

roar echoed through the woods. The bear, untouched, dropped
to all fours and crashed off through the undergrowth the way it
had come. Parsifal, unlike Gabriel, had not been trained to accept loud noises; he plunged back down the road in a series of
wild kicks and corkscrew twists. By the time Conrad got him
under control, Dominic had returned his pistol to its pocket.

"You missed," Conrad said mildly.

Dominic shrugged, essayed a grin, but his eyes were blackly
furious. He prided himself on those guns. "I intended to miss.
I do not like bear and I certainly do not intend to skin and pack
one this afternoon." He considered this briefly. "And I really
do *not* want to sample Hans's attempts at fresh bear."

Conrad shuddered appreciatively. "What now? Did you see
Jussl go?"

"He's after Hans and the pack horse. I hope he hurries; that
stupid pack mare is probably halfway to the Rhine by now." But
he could hear the crunch of underbrush—the measured step of
horses, not bear—and moments later Jussl came into sight; he
was leading his horse and the pack horse through the thick brush.
Hans came close behind; his sleeves were ripped and a long
scratch ran down his right cheek where a branch had slapped
him. He scowled. "This horse was not trained for the hunt. It
didn't fall," he added grudgingly. "But I have no idea why
not."

Jussl handed him the reins to the pack horse and remounted.
"Common sense, Hans. No man would willingly fall from a
horse where yours took you." Hans felt for his water bottle,
swore as he found it gone, took Jussl's and drank deeply.
"There's a hut two hours from here, dry firewood and water. It
would make a good stop for the night," Jussl said. Conrad nodded and waved him on. "There's a ledge just beyond this stretch
of woods," the guide called over his shoulder. "It's steep on the
north side. We'll want to rest there before we go on. The afternoon is building to full heat and there's little shade for the next
part. Not until just short of our destination." He slewed around
in the saddle to look at Dominic. "I heard your gun. Did you
kill the bear?" Dom shook his head; the fury was back in his
eyes. "Or wound it? We cannot leave a wounded bear loose
without warning the villages."

"I missed entirely," Dom snarled; he turned Gabriel and
kneed him hard. Conrad, Hans and Jussl followed. The woods
remained thick: High bushes and bramble edged the road on

both sides, trees curved over the road, forming a cool green cave. But it ended abruptly, like riding through Neustadt's ancient north gate and the long tunnel under the walls. Trees were suddenly few, bushes a few sparse things near the road. Rock was everywhere: piles and heaps of it at the bases of ledges, rock edging the north side of the road where it dropped off sharply. There was no shade, nothing to make shade, save rock; and none of it stood guard between the road and the westering sun. Heat came off the pale granite in waves. Conrad reined in. "You are right, Jussl. We had better rest here."

"An excellent idea," Dominic said. He seemed to have ridden off his anger. "And after our unwelcome guest, I have earned brandy." He dismounted stiffly, rummaged through his pack for the ornately wrought silver flask, uncorked it and took a swallow, then passed it to Conrad, who cautiously sniffed it before he drank, then offered it to Jussl and then to Hans, both of whom refused. Dom took the bottle back, turned away, and walked over to the ledge where he stood with his feet at the very edge.

Conrad sat, decided he had had enough sitting for the moment, got back up and bent over to stretch out his back. The blood ran to his head, invigorating him. He bent back the other way, easing out stiff shoulders as well as he could.

Dominic still stood with his back to them; he was drinking brandy and reloading his English pistol. Somehow he looked rather daunting, Conrad thought; the set of his shoulders, something about his stance. Dom's hands jerked and powder spilled to the rock; he swore under his breath, kicked at the fallen stuff with his boot. *Leave him alone,* Conrad decided. *He is tired and hot, stiff from riding, probably sorry he ever said he would come on this search with me. And Jussl could not have known, but I knew better than to remind him he missed. Dom has no more sense of humor about those pistols of his than about his sword.*

When Jussl hailed him a few minutes later, Dom strode across the rock without speaking to or looking at any of them, shoved the pistol and its ornate silver powder horn home, mounted and rode out ahead. Conrad gazed after him anxiously. He let it go finally and pulled himself into the saddle. Dom hated heat, hated the kind of surprise the bear had given them, hated making what he saw as a fool of himself in front of common men. And brandy made him moody. He would come out of it; he always did. An early stop, a proper hot meal would help.

The road was level, wide and well cared for; it must be the

road that wound along the back of the Scarp and eventually joined the north road somewhere between the passes and the Rhine.

Dominic stayed well out front, the others back and spread out as the road became a steep, switchbacked slope. Here were more trees, enough to shade them now and again, and a faint breeze came down the slope at intervals. Jussl pulled back, let Conrad pass him, and waited for Hans. They began talking about the nearest villages, which they should visit first in the morning, if there might still be time to reach any villages tonight.

Conrad leaned forward in the saddle and pressed his knees into Parsifal's sides: Dom was nearly out of sight and increasing the gap between them much too fast. "Dom, wait!" His words seemed to fall into the dust, muted and possibly unheard. But Dominic, well ahead of him and nearing the next turn, must have heard, for he shifted in his saddle, grinned provokingly and waved an arm, but did not slow. Conrad heard him laugh and yell out, "Catch me then, you lazy creature!" He vanished around the turn. Parsifal picked up his pace.

Rock rose above their heads, shading the road; it was terribly quiet. Conrad felt a breeze but it made no sound; he could not even hear Jussl and Hans arguing behind him. Odd. He never rode alone, had never been by himself in such a place. Silence wrapped him: He found himself liking and fearing it at the same time.

He stared up the road. Gabriel stood at the side of the road not far ahead, nuzzling a white-flowered bush; Dominic was nowhere to be seen. Conrad urged Parsifal to a bone-jarring trot, dragged him to a sudden halt as they drew even with Dom's brown. There had been a slide; rock falling from well above had taken out part of the road. There was fresh dirt; broken trees lay everywhere or stuck up at odd angles from below. Rock and boulders lay on the far side of an enormous hole, fifty paces or more across. Beyond it, the road went on; the hole at his toes fell away at an alarming angle and to an unpleasant depth. Well below him but still short of the bottom, Dominic stood, hands on hips, staring across an extremely unstable pile of scree and the upturned roots of an ancient fir.

"Hssst, Dom." Conrad spoke in a low voice; he was afraid anything approaching normal speech might set the rocks free of their tenuous resting place. Dominic turned and looked up; the hat shaded his face. "Come back up, Dom. It's not safe there."

"It's all right, there's a ledge," Dominic replied absently. He had turned back to survey the rubble. "I think we can get down here but there is one bad place to cross. Where is your woodsman?"

Conrad glanced over his shoulder. "I think I hear them. I can't see them yet." He knelt and peered down at shattered stone and broken trees. "Dom, I do wish you'd come out of there. If it went—"

"I don't *think* it will."

"That's a poor wager, coming from you. Get out of there, now!"

Dominic shrugged, turned and began climbing. Part way up, he scrabbled at rock, yelped and sat down abruptly. "Ah, *merde*, I've twisted my knee." He tried to stand, yelped again and dropped back. "Twisted it properly." He glanced up as a shower of rock slid down over his leg. "Conrad, I'm all right. I do not need your help. Wait—"

"You wait. No, sit still, I'm coming."

It wasn't far, a matter of four carefully set footsteps; Dom's outstretched hand caught his, shifted to grip his wrist hard. "Dom, what are you doing?" Dom leaped to his feet in one swift, graceful movement, took two long steps down the scree and yanked; Conrad came with him. He was sliding, falling—

But before he slid much further, his feet found Dom's ledge. A solid wall of granite rose above it, a sheer drop fell the other way, and it tapered at both ends. It was not very wide. And there was a pile of rock, scree and fallen tree balanced precariously, ready to sweep down across the ledge, shoving everything before it. . . .

There was a sick feeling in the pit of his stomach. "Dominic, what's wrong with you?" he whispered. But he already knew. His friend stood at the widest part of the ledge, eyes black with hate—a stranger's eyes. His teeth were bared in a hellish grin, and he held his dueling rapiers.

Conrad took a cautious step backward; his heel went down on unstable rock and he nearly fell. His right hand crept across his linen shirt, down the sash that held his rapier; his fingers closed gratefully on the hilt. His hardened leather jerkin was on Parsifal's back; he had only worn the sword belt because Dom insisted.

"Dom, you can't do this!" But it was no good: Dom's dreadful old hat was tilted away from his face; the plume had broken away. Augustine's protective amulet was no longer there either. Dominic's fine-bladed swords were describing tight little circles.

There was no time to think. Conrad threw his sword up and grabbed the second rapier as Dominic lunged, one blade high, the other low. Conrad dodged one, caught the other against his sword hilt, nearly fell and an inner warning shouted at him, *Get out of this loose stuff, it'll be your death!* He edged toward his left, toward the smooth rock and the drop-off. Dom's wild little giggle chilled him; the Frenchman pivoted and matched him, step for step.

He wasn't going to make it, Dom wasn't going to let him! But a stone wobbled under Dominic's foot and as he flailed for balance, Conrad spied out solid footing and leaped for it. Dominic lunged, pressed forward; Conrad gave, ducked a wide swipe at his head, deflected one sword and knocked the other into the granite wall: It rang and so did his ears. The click of blades echoed. Far above, he thought he heard voices but he dared not look; Dom was on the attack again. The tip of his lefthand blade caught in the elaborate basketry of the Prince's sword; Conrad jerked upward and Dom's rapier went flying back over his head. It landed with a clatter.

I should be dead by now, Conrad thought dazedly. *He's slow.* No one held so long against Dom; Dom would never make such a novice mistake as the one that had just cost him his offhand blade. Ilse's spell—his own will fighting her? *Or perhaps fighting for my life makes a difference.*

Dominic's eyes had narrowed and the smile was fading. He retreated a half-step at a time toward his fallen sword. Conrad took a running lunge, brought one sword around and the other down in a shining overhand that sent his friend scrambling back a little too far. He executed a furious series of maneuvers to keep Conrad busy, slowly went down into a half-crouch to retake his parry sword. His hand slipped into the basket, but the sword would not move. Conrad's foot was firmly planted on the blade.

Dominic's shoulders moved and Conrad could almost read the thought: One sword or two, it hardly mattered. Conrad swallowed dread and parried a series of swift, brilliant one-sword maneuvers; Dominic's point came up and sliced the back of Conrad's left hand.

Conrad cried out; the sword fell from fingers that would no longer hold it. He turned sideways after the Spanish fashion, put his bleeding hand behind him, and lunged. Dominic, not expecting either the change in style or the attack, lost part of his right sleeve.

He swore and lunged. Conrad parried frantically, falling back a short step at a time. Stone rubbed against his shoulder blades; the ledge was narrowing. *How many more steps to unstable scree, and how far down?*

But Dominic was slowing, and there was a deep furrow between the Frenchman's brows; the smile was gone. "Dom. Dominic! Before God, listen to me, Dom!" Dominic hesitated; his sword came down in a fledgling swordsman's backhand—slow, awkward and easily parried. Conrad knocked the arm aside with his elbow, ripped a talisman bag from his belt, stuffed it down the open throat of Dom's shirt, wrapped both arms around the man and pulled him close, pressing the bag into his bare skin. Dom shuddered, hiccuped loudly and went limp so suddenly he likely would have fallen over the edge if Conrad had not overbalanced them both the other way.

"Dominic!"

Dom's sword fell from loose fingers. Conrad dragged him away from the edge. Dominic blinked and looked up at him in bewilderment. "*Dieu*, you're cut! What have you done?"

"Not much, Dom; never mind."

"That is a sword cut. I have had enough of them and seen enough more to know." The color went out of his face and he sagged back against the rock; when Conrad would have gripped his shoulder in concern, Dom shoved him off. "I did that. Didn't I? I thought—I don't know, it seemed like the kind of dream one gets from too much sweet wine. I thought I hated you, I wanted to—kill—you—" He averted his face and his eyes fell on his offhand sword.

"You lost your talisman, Dom," Conrad said. He was shivering suddenly. "If I had thought to give you one of mine sooner I might have saved myself a scar."

"What have I done?" Dominic whispered. "Ah, God, what did I do? Please, do not smile and give me lies; I remember enough. Ah, *God*." He buried his face in his hands and his shoulders shook. When Conrad touched his arm, he pulled away; rock slithered around them.

"Dominic, don't do that, you'll send us both over the edge. You didn't remove the talisman on purpose!"

One dark eye glared over the fingertips, balefully. "Of course I did not! How many kinds of fool do you take me for?"

"Mostly one who should have become an actor, so much high drama is wasted on me," the Prince retorted dryly. "Would you like back the sword I knocked from your hand?"

"Rapier," Dominic corrected him absently. He let his hands fall then and stared. "*You?* You are not capable!" He sounded a little more like himself. Conrad managed a weak grin. His legs were not entirely steady; he had to grip the rock before he could bend down and pick up the blade.

"Your other is back along that ledge, but you can fetch it yourself. That's a filthy drop and it's your rotten sword, after all." He winced as Dominic gripped both of his hands; Dom groaned and let go abruptly. "It's only a scratch, Dom. Royal blood clots as well as mere noble blood. You're just fortunate I haven't Father's temper; he'd have carved holes in you for that."

Dom opened his mouth, shut it again as cautious footsteps high above reached them; a few loose stones rolled down and Jussl's head appeared silhouetted against the afternoon sky. "What *are* you doing down there?" he demanded tartly.

Conrad smiled and waved, he hoped reassuringly. "We thought we'd try to find a way across—"

"Not a chance of it," the guide replied flatly. "Hans has gone to search out another way, back a turn and higher up. We thought you had gone up that way when we found the horses. I will fetch a rope, if you sirs are ready to come up from there."

"Very much ready, Jussl," Conrad replied steadily, and when the man's head vanished, he went to fetch his sword and Dominic's.

Dominic managed a weak grin as the rope sailed out over scree and landed near his feet. "I thought you were going to make me go get that."

"You owe me." Conrad handed him the rope. "Repay me by leaving that bag inside your shirt for now. When we speak with Gustave tonight, you and I, we will see what else we can do." Dominic merely nodded, wrapped the rope around his back and walked up the slope as Jussl pulled. When Conrad came up, he was sitting a distance down the road, head in his hands.

"It's all right, Dom."

"It's not. You had better get away from me, I'm not to be trusted."

"Dominic, don't fuss it. I'm not hurt, you're protected again. And besides—" He shut his mouth; he had almost told Dom about Nicholas's warning; somehow, he doubted that would make his friend feel any better. "You can ride with Hans or with Jussl in the meantime, if it makes you feel better; I'll stay with the other."

"Better, he says," Dominic grumbled. "Why not say 'safe,' so we can all laugh?"

"All right, safe then. I'm not worried, Dom. It's over."

"You don't know it is. I could—"

Conrad stood and scowled down at him. "One more word and I swear I will personally throw you from that ledge. You make me feel uncomfortable and you embarrass Jussl." Dominic flushed; he had forgotten the huntsman. He pulled himself straight and managed a rueful smile. Conrad had said the best thing possible to stiffen his spine enough to get him on his feet and into the saddle.

Conrad let Gabriel pass, kept Parsifal well back behind Jussl. His hand was throbbing, and he still trembled, in sudden, ugly little moments.

Fortunately, he had to concentrate on his riding and that steadied him. Hans had found a way around the slide that took them up the slope through brush and low scrubby trees, along a flat deer trail and down a slope only slightly less precipitous to the road again. Jussl set off at a canter and Conrad let Parsifal out to stay with him. Hans and Dominic stayed well back of them for the rest of the ride. Well up the slope, hidden by rock, trees and a spell of invisibility, Ilse and the black horse watched them go.

"There is no witch's spell, but blood makes it stronger."
Green & Gold Magyk

18.

When she woke the sky was a deep blue and the mountains pink and orange-edged with sunset. It was cooler in the cave than it had been, but not as cold as the open air had been the evening before; wind blew through the grasses outside the cave but no moving air touched her. Ilse's barrier must do more than keep a prisoner contained. She was glad for it; it would have hurt too much to get the shawl around her shoulders—even if she could use her arms.

She was hungry and her discomfort was growing, but before she could begin to worry either difficulty, there was muted noise outside. She watched as the black horse came into sight and Ilse dismounted; watched without much surprise as the horse simply vanished. The witch caught up several bundles from the ground. Sofia observed her carefully, but could not follow what she did to come through the barrier. Unfortunate; that spell might have a use, even if she had already decided not to escape. *Watch and learn,* she thought, and lowered her eyes submissively as the witch stopped before her.

There was a long silence and despite her resolve Sofia felt her courage falter. Ilse dropped her bundles and squatted in front of her. "Turn, so I can release you." She worked the knots loose; Sofia gingerly rubbed her forearms and wrists while the witch loosened the bonds on her ankles. "There is food. You will make the fire and prepare it for me."

"If you wish," Sofia said softly. She frowned, shifted her weight. "I—I need—"

"You need—? Oh. Yes," Ilse said. "The privy is there." She gestured toward the back of the cave. "Down that narrow way. Take a candle, go." Sofia hesitated, looked at her, and Ilse laughed maliciously. "There is no escape from the privy save the air vent. You could not fit that, even if you could reach it. Go; hasten back, I want my dinner."

"Yes, Ilse." It was hard work, getting to her feet after so many hours on the cold stone floor; harder walking. Her leg muscles were cramped and her left leg was pins and needles.

She came back to find sausage and a bit of hard white cheese on the table, a mound of early vegetables and soft carrots from some villager's gardens. It made an untidy pile. The sooty kettle and two buckets of water stood there also and a knife. "The fire first, you stupid girl!" Ilse snapped as Sofia stood staring blankly at the table.

The firepit needed cleaning before she could lay the fire, and by the time it had settled in to burn properly her arms were soot and ash to the elbow. Ilse held her hands to the flames.

"It took you long enough; I thought Beatrix had trained you properly. Never mind, I am hungry. The first bucket of water is for washing yourself first, the second for the stew. Mind that, Schmutzie Sofie." She grinned nastily as the girl's head snapped up.

"Where did you hear that?" she whispered.

"Why, I might have thought it up myself, might I not? But no—Isabelle shared some charming memories with me, not many days ago. Does that surprise you? She does not like you. That does not surprise you, either, does it?" The smile faded. "Get over there, wash yourself and prepare my food. Our food, if you do not anger me before it is ready to eat. And do not think of any use for that knife that does not have to do with cutting meat and vegetables, I am watching you very closely. Do you understand?"

"I understand." She would have preferred heated water for washing, but any water was better than none. Simply to have clean hands and face was a delight. The knife blade was too small and dull; she hacked and tore at things until they were in small bits, finally dipped water into the kettle, dropped the food in by handfuls. The now heavy kettle pulled at her aching shoulders but somehow she managed to settle it into place next to the fire without spilling anything. She used the knife to rake the coals around the kettle, dropped the knife on one of the rocks surrounding the fire. Ilse looked at it and left it where it was.

The sausage was too spicy; she did not care much for the dried sage Ilse added, and the small piece of garlic would probably make her ill. But the resulting stew was thick and satisfying. Ilse had only one plate. She handed Sofia one of her two cups when the meal was finally ready and signed her to use that for her share. She broke the rest of the bread into two pieces and shared that. Sofia did not like Ilse's sour, flat ale and drank water instead. Ilse shrugged and emptied the leather bottle into her own cup.

She had not spoken during the hour or so it took the stew to cook, or while they ate. Sofia gathered the few dishes together without being told and washed them, but when she set them to dry on the table, Ilse stood and shook her head.

"No. Put them on the floor, beneath it. I have other uses for the table. As for you, you will stay here, near the fire, so I can watch you. You will not let the fire burn down."

Sofia nodded. The air had gone chill since nightfall and even the black shawl couldn't keep it all out. Here, close to the fire, even the stone floor of the cave was warm. "I will stay right here," she added, as Ilse watched her, arms folded across her chest, clearly waiting for a spoken response.

"Good. Put the knife under the table with the other things, set that kettle back in the coals with water. Perhaps I shall permit you tea later, if you're a good child." She smirked; Sofia nodded and bent down to place the wooden plate and cups beneath the table—and to hide the wave of red that flushed her face and darkened her eyes. She dared show no anger; Ilse wanted it.

She stayed on her knees to refill the kettle and slewed around to settle it where it belonged; felt Ilse's eyes on the top of her head as she set the knife inside one of the cups. She moved around the fire, sat next to the sticks and split logs and built it back up a little. When she looked up, Ilse was still watching her and the witch nodded. "Good. Now you are where you belong, aren't you? Among the kitchen things and the ashes, just as your stepmother wanted. All the trouble you've gone to, simply to find yourself another filthy hearth, Schmutzie Sofie." She laughed, then turned away. Sofia managed to keep her hands steady and the second wave of fury abated unnoted.

She found a fat, straw-filled cushion not far from the fire and set it on the clean stone, settled herself on it. Ilse had already forgotten her. *At least I have learned one thing: Ilse cannot read thought. Or emotion, because she wanted anger and was disappointed when I let her see none.*

Hours passed. The cave had filled with a faint, pale green smoke and cleared again; now there was a smell like spiced wine, an undercurrent of pennyroyal to it. Sofia watched carefully, so far in vain; she kept the water hot and the fire fed; she bent to rub aching legs and feet, but Ilse was so deep in her magic she paid no attention. Sofia knew better than to trust that the witch had lost sight of her. She stayed on the cushion and kept quiet.

Ilse was mumbling; Sofia had nearly fallen asleep, but she came awake when the witch spoke Conrad's name. "Conrad and his Frenchman, two village men; Gustave, Augustine, one village man. Three who fear Gold Magic, two who wield it, one who distrusts it, and the Frenchman—who claims not to believe in it. Or did claim. Hah." She nodded in satisfaction. Her face was underlit in blue; it changed her features, made her unrecognizable. She turned away to rummage through the cupboard, turned back to the table and sorted through a pile of things there. "Now. If I—" Her voice sank, vanished, though her lips continued to move. Sofia nearly vibrated with frustration.

The smoke faded, the blue light swung through green to yellow, back to green and stayed steady. Ilse separated out more things, broke off tiny fragments and fed them into the glowing bowl before her. A frown creased her brow; her mouth was hard-set. She shook her head to clear it; her gaze slid around to touch her companion and a smile turned her still hard-set mouth. Sofia stirred uneasily; the smile made her nervous. "You. Girl. Are you virgin?"

"Am I—?" She stared at the witch in stunned astonishment. Ilse giggled. That was even less pleasant than the smile.

"You are, then. Come here and give me your hand."

She forced herself to her feet, held out a hand and gasped as Ilse gripped her wrist and jabbed a needle into her palm, turned the hand palm down over the bowl and squeezed. Two drops of blood fell into the liquid there and as Sofia watched wide-eyed the surface began to fog over, like a pond on a fall morning.

Ilse let go of her hand and shoved her away; her eyes were fixed on the bowl.

Sofia stepped back around the fire and dropped to the cushion with a thump. There was only a needle puncture in the center of her palm, hardly any blood, but it hurt. She sucked at it, then shoved it in her pocket. Her fingers closed around something tiny and metallic there. The rose earring burned her palm, cooled as suddenly. She clapped a hand across her mouth, stared wide-eyed at the witch.

But Ilse was bent over her bowl, her concentration on whatever she saw there total. Whatever that had been, Ilse hadn't done it. She let the earring fall back into the pocket, carefully withdrew her hand. It had already quit bleeding; it itched as much as it hurt. She shoved a handful of small sticks into the fading fire, tucked her feet under her tattered skirts and settled down to watch and wait.

The bowl finally went dark and Ilse set it aside. She leaned against the table briefly, sighed and turned to look across the coals of the fire. "Is that water hot?"

"Yes, Ilse."

"Good. Get the cups from under the table and the ribboned bag from on top of it." Ilse appropriated the cushion and sank onto it with a sigh. "Make me a strong kettle of tea, and I'll let you have a little. There's a small pot somewhere to make it in. There's also a black jar of my aunt's honey and a flat packet under the jar that contains nut cake; hand that to me before you make the tea and I'll portion it."

"Thank you, Ilse."

The witch spat into the fire, scattering ash. "I told you already; I need you yet. For what I need, you must be alert, and therefore well fed." She glared across the kettle. "Do not think I begin to like you, or to pity you."

"No, Ilse."

The tea was a strong mess that in Sofia's opinion needed honey; Ilse gave her a small bit of a hard cake that was almost entirely nuts, seeds and bits of dried fruit. There was an odd taste to it, but it was good enough to wash down the flavor of the tea. Ilse took the last of that, finished the cake herself and yawned neatly, rather like a cat. "I am tired. It has been a very long day. You may sleep here by the fire."

"Thank you, Ilse."

Ilse fished a branch from her sleeve, worked a wooden plug

from one end and filled one of the cups with water from the bucket. She let three drops fall from the hollow branch into the cup and held it out. "Drink it."

Sofia eyed it warily; the liquid was faintly glowing and it smelled horrible. "What is it?" she managed finally.

Ilse moved irritably and Sofia winced away from her, hating herself for it. That movement pleased her captor, however; Ilse eyed her almost benignly and said, "It's a potion to make you sleep and keep you from making a mischief so I can sleep. What, did you think I would let you prowl this place as you chose? Or that I would ease you from the world with poison? Your death will not be as easy as that! Drink!"

Sofia closed her eyes, took a deep breath and drank. It didn't taste until she exhaled and then it tasted worse than it had smelled. Ilse watched as she eased herself down across the fire from witch and table; she tossed Sofia the cushion. "Thank you, Ilse." Already it was hard to make the words come out, and her eyelids would scarcely stay open.

"I have a better," Ilse muttered, and went to fetch it. Sofia heard her footsteps, hardened leather on hard stone, as she walked away from the fire, but she never heard her return.

There was music, a distraction; she shook her head to clear it, and curls bounced against her cheeks. The faint scent of roses teased her nostrils. And a warm hand pressed hers. She opened her eyes and gazed up into Conrad's smiling face. For a moment, she was disoriented; stone was pressing against her shoulders, there was no stone; there was music, there was no music; she smelled roses, not roses, something that smelled of a compounding: spicy stew, burned-out fire and ash, dry herbs and spells. No, Queen's Silver covered her in its fruity-sweet scent; her feet were clad in their petals, moving lightly and exactingly through the complex steps of a French galliard, and there, across a polished inlaid floor as blue as a spring morning sky, Prince Conrad in white and gold, holding the formal pose, his hand outstretched, eager to capture hers once again. . . .

A dream. The realization only steadied her, it did not disturb the dream.

Somehow, she had looked at him an entire evening and not really paid close heed to him. Now she could examine him dispassionately, as though she were the coldly calculating woman she had thought herself then—as though nothing had worked upon her heart as it had then. He was handsome, but not as handsome as the princes and heros in tales: His cheekbones were too prominent and he was too slender, his jaw too wide for perfection, his lips too slender. But she liked him better so, less perfect, more human. She liked the way muscle bunched at the corners of his mouth, the direct and level gaze. He was thin for a German, a rapier, not a two-handed sword. His hands were good hands: as strong, warm and deft as they had looked the first time she had seen them.

He bent toward her as the music ended, took her face in his hands, kissed her hair. She raised her eyes. Something—wrong. Her heart stopped for one long, dreadful moment, lurched and began to pound wildly. *Wrong. Why does he not see?* The Queen, beyond his shoulder, her eyes narrowed, her mouth curved in a malicious smile as she whispered to the Prince's friend. His face was not the same at all; it was thinner, his eyes narrowed and slanted upward, his chin almost coming to a point, his teeth when he smiled tiny and pointed like a ferret's or a fox's. And all around them, men and women and young girls stood and stared at them, at herself and the Prince in their white and gold, and they laughed behind red gloves and whispered to each other, and the faces darkened and changed—like masks, she thought desperately. But no mask was so subtle, so flexible, as the faces encircling them.

She turned, tugging at Conrad's grasp on her shoulder. Why could he not see the danger? There, a woman's cream-colored gown, a woman's pale shoulders, but the head was becoming more catlike by the moment; beyond her, a man whose eyes were pale gold, like a wolf's, and beside him, another wolf. . . .

Her heart thudded so loudly she could hear it above the music. A ferret stood beside the throne, bending over the shoulder of a crowned ermine, and both bared their teeth as Conrad took her hand in his and began to back toward the dance floor, to lead her through the motley crowd. She was afraid; afraid to try to speak, and when she did try, no sound came, and without Conrad's fingers gripping hers, she would not have been able to move. It was like walking through deep water; her legs moved so slowly and faces swirled and blurred as she passed them, bodies closed in behind her, pressing her skirts against her legs. There was breath hot on her bare nape, a hissing, growling, whispery noise all around her.

"Conrad. My Prince—" The words were a ragged whisper,

so unlike her own voice she could not believe she had somehow forced them out. He continued to smile at her, as though he had heard nothing. Sofia looked at his fingers. The nails were so long, tapering—she looked up, met his golden, blazing eyes, and screamed.

Only a dream, waken! But Ilse's potion had her hard in its grip and she could not. Conrad bent toward her. The ballroom grew dark; she backed away, turned and fled. There were bodies everywhere, soft skirts and velvet doublets and short capes, folk who were dark shadows and then nothing but shape and scent and an occasional hard elbow. They were gone, then; she caught up her skirts to run, caught her toe on something hard and un-giving, and fell.

It hurt; her knees took much of the blow, even through the layers of skirt. Her right arm throbbed, her back hurt, and her right palm was scraped. The left fist had come down on soft grass, fortunately, otherwise her knuckles would have been badly skinned. *Fist,* she thought, and the thought echoed. *Why is that?* There was something in her hand. She rose to her knees and brought the hand close to her face.

It was her silver earring, but as she watched it grew large and soft and became a white rose on a thick stem. She bent to inhale the light fragrance and it steadied her until a hidden thorn caught her palm. It hurt; a drop of blood pooled in her hand, the rose turned pink.

Somehow, she had lost her fear. The scent of roses was all around her; the dark was still strong but now comforting; the beast-men and women would not find her, the Prince with coals for eyes and teeth to rend a white throat—he would not come, either.

The rose had gone from pink to pale red to deep red. The rich, musky scent filled her. And then, suddenly and simply, he was there too.

This was a Conrad she had not seen before: There was dust in his hair, his face was smeared with it, and a long, fresh cut ran across the back of his hand. He wore dark, plain garb, and he lay curled on his side, eyes closed. A blanket was rucked around his chest and hips. He looked young and vulnerable; perhaps his hand pained him. And even in sleep, his mouth was hard-set.

Oddly, she was not with him. But others were: The French-man and a lean-faced peasant, both sleeping like desperately exhausted men. A short, stocky armsman with an old-fashioned helmet who sat cross-legged before the fire polishing a three-pointed pike. Beyond him—*I know that man, sleeping away from the fire's light. That is Augustine! Why is he here?* There was another peasant sleeping under a four-wheeled wagon or cart. Horses grazed or slept standing nearby.

None of that mattered. Conrad—

He was *here*, in the mountains—not far away at all. She was certain of that somehow. *No! Conrad, Prince Conrad, go back to Neustadt! The witch will kill you and me both, and her plans for our deaths no longer involve cold steel.* Silence. He could not hear her, of course. *Or, if you will come, save me; Ilse thinks of smoke and fire and I cannot face it.* Smoke and fire: What had she heard this night to tell her that? The dream believed it, and horror was threatening to bury her whole.

Conrad moaned in his sleep, turned to one side and then another. His eyelids fluttered, snapped wide. For one startling moment, his eyes gazed directly into hers, and then he shouted and sat up. That drove her into darkness and silence, where her dream-self huddled, faded rose petals spilling from her hands.

"Grant a sorcerer three things for success: a strong memory;
patience—and a skilled and talented prentice."

Green & Gold Magyk

19.

Jussl led them eastward for over an hour and then down a road
that branched to the right—barely a cart trail at its best, now
overgrown and unused. The main road had begun to level out
and the track was also flat, but hung over with trees; branches
crossed the road and brambles narrowed it so they had to ride
single file. Wild rose scent left Conrad lightheaded. He set his
jaw and urged Parsifal on.

The trail came abruptly into the open—a deserted village near
a stream and a pond. There were houses, huts, sheds—or what
was left of them. Shutters had been taken away, roofs had fallen
in. The tiny church was missing its glass windows and frames,
the altar had been taken away. Jussl rode past the church and
stopped at the last of the houses.

It was heavy log, the only opening a narrow doorway. A large
stone fireplace took up most of the far wall; rough-split wood
covered part of the dirt floor. Conrad slid down from his saddle,
gratefully handed Hans the reins and managed to walk up to the
doorway without limping. Dominic cast him a furtive, guilty
look from under his hat brim and went on down to the stream.

Conrad hesitated, finally shook his head and followed.
"Dominic—"

"Don't come near me, my friend. Please."

Conrad stopped him with a slashing gesture. "Dominic,

you've got my talisman stuffed in your shirt and you left your blades on Gabriel. Stop this. It was not your fault.''

Dominic sank back down to a squatting position, scooped up water in one hand and let it pour back to the stream. "That is not much help.''

"It certainly is,'' Conrad replied vigorously. "Look, Dom; I need you. What Ilse did changes nothing.''

Dominic spun around and glared at him. "Oh, no? The woman used me! That makes no difference?''

"None. She used me, Dom. Why beat your breast and wail about it? I know you've never believed anyone could bespell you; you pride yourself on being so sensible.'' Conrad paused; Dominic tried and failed to bite back an abashed grin. "That's the worst of being such a pragmatist.'' Silence. "It is done with. Why fuss over something past, when tomorrow may bring something worse? But I warn you,'' he added, "lose *that* talisman and I'll have to kill you. I haven't any more charms to spare.''

Dom looked at him long and expressionlessly enough for Conrad to wonder if he'd said the wrong thing. But the Frenchman managed a weak smile. "As if you could—!''

"Let us not try and find out, shall we?'' Conrad held out a hand to help him up, clapped him on the back. "Come on; I would like to face the shade of Gustave with food in my belly. Wouldn't you?''

"I would rather not face him at all,'' Dominic grumbled.

Conrad bent over, stretching his back and legs as he scooped up water and splashed it on his face. Dominic had turned back to look at their surroundings; he seemed to see them for the first time.

"What is this place?''

"Don't know,'' Conrad spluttered; he wiped his face on his sleeve. "Deserted village; ask Jussl. I hope he's got a fire going. That water's like ice.''

Jussl's fire was already warming the hut; Hans had built another outside and upwind for cooking and he sat cross-legged before it, peeling a few vegetables to throw in the pot with the remainder of the previous night's meal. Conrad's nose wrinkled involuntarily: The meat had been edible the night before but a full day on the pack horse didn't seem to have done it any good. At least there would be a hot pan bread to go with it and wash the taste from his mouth; Hans had already prepared the grainy mess and patted it into the smaller of his cook pots.

The food tasted better than it smelled, fortunately. Conrad ate swiftly, then brought out the silver bird and seeds. Jussl and Hans once again went outdoors. Smoke thickened, filled the little cabin, turned the air faintly purple. Dominic sneezed, pinched his nostrils to stifle another, and Conrad held a finger at the base of his nose to stop the tickle.

Gustave was there before the smoke cleared. There was no change in his expression when Conrad told him what had happened, unless the least widening of his eyes indicated alarm. "He is protected again?"

Conrad nodded; uncertain whether Gustave could see him, he spoke. "Yes. The black bag I put in his shirt—he still has that. The one I carried on my belt. But Augustine made it for me, not Dominic."

"That should be all right. Does it smell of marigold, and is it a blue flat bottle inside the bag?" Gustave asked. His voice was faint, flatly expressionless with distance and the oddness of the communication. Dominic inspected it warily and nodded. "Good. It is mostly marjoram oil, and that should seal out magic of any kind. Did it actually bring him back at once?"

"Within moments," Conrad said. He motioned Dominic to keep silent; the Frenchman wore an irritated expression and was trying to insert himself into the conversation.

"So; he is not in present danger. All the same—" Gustave sighed; he let his eyes close. "I feared it would come to this. I will join you, late tonight."

Dom shook his head firmly. "I am fine, you need not."

"That is for me to decide, I think," Gustave snapped. "Where are you? Describe to me, please."

That took time. Conrad finally realized Gustave's wagon must be quite near, along the eastern end of the road they'd travelled all day. Gustave claimed not to know much about his surroundings, or even to have seen them much of the last two days. Finally he seemed to have enough information for Fritz and Augustine. "Before midnight," he said; his voice was fainter, suddenly. "Have Jussl keep the fire burning; sitting in the dark will not hide you from Ilse anyway."

"But—" Conrad let the word hang; Gustave had already vanished. "Damn," he said feelingly.

"I agree," Dominic said. "Why did he need to say that last thing? I will have terrible dreams!"

Conrad put the box and the bird in his pack. "I never thought he would come so far. Not even to get himself in my good graces."

"That is not all his purpose; he hates Ilse also, remember?"

Conrad nodded. He was too tired to speak, all at once: reaction catching up from the afternoon, the long ride, a stew whose meat would never have reached the servants' table under his mother's housekeeping. Bread barely cooked in its center, burned on the bottom, the meal grainy and not completely clean . . .

And then, to have to deal with Gustave yet tonight! Perhaps the old man would be too exhausted to bother him. Augustine was a question mark in Conrad's mind. "Well," he said grudgingly, "perhaps a mediocre sorcerer at our side *is* better than no sorcerer."

Dom cast his eyes at the dark ceiling. "Hah." He thought for a moment, then smiled faintly. "Remember, that cart of his still cannot travel where there is no road. I hope before we lose him again that he creates me a new talisman; you need all the protection you can get." He considered this, closed his eyes briefly, got to his feet. Conrad managed to keep his eyes open long enough to see him out of sight.

He had intended to edge his daggers but fell asleep instead. He woke to the acrid smell of wood smoke and hard dirt under his hip; someone had thrown a blanket over him. He opened one eye as the scent of cut pine and a soft rustling covered other scents and sounds: Hans was bringing in boughs for sleeping. Conrad let the eye close again, considered whether he should bother to wake up. On balance, he wasn't certain it was worth the trouble to move. A sudden, sharp pain against his throat brought him upright, fingers fumbling with the lacings on the leather jerkin, hands pulling the throat wide. Something—the collar of his shirt—

He stared in blank astonishment at Sofia's rose earring. It was uncomfortably warm, almost too hot to touch, and it was a deep, bloody red. His shirt was scorched where the rose had hung.

Dom knelt at his side. "What, are you hurt?" Conrad shook his head; he was momentarily beyond speech. "What's that— did it cut you or something?"

Conrad opened his mouth, tried to speak twice before anything came. It wasn't what either man expected. "Sofia!" he whispered.

Dominic went white to the lips, caught his friend's near shoulder, swung him around by it to grab the other one and shook him wildly. Conrad's head rocked back and forth; his eyes were wide and dazed. "By every saint in my mother's catalog, what are you doing?" the Frenchman shouted. Conrad blinked, shook his head. "Don't do that! Speak to me!"

"Shhh, don't shout, Dom. I'm—I'm all right."

"Prove it to me, my friend," came the grim reply. "Do not sit there looking like a dead man. Do not speak to someone who is not here! Before God, are you trying to make me feel better or to frighten me silly?"

"I'm not—" Conrad began indignantly. He stopped, slowly unfolded his fingers from around the silver rose. Dominic followed his downward gaze.

"Look, there's blood on your palm."

"It burned me. And look, look at my shirt." Jussl shuddered, got back to his feet and went over to the fireplace, where he concentrated on feeding the fire. "It's not my blood." Conrad picked the earring up gingerly by its wire hoop and looked at his hand.

Dominic sat back on his heels; one hand inched across his chest and clamped around on the marjoram talisman through the fabric of his shirt. His grip tightened when Conrad licked his index finger and brought the earring close.

Conrad flinched and jerked his finger back at the last moment, but he licked it once again and this time managed to rub it over the rose. It came away red. "It's not mine," he whispered. "It's hers. Don't look like that, Dom. You wanted to hear; listen to me, then. It went hot without warning, and when it did, I saw her. Not—exactly that. More like—I was part of her. I could see a dark rock chamber, a fire, Ilse standing at a table and staring down into—a scrying bowl, I think. Her hand—*my* hand hurt, like it had just been jabbed with a sharp thing, and there was—cloth all around my hand, and the earring against my hand—"

"Jesu et Marie," Dominic whispered feelingly. "Conrad, take the bag back." But Conrad wrapped his hand around his friend's wrist and shook his head.

"You need it. And—Ilse did not do this. I don't know what it was, but it wasn't her magic."

"You cannot be certain of that."

"I can. Besides, the morning after the ball, when I found it—Gustave told me it could be a link to Sofia. I—I think he was right."

Dominic didn't like it; he very vocally and emphatically did not like it for well over an hour, and he only gave up when Conrad pointed out he had used the same words three times in a row, and had received the same answer each time.

Conrad fumbled with the narrow band of plain collar and rehooked the wire through it, ignoring Dominic's black look, then walked over to pick through the heap of boughs near the door. He piled them into a thick heap, tossed his blankets over the pile and lay back down, resolutely closing his eyes.

Jussl and Hans were watching him; Dominic hadn't taken his eyes off him. If they knew what he had seen beyond what he had told them—Dom *would* think him possessed. He didn't think he had fully convinced Dom that Ilse was not using him somehow.

He wasn't certain what to think. If he believed, then poor lady. Because for one timeless moment, he'd shared more with her than a smarting palm. He had felt the long welts across her shoulders, the dread and fear knotting her stomach. Misery and guilt, determination filled her thoughts. And worry—for herself and for him. How odd. Did he see truly or was it wishful thinking?

He slept again, woke after full dark. The two armsmen were seated near the fire, while Dominic squatted on his heels near the doorless entry, honing one of his daggers. One of the English pistols lay at his feet; the scabbard with his rapiers rested against the wall. He started as Conrad sat up and yawned, then managed a still slightly self-conscious smile. "You startled me; neither of these men has moved or spoken in so long I began to think us all statuary. Jussl suggested we keep a watch tonight."

"Good." Conrad fought another yawn. He drew the silver-and pearl-encased French watch—parting gift from Marguerite—out of his pack and checked it: It was nearly midnight. "No Gustave yet?"

"Not yet. It's quite dark out there tonight, though. I wager they are travelling more slowly than the old sorcerer thought."

"Mmm." Conrad stowed the watch carefully—the mechanism was not so fragile as the older ones, but still could be broken by rough handling. Noise beyond the hut drew his attention, and Dominic set his dagger aside to rise to a half-crouch and peer out. He sat back on his heels and nodded.

"It is a wagon. I can't see people."

Conrad got up and came to join him. "It's Gustave; can't you hear him?" Dominic drew his rapiers and stepped out into the dark. Conrad waited where he was; Dom wouldn't want his company with night pressing him and both blades in his hands.

He was back almost at once, bringing Augustine with him, and Gustave's high, querulous voice rang through the woods. Conrad set his lips in a tight line and squared his jaw.

Augustine looked little the worse for wear; Conrad found himself appalled by the change in the sorcerer. Gustave seemed to have aged twenty years in the past day or so. His skin was a dead white, his lips a trembling, livery slash, his eyes all black under heavy lids. He stuffed a quivering hand into the folds in his gray robes as Augustine came back and wrapped an arm around his shoulder. Gustave shook free of him with an effort that sent him reeling back into the wall.

"Leave be, apprentice!" he snarled. *As ready to win friends as ever,* Conrad thought sourly.

Augustine nodded; his face remained expressionless. "Your leave, Master. I brought—" He held out a small cloth packet and a heavy, footed matte black pottery cup. "Armsman, if there is hot water, I would like to make my master a tizanne." Gustave let his eyelids sag nearly closed, nodded. Augustine drew him across to the fireplace and seated him on Conrad's pile of boughs and his blankets, filled the cup from the kettle Hans offered and dropped the packet in. Conrad sniffed cautiously; it smelled heavily of some tangy herb he didn't know. The apprentice set the cup in Gustave's hands, wrapped the sorcerer's fingers around it and stepped back as Gustave bent forward to inhale the steam.

The results were swift, if not quite miraculous. Color came back to the old man's face; his eyes opened wide and he seemed to take in his surroundings for the first time. He murmured something under his breath, drank off the contents in one long series of uninterrupted swallows and handed the cup back to his apprentice. The face he turned to Conrad still bore traces of fatigue, and nothing could erase the years he had come by honestly, but he no longer looked like death.

"Prince Conrad," he said crisply, inclining his head almost as an afterthought. Conrad looked at him thoughtfully. Gustave spoke as if to an equal in a matter too important for his usual games. Perhaps that was a game itself, but if so Conrad preferred it. "The hour is late, but we need not be underway until mid-morning tomorrow. Have you set watches?" Conrad looked at Dom, who nodded.

"Yes." He could be terse and practical, too.

"Good. Come and tell me precisely what happened this day; de Valois, come here also. If he is guarding now, Fritz will take his place when he finishes with the horses and my bedding. Augustine—drat the man, where is he?" The apprentice had indeed gone out but when he came back he had a suede bag for Gustave. The sorcerer unwound its ties and began setting out bottles and containers before him. "De Valois, give me please a finger's length of your hair and a shred of fabric from an item of your clothing." He held out a hand; Dominic eyed him with evident distrust but finally drew one of his daggers and severed a lock of hair, dragged his shirt hems free and cut a square of fine-woven linen. He squatted on his heels, held out both objects on an open palm. Gustave took them. He opened containers, mumbled to himself.

He turned to Conrad then. "A strand of your own hair. Comprise it of three hairs only, as long as possible—no, cut it by your own hand, with your own blade." Conrad did as he was told. "Tie them about the middle of this bundle," Gustave instructed and held out Dom's hair, wrapped in the bit of shirt. A very unpleasant odor was rising from the shirt fabric, which was now bright blue. "Wrap the hairs completely around once, please," Gustave said. "A double tie—there. Take it by the hair ends—yours, not his!—and put it in your friend's inner pocket."

"Dom, your shirts," Conrad swore. "Which side has the pocket? I cannot *see* it!"

"My left," Dom said, his nostrils twitching. He winced and gasped as the charm came to rest against his chest, with only a single thickness of cloth between it and him. "What is that stuff? It feels like nettles!"

"Never mind what it is," Gustave replied grimly. "It works. It will protect you from any witch, from most sorcerers, and if by chance it fails to protect you, then it will keep you from doing the Prince harm. Hand me the other charm." He held out a hand. Dom's fingers closed around the black bag; he eyed Conrad, Gustave, then hesitated. "At once!" Gustave thundered. "Do you think we have all night?"

"How should I know?" Dominic snapped resentfully. But he handed over the bag and stayed at Conrad's shoulder while the sorcerer opened bag and then bottle, added another ingredient to the thing and mumbled over it for a time. He handed it back, and Dom dropped it back into its bag and into his shirt. His shoulders relaxed and he offered Conrad a weak smile. Conrad gripped his arm in reply, but most of his attention was still on Gustave.

"I will stay as near you as possible tomorrow, Frenchman," Gustave went on. His eyes were on a thin vial he had half-filled with seed of some kind and what looked like sand; he was adding a foul-smelling, thick black liquid to it, watching with satisfaction as it began to steam gently. "If by chance, we cannot remain together, you and I, then Augustine will set himself against your shoulder and remain there. I want your sacred word that you will do that."

"Riddles," Dom snorted. "But if it keeps my friend Conrad safe, then you have that vow, sorcerer."

"That is sufficient. Augustine, you know what to do tomorrow."

Augustine met Dominic's wary look with one of his own. "I know what I must do. Let me tell them, if I may: Men work better together when they understand each other's plans."

Gustave sighed. "My own words coming back to haunt me. Ah, well. Go on, then." He put a thumb over the bottle of roiled black liquid and inverted it, cautiously.

"You and we know from her own lips that Ilse means to end this matter tomorrow," Augustine said. "And from de la Mare's horoscopes, we have the hour—three past midday. But steel may not serve to kill her. And you must reach her with a clear mind, in order to try your steel against her. I can break possession such as she used today, if we are somehow separated from Master Gustave—if our road falls along a path he cannot travel." He hesitated. "That is all, I think."

Conrad considered this in silence for a while. It was not all, quite obviously, but it was all they would learn at present. "I will be glad of your company, after today." He held out a hand; Augustine took it.

Gustave sighed, this time tiredly. "Let us finish. I am badly in need of sleep." He demanded things, one after the other: a bit of leather from Conrad's jerkin, a piece of collar lace. Conrad unwound the collar gingerly; he was afraid Gustave would sense

the change in the rose and demand the story, but he scarcely
gave it a glance, if indeed he noticed it at all. He wanted one
of Dom's rapiers, the hard leather bottle holding powder for his
English pistols. Augustine picked up a bottle of some liquid and
held it near his ear, shook it experimentally. He got up and
walked over to the doorway, where Fritz now sat conversing with
Jussl and Hans. The latter two men looked up, sniffed cautiously
at the bottle. Augustine talked rapidly; Jussl nodded finally, let
the apprentice dip his finger in the liquid, draw a cross on his
brow and smear a little onto the backs of both hands. Hans
shook his head firmly. The pungent odor of marigold filled the
room. *Proof against witches,* Conrad remembered; it was one
of the few herb-uses he knew.

Augustine returned the bottle to its niche and sank down next
to Gustave; he took the sorcerer's cup and poured more hot water
over the herb bag, set it near the old man's knee. Gustave leaned
low to inhale the fragrant steam. "Two last things, both important. Pay attention!" Dominic smothered a full-blown yawn and
tried to look attentive; he was too far from Gustave's cup to have
any benefit from its steam, and unlike Conrad, he had not slept
the evening. The charm in his pocket had stopped itching; it
now spread a soothing warmth over his chest. It was putting him
to sleep where he sat. "I will give you two more things, young
de Valois. The first is a charm I should have carried a night not
long since. It will let you tell real from false."

"But—" Dominic began.

"Let me finish and argue all at once, please," the sorcerer
snapped.

Dominic flushed. "But—"

"Silence, I say!" Gustave shouted. Dominic closed his mouth,
thinned his lips furiously and sat back to listen. Gustave waited
to make certain he intended to stay silent, then handed him a
tiny bottle carved from a beryl. Some liquid sloshed inside; it
was not capped. "Put the cord about your neck; do not touch
or put iron near it, and do *not*, I beg of you, let the liquid pour
from the bottle, or the entire thing is useless! Get your pistols,
please." He brought out a square box, almost as large as his
hand, and broke the wax seal, scattering little chips of silvery
stuff all over his knees. Those that hit the fire sizzled. Inside,
there was a powder that might have been deep gray, littered with
ash. "One at a time—Keep them away from the bottle!" Dominic mumbled something under his breath, held one of the pistols

out with exaggerated care, and let Gustave break a pinch of the ashy stuff over the flint and the powder pan. The gesture was repeated over the other pistol. "The pistols will have to be enough. I leave the musket to your own skills."

Dominic set the second pistol carefully beside the first. "What was that?"

For a moment, Gustave looked as though he would not answer. "Sharpshooter's potion—" Dominic's laugh silenced him.

"What, verbena and rue? That's a liquid; witches use it in France on arrows. It's not much good."

"When I make it," Gustave replied flatly, "it is a powder and it works. Your shot will strike the thing you aim for. Make certain you truly wish to shoot what you aim for."

"I will." Dominic abruptly stopped laughing.

Gustave turned his head and fixed Conrad with a look from which all trace of expression had been removed. "And for you, my Prince—Prince Conrad," he amended crisply. "I have provided you with every protection I know to make. You have the advice of your astrologer, your determination, your own strengths." He tilted his head a little to one side and waited.

"I'm listening," Conrad said.

"Good. Continue to listen. You have also the earring; the girl has its mate. Has it made any sign yet?" Conrad shook his head. He half expected the old man to call him liar, but Gustave merely nodded and went on. "Keep it close—but I see you are doing that—and touch it frequently. If it does somehow come alive for you, but you sense anyone except Sofia von Mencken, then get rid of it at once. Give it to me or to Augustine, or if we are not near, take the little green bottle from your friend's neck and drop the rose in that."

Conrad wet dry lips with his tongue. "What will that do to her, if the earring goes into that bottle?"

"Why do you care what it does to her?"

"Oh." He nodded. "I do not, of course. But how can I know for certain it is Sofia? Ilse could put on her guise, pretend to be her—" He stopped; Gustave was shaking his head.

"No. No wielder of magic—any magic!—can duplicate another's thought. No more than thoughts can lie. Now." Gustave picked up his cup and drained it in one long gulp. "I am done here. Augustine—"

"No." The apprentice leaned forward and held out a hand. "Prince Conrad, your dagger."

"My dagger? Which one?"

"Whichever one you prefer to use. Give it to me, please."

Conrad loosened the strap that snugged the plain hide sheath to the outside of his right knee and held out a long-bladed knife with a very plain, black-enameled hilt. He reversed it, gripped the very point and balanced it thoughtfully, then handed it over. "It's Spanish, Toledo steel and true for throwing."

"If it pleases you, nothing else matters." Augustine gripped the hilt, spat on the point, turned it over in his hands and drew it across the palm of his left hand. Dominic cried out in surprise; Conrad drew his breath in a startled hiss. The apprentice turned his hand palm down, let three drops of blood fall on the blade near the guard, touched the point to the edges of skin. The blood coagulated. Augustine handed the dagger back to Conrad. Gustave, his face dark with displeasure, took Augustine's hand and rubbed sharp-scented oil over his palm.

"What kind of magic was that?" Conrad whispered. The incident had shaken him more than he wanted to admit.

"Green Witches use blood," Gustave spat. But Augustine shook his head.

"You know it is not that, Master. It is not true magic of any kind, and I follow the Gold Way. But I was born in Florence. And we Italians have a saying: Blood calls to blood." He stood and drew Gustave up and out the door with him.

"Knowledge of the herbs and their uses is foremost to the
Green Way, though not all who know the uses are witches."

Green & Gold Magyk

20.

Sofia woke in the gray hour before dawn. She lay still, eyes
closed. Everything ached—hips, legs and feet; her back was still
a raw misery, and she was exhausted from the combination of
drug and unpleasant dreams. The cave felt chill, empty, and she
was certain Ilse was gone. It scarcely seemed worth the effort
to open her eyes and look, and she fell asleep again without
having done so.

She wakened to warm feet: There was early sun coming
through the trees to fall upon them. She eased herself down into
the pool of warmth, lay there until it moved on, then stretched
cautiously and stood.

Ilse was nowhere in sight. Setting about mischief of her own,
no doubt, Sofia thought unhappily. Traps and pitfalls. It chewed
at her to be so helpless; even the certainty that none of these
traps and pitfalls were likely to be fatal ones did not help her.
"If I could do something!"

There was water in the bucket beneath Ilse's table, and buried
under bits of paper, boxes and empty bottles, broken and fragmented herbs was the rest of a loaf—hard, near black bread.
Sofia pulled her shawl close, built a fire. Once that was done
and a pot of water steaming, she could face the bread. It was
nearly too hard to break, and Ilse had taken the knife, but it
finally tore into two pieces. She took the smaller, threw the
moldy corner into the fire and softened the rest in hot water. It

eased her hunger, but did not fully satisfy it; she drank the water, mindful of the crumbs that had fallen into it. There was little to do then but wait.

And think, of course. That had so far done no good, but there was still time. She *could* not give up.

She got to her feet and walked to the entrance; just short of it she was stopped by Ilse's barrier. It felt like a wall, though she could see nothing. It went fully side to side, as high as she could reach, all across the bottom. No escape there. The privy—she could examine it more closely with Ilse away—still showed no hidden way out, there was nothing save the vent, high up in a domed roof, unreachable even by one twice her height.

She hurried back into the main chamber, wary that Ilse might return unseen. Ilse must continue to think her beaten; it was her only weapon. There was no sign of the woman, yet. She rummaged through the piled herbs on the table, found rosemary and settled back down near the tiny fire. Another cup of hot water, this time with a thick pinch of herb in it.

She pulled her tangled hair over one shoulder and did her best to remove snarls and bits of leaf and branch with her fingers; she rebraided it and cast about for a bit of string or cloth to tie it with. There had been a bit of leather tie in her pocket, once . . .

The rose. The silver earring fell into her hand as she felt in her pocket. It was warm against her palm, reassuring. Ilse did not control everything: She knew nothing of this.

The sun was warming the cave entrance when Ilse returned. Sofia sat in light and watched as the black horse came down to earth and unmade under Ilse's legs, lowering her slowly to the ground. The witch gathered up her bundle of twigs and hay, slung a pack over her arm, strode across the shale-littered rock. The barrier didn't even slow her; she dropped a cloth-wrapped packet into Sofia's lap. The fragrance of roasted pork and bread rose from it.

"Eat," Ilse said. She set her horse-bundles beneath the table and squatted down to stir the fire back to life. "There is much of this day left, and though the Prince is not an hour from this place, he has a long day and a long ride before him." She stood, gazed across the firepit; flame underlit her face, heavy lines stood out sharply, her eyes were sunken, her teeth gleamed as she tore bread from the loaf with them and chewed. "And I have yet much to do." She turned away and sighed. "It is so stupid I must do this all myself!"

Sofia's blood thudded in her ears; Ilse was still grumbling about frightened Scarp peasantry, Hel's stubborn temperament, Hel's worthless and terrified apprentices. Something stirred just under Sofia's ribs, and she spoke before she could let herself think. "You need not do it alone. Let me aid you."

Ilse stopped mumbling and stood as if she'd become stone; she turned slowly, crouched down to stare across her knees. Sofia managed somehow not to shrink from that black-eyed, expressionless gaze, but she could not meet the witch's eyes for long. "What did you say to me?" Ilse whispered finally.

Sofia swallowed, managed to speak past a dry throat. "Let me aid you." She glanced up quickly, as quickly away again, fastened her gaze on the bread and meat in her hands and kept it there. "You need—you need an assistant, an apprentice? I—" She swallowed again. "I could do it."

"Why?" Ilse's voice was as low as her own. "Why should you? Why should I let you? Or trust you?"

"Because I—I don't want to die." She choked the words out, drew a deep breath and tried again. "I do not want to die. I will, unless I can be useful to you."

"I could use you and still kill you."

"I know. It is a chance against no chance." She looked up, touched glances with the witch and looked quickly away. Meet those eyes, and Ilse might divine more than she wanted known; she might begin shivering in truth. *A witch cannot read thoughts,* she reminded herself. "You need not trust me. No master trusts any apprentice to work without supervision. I could do nothing to harm you."

"I know that," Ilse broke in impatiently.

"You need me," Sofia whispered. Ilse's head came up sharply. "Not need, then. You could use me. My aid. And I have no life without your protection, not in Saxe-Baden." Silence. "What will you do when Prince Conrad is dead?"

Ilse shrugged. "It does not matter what I do then. Why?"

It was coming together as she spoke; she fought to keep the rising excitement out of her voice. "You cannot simply intend to die; what good is there in that? But you cannot remain in these woods, with every noble in the land hunting you, living among ignorant and superstitious peasantry who do not understand you." The witch was listening. Sofia hurried on. "I know what it is to live where one is not wanted. Why remain here when you have done? If I—if you are kind enough to let me live, or grateful enough for my aid, where in Saxe-Baden am I safe? With the Prince dead, will not every man's hand be against me also?'' She glanced up; Ilse watched her through narrowed, thoughtful eyes. ''There are other lands; Saxe-Baden is not all the world.''

''Other lands?''

''I speak French and Spanish, a little Italian. I learned many things at Court in my two years, simply sitting at the Queen's side and listening. Magic is not so maligned in Milan and in Venice. Or there is the New World, if nothing this side of the ocean will serve. Boats go forth from Italian ports for the Americas.'' Silence. ''Vengeance is a sweet dish, but it tastes better cold.''

''Riddles!'' Ilse snapped impatiently.

Sofia shook her head. ''It is better to live and look back on your revenge.'' She drew a deep breath and brought up the last of her courage with it. She could not tell by the witch's face how well she did; she may as well finish as she had begun. ''You chose me for the ball because you knew I would accept what you offered; not many young women would trade favors with a witch and go cold-bloodedly after Prince Conrad as I did. You know I am sensible. My mother was Spanish; they say witch blood runs through her line.''

''Perhaps,'' Ilse said.

''But the coins stack most heavily on your side of the table. I bear the Prince no love. Wealth and title cannot compensate for a life of slow boredom at Court, for a husband who gets heirs on his wife and takes pleasure with her ladies, or drinks too much and spends all his free time at the hunt. I am neither blind nor blinded by romances: Noble husbands are seldom faithful or caring, and the Prince would have no reason to care for a woman chosen as he was to choose.''

Silence. Then: ''Go on,'' Ilse said.

''My father was a fool. My stepmother wed me to the kitchen floor and the ashes of the great fireplace. My stepsisters wore clothing bought for them with *my* money. They made my life a purgatory, and you killed them for me. I owe no one anything—save you. And you hold the one thing I prize above all: my life.''

''Well spoken,'' Ilse said mockingly, and applauded silently.

''You gave me time to think, Ilse. I used it. To have danced with the Prince—all that was a sweet, pretty dream. Every girl should have such a thing to look back on. Perhaps he might have come to care for me, and I him, but that is gone. This is what is, this is what matters.'' Silence again. ''Let me aid you.''

Ilse sank back on her heels, rocked slowly forward and stayed there a very long, still time. Her eyes were hooded; one hand stroked her chin, then tugged at loose hairs in front of her ear. Sofia became aware she was holding her breath, let it out and tried to remember how to breathe. Ilse leaped to her feet, walked over to the fire. She stood there another long while, staring down at the smoking embers. Finally she spoke over her shoulder. ''Come here.''

Sofia had to try twice to stand; she had gone weak and nearly faint when she'd finally finished speaking, and one leg had gone to sleep under her. Ilse's face gave no sign of her intention. ''Sort out the herbs on the table, each into its own pile. Tell me what each is, and its uses if you know.'' She watched, arms folded across her chest, listened in silence. Turned away to pace across the back of the cave. Sofia stared down at the heaps of rosemary, sweet woodruff, rue and anise root. She had cast all her coins into the water. Ilse finally stopped, so suddenly that pebbles scraped and rattled under her shoes. ''Your words are only that—words. And I doubt you have told me your whole purpose.'' She shoved things aside and cleared a space of table, brought her scrying bowl into place before her. ''You are not the first to offer everything in exchange for life; you will not be the last. So I promise nothing. But if you serve me well—'' She broke off, pressed the bowl aside and stared out toward the trees. ''They say Italy is warm, that oranges grow wild and the winters are pleasant.'' She shook herself. ''Break two stems of the hemlock into bits the size of a thumbnail, and put them in the clay bowl.''

Relief weakened her knees; without the support of the table, she might have fallen. She dared not, dared show no weakness, no fear—nothing but chill purpose, cool cooperation. *Prince Conrad—ah, God, he will never forgive this, whatever else he might have forgiven. If I save his life and mine, I will not let myself care.* She focused her attention on the hemlock then, and let everything else go.

"Spells and charms created by a skilled sorcerer are proof against any witchery; but even the best-made talisman can be worn down by constant assault."

Green & Gold Magyk

21.

Conrad slept poorly; he ached everywhere and even the cushion of pine boughs was not a complete comfort. When he did sleep, it was only a light doze, disturbed by unpleasant dreams: He relived the duel with Dominic. Once he thought he stood in a dark place, only the faint glow of a gutted fire to guide him. Sofia lay close to it, ragged skirts tucked around her feet, a thick shawl over her shoulders.

He woke uneasily, often. He did not want Gustave with them, and it galled him that he had called upon Gustave himself, and so made it possible for the sorcerer to join them. *But then, Gustave clearly intended to come with me all along, else why travel the north road to be nearby? Why was I fool enough not to realize?* Conrad wondered.

He stared out the darkened doorway during his share of the watch, listening to a distant cry of wolves and a nearby owl. How did a man ever know what to believe—magic and power everywhere, so many unscrupulous folk using both.

He finally slept just before sunrise. Hans's porridge was still warm but almost too thick to swallow, the bread too tough to chew even when soaked in tea unless it was left there to become a soggy and shapeless mess that must be eaten with a spoon. Conrad managed to get most of his share down before they broke camp.

Gustave's wagon was already out on the main road, pointing

back east. *He might have asked,* Conrad thought sourly and rather resentfully—perhaps unfairly, since he and his companions had been riding that direction for all of the previous day.

He was beginning to have brief, flickering flashes of bearing—almost as soon as they set out. He glanced at his companions: Even Augustine, riding just ahead and to his right, did not seem aware of them. *Is he a weaker apprentice than I thought, or is it that only I can sense her?*

Dominic was loaded to his ears with witch-proofings but would not come near his friend. Just now he was riding back by Gustave's wagon, talking to Fritz. Gustave was inside; Conrad had not seen him at all since the night before.

They covered a surprising distance, considering the condition of the road which slowed the cart to a walk most of the time, lest it break a wheel. All the same, Conrad was grateful for the stop just after midday. He dismounted, led Parsifal over to a small patch of grass and wildflower and left him there while he walked up and down.

The road had climbed above forest in a series of sharp switchbacks, finally began dropping down again; forest lay just below them, one turn of road away, and there was forest as far as Conrad could see, from mountainside to the edge of this backside of the Scarp. He looked forward to woods: The day was growing unpleasantly, humidly warm.

There was fresh water: a trickle coming down the rock face to form a small pool on the ledge before vanishing in the tall grass and moss at the rock's edge. Hans filled bottles, let the horses drink a little, handed around jerky and plums. Conrad scowled at the stuff behind the pikeman's back but dutifully ate it.

Several paces away, Dominic sat with his back against a tree, listening as Augustine talked. He looked up, met Conrad's eyes and smiled briefly, but that was all. Conrad sighed. He had not realized how much Dominic had done to keep his spirits up until the Frenchman wasn't there to do it.

The earring was a sudden urgent presence against his throat. "Augustine?" He spoke softly, but Augustine heard and came up to him. "This way—where we're going, down there? It's—it isn't the right way. There's another road, I think. Somewhere close by that goes—" He pivoted a little to his right on one heel, pointed off across the rocks. "—It goes that way."

Augustine turned and sighted along his arm. "How certain are you? Remember what de la Mare told you."

"The clear way? I do remember. This is—it is not that. In fact—" He hesitated; Augustine merely waited. "If I tell you this, must you report it to Gustave?" Augustine gazed at him sidelong for some moments, then shrugged.

"That depends upon the thing you tell me. I know you and he do not get on. If it is a personal thing, no. But if it is part of Ilse's magic—"

"No—I don't think it is," Conrad amended honestly. He slid the earring from inside his collar and held it out. "He knows about this; he said it might help me find her. I think it *is* helping; I think I can feel where she is. At—somehow, at the same time, I begin to feel a pull along the east road, the way we presently go. And *that* I think is the clear way Nicholas warned of." He touched the rose lightly. "This—there is no such pull attached to what I feel when I touch it, or it touches me. Sofia is *that* way, the clear way is along the road."

Augustine cupped his chin in one hand, elbow in his other hand. Conrad hesitated, then told him the rest—the sudden heat, the blood, the dreams since. Augustine was frowning now, his eyes unfocused. Finally he reached out a long, square-ended finger and touched it himself.

"This has somehow attuned itself to her. If she holds the mate and has spilled her own blood on it, that may answer all. Keep it near."

"I intend to."

"Do not let anything iron or magic touch it; that could break the join. Or it might alert Ilse to the bond between you—between Sofia's rose and this one." Augustine touched Conrad's shoulder. "I understand why you did not want to speak of this. But I need only tell Master Gustave of our change in direction."

"Why?"

Augustine hesitated. "You will see, if it comes to that." He looked at his fingertip and grimaced. "I should *not* have touched that bauble."

Conrad watched the apprentice enter Gustave's wagon, but he was out and remounted moments later. Conrad remounted, drew Parsifal back as Fritz let off the wagon brake and raised a hellish shriek of metal against metal.

The branch road climbed steeply, straight up a short rise, dipped down and vanished into thick forest and inky shadow.

Jussl drew up next to the wagon; he and Fritz gazed up the slope rather worriedly. Dom rode up to the crest, looked out south, back across the road, then turned and rode back down. He stopped near Conrad.

"It narrows to a mere track just over that hump. We are about to lose our sorcerer."

"How clear is it?" Conrad asked. He wasn't really interested in the answer, just that Dom was talking to him normally again.

He needed to talk, suddenly; he was edgy, like a man waiting for the headsman's axe. Time was running low, days down to hours now; something must happen *soon*.

Something did. Dominic shouted a wordless warning and drew one of his pistols; Conrad threw an arm across his face for protection as the sky directly above them went black. Augustine cried out something—spell or warning, it was lost in a hellish whir of monstrous wings. The sweetish stench of something long dead dropped on them like a flood and left Conrad retching. He could see nothing save blackness at first: That slowly solidified and compacted, taking the shape of an enormous sooty bird with eyes like red witch fires. Parsifal screamed; holding him in check took all Conrad's strength and attention.

Dominic's pistol slapped painfully against his leg. "It wants *you*! Get out of here!" And almost in his other ear, Augustine: "Go! We'll hold your back, go—before God, not that way!" Parsifal tried to bolt down the main road; Conrad dragged him around with an iron hand, spurred him up the narrowing trail. Five shaky breaths up the slope, the darkness and stench were behind them, but terror had gotten under his skin and Parsifal had the bit in his teeth. Conrad crouched low in the saddle and let him run.

The bird-demon was gone. One of Dominic's pistols lay in the dirt at Gabriel's feet; he himself was panting heavily and his face was bloodless. Jussl had been sick at the edge of the road; what was left of Hans was covered by his cloak. Gustave stood on the rear step of his wagon. "Go, the three of you. Fritz will guard me, if that is needed. It will not be; Conrad is gone and the danger follows him. Augustine—you know what you must do?"

"I know."

"Go, then. He gains on you by the moment." Augustine turned away without further word and motioned Jussl to follow.

Dominic leaned low off his horse's neck, scooped up his pistol and shoved it into its case. "You've only one protected shot left; use it with caution," Gustave said.

Dominic looked at him resentfully. "I shot, that horror vanished. If that was not a proper use of a charmed shot, what is? Shall I save them until I am dead?" Before Gustave could reply, he turned Gabriel and urged him up the trail.

Conrad brought Parsifal down to a walk and looked around nervously. The hour was not much after midday, yet the sky was growing dark. He wrapped the reins around his left hand and made a swift search of his person with the right—all charms in place, both rapiers, his daggers.

The sky drew his attention once more. It looked as though someone had spilled ink over writing paper; deep blue sky swirled with a deeper purple. It made him queasy and he looked away. *Magic.* Go, before it began to press down upon him. Parsifal gathered speed until he was running down the narrow trail.

The black things were there before he realized, before he could slow the horse or find anywhere in the thick brush to turn aside. It was like a swarm of mosquitoes, only larger: nasty little black things, shaped like bits of scorched and torn armor metal, ends twisted and warped into points. They moved, not quite flying, floating or fluttering around him—they were all over him, suddenly, whispering, moaning, slithering lightly over bare skin. He flailed at them wildly, brushing them from his thigh, flapping a hand before his face when something touched his cheek . . . he kicked Parsifal, harder than he ever had before; the horse whinnied shrilly but leaped forward, snapping Conrad's head back.

The black things were left behind; he dragged the horse to a trot, glanced over his shoulder. Now that they no longer plagued him, he felt a little shamed by his reaction. They had not even bitten or cut him. Dominic suddenly appeared, emerging from shadow where none should be. He was guiding Gabriel with his knees, waving both arms wildly and Conrad thought he heard a shout to wait. He turned back to face the trail and kept going. Dom could catch him up, and he dared not stop now, lest fear freeze him in place.

He started violently and slewed halfway around in the saddle—someone or something just behind him was laughing wildly. Parsifal leaped high over a fallen tree, nearly unseating him. The trail widened and came out from under the trees; Dominic came up beside him. "*Dieu,* what were those things?"

"Witchery—isn't that enough for you?"

"More than enough," Dominic replied cheerfully. At least for the moment, he seemed to have forgotten his fears of being near his friend, and he let Gabriel pace Parsifal.

"Good. I—what is *that*?" He dragged back on the reins but Parsifal had already slowed nervously. *That* blocked the narrow trail ahead of them. "It can't be bones—can it?" Conrad whispered.

Dominic snorted. "Have you dragons in these mountains? This thing is twenty times the size of a deer—ah, what a stench! The horses will not pass that!"

"They will have to," Conrad replied grimly. There wasn't a choice; the ground dropped away at almost cliff steepness to their right; on the left, rock and tree just behind a berry thicket made a completely impassable mess. "Unless we have come the wrong way." His face bleached. "Oh, God, Dom! If I chose wrong—!"

"What, black nasty things on all possible roads, including the wrong ones?" the Frenchman demanded rudely. "The woman is not God; do not be silly."

Conrad nodded and leaned forward to speak in Parsifal's ear. Dom was right; he would go mad trying to second-guess Ilse.

Parsifal did not want to pass the bones, but he was normally a placid beast and he was finally persuaded. Dom had to dismount and lead Gabriel, and even then had trouble. Conrad turned back once he'd gotten clear; Gabriel had stopped, forefeet dug in, head low. Conrad freed his foot from the stirrup, changed his mind and stayed where he was. Parsifal had no protection without his rider; the rider in question would be lost if Parsifal bolted.

Dominic turned to lead his nervous horse on; a long, bleached armbone quivered, rose from the ground. The claw flexed once, then fell on the Frenchman's unprotected neck.

Dominic shouted in pain and surprise and dropped the reins. Gabriel, freed, tore at the air with his front hooves. He would have turned and fled, but the bony tail had come around to block him, and Dominic's voice rose commandingly: "Gabriel, high! *High!*" Training told: The horse pivoted, reared and brought his hooves down on the thing before him. Sharp-edged shoes cracked across bone. The arm swayed, the claw tightened down, Dominic screamed. A stream of blood ran down his neck. He twisted, caught at it with one hand, fumbled with the other for his blades. Gabriel came down across the bone at the joint, severing the armbone from the rest of the bones; it still held onto Dominic's neck.

Conrad slid from the saddle then, sword drawn, and ran back down the trail. Dom was on one knee, fingers caught between shoulder and claw, teeth clenched hard together; he shook his head when Conrad tried to use his blade as a pry. "Don't— there isn't room," he managed. "Get back—there is another claw—"

"Not without you! Where's the talisman I gave you? Shirt?" Dom nodded faintly, but before Conrad could reach it, something bright and silvery fell to the ground between them. Smoke and sparks blinded them; the bony claw let go and Dominic fell over. When he shoved Conrad aside and forced himself up, there was no claw, no bones of any kind—no evil odor. No blood, only the memory of excruciating pain—which, Dominic thought bleakly, was certainly enough. Gabriel stood beside him anxiously nosing his hat. He stood, pulled himself back astride, and only then noticed that Augustine and Jussl had finally caught up with them. Augustine shoved a short silver rod up his sleeve and dismounted to pick up something near his horse's front feet. He held it up; Dominic shuddered. Mouse bones. Augustine closed his hands over the pitiful little skeleton, whispered something and blew on his fingers. Gray powder fell to the trail.

The trail opened out for some distance, enough to allow them to ride two abreast and at a decent gallop. The wind came so gradually, Conrad barely noticed it. It blew into his face, tearing his hat from his head, suddenly, and only a swift snatch saved it. He dragged down the ties and snugged them under his chin; the wind took it again, half strangling him. He crammed it on, ducked his chin down; this time the wind took it away. *One gone.* The words echoed between his ears as the wind died. The talisman tied to his hat and the hat itself were probably halfway to the Rhine. He set his jaw, gave Parsifal a nudge and rode on.

Dragons, and black night, nasty fluttery black things that now bite—how long had they been riding? The sky was no guide: It had been everything from red to black to purple; lightning had threatened them and brought down a tree almost on their heads just now—real lightning, real tree, it had shaken the ground, shaken Conrad to his very core and terrified the horses. It took time to get them calmed enough to ride on, to find the detour through brush and thick trees.

Conrad brought out his watch, but it was no use. It had stopped at three o'clock, and when he stared at it the hands writhed and reached for him. He shut the case hastily and shoved the watch back in his pocket. There was nothing else in or on that pocket. Somehow, in the last eternity, he'd lost another of Gustave's charms.

His fingertips bled—that had been the black things. God knew what their bite might do to him; his fingers burned and itched as though he'd plunged them into nettles, and the bleeding would not stop.

He kept moving, somehow. And Parsifal at least remained under control. Jussl swore almost constantly at his poor terrified horse until Augustine called a halt and ran his hands over the trembling legs and heaving sides. Gabriel danced at noises and shied at shadows but his training told, and Augustine's mount stayed the course so long as it could follow the other three.

There had been things clearly only illusion: the wall of water sweeping down across the ledge where they rode; the army of Turks on fire-breathing horses riding out of the sky straight for them; the dragon crouched on the road, snorting flaming blood. Those vanished when the four men came near. Conrad was not as certain about the kobold that had run along the road at his right, keeping pace with Parsifal during the rainstorm, muttering and giggling at him. When the tree came down, the shambling, horrid creature had vanished into the woods.

When they finally came to the bridge, Conrad was no longer certain if what he saw was real. It *seemed* to be a flat ledge of silvery-gray rock, a few tufts of grass growing in cracks, from one such enormous crack issued a thundering, booming constant noise. There, if eyes didn't lie, was a wooden bridge, an arched span that a man could cross in ten paces. Beyond it, more rock, but it began to slope down almost at once, and further view was cut off by tall, thick forest.

It felt real. Conrad gripped the near post, looked down and wished he had not. It crossed a cleft nearly as deep as the Scarp itself, a narrow defile cut from rock by the churning white river far below. Spray touched his face.

Jussl peered down and shook his head unhappily. "The horses will not like this at all. Particularly my poor beast."

"Parsifal doesn't mind bridges—normally," Conrad added doubtfully. "But we have to cross—I do, anyway."

"Then we do," Dom growled. "Convince Parsifal, perhaps Gabriel will follow him; he usually does. The rest might come after." Conrad nodded. "And *hurry*," Dominic added. "I feel in my bones this is no place to wait."

"You know you can't rush these things," Conrad replied stiffly. "Think how my bones feel, and be still." He rubbed Parsifal's jaw, talked to him reassuringly, made himself relax—the horse would feel his tension and soft talk would mean nothing. When he thought the horse was ready, he tugged on the reins and stepped onto the bridge.

It clattered underfoot, but Parsifal followed where led. He stopped once, mid-bridge, whickered nervously, moved when Conrad slid his fingers under the strap on his lower jaw and pulled gently. Gabriel shied at the bridge, shied at the noise underfoot and shied again when he reached the far side and a grasshopper bounded away just under his hooves. Dominic had his hands full, and Augustine halted at the far side of the bridge, Jussl behind him.

The Thing caught them by surprise: A brown, hairy creature four times the size of a horse, many-legged and clawed, crawled howling and slavering from the river. Parsifal danced away, halted only briefly as Conrad wrapped both hands in his mane and vaulted into the saddle. The Thing leaped onto level ground with an earth-shaking bound and screamed. Conrad saw a red, malevolent eye and two rows of sharp teeth before he pulled Parsifal around and gave him his head. The horse needed no second urging.

He thought he heard Dominic bellowing furiously and then the loud report of a pistol. But then he was down the slope and into the trees. He reined in as soon as he could. "That horror deliberately separated me from the others!" he whispered. It took an effort and more courage than he thought he possessed to go on.

There was light ahead, a clearing beyond the total shade of

the woods. He knew suddenly what would be there: ledges and caves, a grassy sward of meadow between that and forest. *She is there*. He knew that, too. *And Ilse is*. On an impulse, he freed the silver rose earring from his sadly tattered collar lace and slid it into his left glove. "For safety." It warmed his palm. A moment later he rode into the open.

"When the ancient Greeks fought, they made a fire that burned most marvelously. This was surely a witch's spell, for no man has created Greek fire by ordinary means, or by sorcery. But a witch of means, skill and need may make it in this manner . . ."

An Oral Grammarie

22.

Ilse's face was pale and her mouth set; deep lines crossed her brow. Sofia saw no other sign that the witch's "circles within circles" had cost her anything. She herself felt oddly light-headed, as though she'd been bled; her body vibrated like a lute string. She jumped when the witch turned on her suddenly; Ilse had not spoken to her in so long, it startled her to hear the woman's voice.

"Come, we are finished here." She turned without waiting for an answer and walked out into the afternoon air. Sofia followed. The barrier was either gone, or no longer worked against her. Ilse had given her no praise but she had spoken as though to an equal, or a comrade, just now. As she came into the open, Sofia found herself whispering: *Please let her continue to trust me; please let me learn one thing, however small—please do not let what I did this afternoon count for nothing!*

She followed the witch on down the ledge and into sun. Ilse walked back and forth, muttering to herself, and when she saw her companion, motioned her back. Sofia stopped, gathered her ragged skirt close and sat in a thick patch of warm, dry grass and made herself small, as she so often had at home, the better to escape Beatrix's eye.

Ilse walked up a slight rise, clambered onto a pile of shattered rock and flat stone. She stood there a while, nodded and stepped back, counting her paces on her fingers. At the fifth, she stopped, looked at the pile, nodded again. She turned slowly on one heel, giving the caves, the woods, the meadow, Sofia all the same careful scrutiny. "Remain just where you are, whatever chances. Do you understand me? This is for your protection and mine. Prince Conrad is near." Her eyes narrowed appraisingly, but Sofia merely nodded and kept her thought and her eyes blank. "I am about to build a fire, there." She pointed to the low mound. "It does not burn like ordinary fire; it acts like a lodestone to draw the unwary or the unprotected into its heart. Remain there and you are safe." She fumbled in her skirts and drew forth a slender branch of hawthorne, touched one of the long spines to her tongue, spat in her hand and touched the tip there, then ran it over the ground, all around her.

Sofia turned aside to shield a dry little cough and to conceal her face: The blood pounded through her cheekbones; she could barely see for elation. *She's encircled herself. A circle protects, but it can also be broken.*

When she turned back, Ilse was setting the hawthorne wand upright in the grass behind her. Sofia tried to remember all she knew about encircling. One to protect, a second to imprison—sorcerers calling up demons used two. Ilse had drawn only one.

Ilse brought forth another branch—this one still leafy; small red berries clung to it. Yew, Sofia realized with a pang. They had hung it on all the doors when her mother died. The witch thrust the branch high over her head, took it in both hands and brought it down in a slashing gesture as she cried out. She wavered and sagged briefly at the knees, but upon the bare rock she had chosen, a curl of greenish smoke rose. Ilse laughed, one high, screeching, triumphant outcry, straightened her body and repeated the spell words.

Green smoke exploded toward the sky; Sofia screamed and threw herself sideways on the grass, sheltering her face with her arms. But the smoke was contained on the top of the small rise; it halved, halved again. Hot, bright green flame burned just above the rock; heat and a hellish stench washed over them, and then that too was gone. Sofia staggered to her feet as Ilse bent down to fix the yew branch in the ground before her. The witch came suddenly alert, and Sofia turned to look.

Her heart leaped. The fire was burning so hot the trees beyond it seemed to sway and bend but she could see the man riding toward them, for all the distortion. Prince Conrad, alone, was riding straight into Ilse's trap.

Greek fire. She remembered now, an uncle's tale long years before—fire that the Greeks threw at their enemies. Ships were enveloped in flame that could not be quenched by any means; she had been sent from the room when the uncle began to speak of men shrieking in agony, pleading for escape from fire that burned flesh and bone but did not kill. Her knees gave and she sank to the ground, stuffed knuckles in her mouth to keep from outcry. Warn him now and Ilse would only kill her and then him—there must be another way!

Conrad brought his horse to a sudden halt, slid to the ground and came on. He drew his sword; in his left hand he already held a dagger. By chance or intent, he had brought himself to a point away from the mound. He could have touched Sofia with the tip of his rapier; he could look at Ilse without fire between them.

Ilse made him a deep curtsey. "Your Highness," she murmured.

Conrad waved his dagger hand impatiently. "Enough. I am here, through each barrier you sought to place between me and this place. Give over, and no harm shall come to you by my hands." He tried to say more, but his words were buried under the witch's high-pitched laughter.

"Not by *your* hands, certainly not! Even your father did not dirty himself by setting torch to the faggots under my mother's feet! Do you offer me a better fate? Permit my neck to be wrung before my body is burned? No! I say I shall go free of these mountains and this land entirely! And I shall take with me my new 'prentice. You shall burn, here, in my stead." She gestured; Conrad let his eyes move across the flaming mound.

"Say as you please," he replied steadily. "My safeguards brought me so far and they will hold; my companions are not far behind."

"Your companions are scattered or dead, and the river-monster you fled took the last virtue from the protections you bear. Why do you think I put you to such a maze?"

"No."

"Three amulets gone entirely." Ilse smiled unpleasantly. "And of the rest—there is not enough magic, pooled, to protect a hen from a hawk, young Prince. It was foolish of you to come so far without guards, but you *are* headstrong and foolish—and it will be the death of you."

"No." But he sounded less certain. He turned abruptly away

from her, took one long step and gazed at Sofia searchingly. "Why?" The word was barely a whisper.

Sofia met his eyes levelly. Now the moment had come; after so many dreams and waking hours worrying it, she felt a fatalistic calm. "I had reasons. I thought them good once; you would not." Ilse's laugh broke over them, startling them both.

"She had reasons, and not only for the ball! Who do you think aided me in preparing the hazards you just faced, Prince?"

He felt sick. Sofia made a faint, protesting noise. She was pale, her eyes too bright. When words finally came, though, they were nearly as harsh as Ilse's. "Think what you like, Prince; I cannot change that, whatever I say now. But I will tell you anyway. You cannot know what it is to scheme and fight for the least scraps of food, for clean skirts and slippers that will keep the chill from your feet! To be beaten for things you never did, for merely hoping for a better life. *I* know! And so I know there is little I would not do to break from my father's house and find myself a better life, however I must do it and whatever the cost. And there is *nothing* I would not do to save myself from *that*!" A sweeping, violent gesture took in the fire.

Conrad stared at her, stricken. She let her gaze fall to her trembling hands, stuffed them in her pockets. Sudden warmth against his palm heated the dagger hilt and spread up his forearm.

No! Whatever she said, it was all wrong; and now, suddenly, he read a warning in her eyes. *Think!* He did, furiously. "You have condemned yourself from your own mouth, Lady Sofia," he said flatly. "And though I swore to the Queen you would be brought back alive, I doubt you will long survive that return. And I for one am glad of it." She turned a little away from him and her shoulders slumped. Somehow, he felt he had said the right thing.

He turned back to Ilse. "As for you—" he began, but movement behind the witch caught his eye and broke his thought: Dominic and Jussl had somehow come around behind the caves and were working their way through rock and brush above them.

"As for me," Ilse said evenly, "I know there are two men up there." She pitched her voice to carry across the meadow. "I am protected where I stand, but you are not. One move from either man, and I give you to that fire at once!"

They heard her; Dominic halted at the very edge, held out a warning hand to stay Jussl. But before Ilse could say anything else, Sofia cried out in surprise and leaped to her feet. The witch turned on her angrily. But *she* stopped, staring as Sofia was. Conrad looked at both women, up at Dom and Jussl—they were gazing open-mouthed both at the same spot behind him—and then, warily, he cast a glance over his shoulder. Astonishment brought him completely around. Augustine was suddenly there, a green-gray mist still veiling the lower half of his body. He raised his silver rod, and a protective wall encircled him.

Ilse screamed with rage and yanked the yew branch from the ground; green fire crackled through the air between them, but too late. It flared all around the wall and vanished without touching the man inside. Conrad backed away, a slow step at a time, but just now Ilse had forgotten him. Spell after spell tore across the meadow to singe grass and turn stone red, but the wall held. Within, Augustine held the rod high, let his head fall back and gazed straight into the sky as he began to chant. His words rumbled through the ground, vibrating Conrad's very bones.

Sofia's nerveless legs gave way as air beyond the fire swirled and a sheet of ruddy flame shot skyward. Augustine sagged against his staff, his eyes closed and he fell heavily. The silver wards flickered and were gone. Beyond the Greek fire, Gustave stood.

Ilse was the first to recover. "You!" she hissed, and brought her yew branch up to strike. Gustave swayed, shook his head and hoisted the skirts of his long white robe, swiftly settled them on the ground in an encircling. They glowed a faint silver; Ilse's spell bounced off the air not a hand's distance from the old man's face.

Gustave smirked complacently. "You are surprised to see me, are you not? You pride yourself that you are more skilled than most of your common kind, but *you* could never do what I just did, to transport Being and Body both!"

Ilse laughed sourly. "If yours was the knowledge for that trick, then *I* see whose the skill! Did you kill your man?"

Gustave shrugged. "What matter? I see that anyone may be an apprentice, and a man can always get another—as you have done." On the last word, his hands came up sharply and a triangular-shaped something flew across the fire to strike against Ilse's shield. She bent to pick it up.

"Iron," the witch said contemptuously. "Is that the best you can do, sorcerer? I warned you I was no longer simply a Green Witch." She brought it up and laid it against her cheek. "My mother was burned by such a thing, just there—it took the last of her strength from her.'' She tossed it into the air and cried out a command; it vanished in a flash of light, and something gray and ponderous began to rise from the rocks at Gustave's feet.

The sorcerer hesitated only briefly, then spread his hands and began moving them back and forth. The gray faded, turned pale, then white, then clear—the thing was gone. Ilse had already begun another spell; Gustave countered with one of his own. The Greek fire compressed as something unseen crossed it to surround and beat Ilse down.

There were things seen and unseen—familiar shapes, shapes from tales, bloody horrors for which there were no words. Gustave held his own and gave as good as he got but none of his spells had pierced her circle. His robe circling spell protected him until he extended his arm to counter a spell, and foul, fluttery little black things enveloped it. Ilse laughed and clapped her hands delightedly; Gustave swore and tried to pick them off without success. They swarmed onto his other hand. Blood dripped from his fingers, and when he drew his arms back, they were all over him.

"You have *lost*, sorcerer!" Ilse screamed.

"No—!" But Conrad could scarcely see him for the crawling, fluttering, shapeless black things.

"I can kill you any time I choose! But first, I think you will watch while I feed your Prince to the fire!"

"No—!" It was half a plea; Conrad's lips moved to echo the word, but no sound came. His feet would not obey him and when Ilse beckoned, he found to his horror that he was moving toward her. He wavered, painfully caught between two spells as Gustave shook his left hand free and brought it to bear on him. Ilse shouted and cursed in a fury and shook the branch in Gustave's direction, then turned back to Conrad. Another step, another—he could feel heat on his face, but he could not bear to look. Ilse's whisper hissed into his ear, chilling him, curdling his blood.

"You will die, Prince, but not as easily as my mother did— your skin will shrivel, your flesh crisp and your bones blacken, still you'll feel it to the very last. You'll weep for death, and none will give it to you—'' He could feel heat through the rock, through his boots and his breeches. Ilse's voice beat into him, twisting his guts. Gustave bellowed out another spell; Ilse cursed wildly and turned from Conrad to deflect it.

Something—someone moved, Conrad saw, close by and low. Sofia was on her hands and knees, crawling slowly, moving steadily toward the witch's feet. She could have reached out and touched the branch at Ilse's heels.

Somehow aware of the Prince's sudden attention, she looked up at him, shook her head minutely, turned her attention to Ilse once more. The witch was still occupied with Gustave, who had shaken off more of the black things and was throwing fire and smoke at her; a cloud of insect-sized bats swirled around her hair until she swung the yew branch around her head and they caught fire. She gestured and Conrad's foot moved. He could feel Greek fire tugging at him; the breath escaped him in a long groan.

He heard Dom screaming in furious French, the crack of Dom's pistol, a spang as the pellet struck the witch's shield but did not penetrate. One of Jussl's spears struck the ground not far from her circle. Ilse ignored them.

Sofia felt in her pocket for the earring—it was all she had, but it would be enough since her hand had not healed over yet. She set her jaw and plunged the wire into her palm. Blood welled up; she squeezed it until it bled freely and smeared her hand across Ilse's circle, as far as she could reach. It unmade.

Ilse shrieked and spun around. "You! I will kill you, there in that fire, right now! You and your Prince together!" Sofia huddled away from her with a faint, wordless cry. Gustave shook free from the last of the black things. Conrad leaped away from the fire, caught the witch by her upraised arm and swung her out and away from him. She staggered and fell; Gustave's spell wrapped around her like a net and dragged her across the ground. She shrieked in agony as Greek fire sucked her in.

Conrad stumbled back in horror. Ilse staggered part way to her feet, and for one horrid moment he thought she might break free. But she began to quiver all over, jerked back and forth. Her hair burst into flame, the yew branch exploded, and she fell. Her screams were muted by the shielding around the fire, still horrible to hear, and they went on long after honest fire would have killed her.

"Oh, God and Mary, stop it, make it stop." He was never certain later if he spoke, or if Sofia did; he turned away, caught her close and covered her ears with his hands. But a horrible fascination brought his gaze back to that pool of green fire, the witch at its heart.

Gustave stood at the edge of Ilse's circle and he smiled grimly. "You can hear me, can you not, Ilse? I have more iron here, look you—a dagger! You can die on it, if you are fortunate enough to obtain it. Now—" He laughed; Conrad's arms tightened around Sofia as she shuddered. "What price shall I ask for this favor?"

Sofia hid her face in her hands. "Make it stop, make him stop!"

He wasn't certain he could speak. "Before God, Gustave, let her die!"

The sorcerer turned on him. "Be still! Who are *you* to say what I shall do or not do with her?"

"You know who I am! And I command you as your Prince to end this, at once!"

Gustave slowly shook his head; he froze as Sofia screamed wildly. Conrad stared in horror. The witch—blackened and shriveled beyond recognition—somehow came half upright and reached. Two long, slender snakes writhed out from the fire, wrapped twice around the sorcerer's waist and dragged him into the flame. Gustave's wail soared skyward, descant to Ilse's constant shrilling.

"Conrad, get down!" Dominic's voice, overhead and behind him. A moment later, the sorcerer's voice was mercifully stilled. Conrad turned to see the Frenchman crouched on the rock ledge, smoking musket balanced across his knees. Somehow, then, he himself was on his feet, the Spanish dagger point between his fingers. *Blood calling to blood,* he thought grimly, and threw. Ilse fell sideways across Gustave, dead. He turned hastily away.

Jussl had come down from the ledge to help Augustine; Dom was on his way. The Greek fire was dying, already only a dull green flame in the very midst of the circle.

"What will you do with me?" He looked up to see Sofia before him. She met his gaze levelly; he could read nothing there save exhaustion. He reached into his doublet and brought out a rumpled handkerchief, pressed the cloth against her bleeding hand and folded her fingers over it.

"Some of what I said here was true, not all. I promised Mother I would bring you to her, unharmed. She has been greatly worried for you."

"She is a kind lady." Sofia touched the handkerchief to her eyes. "What I did—"

"I know."

She shook her head. "You cannot. I won't ask sympathy or understanding; I have no right to them. I—I never intended treason, before God, I never did."

"I know." Somehow in *this* moment, he could believe it. "No one thinks you intended treason."

"I—" She nodded. They would think her a witch, she realized, whatever she said or did. He would. She didn't dare think of that just now; she'd weep and never be able to stop.

"Can you ride?"

Her eyes closed and her shoulders sagged. "If I must, I can." She brought up a tired little smile. He looked so utterly exhausted himself; she must not be a burden. "I—thank you for your kindness, your Highness." In spite of weariness and the nagging worry buried under it, Conrad smiled.

"We two of all the men and women in this world need not be so formal." He peeled off his left glove, let it fall, picked up the silver rose and held it out. "Thank you for my life, Lady Sofia."

"And you for mine." Sofia's face was solemn, her dark eyes unreadable as she reached into her pocket and brought out the mate.

"Mischief set by a witch . . . can outlive her, to cause woe after."

An Oral Grammarie

23.

In the end, Conrad was persuaded to take Sofia and Dominic, and return to Neustadt as quickly as Sofia could manage; Jussl rode on ahead to alert the Queen. Augustine remained behind to seal the witch's cave until better provision could be made. He would need an extra day to bring Gustave's cart; that could not be left where it was or sent on its way with only Fritz to guard it. And Augustine would use it to bring the box in which he had placed the mingled ash and bones—Ilse's and Gustave's.

Sofia rode before Conrad most of the way; Hans's horse was available to her but she could not ride it sidesaddle and would not astride. She slept most of the journey, waking only briefly when they stopped to rest the horses. She stirred at Neustadt's gates, when Conrad must call out the guard to let them through. The town clock tolled five—nearly day—as they rode up damp, deserted streets; Conrad could feel the tension in her.

Henriette must have left word to be wakened when they reached the palace gates; by the time they had dismounted and Conrad had Sofia steady on her feet—she would not permit him to carry her—the Queen was at the head of the stairs in her night robe and cap, long ribboned braids flying as she came down to greet them. She hugged her son and immediately bundled Sofia away with her.

Things blurred. Conrad later remembered taking a long, hot bath, being put into a clean long shirt and fed a thick soup, fresh bread, a cup of his mother's Florentine red wine. The sun reddened his balcony when he finally climbed into his bed; he did not waken until after dark. Dominic did not put in an appearance until very late the next morning.

The Regent's Council fussed at him, listened to his story aghast and fussed more when he finished it. He bore it in silence, heard them out patiently and with every sign of meekness. And he got from it the one thing he wanted: Sofia would be exonerated of witchcraft and treason alike. There would be no trial.

Conrad himself, now that he was partly recovered from his adventures, was concerned about the matter of witchery—many of the Nobles Council and the Regent's Council were, he thought—but they recognized a trial would create more difficulties than it solved. And Sofia had surely suffered enough.

He saw her twice, only briefly those first days. She sat with Henriette's other ladies at a formal evening meal—pale and to his eye unwilling to be there at all. *She reckons without Mother, who will have her here regardless,* he thought uncomfortably. Once again, when he had come to the Queen's apartments, he saw her—she lay upon a couch near the balcony, sun touching her face, and she slept.

He thought she avoided him; he rather wished she would not, and the thought surprised him. All the same, if she sensed his discomfort, his fears—perhaps it was better this way.

Henriette came with his breakfast several mornings later, waited until the servants laid it out to speak. "You have said nothing of her at all."

Conrad shrugged, bit into a ripe peach. "What should I tell you? That you were right?"

Henriette waved that aside impatiently. "Of course I was right. But you avoid her. Why is that?"

"I don't—I have had things to busy me. Say rather she avoids my company. But—I simply cannot talk to her, and—if you had seen her, Mother, with Greek fire at her right hand and Ilse at her left! Her words then, what I thought she was trying to tell me—" He spread his hands helplessly. "What if I was wrong? But I cannot find words, and she is not there to hear them."

"Bah," Henriette said good-naturedly. "I warned you she

was a strong young woman—fortunately for you, my son! But you young! All this diffidence." Conrad scowled over his bread.

"What can I say? I apologized once for threatening her with murder; she apologized for bespelling me. What more can we say to each other? And—Mother, what does that leave!" Henriette merely looked at him, and he sighed. "It is too bad; she was so fair when I first saw her. She still is. With all that is between us, though—" He stared at his bread, stirred himself and began to eat again. "Mother, what if we *are* both wrong you and I? I—truly, I find myself fearing to turn my back on her. If we had gone ahead with the test—not a trial, of course, but the test Gustave proposed, the slippers—?"

"And when gossip spread across the court as it does, and beyond, then what for the Lady's reputation?" Henriette said flatly. "And for the repute of the Court itself?" Conrad sighed, shook his head. "Well, never mind." Henriette stood. Conrad came halfway to his feet and she motioned him down. "Never mind, finish your food. What plans have you for today?"

Conrad tucked bread into his cheek. "Something needs doing about Gustave; we cannot simply have his ashes thrown away."

"Speak to the bishop; he will know how best to handle that. A state funeral, I fear; but a small one."

"If you say. Not everyone saw through him as I did, after all. Something must be done about that girl, Isabelle, and at once. I am uncomfortable sharing a roof with her."

"You have nothing to do with her; imagine the plight of those who must visit her!" Henriette exclaimed. "But she is nearly well enough to travel. Friends offered her a place in the City, but it seemed cruel to put her where she might see the ruins of her home. An uncle has offered her a home in Saar. A banker. She won't go to rags and dirt, at least." She looked momentarily quite angry. "You realize *she* is trying to force the test; nothing would please her more than to see Sofia named a proven witch."

"If—"

"Do not say it; you know it isn't the truth."

Conrad shook his head. "Before God, Mother, I truly wish I did! But perhaps this way—obviously *we* cannot demand the test, but if it were put upon us—?"

"No," Henriette said forcefully. "It would do us no good, and it would do Sofia immeasurable harm to be put to such a test. Let it go; Isabelle will be gone soon, and the matter will be forgotten. But *I* want to be rid of Isabelle, Conrad, before she causes poor Sofia any more grief.''

Conrad waved that aside; so long as Isabelle was gone, and soon, he scarcely cared where she went. "There are my words for the confirmation ceremony—''

"That is four days away; you'll know them. Come this evening and play chess with me. Your friend Dominic played yesterday afternoon. He is quite good, but I took two of our three games.''

"He and I are evenly matched; you'll get no better challenge from me, Mother. But I'll come.'' He smeared cheese on his bread and smiled. "It seems forever since I thought of chess— anything civilized.'' Henriette smiled. She was still smiling as she collected her two young ladies from the bench in the hallway and went down to her rose gardens. *Silly children; I'll be a gray-haired crone before I see grandchildren, if I must wait for those two to act.*

He came late, freshly washed and combed, neat in dark blue plain doublet and breeches, darker blue boots. Light from the Queen's candles turned his hair silver as he knelt and kissed her hand. "My mind is all wrapped in 'sacred oath of honor' and the rest; I warn you, I'll be easy prey tonight.''

"You had better not,'' Henriette said mildly. "I like a proper challenge at the board. If I catch you mooning or mumbling to yourself, I'll kick your shins as I did when you were a boy and squirmed at services.'' She set the board between them, waited until Conrad had seated himself and began setting up her pieces. Conrad picked up the black queen and studied it. He had always liked this particular set: They were carved and inlaid; white with pearl, black with chalcedony so dark a gray it was sooty. The Queen stood almost as tall as his forearm, and her face had been modeled from life.

Soft music touched his ears and he turned his head. Most of Henriette's ladies were gathered beside the balcony, where two of them played and one sang. Sofia might be there—He brought his attention back to the board when Henriette tapped his leg gently with her soft slipper and indicated her move. A simple beginning; he moved a pawn to cover hers, put both elbows on the table and rested his chin in them.

A clock chimed ten, and then the half; they finished one game—Conrad won it after a hard fight—and began another. The music went on, instruments only. He sensed movement around them as one or two girls came to watch. Seven moves; he'd lost a knight already and was plotting his next move when the Queen started to her feet. "The hour—I forgot. No, Conrad, stay where you are; I will not be long. Marie, Honaria, come with me. Sofia, take my place, please."

"Madame—"

"At once, please," Henriette said firmly and hurried from the room. Conrad stood staring across the table at Sofia, who stared back at him, stricken. She touched one hand to her face, straightened her shoulders and sank onto the Queen's stool.

"Your Highness. If you prefer it, I will leave."

"No." The word slipped out, louder than he'd intended. Sofia started nervously. He managed a smile, spoke more quietly. "She *did* make that an order."

"I will stay, then." She leaned forward to study the board. "Whose move is it, and which was the last?" He told her, made the move he had worked out, sat back while she contemplated the board. Why had he not realized what Henriette intended? There was so much of this kind of thing in Paris, how had he missed it here? And—why was he not already gone, or at least resentful?

Her attention was fixed on the board, her fingers tracing various paths across the table as she thought her way through likely moves. She was too thin, still, but her face was relaxed. Her hair had been dressed in curls but plainly; her gown was as severely unornamented as his doublet. But a damask rose bud held hair away from one side of her face, and she wore the silver rose earrings. She picked up her bishop, hesitated, moved it.

"A good move," Conrad said. His voice was a little breathy. It was a very good move; it took him some time to work out her strategy and counter it, and he looked up to see her eyes on him.

Sofia won the game finally; a second went to draw. After three slow moves, he looked up again to meet her eyes, and gently pressed the board aside, caught her hand under his when she would have risen. "Wait. Please."

"As you wish, Your Highness."

"Prince Conrad, if you must be so formal. Remember?"

She nodded. "I do remember. I—wonder that you can think of it at all, and still bear to touch me."

He leaned forward and slid his free hand under hers, so it was now captured between both of his. "I can bear it. Do you still fret that? Please, don't.'' She nodded once, and he thought her fingers relaxed a little. His next words surprised them both. ''Lady Sofia, marry me.'' Her head came up slowly, and she would have shaken her head but he went on. ''I—Do not answer yet, listen. Think on it. My reasons are sensible ones; you, I know are a sensible lady. My father's Will still holds; I must wed, and before year end. You are noble and fair; the people would like you. We share interests; think how few husbands and wives can say that. We could become friends, at least.'' A corner of his inner self was aghast, another hastily justifying his words: She must be at Court anyway; the Queen insisted. She would be no more danger to him than she was now, she would still have her own separate apartments. . . .

Sofia shook her head sharply. ''You cannot! You were under a spell when we talked. How can you know, how can I? Think of the gossip, Prince Conrad! And there were so many other women at that ball! Any of them might suit better—''

''No. Do you think I did not study them carefully? There were hours before Ilse came into the palace with her spells and with you; there was no one. Marry me; satisfy my father's Council and his Will. We can ride, or play music. Or chess. I will give you a peregrine falcon as a betrothal gift—you see, I do remember!'' Silence. ''It is a sensible thing I ask of you.''

''Sensible.'' Sofia's head drooped, and a tear spattered the table.

Conrad tightened his fingers on hers, then let her hand go. Whatever else was churning inside him, his desire to save her from harm, from hurt, from any pain at all was still high. ''I have upset you. I never meant to.''

''How can you possibly trust me, after I aided Ilse not once but twice?''

The question would have frightened him, if he'd let it. He wouldn't. ''I can. But—you. If you could not bear my presence, if you could not bear to marry me, say so, please, and I will not ask again.'' She shook her head, wiped her cheeks with a little square of lace.

''Never that. I—if it is what you want, if you are certain, then—then yes.'' She looked at him with brilliant eyes and wet lashes and smiled tremulously. ''Perhaps it is sensible; a clean repute for me since you would never marry a witch—hush, let me finish—and surely sensible for you, to avoid another ball and another round of terrible choices. But the Queen, the Council; how could they ever permit it?''

"The Council understands it has no say in the matter, so long as the lady is noble and of Saxe-Baden. As for Mother—why do you think she had me come here tonight, save to see us together over that board before she fled this room?'' He stood as the clock rang midnight, touched his lips to her hand and kept her from a curtsey. "From now on, you must not. A lady does not curtsey her trothed lord.'' He walked from the room in a haze; she slowly sank back into her chair and watched him go.

The palace buzzed with the news the next morning; by mid-afternoon, Dominic came back from a card game with a report that the news had spread to the La Modes and he'd heard it cried across the market. Conrad had been right in one thing: People were pleased with his choice. And if there were still any rumors connecting Sofia with magic of *any* kind, Dominic did not mention them.

The Queen convened the Regent's Council at midday and won their approval; the investiture was lengthened by a brief ceremony that would let Sofia speak the oath of service and fealty to the crown, Conrad the responding oath of protection necessary before the troth could be formally recognized. That would be done at the end of the ceremony, after Conrad was officially proclaimed Crown Prince and Heir.

The days went by in a haze: He slept when men pushed him into bed, ate when food was given him. He saw less of Sofia than ever, and found himself sorry. Dominic spent a good deal of his time with the would-be fashionables, and, if Conrad had heard him correctly, he was thinking of creating a hotel society of his own—for at least the next few years. He couldn't be certain that was what the Frenchman had said: Too much happened too quickly, the words of his oath would not stick with him, and he found it hard to believe Dom would not tear back to Paris at high speed once he had the opportunity. Then again, there was an attraction in being the largest fish in the pond, instead of one of the smaller sprats.

His own uncertainty was buried deep just now; he wondered now and again how long before it would rise again. But he found himself doubting Henriette's vision at odd hours. Give Sofia the test—*he* would not be the only one to shed terrible doubts of her, if she passed!

If.

People everywhere in the halls, at all hours of day and night; most of them he did not know. A few looked vaguely familiar; one gaunt young woman in a yellow ill-matched to her skin and pale hair. It was only after he returned to his rooms much later that he realized this was Isabelle—Sofia's stepsister. She looked dreadful, but she was on her feet and walked without aid; surely she was well enough to be gone by now! But he forgot about her almost at once: Nicholas was waiting for him with horoscopes to pick the most auspicious wedding date, his tailors with clothing for the ceremony.

They woke him while it was still dark; there would be no food until it was all over, but the dressing seemed to take hours, and it was nearly dawn when he was bowed into the hall. Men waited there for him: Eino Trompe and a hand-picked guard; Augustine—now called sorcerer in charge only because Conrad could not name him chief sorcerer until after he was confirmed Heir—and four gray-clad apprentices; the First Steward and half a dozen household. Dominic, dazzling in black figured velvet, white lace and pearl-covered gloves. Conrad's noble dressers fell in behind him.

The throne room was nearly as large as the ballroom, and at the moment as full as that room had been. The Queen was already seated on the dais; the King's throne had been set away from hers for the day, a separate, ornate chair was brought in for the Heir. Henriette was a blur; it all was. Ladies clustered behind the Queen; he did not see Sofia among them.

The investiture itself went quickly: the Queen's demand, the Council's response—his oath to uphold the kingdom and protect its people, which came word-perfect for the first time. The various oaths after, beginning with the Queen's, those took time. Henriette was followed by the Regent's Council. There was a little pause, and Sofia came along the base of the dais to kneel before him. She wore white and gold once more; a rope of pearls was looped through her hair, pearls edged her bodice and gloves. Her voice was so low, Conrad barely heard her, and surely no one else could have. He stepped forward to hand her to his side.

"No!" An outraged, shrill female voice echoed across the high ceiling and Isabelle pushed her way onto the steps. Eino Trompe edged forward; Conrad motioned him back. "This is not right, I *know* her!" Sofia clasped her hands together and held them in a fold of her skirts; she might otherwise have been carved out of ice. "She—my mother married her father, I lived in the same house with her! All that has gone awry—my mother is dead, and my sister!" The nervous whispers ceased; Isabelle suddenly had the full attention of everyone in the throne room. "Our house burned to cinders, the servants harried—and she! She went to the ball and then across the Scarp with a witch, a woman proven witch, and despite all this, comes back to Neustadt on the Crown Prince's saddlebows?" Silence deepened. Isabelle was white to the lips but she must have rehearsed those words over long hours; they fell much too glibly from her thin lips. "And now he will marry her—the witch Ilse is dead, a King's sorcerer dead, and Sofia von Mencken becomes an honored guest in the King's household, and then betrothed to the Crown Prince?"

One of the Queen's ladies stirred; subsided as Isabelle fixed her with a mad, black glare. "I demand honor for the soul of my mother and the soul of my sister!" Her shrill voice echoed.

Conrad shook himself and when Henriette came across to lay a protective arm over Sofia's hand, he waved her back.

"And what test, I wonder, would you devise?" he asked finally. Isabelle's eyes glittered, but she made no reply. Conrad gazed down at her, and the knot that had built around his heart for long days suddenly loosed. "Lady Sofia has been cleared of all complicity with the witch Ilse," he said finally. "And there is no need for this—"

"I will take the test," Sofia said quietly. She had detached her hand from Henriette's protective arm.

"As it chances, there is a test devised by my father's chief sorcerer. Augustine, go and fetch Gustave's green short cape—with care." He heard rather than saw his own chief sorcerer leave the room and return. The shabby green short cape in his hands, Conrad turned to face Sofia. She met his eyes squarely and without fear. "Lady Sofia, I bear the petals which were slippers, shaped to your feet; I was present when they left your feet and when they unmade. If they again become slippers, if they reshape themselves upon your feet, then by Gustave's own words we will know you as a witch."

Sofia turned to gaze down at her stepsister; her face was unreadable. She nodded. "I am willing. God knows me innocent." Isabelle laughed sourly and Sofia added gently, "Not perhaps innocent of feelings of dislike, bitterness, anger—or of the desire to live and to save the life of another. But those are human things, and God knows me for human, too.'' Isabelle glared at her, set her mouth in a tight, angry line, and stood back to wait.

Conrad handed Sofia into his chair; his fingers were suddenly cold and they wanted to shake; her fingers were stiff and unresponsive but her eyes were momentarily warm when they met his. Augustine came forward with the green cape, and Conrad stood aside as his sorcerer mumbled over the fabric and finally spread it flat.

Sofia lifted her skirts, revealing exquisite, tiny feet in white furred slippers. Augustine removed these and took hold of her heels, lowered them gently into the faded rose petals. And after what seemed hours and could only have been moments, he lifted them again, pulled the cloth aside, and set her feet back in the white slippers. He stood and turned to face the crowd. ''There was no reaction at all; she is innocent,'' he declared.

Innocent. Conrad's knees wanted to buckle; he didn't dare let them. Any more than he would ever tell Sofia how he had doubted her. He reached for her hand; before he could take it, a blur of yellow fabric and yellow hair was between them.

''No!'' Isabelle's scream tore the room apart. Her fingers wrapped around Sofia's wrist. A long knife was in her free hand, then at her stepsister's throat.

''Do not dare move, or she is dead at once!'' she shouted as Conrad cried out in horror.

Sofia had not moved at all. ''Isabelle,'' she said quietly. ''No one but you and I care for my death; you make this difficult for yourself.''

Isabelle laughed, that horrid, cutting laugh. ''He cares, Schmutzie Sofie. Look at him, look at his face! For you! He must be mad!''

''Mad,'' Sofia said evenly. ''You are the one mad, Isabelle, to think you can kill me and simply go away.''

''Perhaps I don't intend to go—perhaps I don't care any more,'' Isabelle said. The knife pressed nearer, breaking skin. Sofia felt blood slide down her neck. ''She spoke to me, you know. Ilse did. I was—I was sick, there was a horrible smell everywhere, the noise of wagons—I can't remember. *She* knew what you were, Sofie. She knew; however you've fooled the Queen and the Crown Prince—you never fooled me!''

''No.'' Sofia stood quite still; her hand clamped down over Isabelle's suddenly. ''You never fooled me either, Isabelle. You were a wicked, nasty, stupid young woman, and for eight years you and your mother and sister made my life a hell. Look at me, Isabelle. I have everything you wanted. You have nothing, Isabelle.''

"Sofia, no—" Conrad whispered, stricken. Little sound came with the words.

Sofia laughed. Her smile was complacent; only Conrad could see the black terror in her eyes. "Everything, Isabelle. A Prince, wealth, fine gowns—a crown, Isabelle." She caught her breath in a frightened little cry as her stepsister pulled the knife from her throat to slash, to maim. She missed; Sofia's hand was torn from the dagger hilt, her heel caught on the step behind her and she fell. Isabelle had the blade poised when Conrad grabbed her by the waist. Eino Trompe yanked the dagger free.

Isabelle was screaming wildly. The throne room echoed with her cries, the shouts and cries of the gathered people. Augustine hauled the girl about by the shoulders; one of his apprentices upended a small bottle in his palm and smeared liquid across her upper lip. She collapsed; the assembled nobles went silent. Augustine handed her to guards, who took her away.

Conrad bent down to help Sofia back to her feet; her face was white and he swore. "May she never know a happy day."

"No." Sofia shook her head. "That is not right. Poor thing; all her near kin dead, taken by a witch's spell. I hated her once; perhaps I still do, although a good woman would never admit it. I will be glad when she is gone forever, and I need never see her again. I cannot wish her ill." She gazed up at him; her eyes were solemn. Conrad drew her along the step, and her fingers curled around his. He kept her hands firmly in his, his eyes fixed on hers, until the last of the Saxe-Baden came forward to give the fealty oath.

—And so, Marie, as you see there has been no end of trouble here. Poor Leo must have turned right over in his catafalque. Rumor surely has reached you by now, and I only assure you the most exaggerated of it may well be truth. But certain good has come of the matter. The villages upon the Scarp show enthusiasm for their Prince, and Conrad has made it clear there will be no persecution for simple magic. He has the admiration of the army for this wild trick of sneaking off to nearly single-handedly track the woman Ilse, which I suppose is good—The wretched boy!

You have lost young de Valois, I fear (I know you will say this is all to the good; surely he never won so many games of chance and broke so many hearts as you maintain!). He has offered little Sofia a good price for the land where her father's house stood; he intends a hotel, a place to have readings and ballet, opera. I admit with relief that since he has taken them in hand, one seldom sees young clothing-conscious nobles in garish overdress; perhaps next he will teach them proper manners. And I have hopes for this salon of his; we are not barbarians here, but we presently have very little decent entertainment.

The wretched Isabelle left that same afternoon to join her uncle. I hear that notwithstanding the sudden advance in her status· from impoverished to upper bourgeoise she is unhappy there. But she curbs her tongue where Sofia is concerned, and that is all we dare ask.

The wedding is set for two months hence. I hope you can see your way to the journey east. Conrad and Dominic both tell me the French roads are excellent, ours at least passable. Nicholas wanted a date in three weeks time, but of course that was impossible; there would be no time to make Sofia's gowns. A Princess has certain obligations, after all.

I laugh so at those silly children. So *pratique*, they think themselves, setting up their lives over a chessboard, as though they were pieces upon that board! Such sensible reasons to wed. If either of them wishes more than mere sense, they do not speak of it. One cannot blame them, I suppose: They are both stubborn and proud, both the kind to hide what they feel. And they have gone through so much, for and with each other. And yet—I know them both so well. I see it in her eyes when he does not look at her, in his when her head is turned away, it is truly a story from the Courts of Love, in all its splendor.

Or it will be, once they both recognize it.

I truly hope to see you for the wedding; if not, then before I become a grandmother—for that, I am serenely confident, will be long before my son is crowned King.

Yours,
Henriette

AUTHOR'S NOTE

This is a fantasy set in an actual period of history, in a recognizable part of the world. To wit: the Germanies of the early 1600s.

There is a fine line to tread in such a fantasy: accuracy of detail balanced against desire to tell a story. I went to some lengths to make certain that details were correct or at least logical; I hope, without cluttering the story with extraneous "historical" detail.

There was a wild array of tiny Germanic kingdoms in the seventeenth century; there was no actual Saxe-Baden, Upper Hesse, Saar, or Lower Hesse. There was at least one Leopold I and doubtless many Conrads; my Leopold I is his own man, as is my Prince Conrad.

There were many books dealing with alchemy and witchcraft, numerous herbals. Mine are an amalgam. And while the Key of Solomon is authentic, my translations are freely made to fit my story. I would like to acknowledge Lesley Gordon for *Green Magic* (Viking, 1977), which was invaluable as a general source.

With one exception, the roses are authentic: I chose not to imagine a time when the hybrid tea rose called Sterling Silver did not exist. The Language of Flowers, often thought of as a Victorian indulgence, was also practiced in the 1600s.

Thanks to Vicci for the map. And to the Victoria and Albert Costume Wing for Prince Conrad, who stands just inside the doorway.

CLASSIC SCIENCE FICTION AND FANTASY

__DUNE Frank Herbert 0-441-17266-0/$4.95
The bestselling novel of an awesome world where gods and
adventurers clash, mile-long sandworms rule the desert, and
the ancient dream of immortality comes true.

__STRANGER IN A STRANGE LAND Robert A. Heinlein
0-441-79034-8/$4.95
From the *New York Times* bestselling author—the science
fiction masterpiece of a man from Mars who teaches
humankind the art of grokking, watersharing and love.

__THE ONCE AND FUTURE KING T.H. White
0-441-62740-4/$5.50
The world's greatest fantasy classic! A magical epic of King
Arthur in Camelot, romance, wizardry and war. By the author
of *The Book of Merlyn*.

__THE LEFT HAND OF DARKNESS Ursula K. LeGuin
0-441-47812-3/$3.95
Winner of the Hugo and Nebula awards for best science fiction
novel of the year. "SF masterpiece!"—*Newsweek* "A Jewel of
a story."—Frank Herbert

__MAN IN A HIGH CASTLE Philip K. Dick 0-441-51809-5/$3.95
"Philip K. Dick's best novel, a masterfully detailed alternate
world peopled by superbly realized characters."
—Harry Harrison
